The Harry Starke Series

Books 13 - 15

Blair Howard

ISBN: 9798354178315

The Harry Starke Series

Books 13 - 15

Apocalypse

The Harry Starke Novels Book 13

By

Blair Howard

This one is for my lovely and ever-patient wife Jo.

Chapter One

The assassin waited patiently, parked in the shadow of the giant Finley Stadium scoreboard on Chestnut Street. He checked his watch. It was a little after midnight. *Soon*, he thought as he checked his side-view mirror.

He reached under his jacket and withdrew the Ruger Mark IV .22 semi-automatic. For a quiet moment, while subconsciously monitoring for movement in his mirrors, he lovingly caressed the rosewood grips, savoring the silky texture of the polished wood. He ejected the magazine, cleared the chamber, reinserted the ejected round into the magazine, checked the load, and then reinserted it into the weapon, slamming it home with the heel of his palm. Finally, he worked the action and loaded a round into the chamber, set the safety, and returned it to the holster under his arm.

It was a warm night in mid-May. Chattanooga FC had played Detroit to a 1-1 draw earlier that same evening, so the bars and clubs on Chestnut were teeming with happy hometown supporters.

The minutes ticked by. His eyelids began to droop. His chin fell to his chest. It was enough to jerk him back to full consciousness. He cursed silently, checking the car parked in front of him, then his mirrors: nothing. He heaved a sigh of relief, shaking his head, disgusted with himself, and turned in his seat to search the floor behind the passenger seat. Locating the package of small containers, he grabbed one, turned back to peer out the windshield, and twisted the cap off the small bottle. Raising it to his lips, he gulped the contents, and two swallows later the energy drink was gone. Then he rolled down his window and settled back to... wait.

It was after one in the morning when he finally spotted the mark... walking toward him from the wrong direction.

Damn! What now?

He'd intended to shoot the mark from inside his car—through the passenger-side window—as the target passed by, but the man was now approaching from the front, so he wouldn't be passing at all.

He looked across the street, studying the revelers gathered at the Southside Social, considering his options. *I can't let him get away. It has to be done tonight, now, before he can meet with his handler. But if someone... Damn, damn, damn... Ah, what the hell. It is what it is.*

He waited until the man stepped off the sidewalk and was about to open his car door, then he opened his own.

"Hani," he said, loudly, as he exited the car. "A moment, if you please."

The man looked at him, wide-eyed and startled, then he panicked, fumbling to wrench the car door open, but it was too late. The assassin took several quick steps, arm outstretched, gun in hand, and was upon him.

Without a word he fired a single shot into the man's head just above his right ear and a second into the back of his head as he went down. The muted crack of the subsonic .22 rounds attracted no attention from the revelers across the street.

He turned away quickly, smoothly slipping the weapon under his jacket as he slid into his car—the engine already running—and pulled out, steering around the mark's body and slowly drove away, heading south on Chestnut. He cruised down one block, turned east on W. 20th, continued four more blocks until he made a right onto Market Street, took the eastbound ramp onto I-24, then slid expertly into the traffic, matching its speed as the hint of a smile crossed his lips at the thought of a job well done.

Chapter Two

"**H**ey, Harry. It's good to see you again after all these years. Take a seat. Sit down."

Nice, huh? Well it would have been but for the fact that Greg Parker was seated in my chair, behind my desk in my own private office. I did as he asked. I took one of the guest chairs in front of my desk and sat down; a new and more than a little weird experience for me.

It was during the middle of the afternoon on the 21st when it began. The time was just after two-thirty when I pushed the street door open and into my outer office, a.k.a. the bull pen. Jacque, my partner and PA, had risen from her seat and stepped around her desk to meet me. She had her finger to her lips, shaking her head.

"There's someone in your office," she whispered. "He looks like a fed. He's been in there waiting since nine o'clock."

"Who is it? Did he give a name?"

"No. He just said he wanted to see you, and that you wouldn't mind if he waited in your office. He also said to mention Hannah. He said you'd know. Does that ring a bell?"

Oh hell! Yeah... It rings a bell. Son-of-a-bitch!

The thought was mine, and I didn't want to share it with Jacque, so I nodded and pushed through the door into my inner sanctum, a normally inviolate territory that no one, not even Jacque, would dare enter without being invited.

Scowling, I said, "Not funny, Greg. This office is private. It's the only freakin' place I can really call my own, and I don't appreciate you busting in when I'm not here, much less taking over my chair. That's like stealing and wearing my underwear. What the hell do you want?"

"I'll get to that in a minute. In the meantime, Hannah said to tell you hello and that she's looking forward to seeing you again."

"Tell her thanks, but no thanks."

"Aww c'mon, Harry. You never were one to hold a grudge, a little ill-will perhaps, but nothing more." He was right. I wasn't, and I didn't. What I did do was dislike Greg Parker with a passion. But that's now. Back then, it was a different story. During the early nineties, Greg had been one of the best friends I'd ever had. We were at Fairleigh Dickinson together. He graduated with a bachelor's in forensic psychology in '95; I graduated with a master's in the same discipline two years later. Hannah Gordon was, at the time, my girlfriend. She and Greg graduated together. I never saw nor heard from her again. She and Greg were married six months later, and they now have two kids, both girls.

Getting back to Greg, he was... is one of those people who learn easily, a natural, and the FBI recruited him right out of Fairleigh; he's never looked back. This was the first time I'd seen or heard from him in more than ten years.

"What the hell do you want, Greg? I need my office. I have a business to run here."

"And it's good to see you, too, my friend."

"Get on with it or get out."

He heaved a sigh, shook his head, and stared at me across *my* desk. I always wondered what it would be like from the other side. Now I knew. And I didn't like it, not at all.

"Harry. A lot of water has passed under the bridge since those days back in Virginia, and I know we've not stayed in touch, and I sincerely regret that. I also know how you must feel about what happened, but I'm here on a matter of national security, so you need to put aside your animosities and get with the program."

I was dumbfounded. "Screw you, Parker. You always were an arrogant sonofabitch. It was always all about you. First, get this through your head: there's no animosity, and never was. I forgot about you a long time ago. As to Hannah... Well, when she went off with you, I figured I was well rid of her. Now, Mr. Big Shot FBI, tell me what you want or go before I throw you out."

"Fine. Have it your way. Here's the way it is, the way it's gonna be. I need insider help here in East Tennessee and you're it."

"Get the hell out of my chair and my office. I don't, and I won't, work for the government in general, and that applies most especially to you in particular. I quit organized law enforcement more than ten years ago. Since then I've been shot three times and beaten almost to death. I'm tired of getting shot at. I promised Amanda there'd be no more, that I was done with that life. Greg, I have a kid on the way... I won't do it."

"Yeah, you will, Harry. First, you'll listen to me; then when you know what it's about, you'll pitch in. I know you too well. Oh, and if you won't listen, I'll have your ass hauled to the Federal Building; there you will listen. Gimme a break, will you, and ten minutes?"

I almost told him to go ahead and do his worst, but I caught the look in his eye. He was concerned. I weakened, but only a little, and nodded.

"So tell me. I'll listen, but it won't do you any good."

He nodded, looked me in the eye, and said, "This is strictly between us, Harry. Not a word of it must leave this office. Agreed?"

I nodded.

"First, I need to tell you what my role in all this is. I'm Special Agent in Charge (SAC) for the National Security Branch at our Knoxville regional office. The NSB is a service within the FBI charged with the responsibility of protecting the United States from attacks by weapons of mass destruction, acts of terrorism, and espionage undertaken by foreign powers. We accomplish that by investigating threats to national security. We then provide information and analysis to other law enforcement agencies, and we further assist by developing the strategies and capabilities that will keep y'all safe and secure. But I'm sure you knew all that, right?" He grinned as he said this. I stared stoically back at him.

"Harry, I was here three years ago in July when Abdulazeez attacked the recruiting and Naval centers. I would have dropped by then, but... well, you know. Sorry. Anyway, that was a bad business, very bad. Now we have another situation, centered right here in Chattanooga, that could make the last attack look like... well, if it happens, it would be an apocalypse by comparison."

He stared at me, waiting for a reaction. I didn't give him one.

"Gee, Harry. You always were a tough one to communicate with. Okay, so what if I told you we're expecting an attack on one of the nuclear plants?"

That... got my attention. I sat up straight in my seat and said, "Go on."

"Two weeks ago, an illegal immigrant was gunned down outside a bar—"

"Yeah, I remember," I interrupted him. "So what? It happens all the time."

"This one was special. He was an Iranian."

I stared at him for a moment before asking, "How come I didn't know about that? The word here is that his name was Hani Shammout, a Syrian refugee."

He nodded, saying, "Very few people do. We kept it quiet. The refugee thing worked for us, up until a couple of weeks ago anyway. His name... Well, he wasn't Syrian and he wasn't a refugee. His real name was Vahid Shahini. He was an Iranian, a spy, a major in Iran's Revolutionary Guard Corps, the IRGC; the Quds Force, to be precise. We turned him. He was working for us."

"The Quds Force? What the hell is that?"

He smiled across my desk at me. I had the distinct impression he was mocking me.

"It's a highly secret, special branch of the IRGC tasked with clandestine operations outside of Iran's borders. The unit was formed in 1980, as far as we know, and has played an active role in providing training and weapons to extremist groups across the Middle East, including Iraqi insurgents, Lebanese Hezbollah, Hamas, and others. They are thought to be responsible for the assassination attempt on Saudi Arabia's ambassador to the United States back in 2011 and, according to a New York Police Department intelligence report released in 2012, they were linked to nine foiled plots here in the U.S."

"Okay... and?"

Parker obviously wasn't used to being interrupted, because he glared at me and shook his head before continuing.

"The group's commander is Major General Amir Rostamzadeh who, from what we think we know, reports directly to Iran's Supreme Leader. Under his, Rostamzadeh's, direction, the Quds Force controls many strategic industries throughout the world. They have a very competent cyber unit. They exert control over a wide range of international commercial services. They have a vast black-market network that includes, among other things, smuggling; and that, Harry, is what brings me to you. In March of 2017, Shahini, along with an unknown number of—I'm going to call them terrorists—were smuggled across the Mexican border."

"Okay, okay, okay. I get the picture. They are bad-asses, but I'm just a small-town PI. How d'you figure it's any concern of mine?"

"Does the name Lester Tree mean anything to you?"

It did. I blinked, then stared at him, barely breathing.

By now, those of you who know me, know that I pride myself on my ability to maintain a "poker face." The reference to my old pal Shady Tree, however... well, let's say Parker copped the tell immediately and grinned.

"Ah," he said. "I see that it does."

I nodded, slightly. Lester "Shady" Tree had been a thorn in my side for as long as I could remember; since my early days as a cop when I put a bullet through his arm, to my several run-ins with Congressman Harper and his hired assassin Calaway Jones. I'd sent Shady Tree packing during that last episode with a warning never to set foot in Chattanooga again. *Does the idiot think I was kidding?*

"And he's back?" I asked. "How do you know? And are you telling me he's been radicalized?"

He shook his head, and looking at me thoughtfully he said, "I don't know if he's been radicalized or not. I *do* know that he's up to something. Shahini was one of six Iranians posing as Syrian refugees. I have no idea where Tree is, which is why I'm here. I need to find him, and quickly. He's the one link we have to the rest of Rostamzadeh's infiltrators. I need you to find him for me."

I shook my head and said, "There's no way that piece of garbage will show his face here. Last time I ran into him I told him I'd put him on crutches if he did."

I paused, stared across my desk at him, and then said, "You're serious!"

He nodded earnestly. Removing his iPhone from his inside jacket pocket, he flipped the lock screen, searched through the contents, then handed it to me. I looked at the fuzzy, shadowy image. It was a close-up of the driver-side window of a car. The picture appeared to have been taken with a telephoto lens at night by the light of a street lamp. The car window was open. The driver was just a silhouette, unrecognizable, but there was something eerily familiar about the profile of the nose, chin, and brow. Suddenly, I felt cold.

"This could be anybody," I said, my voice lacking conviction. "Where was it shot?"

"On Chestnut Street, at the rear of Findley Stadium—"

"No shit!?!" I interrupted him. I was astounded. "You're saying this is the trigger man? If so, it's not Shady. He doesn't do murder. At least he never has in the twenty or more years I've known him. How did you get this?"

"Yes, well, that's as it may be, but he's in with some bad people. And he may no longer be the Lester Tree that you knew. The photo was taken, along with several dozen others—this is the best one—by an undercover agent that I had following Shahini. He was upstairs in the Southside Social Club; saw the whole thing. The shooter was good; the entire event lasted less than twenty seconds from start to finish. Tree, if it was him, was out of his car, put two in Shahini's head, and back in the car and rolling away before my agent realized what was happening. He's disappeared, Harry, so we need to find him, right away."

I stared down at the image. It faded. I tapped the screen. It returned. The more I stared at it, the more the sinking feeling in my gut deepened. I looked up at Greg. He pursed his lips, shrugged, and held out his hand. I handed him the phone.

"Send it to my phone, will you?"

"Number?"

I gave it to him, and he sent it.

"And you think they're targeting Sequoya Nuclear Plant?" I asked.

"Either that or Watt's Bar. We don't know which, not for sure, but we assume Sequoya. It seems most likely."

"Come on, Greg. Those places are like fortresses, especially now, and if what you say is true, why are we not swamped with feds..."

"No, Harry, not fortresses. You'd think so, but you'd be wrong, and you're not 'swamped with feds' because we don't have them. We're investigating more than a thousand threats spread throughout all fifty states. This is just one of them. And..." He shook his head and stared down at the desk for a moment. Then he looked up and said, resignedly, "The problem is, all we have are rumors. We have no credible evidence. And, well, as I said, we just don't have the manpower to..." Again, the shrug.

"So," I said, "you're here because you think I can lead you to

Tree." I shook my head. "He's not here, Greg. He wouldn't dare show his..." But then the more I thought about it, the less sure I was. Shady didn't earn his nickname just from the reference to his last name, Tree, he was... well, shady, a shadow that had managed to survive the ghettos for almost forty years without ever joining one of the numerous gangs. He was a crafty, nefarious sonofabitch that could manage to hide in the middle of an open field. But murder, terrorism? No, I didn't think so.

"You're not sure, are you?" Greg asked, leaning forward, his elbows resting on the desktop.

"Nooo... How credible is the threat, Greg? Wishful thinking or... what?"

"I told you, all we have are rumors, but it's more than wishful thinking I'm afraid. There's all kinds of chatter in the air. Something big is definitely coming, but where... we don't know for sure. There are five other major threats around the country that we know of, all of them as iffy as this one. This one could be a decoy, but so could the others. We just can't afford to take any chances. Now, are you in or not?"

"Get out of my chair, Greg. I can't think sitting here." He did, and we swapped seats. Suddenly, I felt a whole lot more comfortable, but yet uncomfortable at the same time. Have you ever felt like that? If you have, you know what I mean.

"Well?" Greg asked.

I stared at him, my elbows on the arms of my chair, my fingers steepled at my lips. *The man's not fooling. He's scared.*

"Greg," I said, quietly. "I think you're exaggerating. You always did. There's no way they could get that much explosive inside Sequoya or Watt's Bar. Even a truckload like what Tim McVeigh used in Oklahoma wouldn't do the amount of damage you're describing, not to a nuclear plant. The containment is shrouded in concrete. Even the Mother of All Bombs couldn't get through it..." Then I noticed something in his eyes; something that hadn't been there before.

I slowly shook my head as I said, "No way?"

He nodded, his face a mask. "The word is that two 1960s era SADMs—Special Atomic Demolition Munitions, the so-called backpack nuclear bomb—have surfaced somewhere in the Middle East. We have no idea what's happened to them. We think at least one of them is here in the U.S., possibly both of them."

"Holy shit! Are you serious?" I asked.

Nodding, he said, "As I ever was."

"But why here? Surely one of the major cities would be the better, more obvious target. It makes no sense—"

"No, Harry. It makes perfect sense," he said, interrupting me. "It's the unexpected, so they think that provides them with the best chance of success. And you've got to admit, they're right. The security in this neck of the woods is virtually nonexistent. They only need to get the device within a quarter mile and... well, life as we know it around here will cease."

"Oh come on..."

"I'm not kidding, Harry. A one-kiloton blast close to either one of those plants would... Harry, did you know that there's a public access parking lot within two hundred yards of the main building and right next to the switchyard at Sequoya? Do you have any idea of what the EMP blast alone would do to that?"

I shook my head, saying, "I've heard of those things, the backpack nukes, but I'm not buying it. I need to know more."

"More?" He sounded incredulous. "What the hell more... Okay, okay, you got it."

He thought for a moment, then said, "It's not widely known..." He paused, then began again, "It's not widely known that for almost twenty-five years during the sixties, seventies, and eighties the U.S. Army Special Forces packed miniature nuclear bombs; oh, don't look at me like that, it's true. The devices were technically known as the B-54 Special Atomic Demolition Munition—SADM—which they carried in a backpack, *on their freakin' backs.*"

I smiled at the sarcasm, but what he was telling me wasn't funny. Not in the slightest, and he was right... I didn't know.

"From what we now know," he continued, "though most of it is still classified, Soldiers from elite Army engineer units, Special Forces units, Navy SEALs, and even Marines, were trained to use the 'backpack nukes' on what were considered potential battlefronts from Eastern Europe to Korea to the Middle East. These elite units were to be inserted—by parachute or SCUBA—behind enemy lines to..." He paused to make quote marks with his fingers, then continued saying, "... to 'take out strategic installations or render vast tracts of land uninhabitable.' Harry, many of these SADMs or MADMs—the larger versions—were more powerful than the nuclear bomb dropped on Hiroshima, and quite obviously would have obliterated any battlefield or strategic installation and irradiated much of the surrounding area. Fortunately, they were never used."

I nodded slowly as I nibbled the side of the forefinger of my left hand.

"D'you realize," he continued, "the consequences if they manage to set one of these things off here? It will effectively wipe out a big swath of Southeast Tennessee at best. At worst... Who the hell knows? C'mon, Harry. Get with the program. The clock is ticking."

"I can't," I said as he glared at me across the desk and opened his mouth to speak, or maybe even yell, but before he could, I quickly continued, "I'm not saying I won't, but I have to talk to Amanda first —the baby is due anytime—and I need to talk to my partners. So you're going to have to give me some space."

That was what I said, and most of it was true. What I didn't tell him was that I needed to do some research, and I hoped I had just the guy I needed to talk to working for me. Yeah, I was having a hard time believing all he'd told me. The problem was that aside from my disbelief, I was able to make some sense of it, even though it was akin to a spy novel, something that might have been written by Tom Clancy. The other problem was, of course, supposing I didn't lend a hand and all his lies were true, what kind of a chump would I be, always presuming I survived such an event.

"How imminent is the threat?" I asked.

He shrugged, saying, "They're here. What more can I say?"

"How about the local police?" I asked. "The Sheriff's Office?"

He shook his head, his lips tight. "No, not yet. We need to keep this contained, at least for now. The fewer people that know, the less chance this mess gets leaked to the public..."

"Hell, Greg. The public needs to know."

"Panic, Harry. We can't have that. We don't need for them to know yet. There are less than thirty thousand people living within a ten-mile radius of Sequoya. We can evacuate that many within hours if we have to. The city and its surrounding areas would take a little longer, but it's doable."

What he was saying made sense. No, what he was saying was unacceptable, but he was right about one thing. Panic in the streets was the last thing we needed, but I had my doubts that something this monumental could be contained. I shook my head but said nothing. My brain was spinning.

I looked at my watch. It was almost four o'clock; we'd been talking for nearly an hour and a half.

I folded my arms, sat back in my chair, and stared at him for a long minute before saying, "I dunno, Greg. As I said, I need a little time. Can you come back tomorrow morning, say at nine o'clock?" I asked.

He nodded and said, "Yeah, I figured it would take a while. I'm booked in at the Read House along with a half-dozen agents for the duration." He stood, and then held out his hand across the desk.

"I'll be here at nine in the morning," he said as I stood and shook his hand. "And, one way or the other, I'll need an answer, yes?"

I nodded; he returned the nod, and then he left, leaving me with the feeling I was about to step off a cliff into the abyss.

Chapter Three

I watched the door close behind Greg Parker, then picked up the office phone and buzzed Jacque.

"Yes, Harry?"

"I need for you, Bob, and T.J. to join me, now. Have Heather hold all our calls. We'll be a while."

"Of course. Coffee?"

"That would be nice."

If you've not already met me and my staff, let me take a quick moment to introduce you to them.

Me? I'm Harry Starke, an ex-cop-turned-private investigator, and a very successful one, if I do say so myself.

Jacque Hale is my personal assistant and one of my two business partners. She's Jamaican, thirty-four years old, looks like a teenager, and never seems to age. She's tall—five-nine—has skin the color of coffee and cream, bushy black hair, and big dark eyes. She's not exactly beautiful; although attractive, she's somewhat skinny, and radiates a captivating smile. On thinking about it, she looks a little like Alicia Keys. She also has a rather dry sense of humor. She has a master's degree in business administration and a bachelor's in criminology, which is one of the reasons I hired her even before she got out of college. The other? Hell, I like her. We get along, well, most of the time. I don't know what I'd do without her.

Bob Ryan is my other partner—there are just two, Bob and Jacque —and he's also my lead investigator. He's a hard-ass, an ex-Chicago PD cop as well as an ex-Marine, and he's been with me almost since the day I first opened the agency. He's forty-seven, a year older than I, a big man who stands six-two and weighs in at two-hundred-forty pounds of solid muscle—twenty-five more than me—with a wry sense of humor and a deep voice, almost a growl, menacing even when he's being nice, which he rarely ever is. I said he was a bad-ass; uh, yeah, that's a bit of an understatement. The man can kill almost without thinking, and he has on several occasions. Unpredictable? Yes. He's even saved my life at least twice when we found ourselves in hostile situations, and he saved my wife, Amanda's, too. He's the older brother I never had.

T.J. Bron is something of an anomaly. Not more than three months ago, the man was on the streets, homeless, and ready to cash in his chips, that is until he discovered the body of a young woman in a back alley. Kate Gazzara was the investigating officer and saw some-thing in him nobody else did, so she brought him to me. Turns out he's a highly decorated Vietnam vet—two tours, the first beginning in 1968 and then again in 1972—an ex-Marine down on his luck... Nope, luck had nothing to do with it; he was the victim of a shady bank officer who accused him of stealing from the bank, but he didn't do it. He did some time, and it ruined him. He lost everything: wife, kids, home. He has a degree in accounting, and at the time, I happened to be looking for a financial investigator. Bearing in mind the man's military record, including his earning of a Silver Star and two Purple Hearts, I figured I could take a chance and hire him. So I did. Jacque found him a place to live and here we are. At sixty-eight, he's way older than the rest of my team, but he's also in better shape than most of them; this being due to a rigorous workout regimen he started the day Jacque took him in hand and that still continues. He's six feet, 190 pounds, with white hair and a heavily lined, deeply tanned face. I wanted him in on the meeting because I had a feeling that if anyone on the team knew about these SADM bombs, he would be the one... And he did.

They all arrived at my office door together, coffee in one hand—Jacque had two, one for her and one for me—tablets in the other.

I waited until they were seated and then began to relate the details of Greg Parker's visit.

"Okay," I said, then sighed before continuing, "I have a lot to tell you and I don't want this to take all day, so please keep your questions and comments to yourselves until I'm done."

The more I talked, the wider their eyes opened in response to the craziness. By the time I'd finished, they were either stunned or in open disbelief, depending upon the individual.

Bob Ryan, the first to speak, said, "Hogwash. I've heard of those suitcase bombs; they're an urban legend. The Russkies were supposed to have had 'em and when the Wall came down, more'n fifty of 'em disappeared, so they say. That was thirty-odd years ago. If they did exist, and if they did go missing, how come they've never been seen since? The answer is, they didn't..."

"With all due respect, Bob," T.J. Bron said, leaning forward in his chair, his hands clasped together, "what we're talking about here are not suitcase bombs. Maybe the Russians had 'em, maybe they didn't. What we're talking about is the SADM, an entirely different weapon. I know. I was part of a team that would have deployed one had our government been insane enough to order it. And what Harry says is entirely feasible, though quite fanciful—"

"Fanciful," Bob interrupted him. "You can say that again. Do you seriously think that the U.S. military could lose a couple of nuclear weapons, even small ones?"

"What do you think?" T.J. responded with a smirk.

"Would they even work today?" Jacque asked.

"Probably not," T.J. said. "There was even some doubt back then that they would work and being close to them was a nightmare;

deploying the thing would have been a suicide mission. Oh, and one more thing, Harry, your friend Agent Parker was exaggerating the effect one of those things would have. I'm not sure it would even take out a nuclear plant. They came in several... I'm going to say sizes; the smallest had a yield of only ten tons, not quite as big as the MOAB, The Mother of All Bombs, we dropped on Afghanistan; it was eleven tons. The largest SADM, as far as I remember, was one kiloton. There were bigger versions up to ten kilotons, but they were far less mobile. The one-kiloton SADM would make one hell of a bang, but devastate Southeast Tennessee and its surrounds? No! Nothing like it. If it was detonated at Sequoya, the effect on Chattanooga would be negligible. It might rattle a few windowpanes, but even that's a stretch, and even if it managed to breach the containment building, the prevailing winds would take the fallout north and east toward Decatur."

"A nuclear friggin' bomb?" I said, aghast. "Are you out of your mind? You're talking like it would be no big deal."

"If the target's Sequoya, it wouldn't be that big of a deal. Downtown Chattanooga? Now that would be a little different. Even then..."

"What are the chances of them being able to pull it off?" I asked.

T.J. shrugged, thought for a moment, and then said, "It's hard to say. The weapon is small enough to fit in the trunk of a full-size car or an SUV. Getting it close enough to Sequoya to do any real damage... I'm not familiar with the area, but I'd say they'd need to get it inside the perimeter. If they had someone on the inside, their chances would go up exponentially. Then again, engaging the thing would be another problem. Back in the day, the triggering mechanism was a combination of both mechanical and electric: the timer was mechanical with a thirteen-minute lead; the trigger was electric and battery powered. If they're planning on using the original system, it would almost certainly have to be deployed by a suicide bomber. But if it's not activated utilizing the original system, they would have to completely rebuild the triggering system, which wouldn't be that big of a deal for someone who knows their stuff."

"I don't believe it," Bob said in a low voice, shaking his head.

I stared at him. I could tell by the look on his face that he wasn't quite as sure as he would have us believe.

I looked at T.J. and said, "T.J.?"

"It's possible, though hardly probable... but I'd say it would be best to err on the side of caution, because even though it's improbable, we need to be ready. The consequences would be unthinkable."

"Why here?" Jacque asked. "Why not downtown Manhattan or Los Angeles?"

"I asked Parker that myself. His answer was that we're a relatively soft target, and he's probably right. Security around here seems almost nonexistent. And who the hell knows how these fanatic minds work? That being the case, it makes sense, sort of."

"I should have offed that Tree sonofabitch when I had the chance," Bob said. "You think it's him in the photo?"

"I don't know. The profile... Yeah, it could be. You're right, though. We should have put him away when we had the chance," I said wryly. "Hell, I've had a dozen chances to do just that, but somehow I always let him go. If anyone deserved it, he did. But that aside, we have to deal with the facts that he might be here and that he knows the territory better than most."

I thought for a minute and then continued, "T.J., you're not part of this. If we get involved, people could die. I can't expose you to that. Bob, Jacque, you have the vote. Are we in or are we out?"

"Wait just a minute," T.J. Bron said. "I'm the only one here that knows how this thing works. You need me."

I looked at him, shaking my head. What he said was true, but if things got rowdy, and I knew they would, well... at the risk of offending some folks, I didn't want to put the older man in harm's way, and while that's not quite what I told him, it didn't go down too well.

At first, he glared at me as he considered my explanation, but then his look suddenly changed to a smirk and he said, "You think you're a better man than I am, do you, Harry Starke?"

"No, it's not that—"

"Yes it is," he interrupted me. Out of the corner of my eye, I could see that Bob was grinning. "You think I'm too old, that I can't handle my end in a fight. Well, I venture to say that I could do a whole lot better than you... Calaway Jones, her name was, wasn't it?" Now he was grinning a little. "Didn't she almost do you in?"

"That's not—"

"Tell you what, Harry," he said, interrupting me again. "I'll take on the grinning buffoon here," he said as he nodded in Bob's direction, then continued, "and if I can't subdue him in less than ten seconds, you get your way. How does that sound?"

I didn't like the sound of it at all, and by the look on her face, neither did Jacque.

"That's not going to happen," I said.

Now T.J. really was smiling, a large grin on his face. "I thought not," he said with a smirk.

"Wait just a damn minute," Bob growled, rising to his feet and taking a step forward. "I'd like to take grandpa up on that. Oh, don't worry, Harry. I won't hurt... Arrrrggghhh?"

To this day, I have no idea what exactly happened at that moment. All I remember is that T.J. suddenly leaped out of his seat, moving so quickly I could barely track his movement, and then took two steps forward, ducked slightly, dropped his right shoulder, swung his right fist upward and across Bob's chest, and caught him on the jaw with a hard blow. After that he seemingly followed through with the punch, his fist streaking on past Bob's head, and then, like a striking snake, he reversed its direction, the outside of his right fist slamming hard against the right side of Bob's neck at the same instant his left arm came up under Bob's, grabbing a handful of hair at the back of his neck, and pulled. Bob's head jerked back exposing his neck to T.J.'s right hand.

"Don't move an inch," he growled into Bob's ear, just barely loud enough for me and Jacque to hear. "You do, and I'll open you up like a can of spam." They remained like that for a long moment, then T.J. released him and stepped back, only then opening his fist for all to see the Kershaw pocket knife. It was closed, but when he depressed the catch, the three-inch blade snapped open.

"Had that been for real," he quietly said before stepping forward again and continuing, "the first blow wouldn't have been my fist, see?" He held the knife like a dagger but with the spine of the knife laying against his forearm so that the edge of the blade faced away from him, aiming it toward Bob.

"Instead of connecting with your chin, the blade would have opened your chest from gut to shoulder, like this," he said, imitating the first upward sweep again; this time in slow motion, the blade arched upward from Bob's waist to his shoulder, only inches away from his chest. "And then, coming back," he continued explaining as, again in slow motion, he swept the knife down, the blade glittering under the office lights, and then stopped, the tip less than an inch from Bob's throat. "I would have slit your throat from ear to ear..."

T.J. grinned at him and said, "Now, you had enough of grandpa, or d'you want more?"

"That's enough, T.J.," I said. "You made your point. You can sit down now. Where the hell did you learn that stuff?"

"Special Forces. I told you I was part of a team that carried one of those things." He looked at Bob. "No hard feelings, Son?"

Bob grinned at him. "Not hardly," he said, rubbing his jaw. "There was no need to hit me so hard; it hurt, damn it. Yeah, okay, you win. I'd rather have you with me in a fight than against me."

"All right, Boys," Jacque said. "Now that the flow of testosterone has subsided to a trickle, let's get back to business. As far as I'm concerned, it's a go, and T.J. is in. Bob?"

He sat down, still rubbing his jaw. "Yeah," he growled, "it's a go, and T.J.'s in."

I gazed at the three of them, one after the other, shook my head, and shrugged, then said, "Okay, it's a go; he's in. All we have to do

now is find Shady and waterboard him... *Joking*, Jacque, just joking."
She looked horrified, eyes wide and mouth hanging open. Bob was
smirking. T.J. was a sphinx.

"Bob," I looked across the desk at him, saying, "I'll pay $1,000 to
anyone who will tell us where Shady Tree is. Get the word out on the
street, will you? Jacque, you call Benny Hinkle, though I can't for the
life of me believe he'd show his face in the Sorbonne. Still, Benny
may have heard something. When you've done that, call Kate. See if
she's heard anything about Shady being back in town, but don't
mention anything else. If she asks you why you want to know, tell her
it's me that's asking, but you don't know why. T.J., you go to that
nightclub on Chestnut. Ask around. See who was working that night.
Talk to them. Somebody may have seen something, and make sure
you specifically ask if anyone saw someone taking photos with a cell
phone at one of the tables on the balcony overlooking Chestnut.
Okay, that's it. I need to go home and talk to Amanda. I'll be in early
tomorrow, no later than seven. Parker will be here at nine; we'll talk
before he gets here. Let's go." I stood and followed them out of the
room.

On the way out, I called Amanda to make sure she was at home
and to let her know I was on my way, and then I headed up the
mountain.

Chapter Four

She was waiting for me when I arrived. Even almost nine months pregnant as she was, she looked stunning.

I nodded at her distended belly, smiling, and said, "Still no sign?"

"No, not yet... Harry, it's only four o'clock. Why are you here?"

"I have something I need to discuss with you, and I'm hungry. Have you prepared anything?"

"Of course. As soon as I knew you were coming I made a salad."

I wrinkled my nose and asked, "Salad? Amanda..."

"Oh come on. Just take a look. I have crusty bread. You can make a nice sandwich."

Dinner was sounding a little better, so I asked, "Drink?"

"Oh... I take it you're going out again?"

I nodded. "Maybe."

"Well, in that case, we have non-alcoholic sangria, orange juice, Dr. Pepper, coffee, or iced tea."

I sighed. "I'll have a Dr. Pepper."

The salmon salad sandwich wasn't at all bad, the Dr. Pepper was icy cold and, well, there's not another taste like it in the world, not that I know of.

I finished the sandwich, pushed my plate to one side, and looked at her across the table. There was just a hint of an enigmatic smile on her face. I had the durnedest feeling she knew what was coming.

"So," she said, unable to wait any longer, "are you going to tell me, or not?"

"I will, but first you have to promise me that what I tell you stays here. You can't tell anyone, especially not Channel 7."

Amanda, when she's not pregnant, is an anchor at one of the local TV stations.

"I mean it. You have to swear you'll keep it to yourself."

"Oh, don't be childish, Harry. You have my word; I won't say anything to *anyone*. Is that good enough for you?"

So I told her. Everything. I didn't leave anything out. It took a while. Finally, I stopped talking and looked at her. Most of the color had drained from her face, and she was no longer smiling. Ha, you think?

I waited for her to speak, and I studied her as I continued waiting, then finally she said, "Damn you, Harry Starke." Then she threw down her napkin, stood, and walked out of the kitchen heading toward the patio.

I sat for a moment, and then I followed her. She was standing beside the pool, the low patio wall in front of her, her legs akimbo, her arms folded, staring down at the city and the river below.

She must have heard me coming, but she didn't even turn her head. Instead, she said in a low voice, "You said never again, Harry."

"Yes, I know, but..."

"That's it, isn't it? There's always a 'but.' You'll never change. There will always be 'just this one more and I'm done.' I've heard it so many times. I don't believe you anymore."

"Amanda..."

"No, Harry. There's nothing you can say. Go save the damn world. Get yourself killed. I can manage without you. So can your child," she said, bitterly. And then she turned, brushed past me, and hurried back into the house.

For maybe five minutes, I stood there staring at the incredible view, but I didn't see it. I was lost in thought. I'd never seen her like this before. She'd never said those things to me, or anything like them. She was...

I went into the house. I expected to find her in the kitchen; she wasn't there. Nor was she in the living room. I found her in our bedroom, sitting on the bed, crying. *Oh shit!*

"Hey," I said as I sat down beside her and put my arm around her. *Well at least she didn't shrug it off.* "It's going to be okay."

"No it isn't!"

She stood and walked to the window, cupped her left elbow in her right hand, and sucked on the side of her forefinger.

"Yes, it is," I said.

I stood, went to her, slipped my hands around her waist, and massaged her belly. *Damn! That was a kick.*

"Hey, it kicked me."

"Consider yourself damn lucky I don't do the same," she said, angrily pushing my hands away.

"Come on, Amanda. All I have to do is help Greg find Shady. That's it. That's all I'll commit to. I promise."

She turned. Her belly touching mine, her face close to mine, tearstained with mascara.

"You promise? You really promise?"

I put my arms around her waist—well, as far as I could—and pulled her to me. Okay, she was already touching me, so I slid my hands up her back to her shoulders, leaning forward I kissed her, and suddenly my heart was in my mouth as a wave of emotion swept over me. I always knew I loved this woman; but never, until then, did I know just how much. And I think at that moment she could feel it too.

She let go of me, leaned back in my arms, and stared up me.

"Tell me," she said.

"I love you..."

She laughed, sniffling and wiping her nose on her sleeve, and said, "Not that, you idiot. Promise me that when you find Shady it will be over, and that you'll tell Greg that's all you will commit to in helping him with his problem."

"I do, I promise." *Oh hell, how am I going to do that?*

"I have a bad feeling, Harry. I don't want to lose you; I don't want our child to grow up without you."

"That's not going to happen..." I started saying, but right then, something happened, and I stopped talking.

I've always been blessed with... I dunno, Amanda and Kate call it second sight. I've never thought anything of it. Anyway, I suddenly had a vision. I was in what appeared to be a hospital room, looking down at the bed. It was dark, so dark I couldn't see who was lying on the bed, but I had the distinct feeling it was me. It lasted but a few seconds, until I shook my head to clear the image, and then it was gone. *What the hell was that?*

"Harry, you shuddered. What is it? What's wrong?"

"Nothing, My Sweet. Nothing at all. It was just one of those 'Somebody just walked over my grave' moments."

"Oh God. You had one of those visions, didn't you? Tell me."

I wasn't going to tell her what I saw. That would upset her, a lot, and that was something she didn't need right then, not in her condition. They say there are times when it's okay to lie, a little. I figured this was one of those times.

"There is nothing to tell. I told you. I shuddered. It was involuntary. That's all there was to it."

By the look on her face, the questions I saw in her eyes, I wasn't sure she believed me, but she didn't pursue it, so I guess I got off light.

"Are you going out again?"

I looked at my watch and said, "No. I was planning to spend the rest of the day with you." And I did.

Chapter Five

I was up at four-thirty the following morning and ran my usual five miles, then did a couple of laps in the pool to cool off, took a shower, and ate breakfast with Amanda. Breakfast wasn't the usual happy moment I'd come to enjoy. She was quiet, and I didn't push her as to why; I already knew.

"I have to go," I finally said.

She nodded and followed me to the car. I turned, wrapped my arms around her, pulled her to me, held her tightly, a little *too* tightly and for a little too long. Eventually, I leaned back in her arms, and looking into her eyes, I smiled. She didn't smile back.

"What time will you be home?"

"I don't know. Depends. If we find Shady fast, then no later than usual. If not..." I didn't need to finish the thought. She knew me well enough.

She put the palms of both hands on my chest and pushed. "Go on," she said, blinking away the tears that threatened to fall any moment. "Go get him. Be careful... and don't forget to tell Greg what you promised me. I'll be here when you get home."

"You sure you'll be alright?" I released her, stepped back, and looked down at her belly.

"Don't worry. If the baby comes, yours will be the first number I call... after 911." She laughed, but there was little humor in it.

I nodded, kissed her on the lips, then climbed into the car and started it. Pulling out through the gates onto Brow Road, I glanced at the rearview mirror. Amanda was standing at the gate watching me go; I felt like shit.

I arrived at my office some fifteen minutes later; it was just a few minutes after seven. I was the last to arrive.

"Okay, everyone," I said as I walked into the front office. "Conference room, now. Parker will be here soon, and I want us all to be on the same page."

It didn't take long to follow up on the results of Bob's and T.J.'s assignments from the previous afternoon.

Bob had put the word out to several of his street contacts, but so far, he hadn't heard back from any of them. T.J. had no luck at all. The waitress that had been on duty the night of the hit was no longer working there, and he'd received nothing but confused looks from the rest of the people he'd talked to.

Lastly, I related a little of my conversation with Amanda and what I had decided as a result of it. Jacque looked relieved, Bob just shook his head, obviously not fully understanding; I didn't bother to explain further. T.J. was as enigmatic as he always was: calm, collected, with a slight smile on his lips.

By eight o'clock that morning, we were done talking, and I was done waiting. I called Parker and asked him to hurry his ass up. He didn't. It was nine o'clock on the dot when he finally arrived.

"You ready, Hero?" he asked, sarcastically.

"Thanks for putting yourself out, Greg. I really appreciate it."

"Screw you, Harry. Talk to me."

I nodded at Jacque, saying, "Get the others, please."

I turned to Greg and said, "My office."

I took my seat behind my desk and waved him to one of the two guest chairs in front of it. When the others arrived, I indicated to Jacque for her to take the other seat by Greg and for Bob and T.J. to turn two of the big chairs at the coffee table around so that they too were facing my desk.

I stared at Greg over my steepled fingers; he waited. And I made him wait some more. No, I wasn't trying to make him uncomfortable; I just wanted to clear my own head to be sure I knew exactly what I wanted to say. He stared back at me, obviously not happy, but he waited without interrupting my thoughts.

Ultimately, I said, "Two things, Greg. The first is that I have only three people, including me, that I can spare: me, Bob, and T.J.; Jacque will coordinate. The second and most important thing is, at least to me, that when we find Shady, if we do find him, if he's here, then it's over, done. I will not allow myself or my team to be sucked into a protracted hunt for terrorists and a super bomb. If that's agreeable, we're in."

"That's not exactly what I was hoping for," he said, quietly. "You guys know this area better than any of my agents, even those in the local office. I need that expertise, Harry. I need you in until the thing is found—if it exists—and neutralized or, if the worst happens, until the damn thing blows Sequoya all to hell."

I responded, shaking my head, "Not happening, Greg. I gave you my terms, now take them or leave them."

"You talked to your wife, didn't you? This is her doing, damn it! Friggin'..."

Jumping to my feet, I said with a raised voice, "Don't even think of finishing what you were about to say. You talk about my wife with respect or get your fancy tailored ass out of here. You hear?"

"What I was about to say was..." My iPhone buzzed. Greg paused.

I looked at the screen, answered the call, and said, "Yes. Okay. Later." I hung up.

"Friggin' hell, Harry," Greg continued. "What I was about to say was that I need you in this thing. I told you manpower was stretched to the breaking point. I cannot get additional agents assigned to this case until I have something more. Harry, I have a bad feeling about it. My gut tells me that we are the target, but as far as the director is concerned, gut feelings are only one step removed from bullshit... Look, what if we do find him? What if I'm right? Are you still going to walk away?"

"Listen to me, Agent Parker," I said, leaning forward and folding my arms on the desktop. "I told you that we'd help you find Tree and then that was it; we're out, all of us, gone. And I don't care what the hell else we find. If they have a bomb, you'll get all the manpower you need from the FBI, military, CIA, and God only knows who else. You won't need me. Unless they plant the thing here in my office, and I mean right here in this room, I'm out. Got it?"

He leaned back in his chair, glaring at me through eyes that had become little more than slits. After some time, he lowered his head, shaking it, then looked up at me, nodded, and said, "Yeah, I got it."

"Good," I said, leaning back in my chair. "Just so long as we're clear. Now, talk to me. What's your plan?"

"Other than finding Tree, I don't have one. This is your neck of the woods. I figured you'd know all the angles."

I nodded, and then looking at Jacque, I said, "You called Benny Hinkle. Tell Agent Parker what he said."

"He said he didn't know where Shady Tree is. The last he'd heard was a rumor that Tree was in Nuevo Laredo working with one of the cartels, but that's all it was, a rumor."

I glanced at Parker; he was smirking.

"You think that means anything?" I asked. "It doesn't." Parker said nothing. He just leaned back in his chair, his arms folded across his chest, the smirk now a wry smile.

"I'll tell you what it does mean," I said. "It means he's not here, at least not yet. If he was, Benny would have heard something."

"He's here," Parker said.

"And you know this for sure? How?"

He simply shrugged and smirked.

"Why do I get the feeling you're not telling me everything you know?" I asked.

Again with the shrug and the smirk.

I turned back to Jacque and asked, "Did you ask Benny to keep his eyes and ears open?"

She nodded. "That I did. He said he'll call you if he hears anything. And, as you know, I also talked to Kate. She hasn't seen or heard anything of Shady either. She also asked what we were up to and why you wanted to know about him. I did as you asked and told her I didn't know. She wasn't happy. She said she wants to see you."

"Yeah, I know," I said, dryly. "I called her on the way in. That was her calling me back."

"Who the hell is Kate?" Parker interrupted me.

"Lieutenant Kate Gazzara, local PD. She's a friend. If she can help, she will."

That, I thought, *might be a bit of a stretch. If I can't be completely candid with her, tell her what's going on, she could even become a problem; it wouldn't be the first time.*

Kate had been my partner for almost eight years until I left the PD... Actually, she'd been more than just my partner, until... well, that's another story. For now, let's just say I know her very well and that she's my "go to" inside the Chattanooga Police Department, at least she was.

"Greg," I said, leaning forward again. "We need to bring Kate in. She has the ear of Chief Johnston. He also needs to be included..."

"*Whaat?*" Greg was pissed. "The local PD? Are you out of your mind? Did I not lay it out for you? You bring in the PD and then the media will have it ten minutes later. Hell, why don't you bring in the sheriff as well?"

I smiled. The sarcasm was what I remembered most about him.

"I thought about that but decided not to. But you know, Sequoya is within his jurisdiction. It would make sense to bring Whitey in, don't you think? I know him; he can be trusted."

"Oh yes, that makes perfect sense." He looked at Jacque and said,

"Has the mail run yet?" Then he looked at me and said, "Why don't we bring in the mailman and the friggin' FedEx driver while we're at it?"

I heard Jacque trying to suppress a giggle, not very successfully.

Parker stood, glared at me, then angrily said, "I should have known. Four years at FDU with you... What else could I expect from...?" He paused, shook his head, then continued, "Ahhh, I can see now that this was a mistake, a waste of time. What the hell happened to you, Harry? I guess you found yourself a trophy wife and she turned you into a damn pussy; you're friggin' pussy whipped, that's what you are. I don't know what I was thinking. You and your..." He looked around the room. "You and your team can stay the hell out of it. I'll do without you... And by God, you'd better keep your mouths shut." He walked to the door, opened it, and stormed out slamming the door behind him.

The room was silent for a moment, then Bob quietly said, "I think he's pissed at you, Harry."

"No shit?" I said, caustically.

Pussy whipped? Me? Nah... Am I? I looked at the door through which Parker had just made his exit. *Son-of-a-bitch, I hope to hell not.*

I looked at Jacque, then at Bob. Neither one of them would look me in the eye. I looked at T.J. He smiled and winked at me.

"Well..." I said, looking at each one of them in turn. "Is that what you think too?"

Jacque just shook her head.

"T.J.?"

He shrugged. "What the hell do I know?"

I looked at Bob quizzically.

"Honestly?" he asked.

"Yeah, honestly," I growled, "but be damn careful, Bob."

He smiled. "You're not the man you were two years ago. Pussy? Hardly. Pussy whipped? I don't know, but *you* do. That's why you're asking the question."

I stared at him, not liking what I was hearing. The problem was that deep down I had a feeling he was right. I also knew there was little I could do about it, even if I wanted to. I now had a family and that brought with it new responsibilities, responsibilities I'd never had before.

I looked at Jacque. She smiled and shrugged.

I looked at T.J.

"Don't look at me," he said, smiling. "I hardly know you."

I leaned my chair back as far as it would go, laced my fingers together behind my neck, and stared up at the chandelier.

"Greg was right," a little voice inside my brain said. *"It's time you got out, Harry."* I tried to ignore it; I couldn't, and the more I thought about it, the angrier I became.

"Get out," I growled, not taking my eyes off the chandelier. "All of you... Out! I need some time alone. T.J., go on back to the night-club. Keep digging. See what you can find out. Bob, I'll talk to you later. Jacque, I don't want to be disturbed unless somebody's dying."

And they left.

Pussy whipped, my ass.

Chapter Six

They hadn't been gone from my office more than a couple of minutes when I decided I needed to get the hell out of there myself. I looked at the lock screen on my phone; it was ten forty-five. I looked at the cupboard where I kept my booze. A stiff jolt of scotch would have gone down well, but it was too early and I was driving. *Here we go again. Three years ago, I wouldn't have given a damn.*

I let the chair fall forward into its upright position, opened a lower desk drawer, and took out my shoulder rig and VP9. I hadn't worn or used either in a while, favoring instead a much lighter Glock 43 and sticky holster... *Maybe that's part of my problem; suit and friggin' tie!*

I stood, slipped out of my suit jacket... *Maybe that's another sign... Damn, I miss my old leather jacket and jeans.*

I dropped the Glock into the drawer, donned the shoulder rig, drew the VP9, ejected the mag, turned the weapon ejector-side up, worked the slide to clear the chamber, flipped the gun into my left hand, and caught the round in my right before it hit the desktop... *Pussy whipped, my ass! You're as sharp as you ever were, Harry.*

I returned the round to the mag, slammed the mag back into the grip, worked the slide to jack the round back into the chamber, and shoved the gun back into its holster. Then I put on my suit jacket, grabbed two extra mags, slipped them into my jacket pocket, and headed for the door.

On the way out, I told Jacque I'd be back by six and then left. Outside in the lot, my metallic-gray Range Rover reminded me again of the changes in my life. Time was I'd have laughed at the idea of driving such a... *Pussy wagon? Hell, it's got to go!*

I climbed into the car and headed for Carter Shooting Supply on Highway 58. I checked in, purchased a box of ammo, and went out to the range. It being early afternoon, I had the place almost to myself. I plugged my ears and then put forty-five shots downrange at fifteen yards as quickly as I could pull the trigger and change the mags. Then I pushed the switch to bring up the target and watched distractedly as it rolled slowly toward me. I was somewhat encouraged to see that all forty-five hits were within a six-inch group, and at least twenty were within a two-inch group: the center of the target was a gaping hole. *Pussy, my ass. You still got it, Harry.*

I cleared the VP9, then reloaded the three magazines. Slapping the first mag into the grip, I then chambered a round, holstered it, slipped the other two mags into my pocket, and headed out the door back to the Range Rover. *Pussy car!*

I climbed inside, hit the starter, then the Bluetooth, and called Kate.

"Harry. What's up?"

"You busy?"

"Not especially. Why?"

"You want to meet me for coffee?"

"Sure. Where?"

"Hell, I don't know. Anywhere. You name it."

"Wow, you're in a good mood. How about Starbucks at the Read House?"

"Yeah, okay. I'll meet you there. Now?"

"Give me..." I looked at my watch. "Say fifteen minutes?"

"Make it twenty. See you."

Even on a Thursday in the early afternoon, it took me twenty-five minutes to make it from Highway 58 to the Read House downtown. Kate was already seated, waiting for me.

I've known Kate Gazzara almost all of my professional life, from when she was a rookie cop to the present in her current position as a lieutenant in Chattanooga PD's Major Crimes unit. She's a commanding presence, almost six feet tall, long tawny hair, and startlingly huge hazel eyes. She was wearing jeans and a tan leather jacket. Her hair was tied back in a ponytail. As always, she looked good.

I sat down opposite her. There was coffee already on the table waiting for me. I thanked her, took a sip, and looked at her.

"So," she said, smiling. "What's wrong? Jacque called me, said you were looking for Shady. I haven't seen him in months, Harry. Why do you want him?"

"What makes you think that... that there's something wrong?"

"Come on, Harry. You never call me these days unless the world's about to stop spinning. What's up?"

"Let me give Jacque a quick call."

I did and told her I wouldn't be back. Then I looked again at Kate.

"Kate..." I paused. I didn't know how to say it. She was always, well, almost always, my go-to when I needed help, and she reciprocated more often these days than I did. She was the one person, other than Amanda, that I could talk to without reservation, but what I wanted to ask her this time... Hell, I just blurted it out.

"Kate, have I changed lately, that you've noticed?"

She narrowed her eyes. "Yes, of course. We all have. It's the natural order of things. We get older, we change..."

"That's not what I meant..." I sighed and continued, "I met an old friend today... No, not a friend, a piece of... Greg Parker—you never knew him. He's FBI, SAC Knoxville, or some such—was in my office when I arrived yesterday morning, and I do mean in my office, in my chair. Why? I'll tell you in a minute. Anyway, we were at Fairleigh Dickenson together, but that's another story. He asked me for help with a case he's working on. I said I would, but that it would be limited, that I was done with the wild life... Kate, he said I'd changed, that I'd turned into a pussy, and that I was pussy whipped. You don't think..."

She burst out laughing, loud, long, and raucous; when she finally stopped, there were tears in her eyes.

"And you didn't smack him in the mouth?" she asked. I didn't answer. "There's your answer then. I guess you have changed. The Harry Starke I knew would never have let a taunt like that pass unanswered."

She picked up her coffee, put it to her lips, paused, studied me over the rim of the cup, then slowly lowered it back to the table.

"You're serious," she said. "Harry, you can't let that kind of thing get to you, for Pete's sake. He was probably joking."

"No, he wasn't, and the tough thing is, I think maybe he's right. Ever since I married Amanda, and especially now, I seem to have sunk into some sort of rut. Hell, I made Jacque and Bob partners, and then I turned over most of the running of the business to them. Shit, Kate, I don't do much of anything anymore... And... And..." I paused and looked her in the eye. She looked right back at me. "And Amanda's kinda laying down some rules."

"And so she should. You were a wild one, Harry. She loves you; she doesn't want you to get hurt, and she sure as hell doesn't want to lose you. You can't blame her for that. She killed for you, Harry. She saved your life."

"I know. And I don't blame her. What I have a problem with is me. I've grown complacent and let myself slip into some kind of stagnancy, but I didn't even notice it happening... I don't like it, Kate. I've either gotta get with the program again or I've gotta get out."

"Harry, you're taking it far too seriously. Obviously, this... Parker person is some kind of asshole and you pissed him off."

I sighed, nodded, then said, "Okay, that's enough of that. Thanks for letting me get it off my chest. Now I need to talk to you about what Parker was doing in my office."

I spent the next fifteen minutes filling her in on the two meetings I'd had with him, ending by telling her how he stormed out virtually telling me to go to hell. *Screw him and keeping it to myself. We're not talking a couple pounds of C-4 here.*

While I was talking, she sat perfectly still and listened; watching her, I saw the color slowly drain from her face.

"You've got to be frigging kidding me..." She was stunned. "A nuclear bomb? Here? In Chattanooga? Harry, we can't keep this to ourselves. I certainly can't... I can't," she repeated. "If nothing else, I'll have to brief the chief."

"Yeah, I figured you would, but look, everything I've just told you is FBI speculation. They have no evidence. They don't know anything. They have no proof; their only source is some internet chatter and an informant that was gunned down on Chestnut two weeks ago. Parker admitted to me that there were at least four other possible targets. This all may be just a great big nothing... and me? I just can't believe it. The whole idea could have been lifted from a Jack Reacher novel."

"But it may *not* be a great big nothing," she said, visibly agitated. "We can't take that chance. We're talking about a possible nuclear explosion, for God's sake, right here... But Parker's right... and you're right too. The fewer people who know about this the better. Panic in the streets is the last thing we need... But you're not done with it, are you?"

Shrugging, I said, "Hardly. I promised Amanda I'd find Shady and then quit, but I dunno. If we do find him, and this turns out to be for real, I won't be able to walk away from it, you know that."

She nodded. "No, you won't. Look, I'll call Chief Johnston and set up a meeting. Oh, don't look at me like that. I have to; you know I do."

I sighed and nodded. "In the meantime, we have to go after

Shady. I have a feeling that time's short." Just how short... Well, if I'd known, I would have panicked myself.

She made the call; I listened. She gave him no details, just that she needed to meet with him and that she'd be bringing me along. He wanted to do it the following morning, but she insisted that we see him before then. He agreed. An appointment was set for us to be at the PD on Amnicola at eight o'clock that evening. Then she hung up, but she wasn't yet finished.

She looked at me, shook her head as if to tell me not to interrupt, then she hit the speed dial and raised the phone to her ear.

"Whitey," she said. I half-stood, both hands on the table, shaking my head. She raised a hand to stop me. Slowly, I sat down again. Oh, was I pissed!

"It's Kate Gazzara. I have a meeting with Chief Johnston at eight this evening. Can you attend?"

I'm not going to go into the conversation that was generated by that question. Let's just say that Sheriff White took a bit of persuading—she told him nothing about why he should be there—but in the end, I guess she must have piqued his curiosity, because he finally agreed and she hung up.

I stared at her. She stared defiantly back at me.

"He has to know, Harry. He's the sheriff for Pete's sake, and Sequoya is in his jurisdiction."

I didn't like it, not one damn bit. She was right, of course, but now we had two more loose lips to deal with, and how many more there would be after they were in the loop, only God knew.

"Yeah, okay. Look, I need to talk to Benny. If anyone can find Shady, it's him... Always supposing he's even here, which is doubtful. You want to join me or d'you need to go?"

"Need to go? Are you kidding? Let's go talk to him, now."

I suppose now would be a good time to fill you in about Shady. Those of you who've been following my career know all about him. If you don't, here's a quick rundown.

Lester "Shady" Tree is something of an enigma among Chattanooga's black community... Well, he was, but he hasn't been around lately. A well-educated, long-time, small-time ambitious criminal whose career escalated when a local, corrupt congressman took him under his wing; a relationship that lasted until the congressman was put away for what certainly would have been the rest of his life, had he not died violently in prison. That rise in Shady's fortunes elevated him from small-time thug to the head of organized black crime in the city. He and I had several altercations over the years until I finally ran him out of town about a year ago. It didn't surprise me that he'd gotten himself into a bad crowd, though I was sure that whatever the enterprise was, Shady would be close to the top of the tree—no pun intended.

I said he was well educated, and he is, but if you don't know him, you might never know it. When he's in the ghettos, he reverts back to the subculture, speaks Ebonics and dresses in the stereotypical way you would expect, including shoulder-length dreadlocks and orange sneakers. Take him out of the ghetto and he speaks better English than the average college professor.

He's arrogant, self-confident, and vicious, with a penchant for straight razors. He's committed almost every anti-social crime you can think of but has always drawn the line at murder, which makes me wonder what the hell he's gotten himself into. I guess we'll soon know.

Chapter Seven

I t was just after five that afternoon when we arrived at the Sorbonne. Inside, it was a dark, empty cave. Well, almost empty. There was a couple seated in a booth at the far end of the room and a somewhat rough-looking individual seated at the far end of the bar, close to the restrooms. I watched him watch Kate as she walked to the bar and asked Benny to join us.

The little man nodded as she spoke to him, then put down the glass he was cleaning and threw the washcloth into the sink. He beckoned to Laura, his partner, barkeep, and main draw for the business. He whispered into her ear and looked across at me, then nodding, he pointed to Laura and quizzically raised his eyebrows. I nodded.

Laura walked to where the man was leaning his elbows on the bar and said something to him I couldn't hear. He shook his head, so she came around the end of the bar and sat down beside Benny who was now seated opposite Kate and me.

"Whadaya want, Harry? I don't have no time for casual conversation. I gotta business to run."

"So I see," I said, sarcastically, looking around the vast empty space that constituted the inner delights of Benny Hinkle's "business," the Sorbonne...

In case you're not familiar with Chattanooga's sleaziest nightclub... Well, I really don't need to say more, because that's what it is—Chattanooga's sleaziest den of iniquity—the haunt of every lowlife that can afford Benny's exorbitant prices and watered liquor, as well as many of the Scenic City's beautiful people too, the so-called movers and shakers. Me? Yeah, I've been a patron for as long as I can remember; it's part of my job... at least it was...

Benny? He's a fat little creep, maybe five-six and almost as wide. If I were a believer in such things, I'd say he was one of the "undead," a greasy, unshaven slob that emerges from the even darker regions of the Sorbonne, his office—if you could call it that—where he lives, only coming out at night to take advantage of his unwary customers...

Ah, maybe I'm being too hard on him. Ours is a somewhat symbiotic relationship, at least it was when I was a cop. He was my CI—confidential informant. Now we simply tolerate each other, at least as much as we can. Yes, he's been helpful on occasion, and I think he trusts me, at least a little.

Laura Davies, Benny's long-time sidekick and "business partner," is something else again. I've never been sure if theirs is a romantic or financial arrangement; I'm of a mind that it has to be the latter. Laura is, in fact, a respectable married woman with two lovely kids, a boy and a girl. It takes all sorts, I guess. Laura is the quintessential Southern barkeep, Chattanooga's answer to Daisy Duke. *Wow, now that dates me.*

She usually dresses to please her customers—with whom she flirts unashamedly—tops designed to barely cover her more-than-ample breasts and cutoff jeans that barely cover her amazing ass. But, my friends, it's all a façade, an act that earns her more in tips than her tight-assed little boss, partner, whatever you want to call Benny, could ever afford to pay her.

I looked at her, then at Benny. His piggy eyes were half-closed; he looked like a great fat rat.

"Jacque called you earlier today, right?" I asked him.

"Yeah. She said you was looking for Shady. I ain't seen 'im. Laura ain't neither."

"I'm sure Laura," I said, looking at her before I continued, "doesn't need you to talk for her."

She flashed a tight-lipped smile.

"I didn't ask if you'd seen him. What's the word around the city? What's he been doing? Where is he? Is he back in town?"

"Jeez, Harry. Slow down. None o' the above. I ain't seen his ass since you ran 'im off. That was what? Nine? Ten months ago?"

"How about you, Laura? Anything?"

She shook her head and said, "No. Not a word."

"And you've heard nothing about him smuggling..." *Whoops, almost let the cat out of the bag.* "...opioids?"

"I told you, Harry, I ain't seen 'im. The only thing I heard was that he was somewhere in Mexico, Nuevo Laredo I think it was. The word is that he has hooked up with one of the cartels. Other than that, I ain't heard nothing about that piece o' crap in months, an' I hope to hell I don't. Now, can I get back to my business? That guy looks like he needs a refill."

No, he doesn't. He's watching us!

I'd been watching the creep out of the corner of my eye. I could see his face in the mirror behind the bar; his eyes were on us, watching, prying, trying to listen. I took a mental photo of his face. He was black, long thin face, mustache and goatee beard, and wearing a red ball cap turned backward on his head. He looked vaguely familiar. I was sure I'd seen him somewhere before, but where? I couldn't remember.

"Benny, Laura, I think Shady's back in town. I have to find him, and quickly. I need you guys to ask around, put the word out; there's a $1,000 reward for his location..."

The man at the bar had an iPhone in his hand, close to the bar top, as if he was playing with it, only he wasn't; he was taking photos.

"If you'll excuse me for just a minute," I said. "I'll be right back..."

I slid sideways out of the booth just a microsecond too late; he clocked me. By the time I'd turned and stood upright, he was up and away, heading for the back door. I chased after him, but he'd been ready for me. He must have cased the joint well, because as he exited the back door into the passageway that led past Benny's office to the Prospect Street exit, he stopped and dragged a thirty-gallon keg of beer against the door. It didn't take a lot of effort to shoulder the door open, but it gave him the time he needed to make his getaway. I heard the motorcycle's engine roar to life, and when I exited onto Prospect, I caught a glimpse of its brake light as he made a left turn and headed toward Market Street. *Damn it. I am out of shape.*

I returned to the booth and sat down in my seat.

"Well?" Benny asked. "What the hell was that about?"

"Who was he, Benny?"

"I dunno. I never saw him before tonight."

"Laura?"

She shook her head.

"You're sure you've never seen him before, Benny?"

"I told you, no!"

"Laura?" I looked at her.

"Never!"

I turned to Kate and asked, "How about you, Kate? Did you recognize him?"

"No, but then I didn't really take a whole lot of notice of him, either. But you did, right?"

"Yes... No, not really. He looked familiar, but I couldn't place him. He was watching us, listening, and I'm damned certain he was also taking photos of us. I'm of a mind that we were the reason he was here."

Who the hell was he? I thought. *What the hell was he up to? He had to have been in here for a reason. Waiting for someone...*

"Okay," I said as I turned to Benny before continuing, "if he comes in again, and I'd bet money he won't, I would appreciate it if you'd call me."

"You got it, Harry," Benny said.

I looked at him, skeptically. Laura winked at me. I shook my head. She shrugged.

"Benny," I said. "Look at me." He wiggled uncomfortably on his seat, but he did it.

"If I find out you know who that guy is? I'll castrate you. You understand?"

"I told you, Harry, I don't know who he is. Look, I gotta go... I gotta go." He started to rise.

"Sit the hell back down," I growled at him. He did.

"Here's the deal. You too, Laura. First, I want to know who that guy is. Second, I'll pay either one of you five grand to find Shady Tree for me. You can use it however you like: to pay for the information, or you can keep it and split what's left, whatever. We've got to find him. It's a matter of life or death." *Oh jeez, I can't believe I just used that old, worn-out cliché.*

"You'll put the word out?" I asked.

"Yeah," Benny said. "Can I go now?"

I sighed and nodded, then peering at both of them I said, "Yeah, go on. You too, Laura, and thanks..."

She slid out of her seat and stood to one side while Benny slid out and waddled back to the bar.

"How the hell d'you live with him?" I asked her.

"Fortunately, I *don't* live with him. If I did... Well, I'd have to kill him," she grinned as she said this, but I had the feeling she wasn't entirely joking.

"He's not so bad," she continued, "and I can handle him."

"Yeah, I know you can, but why would you want to?"

She smiled and said, "Let's just say the pay is better here than it is at Walmart. I'll do what I can to find Shady for you, but it may take a while." And then she was gone.

We left too. My hopes for anything helpful from either of them were pretty low.

Chapter Eight

I called Amanda to let her know that I was going to be late. She asked the questions I thought she would. I told her I was with Kate and that we had a meeting with Chief Johnston. She asked if I'd kept my promise, and I was happy to be able to tell her that I had. What I didn't tell her was that I might not be able to keep said promise. So I ended up feeling like shit anyway.

Kate and I had dinner at the Boathouse on Riverside. It wasn't the most enjoyable couple of hours I'd ever spent with Kate. The conversation was stilted, and I knew she felt uncomfortable being alone with me like that, but what the hell was I supposed to do?

It was just a few minutes before eight when we arrived at the PD on Amnicola. Kate signed me in and I followed her along the corridor to Chief Wesley Johnston's office. He was waiting for us, sitting behind his desk, which happened to be an artifact that was even bigger than mine. He was in uniform, and even this late in the day, it still appeared crisp and perfectly pressed; the four gold stars on his collar glittered in the artificial light when he moved. He's a big guy, is our Wesley, a commanding presence, a no-nonsense administrator who demands respect and obedience from his underlings. The respect? He gets it because he's earned it. The obedience? Not so much, which is why he and I didn't always get along. He has a big head... No, I don't mean he's arrogant. It's big and round, shaved and polished to a shine. His mustache—Hulk Hogan would have been proud of it—precisely trimmed and coifed, was the perfect accessory.

There were two other people in his office, both seated in guest chairs some distance from the great desk: Sheriff Jordan White and someone I'd run up against many times during my eight years as a cop —Assistant Chief Henry "Tiny" Finkle—a greasy, slimy little bastard of whom I thought I'd seen the last.

"Starke, Lieutenant," Johnston said as he nodded at the two empty guest chairs. "Sit down. Tell me. What's so damned important you couldn't tell me over the phone, and why does Sheriff White need to be here?"

"And good evening to you too, Chief," I said, sarcastically. I didn't sit, neither did Kate. She remained standing just inside the door. She knows me too well, and she knew what was coming.

I turned and nodded to the Sheriff.

"Hey, Harry," White said, half-standing, leaning forward and offering me his hand, which I shook. "Long time no see. How's Amanda? Must be getting close, yeah?"

"Yeah, Whitey. Any day now. It's good to see you too."

I turned again, and glaring at Finkle without taking my eyes off his smirking face, quietly asked, "What's he doing here, Chief?"

"I asked him to sit in. D'you have a problem with that?"

"Yeah, I do. This is supposed to be a private meeting between the four of us. The subject is sensitive. Please ask him to leave."

"Sorry, Starke. That's not going to ha... Hey, wait a minute. Where are you going?"

"I'm leaving. If I wanted the specifics of this discussion to be leaked to the press, I'd do it myself, not leave it to rat face here," I said as I nodded in Finkle's direction; his smirk was gone. "He goes or I go. Your choice."

"Henry," Johnston quietly said. "Do you mind?"

He did, but he rose from his seat anyway. His face was a mask of fury. I didn't care. Kate might have to put up with him, but I didn't. *Sneaky little bastard.*

I waited until he was out of the room and then pushed the door shut with a bang, just to let him know it was me. *Petty? Hell yeah!*

"Sit down, Harry," Johnston calmly said in a low voice. *Harry now, is it? He must be remembering the good times. Nah, there weren't any.*

I sat down and so did Kate. I glanced around at White. He was smiling. He didn't like Finkle any more than I did.

I looked again at Johnston. He was leaning back in his chair, elbows on the arms, fingers steepled in front of him, with a tight smile on his face.

"This better be good, Harry," Johnston said, his eyes narrowed almost to slits.

"It is... No, Chief, it's bad, very bad."

I spent the next fifteen minutes filling them in on the events of the last couple of days. I also showed them the photo of what might or might not have been Tree, the one taken from the nightclub balcony. I continued providing the details until, finally, I figured I'd said enough.

I paused, looked first at Johnston, then at White. Johnston stared stoically back at me, slowly rocking his chair back and forth. White... well, he looked shaken, something I'd never seen before.

"Look," I said. "I don't know how credible the threat is, so it may be all smoke and FBI bullshit, but no matter; what I've just told you can't leave this office. I'm sure you both understand why, and now you also know why I wanted Finkle out of here. If one whisper of this gets out, you'll be dealing with... Well, you both know that better than I do. Any questions?"

Johnston looked at White, his eyebrows raised in question.

"I know Greg Parker," White said. "I'm sure you do too, Chief, and whatever you may think of him, Harry, he's the real deal. I think we have to take this seriously. Don't you, Chief?"

Johnston nodded, thoughtfully, and raising the tips of his fingers to his pursed lips he said, "He is the real deal, but you said there are four other possible targets, Harry, so the odds are one in five in our favor—"

"I disagree," I said, interrupting him. "If Lester Tree is involved, and we don't yet know for sure that he is, then Sequoya it is. You can count on it. He knows the area. He knows our security, or lack of it. Sequoya is the quintessential soft target... Well, Watt's Bar is also a possibility, but my money's on Sequoya. Have you been up there? Hell, you can drive right onto the property. Google the place. You wouldn't need to get farther than one of the parking lots and you're close enough. A one-kiloton blast would take out the entire facility."

"I don't buy it, Harry," Johnston said, shaking his head. "Tree is a piece of shit, for sure, but I can't believe he's capable of what you're suggesting. To my knowledge, he's never so much as killed a bug. Now you're saying he's capable of killing thousands of people..." he said as he continued shaking his head.

I thought about it for a minute, then said, "Maybe you're right. I do know him as well as anybody and, yeah, I wouldn't have thought he had it in him, but we can't afford to take that chance. He may not be the one who will pull the trigger, but if he smuggled these terrorists into the country, he knows who and where they are. We have to find him, and fast!"

Johnston looked at White and asked, "What do you think, Jordan?"

"I hope to hell you're wrong, Harry. Sequoya is pretty isolated. Even so, the number of casualties from a one-kiloton explosion would be significant, probably in the thousands. We can't let it happen. Harry's right, Chief. If Tree is the only link we have to these... Iranians? We have to find him. He's the key. I... I should put Sequoya on notice..."

"You do that," Kate said, "and I doubt we can contain it. Could you deploy some deputies?" White looked at her, skeptically. She shrugged and suggested, "You could make it an undercover op.

There's an RV park on Igou Ferry Road, just across from the plant... Damn, that's the ideal spot to plant the bomb. It's close enough and open to the public. They could run a camper in there anytime and it wouldn't be noticed."

"She's right," I said. "That RV park can't be much more than a couple of hundred yards from the generating plant, and it's just across the road from the switching yard."

"Yeah," White said, leaning forward in his chair, his hands clasped together. "I know where you're talking about. It's a gimme. What's worse though, is that there's really nothing to stop them just driving right on into the complex... Let me think about it. In the meantime, we need something more definite; we need Tree."

"There's no telling where he might be," Kate said. "We'll need every resource we can muster if we're going to find him with all possible haste."

"I've spread the word on the streets that I'm offering a thousand bucks for his location."

"Oh yeah, Harry," White said, sarcastically. "That'll do it. *Only a thousand?* Are you sure you can spare it?"

I shrugged but didn't answer.

"Lieutenant," Johnston started to say, thought for a moment, then continued, "we need to put out an APB on Tree, but you're to provide no information as to why we want him, just that he's probably armed and dangerous. Make sure it's understood that we need him alive, no matter the cost. If he dies, we're screwed. Go see to it, will you, please?"

She nodded, rose from her seat, and left us.

"Jordan," he said. "How about you? You want to call it in to your people?"

He nodded in agreement and said, "Yes, I'll do that. I also think we should send an advisory to the tri-state sheriffs and PDs. He could be anywhere: Dalton, the North Georgia mountains, Cleveland... Hell, Sequoya is closer to Cleveland than it is to here. He could be hunkered down somewhere up there."

"You're right," Johnston said. "I'll have my people do that. In the meantime, Harry, what will you be doing?"

"There's not much I can do, except wait... and hope." I looked at my watch. It was almost nine-thirty. I needed to get out of there.

"I'll be at Benny Hinkle's until late," I said, rising from my seat. "If anything comes up, call me. I'll be back in my office at seven in the morning. Oh, and one more thing, Chief; I need access to Kate, for the duration. Can you arrange that?"

He looked at me, skeptically, and considered the request, then nodding he said, "Yes, I'll see she gets the word. Keep me and Sheriff White informed. If we hear anything, we'll let you know."

I closed the door behind me, leaving Hamilton County's two top law enforcement officers alone: to talk, to think, to plot, to scheme? I didn't care. I wanted Shady Tree.

Chapter Nine

A manda was already in bed and asleep when I got home, which didn't surprise me because it was almost one o'clock in the morning.

"Hey," she said sleepily as I crawled into bed beside her, then asked, "Did you find him?"

"Tree? No, not yet."

"Did you tell Greg?"

"I told you I did. Now go back to sleep."

I was glad I didn't have to lie to her, but it troubled me that I hadn't been entirely honest with her either.

As you can imagine, I didn't sleep much that night. There were no visions of sugar plums dancing around in my head, just old newsreel images of cataclysmic explosions, ruined buildings, burned bodies, and women and children with horrendous wounds.

I tossed and turned through the early hours until I could stand it no longer. By four in the morning, I was out of the house and running swiftly along East Brow Road toward Covenant College, a round trip of nearly eight miles that usually took me about an hour and fifteen minutes to complete. That morning I did it in sixty-five minutes. Not a record for me, but close.

At fifteen after five, I was swimming laps in the pool. By six, I was out of the shower, dressed, and ready to leave; except that Amanda had coffee and scrambled eggs waiting.

I almost left without partaking of either, but my conscience wouldn't allow it. So I sat down at the kitchen table across from my wife and hurriedly ate, for the most part in silence, and also managed to gulp down a cup of black coffee.

"Why were you so late last night? Are you not going to tell me about what happened yesterday?" she asked. She sounded... Distressed is the only way to put it.

"There's nothing to tell," I snapped at her. "No Shady, no bomb, no big deal."

She looked at me as if I'd slapped her. I felt like crap. She didn't deserve the back end of my black mood.

"I'm sorry. I didn't mean... Look, Greg's gone. After I told him how it was going to be, he stormed out of my office, madder than hell. By the time I got home and into bed with you, I'd talked this thing to death... a dozen times: with my people, Kate, Chief Johnston, and Whitey White. We got nowhere, except we all agree that we need to find Shady."

"But if Greg's gone... does that mean that you..."

"*No!*" I said almost shouting the word. "It doesn't mean anything. We find Shady, we hand him over to Greg. That's it. Done and finished." I sat back in my chair and sipped on my coffee. She didn't look convinced. *Damn it!* I thought, exasperated. *What the hell am I supposed to do? Let these creeps blow up a nuclear plant? I don't think so.*

But I couldn't tell her that. Suddenly, I wanted out of there. I had to get away before I said something I'd regret.

"Look, I promised I'd be at the office by seven." I looked at my watch. "And you know what the traffic is like at this time in the morning. I need to go."

I stood, stepped around the table, leaned in, and kissed her, then said, "I love you. Take care of our baby. I'll see you later, okay?"

She nodded and I left feeling pretty despicable.

* * *

Kate was waiting for me in an unmarked cruiser when I arrived at my office that morning. I parked the Range Rover beside it, and we entered my office through the side door. She wasn't the only one waiting for me. When we entered, Greg Parker was sitting on the edge of Jacque's desk, a cup of coffee in his hand.

"What the hell are you doing here?" I asked, brushing past him. "You can go back to the hole you just crawled out of. There's nothing for you here."

"No can do, Buddy. You either work with me or you're out of it. I'll lock you up if I have to. Now get the chip off your shoulder and let's talk."

I glared at him, nodded, and pushed open my office door. Now it was his turn to brush past me.

"Over there," I growled, pointing to one of the guest chairs.

"I need coffee," I said to Kate. "Can I get you some?"

She nodded and said, "Black, but not that strong stuff you drink."

I smiled at her, ignored Parker, and went to get it. I returned with two cups: one for me, one for her. Parker would have to fend for himself.

I sat down behind my desk and sipped my coffee, glaring at Parker, then said, "You told me and my team to go to hell yesterday. Why are you here?"

"That's not quite what I said, Harry—"

"Close enough," I interrupted him. "Why are you here?"

He sighed, shook his head, and flipped through the screens on his iPad.

"D'you know who this is?" he asked, approaching the desk and turning the iPad for me to see the screen.

My heart sank.

"Yes. It's Duvon James who is also Tree's chief lieutenant. Where did you get that picture?" I asked, still staring at the photo.

"One of my agents shot it yesterday." Before I could comment, he pulled the iPad away and flipped the screen again.

"How about this guy?" Again, he held the iPad for me to see. I felt the hair on the back of my neck prickle.

"No, I don't know him, but he was in the Sorbonne last night. Benny Hinkle said he didn't recognize him either. He was watching us, taking pictures. I tried to grab him, but he got away. Now, are you going to tell me where you got them?"

"This one, the guy you say was in the nightclub, also works for Tree. His name is Marquis Lewis. He was with James in the club on Chestnut around eleven last night."

"So, he's here then, Tree?" Kate asked.

"It would appear so," Parker said.

"Your guy followed them, right? You know where they are?"

He shook his head and said, "Nope. Apparently, they were arguing about something; my guy couldn't get close enough to hear much, just a few words. He clearly heard James say '... he made you? You dumb...' But then he caught Larry watching him and shut up. Well, not quite. He leaned across the table and whispered something to the guy you saw. Then they finished their drinks and left."

"Why didn't Larry follow them?" Kate asked.

"He tried to, but they left on motorcycles, each traveling in an opposite direction. Larry figured he'd better stay on James, but as he ran down the stairs, some dickhead bumped into him and sent him flying; he has a sprained ankle."

"What a damned cluster—" I interrupted myself. "Ah hell, that wasn't a coincidence. Did anyone talk to the guy that ran into him?"

"No, and it wasn't a guy. It was a young black woman with big teeth."

I almost laughed but stifled it before saying, "That's all he could remember, big teeth? I bet she doesn't have them now. They're onto us, Greg. I thought the guy in the Sorbonne looked familiar. I must have seen him before when he was with Tree some other time."

I looked at Kate. She shook her head; she looked dejected, and I didn't blame her.

"So, Tree is here, then!" she said. It was a statement rather than a question.

"It would seem so," Parker said, placing his empty cup on my desk.

"And he knows we're onto him!" I said.

This time he merely nodded.

"So when does the cavalry arrive?" Kate asked.

He turned to look at her before asking, "More agents, you mean?"

She nodded.

"Well," he said, sucking his breath in through his teeth before continuing, "I have fifty agents on the way. That's all I could get right now, but they won't be here until Monday... I've pulled four out of Knoxville, although..."

"Fifty? Monday?" I asked, shaking my head. I was about to make a caustic comment, but my iPhone buzzed and began to travel across my desk. I grabbed it and put it to my ear.

"Hello!"

"Harry, m'man. Long time no see. How the hell are you?" I almost dropped the phone. It was several seconds before I could speak again.

Both Parker and Kate could tell by the stunned expression on my face that something was wrong; they both leaned forward in their chairs.

Kate mouthed, "What?" at me.

"Shady," I whispered just loud enough so they could hear. If I said they looked stunned, I'd be lying. They were flabbergasted.

"I've been thinking about you, Shady."

"The hell you say? Well, I just bet you have. Now, why don't you put me on speaker? I'd sure like to say hello to Agent Parker and the lovely Kate."

"Shady, the last time we met, I ran you out of town and made you a promise. Remember?"

"I do, Harry; I do. Something 'bout putting me on crutches, wasn't it? But this time we ain't gonna meet."

I beckoned for Kate to get up as I went around the desk to her.

"Go to Tim," I whispered. "Ask him to triangulate this phone. Quick."

Let me introduce you to another member of my staff. Tim Clarke is a geek, one of a rare breed of weirdos that eat, sleep, and dream in binary code. He's been with me since a month after he dropped out of college when he was just seventeen. I found him skulking in an Internet café only one small step ahead of the law. Yeah, he was a hacker then and still is when he needs to be... Well, he kind of fudges around the edges of legality, once in a while—eh, who am I kidding? He's a hacker; always will be. He never did get caught, although to hear him tell it, he came close a couple of times. He says he's reformed, and maybe he has. I sure hope so, because long ago, I turned him loose to handle all of my IT requirements. I said he was a geek, and he is, in every sense of the word: he's skinny, wears glasses, is twenty-five years old but looks fifteen, and speaks in tongues... well, a language known only to himself. He's also the busiest member of my staff.

"Harry, you still there? I know you are. You trying to trace this call? Go ahead. Have fun. Now put me on speaker like I asked."

I sighed and did as he requested.

"You're on," I said. "Now, tell us, what do you want?"

"Not a damn thing, other than to ruin your day, which I'm pretty sure I already did."

Kate returned, nodded, and sat down.

"Agent Parker. How you is? Cat got your tongue? I guess he does. How 'bout you, Kate? You wanna say hello to an old friend?"

"You're no friend of mine, Tree," she said, barely loud enough for him to hear.

I waved at both of them, got their attention, then mouthed at them, "Don't mention the bomb." They both nodded.

"Well, anyway," Tree continued, "I knew y'all know I'm here, so I figured I'd tell you hello. Harry, you clocked my boy, Marquis, last night. I didn't think you knew him. Well done.

"So, I bet y'all are wonderin' how I got onto you. Well, I'll tell you. I've had my people watching you, Agent Parker, and the rest of your clowns, right after we tapped that informant of yours on Chestnut. I've had two guys following you, Parker, ever since you rode into town. That's how I knew you was also a part of it, Harry, an' you too, Kate. Agent Parker visits you, I put tails on both of you. Jeez, Harry, you gotta get a life; you're so predictable. I put Marquis in the Sorbonne to wait an' see, an' sure enough, in you all walk. What you didn't know was that I also had Duvon tailing you too. Didn't make him, did you?"

"We need to talk, Shady," I said.

"We *are* talking, Harry. What would you like me to tell you?"

"I don't suppose it's any good me asking for a face-to-face?"

"You're right; no good at all. You think I'm stupid, Starke? Yeah, of course you do. You always did."

"You want to tell me what the point of all this is?"

"Sure. I just wanted to jerk your chain a little. Gotcha, Harry. Well, times up. Gotta go..."

"Hold on, Shady. You owe me one. Twice I let you off the hook; once when your boy Gold killed my brother and again less than a year ago. Talk to me."

"First, I don't owe you shit, but I'll humor you. What you want to know, Harry? As if I couldn't guess."

"What's going on? What are your Iranian friends up to?"

He was quiet for a moment, then said, "They ain't my friends, just clients, an' they pay well. They need a little help findin' their way around. I'm a guide, that's all."

"Why are they here, Shady?"

He laughed at that.

"From what I heard, they're here on a mission, something 'bout makin' a big splash, whatever that might mean. But then again, I'm sure Agent Parker knows, right, Greg?"

"You can't do this, Shady," I said. "You're not much, but you're not a killer. You let these terrorists do what they're planning, and you're as bad as they are, complicit too."

"Yeah, well. For a million bucks, there ain't much I won't do. By the way, Harry, how's that pretty blonde wife of yours? Amanda, right? Duvon tells me she looks like she's about to drop little Starkey any time now. You need to keep an eye on her; wouldn't want anythin' nasty to happen to her, especially now she's gonna make you a daddy."

"You keep him the hell away from her, d'you hear?"

"Oh c'mon, Harry. I just inquirin'. I always thought a lot of Amanda; you know that."

"You sonofabitch. I'm coming after you, Shady, and this time it will be the last. This time I'll keep my promise."

"Put me on crutches? Good luck with that... So, I guess it's you an' me again, Harry. One last time, eh? Just like old times. Only this time... I win, an' I win big. I get my money from the warriors an' I'm outta here, never to be seen again..."

It was at that moment that Tim burst in. "He's just a couple of blocks away in the parking garage down the street," he shouted and gasped.

"Hey, Tim," Shady said loud enough for him to hear. "That I am. Good job, buddy. Well, I guess it's time for me to go. Have a nice day, y'all." And he hung up.

"Oh hell, Harry, I'm so sorry." Tim was horrified at what he thought he'd done.

I laughed, though I didn't feel like it.

"Don't worry, Son. He was just playing us. He knows more about us than we do about him. Did you get his phone number?"

"I did."

"How about his GPS? Can you track it?"

"It depends. If he has his location services turned on, yes. If not, it will still be possible, but not very accurate. I'll give it a try." He turned and left, only to return five minutes later.

"I found it," he said, excitedly. "I can take you right to it."

And he did. Twenty minutes later, the four of us were standing in a circle under a tree on Riverfront Parkway, in the shadow of the Market Street Bridge, staring down at an Android smart phone nestled in the grass.

Kate pulled a latex glove from her jacket pocket and put it on, then she picked up the phone.

"It's turned off," she said.

"It's still transmitting location services though, see?" Tim said, holding his iPad so that we could see the blinking icon.

I looked around. There was no way to tell which way Shady had been traveling when he tossed the phone. We were so close to the bridge that he could either have been on it or on the Parkway where we now were.

"Bummer," I said, more to myself than to the others. "Why'd he toss it? All he had to do was pull the sim card."

"I could try to track his movement over the past several days," Tim said.

"Yeah," Parker said, reaching for the phone. "I can do that. I'll send it to Quantico."

I grabbed Parker's arm, and at the same time, Kate, still clutching the phone, took a step back.

"That will take a month," I said. "We might have only hours. Why don't you let Tim do it? He's the best there is."

Parker looked at Tim and asked, "You can do it?"

Tim nodded and said, "Yes, I think so."

Parker nodded and said, "Okay, you've got today. Then it's my turn, understood? Take me back to my car, Harry. I need to go to my office."

"Are you coming in?" I asked Greg as I parked the car.

"No. I don't have time. Don't forget, Harry, your boy has today and then I want that phone. Let me know what you find, if anything." Then he turned, walked to his own car, and without a backward glance, he got in and drove away. *What an ass! You sure as hell haven't mellowed over the years, Greg.*

It took Tim less than an hour to map Shady's comings and goings. In the meantime, Kate went back to the PD. Even though she didn't say so, I figured she was going to update the chief. Although Tim had what I needed, it soon turned bittersweet.

He came barging into my office clutching his laptop in the crook of his arm and waving the Android in his free hand; boy was he excited.

"Okay," he began. "There are more than five hundred calls—"

"Hold on, Son," I said, waving him to one of the guest chairs. "Take a breath and slow down."

He sat, but slow down? That was like telling a Jack Russell terrier puppy to stop biting your ankles.

"More than five hundred calls on his phone," he repeated while waving the Android at me. "Incoming and outgoing. I pulled the sim card and read it, see?" He pointed to the small device plugged into one of the USB ports on his laptop. "I got all his texts too, and was able to isolate most of them, as well as his calls. There are a lot of international calls, most of them to Middle Eastern countries, but Iran in particular. See, it works like this..." He waggled it in the air.

"The handset, from time to time, communicates with the nearest tower to let it know it's active. See, when you get a call, the network needs to know which tower to route the call through. This information is stored in one of two nodes: either the Home Location Register or the Visitor Location Register. You get a call and the system does a lookup; it checks the nodes to find your current location and then routes the call. Unfortunately, that doesn't give us a pinpoint location, just the location of the cell tower, and the other bad news is that the cell phone itself could be anywhere within a quarter-mile radius of said tower. However, smart phones are now equipped with A-GPS..." He paused and grinned at me. "That means Assisted-GPS, so now we get not only the location of the tower but also the coordinates—"

"Oh, for Pete's sake, Tim," I interrupted him. "Cut to the nitty. Can you locate him or not?"

He nodded and said, "I can. Many of the calls were made to and from locations all over the tri-state area, and even more in Southern Texas." He paused again and grinned at me. Then he caught the look I was giving him, because he rushed on to finish his explanation. "Some, more than fifty, were made from this location." He pointed to the image on his computer. A map was displayed on the screen, and blinking slowly right in the center of the map was a small red dot.

"Some were made late at night. I think this must be where he's living."

I pulled a face and looked at him skeptically.

"Whaaat?" he asked.

"You don't think it's weird? That we were able to find his phone, and that he tossed it with all his calls still logged? He's not that dumb. In fact, he's frigging smart. He knows better than to leave the sim card in it. He's a frigging drug dealer for God's sake; he knows better than anyone, maybe even you, how things work. He wanted us to find the phone and the numbers."

"You think?" Tim looked horrified. "But... that means..."

"That it does, Tim. He's up to something, but what?"

I thought for a minute, then picking up the office phone, I called Jacque and asked her to send in Bob and T.J.

Bob entered first and dropped into the seat beside Tim. T.J. pushed through the door half a minute later and sat down beside Bob. "What's the haps, Harry?" Bob asked.

I explained what Tim had found but in far fewer words, and then I told him my doubts.

Bob nodded. "You're right," he said, "Shady's not that dumb. A trap, you think?"

"I do. As I've said before, Shady's many things, but stupid isn't one of them. He didn't make that call to me for fun, or to taunt me, and he made sure he stayed on the call just long enough for Tim to trace it, then he tossed the phone; tossed it for us to find. So yeah, I think it's a trap. The problem is, we have to walk into it... at least I do. We need to talk to the SOB. If there's a bomb, we need to find it, and fast. He's the only link."

"Harry," Bob said, "you need to leave this to the feds. You made Amanda a promise. You need to keep it. Let them walk into the trap."

I looked at him, then at T.J. who was slowly nodding his head, a slight, enigmatic smile on his lips.

"I can't. He'll be waiting, watching," I said, "and if I do that and someone besides me goes... If he thinks we're onto him, if the feds go charging in, he'll fade away like smoke. No, it's me he's after, and if he doesn't get me... Well, you heard what he said; he'll go after Amanda. I have to go to him, now, today!"

Oh hell, what am *I going to tell Amanda?*

"Tim, I need that address."

"Umm, there really isn't one, per se. It's in the railroad marshalling yards off Wilcox. See? Right here," Tim said as he flipped between screens from map to satellite, then turning the laptop so I could see it, he pointed to a spot showing on a Google map of the area. The little red icon was flashing over a small area inside the yards.

"There's an old road just past Wilcox Boulevard, here, on the right by the railroad crossing at Curtain Pole, right there." He pointed to it. "Just where the road forks at Amnicola and Riverside. It looks like there's a barrier across the old road, but it's not much. I'd say you can drive around it..."

"You've got to do better than that, Tim. Those yards are huge."

He nodded, turned the laptop so he could see, and tapped the keyboard a couple of times before turning it back to face me again.

"I zoomed in. It's one of those sheds. I can't pinpoint the exact one, but it's one of them."

The flashing icon was now stationed over a small group of buildings: three sheds and what looked like an old railroad car that was painted a weird shade of green.

"Yeah, I see it now. If I go around the barrier here," I pointed to it before continuing, "then bear right and follow the road, and then take the first left and keep going for maybe a couple of hundred yards..." I paused and stared at the layout. "And there's no way to tell which shed they're in, if any?"

"No. What you have here," Tim said, "is just the location the calls were made from. The phone would have to be on-site right now to pinpoint it closer."

I stared at the screen; I didn't like what I was seeing. For one thing, it was a satellite photo and I knew it wasn't in real time. There were no signs of life around the little group of buildings: no cars, no people, nothing. They looked... isolated.

"If he's there..." I started to say but paused to consider the possibilities, and then said, "If he's working with a gang of terrorists, and if they have a... We have to find out, and quickly. They may already be executing their plan. We need to go take a look, right now. Tim, I need a hard copy of the map." He nodded, tapped the screen, sent it to the printer, then jumped up and went to get it. He was back almost immediately. I took the map from him, folded it, and slipped it into my jacket pocket.

"Bob, T.J.," I said, "we need to go check it out."

I stood, removed my jacket, opened my desk drawer, took out my shoulder rig, and slipped into it.

"Bob," I started to say as I slipped into my jacket before asking, "You carrying?"

He grinned. "Does Dolly Parton sleep on her back?" He held his jacket open to reveal a rig similar to mine, but his held a Sig Sauer .45, model 1911.

"That it?" I asked.

"Sure is."

I shook my head. The Sig held only seven rounds, eight if he kept one in the chamber. I'd lost count of the number of times he'd been caught short. Well, it's what he liked, so...

I looked at T.J. and said, "I know you're not. But I have something in the car for you if we need it. Okay?"

"Whatever you say, Boss."

"Okay," I said, heading for the door. "Let's go." And we did.

Chapter Ten

"Harry, you don't think..." Bob began to say as we climbed into the Range Rover.

"Think what?" I didn't wait for him to answer. "Yeah, I do think. I think that, trap or not, I'm going to get him if he's there, and I mean right now. You got a problem with that?"

He pulled the seat belt around him, sighed deeply, resignedly, and said, "Yeah, that's what I figured. No, Harry, no problem."

It was a drive of only a couple miles, most of it along Riverside Drive. The old road Tim had shown us on the map was easy to find. It was almost directly under the railroad crossing signals.

Fortunately, the steel barriers only stretched across the road itself. The grass areas on either side were no more than ten yards wide, neatly mowed, bounded by a secondary road inside the yards, and appeared to be easy to navigate.

I slowed, turned right off Riverside, and drove slowly around the north end of the barrier into the southern end of the marshalling yards, maneuvered onto the secondary road, and turned right, following Tim's directions to our destination, or should I say destiny. Whatever, a minute later, I rounded a bend and spotted the faded green paint of what was indeed an old railroad car and slammed on the brakes.

We were maybe a hundred yards, perhaps a little more, away from the railroad car facing a vast expanse of open ground.

I surveyed the scene. I didn't like it. It was too open. I could see all three sheds beyond the railroad car, one behind the other. If it *was* a trap, they were waiting, and they would already have seen us. I hoped to hell I was wrong, but that friggin' sixth sense of mine told me I wasn't.

I weighed my options. I didn't have any. I had no choice. I took my foot off the brake and let the car roll slowly forward on an idling engine, toward the railroad car, expecting at any moment to be greeted by a hail of gunfire. It didn't happen.

I turned in front of the railroad car, parked, rolled down my window, and cut the motor. We were now out of sight if anyone was peering out of any of the three sheds, but I didn't feel any less uncomfortable. If Shady intended to trap us, he'd picked the ideal spot: isolated with a wide-open field of fire. We sat still, listening. All was quiet. I removed Tim's map from my pocket, unfolded it, and stared at it. It didn't help. The only cover I could see between us and the first shed was a clump of trees lining the back side of the railroad car and alongside a section of railroad track.

"So, what's the plan, then?" Bob asked, shifting in his seat to look at me.

"The plan is that we take these three sheds one by one, starting at the far end." I flicked the map with my finger. "If he's there, we'll get him."

"That's a plan? Hell, Harry... He's set us up. The sonofabitch is waiting..." He leaned forward, looked out through the windshield, and then continued, "And what about this piece of junk right here?"

He was talking about the railroad car.

"It's vacant, see the dust on the steps and the crap around the doorframe? Besides, if there was anyone in there, we'd know it by now." *And oh boy, did I hope I was right!*

"There's gotta be a back door to..." he said, leaning back in his seat.

I glared at him.

"Okay, okay. Let's do it. What goodies have you got stashed in the back?"

"Not as much as I'd like," I said as I slid the VP9 out of its holster, ejected the mag, and checked the load for the third time. Why? Habit and training, I guess. I retrieved its suppressor from the glove compartment, screwed it in place, slammed the mag into the pistol, jacked a round into the chamber, and then returned it to the holster under my arm.

"Let's see what else we have," I said.

We exited the vehicle and I opened the tailgate. I keep several lightweight tactical vests and a steel gun case in the rear. It's bolted to the floor and double locked. I opened it up, lifted out two suppressed Ruger AR15s, and handed one to Bob. I gave my spare VP9 to T.J. along with a couple of extra mags and a suppressor.

"It's already loaded, Bob," I said as he ejected the AR15's mag. "One in the chamber and twenty-eight in the mag."

"If you don't mind," he growled, "I just want to make sure for myself."

I nodded and said, "Okay, when you're done, check out the vests and see if you can find one that fits—that gray one is mine—and then grab a couple more mags as well. You too, T.J., grab yourself a vest." I paused and looked at T.J. "Are you sure you're all right with this? It could get hairy."

"Ha!" T.J. grinned, saying, "You kids don't know the meaning of 'hairy.' The stories I could tell you, my friend. Yeah, I'm fine with it. First time in ten years I'm enjoying myself. I should thank you. Let's do it."

I nodded, grabbed a handful of plastic cable ties from behind the gun case and shoved them into one of the vest pockets, and then turned back to Bob. "Bob, how many mags d'you have for that Sig?"

"I have a couple of spares. Why?"

"Twenty-one then; twenty-two if you have one in the chamber. Here, you might also want to take this with you," I said as I handed him a Smith & Wesson Model 69, 44 Magnum and a box of shells.

"Oh hell, Harry, not that friggin' revolver again? It only holds five and kicks like a damn horse. I thought you'd gotten rid of the thing." He grabbed the Colt, shoving it into the waistband at the back of his pants, then stored the box of cartridges in one of the vest pockets.

"Gotten rid of my old friend?" I smiled at him. "Not likely. You ready?"

I knew he wasn't; he was still buckling the vest.

"Gimme a minute, will you?"

"We don't have a minute. We have to find that damn bomb. And listen, don't use either the Colt or the Sig unless you have to. The less noise we make the better. Oh, and one more thing. I want Shady alive and in one piece. You got that, Bob?"

He didn't bother to answer. He finished buckling the vest, then grabbed the AR15 and worked the action.

"Okay, okay. I'm ready. How d'you want to play it?"

"T.J.?" I asked. "You ready?"

"Ready when you are, Boss."

"Right, okay then." I spread the small map out on the floor of the Rover and pointed. "We'll circle around to the right on the back side of these trees here. They should give us some cover; not much, but some, and they won't get us all the way there, but they will shorten the run across the open yard. Ready?"

They both nodded.

I left the Rover's tailgate open when we started to circle around the east end of the railroad car, but there we stopped. *Shit! That's not on the map. They must have removed some trees.*

There was a wide gap between the railroad car and the trees. I looked back at Bob, nodded, then ran as fast as I could across the gap. Bob followed close on my heels; T.J. was right there with him. From there, I kept going and didn't stop until I reached the end of the line of trees. Once there, I dropped and lay on my gut facing the last shed in the line of three. It was at least fifty yards away. *Damn! It's too far, too exposed.*

Bob and T.J. dropped down beside me. "You sure as hell miscalculated that," Bob whispered. "I didn't like that one bit; I already feel like I'm friggin' naked. I don't think these cheap vests would stop a twenty-two, much less a two-two-three, or even a nine."

"They weren't cheap, you butthead. Dwayne Johnson wore one in *The Fast and the Furious.*"

"Oh goody. That makes me feel a whole lot bett..."

He was cut off by the crack of a bullet smacking into a tree trunk just a few feet to his rear.

"Shit," he whispered. "They made us. I felt the wind of that one. We make a move and we're dead. I'm telling you, Harry, we can't do this by ourselves. We need backup. Call Parker, or even Kate."

"No time," I said. "If that bomb's on the move, we need to know, and much sooner than later. Follow me and keep your ass down."

I crawled on my belly—I'd learned the military low crawl when I was a rookie cop—I'd never had to use it until then, and I have to admit, it didn't go too well. By the time I'd gone ten yards, my knees were sore as hell, and Bob had overtaken me; I'd forgotten he was an ex-Marine.

We crept through the trees, almost back to where we'd started. In fact, I could see the green paint of the railroad car just a couple of dozen or so yards away.

"Stop," I whispered, hoarsely. "We've come too far. I'm going to make a run for that first shed; cover me... Wait. Where the hell is T.J.?"

My question was answered by an explosion of gunfire. He was running, head down, toward the shed at the far end of the clearing from where the gunfire had come, and man, could he go. He dodged right, then left, and then he was there, breathing heavily, his back against the shed wall, but not for long. He took three steps forward and hurled himself against the door, which offered little resistance to his one hundred and ninety pounds, and then he was inside, firing the VP9 as fast as he could pull the trigger.

"Crazy sonofabitch!" I shouted. "C'mon."

I leaped to my feet and burst from the trees running for the shed at the center of the trio... and then they were shooting, and so was Bob. I could hear the muted cracks of subsonic rounds from the shed windows and the louder crack of Bob's AR15. I felt something pluck at my pant leg but didn't stop. I slammed into the shed door; it burst open and I fell inside. I felt rather than saw Bob fly over the top of me, his AR15 spitting fire. There were two men in the shed, but by the time I was able to haul myself up, they were both dead.

"*Damn it all to hell, Bob!*" I shouted. "I told you I wanted him alive."

"He ain't one of 'em. And that piece o' shit there was about to put you away. Where d'you get that stupid ragin' bull stuff anyway? It's gonna get you killed one of these days."

I stood, leaning one hand against the shed wall for support with the AR15 dangling from my other hand. I could feel the adrenaline pumping through my body.

I looked at the two bodies. One was lying on its side, his right hand still clutching a semi-automatic pistol, his left hand under his chin. He could have been asleep, except that he had two small holes in his forehead, both oozing blood. The other body was in the far corner of the shed, on its ass, back against the wall, arms by its sides, chin on its chest, and a heavy semi-automatic pistol in its right hand.

"They look like Iranians," I said. "Hell, what do I know? They're Middle Easterners, for sure. Where the hell is Shady? And T.J.?"

I listened for a minute. All was quiet. Either T.J. was dead and Shady was long gone or it was all over and Shady was dead. Either way, we were screwed. Thankfully, it was neither.

"You guys hurt?" T.J. asked from the doorway, but without waiting for an answer, he continued, "I guess not." He shoved a subdued Lester "Shady" Tree inside, his arm so far up his back that I could see his hand over his shoulder.

"This the guy you're looking for? I hope so, because the other two got away, out the back window, but not before I winged one of'm. Don't know how bad."

"Is he hurt?" I asked, now leaning with my back against the wall.

"Nah... well, he probably has a headache where I smacked him upside the ear with this." He waved the VP9 in front of Shady's face. Shady flinched but kept quiet.

I took a step forward, lifted Shady's chin with my finger, and said, "Well, well, here we are again, Shady. This really isn't your lucky day."

"Screw you, Starke... *Owww!*" he yelled and clamped his eyes shut as T.J. jerked his arm even further up his back, something I wouldn't have thought possible.

"Easy, T.J.," I said. "I need him in one piece, at least for now."

When T.J. eased up on the pressure, Shady opened his eyes.

I smiled benignly at Shady and said, "Tie him up, Bob." I took the cable ties from my vest pocket and handed them to Bob.

There were a table and three chairs in the shed. T.J. shoved him down on one of the chairs, and Bob strapped him to it. "He's all yours, Harry," Bob said, pulling the last tie tight.

"I think it might be a good idea if one of you checked the other shed," I said. "Make sure it's clear."

"My pleasure," T.J. said. "I'll be back."

Bob asked, "You going to call Parker?"

"Hmmm, no! Not right now. I'm going to have a quiet word with our friend here, and then we'll see."

Bob nodded and stepped back.

"So," I said, pulling up a chair and placing it in front of him. "It's been a while. How've you been, Shady?"

He glared at me but said nothing.

"So that's the way it's going to be, is it?"

Still no answer.

"Okay, Shady," I said. "I don't have time to play with you. I need some answers and I need them now. Tell me about your Iranian friends. What are they up to? What are they planning?"

"Screw you, Starke," he snarled, "an' you too, Ryan."

It was at this point that T.J. returned, the VP9 hanging loosely by his side.

"An' screw you too, granddad." He hawked deep in his throat, coughed, then turned his head and spat a gob of something nasty in Bob's direction. It flew past him and smacked fatly down onto the linoleum. Bob stepped forward and slapped Shady's face, hard. So hard that it wrenched his head sideways. At first, I thought he'd done some serious damage to him; he hadn't, though, and only a thin trickle of blood ran from the corner of Shady's mouth onto his chin.

"Well, if you won't tell me," I said, "then I'll tell you."

I set my AR15 down on the table, then slipped the VP9 out of its holster and placed it beside the AR. He looked apprehensively at it. I think if he could have rubbed his nose, he would have.

I smiled at him and said, "Not this time, Shady. I have something a little more... shall we say, persuasive? But I really do hope I won't need to use it. It would be *very* messy, I imagine. So, let's talk.

"We know that your friends have somehow acquired a small nuclear device, perhaps two of them. I say small as if such a weapon could ever be called small, but we think the yield could be as little as ten tons of TNT, which would still make the Oklahoma City bombing look like a firecracker, or possibly up to as much as one kiloton... That's one thousand tons of TNT..." And right then, as he looked into my eyes, I knew that not only did he know what was planned but he also didn't care.

"You sonofabitch, Shady. Are you friggin' crazy? D'you know what will happen if they set that thing off?"

He didn't answer. Instead, he glared defiantly back at me.

"Look... Shady. You and me, we go back a long way. We've never seen eye-to-eye on much, but even you can't want this to happen, right?"

He didn't answer.

"T.J.," I said without looking up at him, "would you go get the car please?" I fished in my pants pocket and held out the keys. "Also, you'll find my briefcase on the back seat; I'll need it."

He took the keys from me and left.

Bob leaned against the wall while I sat watching Shady's face, looking for a tell. He remained still, the look on his face was set, impassive.

"I hope you're thinking about the consequences of keeping silent," I said, conversationally. "If you don't tell me what I need to know, I'm going to hurt you. And I do mean HURT... you." I shouted the word "hurt," and if he hadn't been strapped down, I swear his head would have hit the shed roof. As it was, the chair came off the ground at least an inch.

"I parked it around back, out of sight," T.J. said when he returned a couple of minutes later.

"Where d'you want this?" he asked, holding out my briefcase.

"On the table, please, T.J."

He set it down and stepped away.

"You ready to talk, Shady?"

"Screw you, Starke. You'll get nothing outta me."

"Shady," I said, shaking my head, "you've heard the old saying that 'the end justifies the means,' right?"

He stared at me, didn't answer, but I could tell he was apprehensive.

"There are times," I gently continued, "when we have to do things, bad things, things we'll later regret. This is one of those times. You've heard about waterboarding, I'm sure." He didn't acknowledge it one way or the other, but the question was rhetorical anyway. "Well, no matter. What I have planned for you is far worse and will get the answers I need a whole lot quicker.

"Shady, I'm going to regret what I'm about to do, but not as much as you will. Now, you know what your friends are planning, and you know that I know that you know. And we both know that you're going to tell me, eventually. It's inevitable."

He seemed to have retreated into some sort of a trance. He stared at the wall, unblinking and focused on something, a fixed point somewhere along the wall behind me. I turned around to look. There was nothing there that I could see, but his eyes never left the spot; his lips never moved.

"Come on, Shady," I said. "Talk to me. You know what will happen if that damn thing goes off. Thousands of people will die. I know you. You're not a killer. Tell me."

He didn't answer. He continued to stare at the spot on the wall.

I nodded, then shook my head and sighed. I knew I had to get it out of him, and I knew it had to be the truth, which meant I had to get tough with him, really tough.

"Do you remember my promise? The one I made to you last time? I said I'd put you on crutches, and I will."

I turned and looked at T.J., then said, "There's a roll of paper towels in the back of the car. I'm going to need it. Would you mind?"

He didn't, so I waited until he returned with the roll and set it down on the table. By then, I had Shady's attention.

I stood up, moved the chair back away from the table, opened my briefcase, took out a pair of cable cutters, and closed it again.

I turned to Shady and dangled the cutters in front of his face. They were about double the size of heavy-duty pliers and had a cutting head that reminded me of a parrot's beak: two small curved blades, shiny and sharp.

"One last chance, Shady."

He didn't answer, but his eyes were wide and he was looking decidedly uncomfortable. He turned his head and looked up at Bob. Bob just shrugged. Shady turned again and looked up at me.

I glanced at Bob and found him staring at me, slowly shaking his head, his lips pursed.

"You ready to lose some fingers, Shady?" I asked, quietly. "I can do all ten then start on your toes. But we won't get that far... at least I hope not. Two fingers and a thumb, perhaps, and you'll tell me what I need to know... Damn it, Shady, you and I both know you will. It's just a question of how many fingers you decide to lose before you do. So why don't you just get it over with right now? No pain and you get to keep all of your fingers. What do you say?" He said nothing. He returned his gaze to whatever it was he'd been staring at on the wall.

I nodded, then said, "Okay then. So, let's begin, shall we?"

I put the cutters on the table, repositioned my chair, tore several paper towels from the roll, and then sat down in front of him, folding the towels and placing them on my lap. Then I picked up the cutters, held them up in front of my face, opened them, and stared at Shady through the gap between the blades. Up until that moment, it had all been for show. I'd been hoping the threat alone would be enough to get him to talk; it wasn't. He watched with his eyes opened wide, every move I made, but he still said nothing. *Oh hell; son-of-a-bitch! I really was hoping it wouldn't come to this.*

"Ready?" I asked, amiably, though I really felt like shit. Then I looked up at Bob and nodded. He took a knife from his pocket, opened it, reached down, and cut Shady's left hand free. Then he put the knife on the table, grabbed Shady's wrist, and forced his arm out toward me.

"You right-handed, Shady?" I asked. He didn't answer; he couldn't. His mouth was working but no sound came out.

"The pinky finger first, I think, Bob. Nice ring, Shady. A present from someone special, no doubt." It was gold with a blue stone and really quite nice.

Shady's hand was curled tightly into a fist. He tried to keep it that way, but he was no match for Bob. Bob jerked the finger straight so I could slip the beak of the cutters around the base of the pinky finger, then I applied a little pressure.

Shady squeaked. Then he found his voice and screeched, "Stop, for God's sake, Harry. Okay, I'll tell you what you want to know. Just gimme a minute, will you?"

I did, but I didn't remove the cutters from his finger.

"They, they do... do have a bomb, a small one, point-five of a kiloton, I heard one of them say."

Okay, I thought, *that's the equivalent of five hundred tons of TNT. Sonofabitch is big enough to take out just about anything and leave behind a crater the size of... I dunno, a friggin' big one.*

"What's the target, Shady?"

"They plan to take out..." I caught the look in his eyes, the twitch of his eyelid, the tell. He was about to lie to me. "... the Sequoya nuclear plant."

That gelled with our thinking, but I was sure he was lying. Even if he wasn't, I had to be sure.

Suddenly I felt cold all over, really cold. I'd never done anything like this before, but... I took a deep breath, and... *Oh jeez. Here we go!*

I slammed the cutters closed and the finger spun sideways, blood spraying from it and the stump remaining on his hand. Blood spattered my face, my shirt, my hands, and the paper towels on my lap. *Holy crap!*

The finger landed on the floor a couple of feet to the left of the chair, the ring clinking against the wood as it rolled across the floor.

For a couple of seconds, Shady could only stare down at the stump, speechless, and then he howled; he closed his eyes, threw his head back, and he screamed.

I too stared at the stump, mesmerized, shocked, in disbelief; it was so easy. For a moment, I sat frozen, then I looked up at Bob. He was still holding Shady's wrist, but his face was white. T.J. was leaning against the wall just inside the door, his arms folded, legs crossed at the ankles, a slight smile on his lips. *Damn, you're one cold sonofabitch.*

Suddenly, I felt physically sick. I gave no hint of it, but I can tell you, it took a minute before I was able to get over it. Shady, not so much. He sat still, but with his head down, chin on his chest, and breathing jerkily.

"You bastard," he groaned. "You crazy bastard sonofabitch. You cut my finger off, ow, ow, oh hell. Have you gone mad, Starke? What did you do that for? I told you what you wanted to know," he whispered.

"No you didn't. I didn't believe you, Shady. Want to try again? Ring finger next, I think, Bob."

Bob jerked open the chosen finger—the blood from the pinky stump leaking out between his fingers, dripping onto Shady's pants— and held the finger ready.

"Oh jeez, NO!" Shady gasped, his face twisted in pain. "For God's sake stop. I'll tell you what you want to know."

"The truth this time, Shady, and I'll know if it's not."

He nodded frantically, then started rambling, "I don't know what it is, what they're planning to hit... *no, no, nooo!*" He yelped as I set the cutters around his ring finger and applied a little pressure.

Oh jeez, I don't know if I can do this again.

Fortunately, I didn't have to; the threat, this time, was enough.

I looked into his eyes as he said, "I don't know, Harry. I swear I don't. Please don't do any more."

This time he was telling the truth. I could tell.

"Tell me what you do know, Shady," I said quietly without removing the cutters from around his finger.

"These guys, they're fanatics, Harry. They hate us, Americans, all of us. They only tolerated me 'cause they had to. They needed me. They didn't tell me nothin', well not much, but I've seen it, Harry, the freakin' bomb. It looks like a hunk o' junk, but it isn't. It's in a big green canvas backpack thing. That's what they needed me for, to get it and them into the country. I smuggled 'em across the Rio Grande just south of Piedras Negras. There's a dirt road that runs just this side of the river. Me and Duvon and Marquis went during the night and transported 'em in a rubber boat. Then we brought 'em here. That's it. That's all I know. I swear... Whaaat?"

"Cut to the chase and stop blathering, Shady. How many of them are there?" I asked.

"There's seven of 'em, now. The guy in charge is a greasy bastard called Captain Majid Hammad. It was 'im I heard talking about the bomb. There were ten, but you just got them two," he said as he looked at the body in the corner. "And they popped another of 'em a couple weeks ago. Turns out he was some sort of spy, CIA..."

"Don't bullshit me, Shady..." I said, tweaking the handles of the cutters, a rivulet of blood appearing before it dripped onto his pants.

"Ow, ow, ow, son-of-a-bitch! Don't do that! I'm telling you the truth. They popped one..."

"No, Shady, you killed him. Someone got a photo of you that night. Now talk to me and don't give me anymore crap, or you'll lose another finger."

"There's seven of 'em. I told you!"

"Where are Duvon and Marquis?"

He shuddered involuntarily, his head twitching, and I could sense he was about to lie to me again.

"Don't do it, Shady. Don't lie," I said, then twitched the handles again, more blood dripping onto his pants.

He squeaked, "I wasn't gonna. I swear."

Suddenly, his whole demeanor changed. He tried to sit higher, but his bonds held him down. He blinked, looked at his hand, then said... no, he snarled, "Screw you, Starke. You'd best kill me now, 'cause if you don't, I'll make you pay for that finger, in spades."

"I'm not going to kill you, Shady. You're going down this time, but before you do, if I have to, I'll take every last one of your fingers. So, d'you want to lose this one, or what?" I tweaked the handles. Shady sucked in his breath, tilted his head back, and squeezed his eyes closed. "If not," I continued, relaxing the pressure a little, "you'll answer my questions, and you'll tell the truth."

He lowered his head and opened his eyes. The hate in them was plain to see.

"So ask," he said, sullenly.

"Where are Duvon and Marquis?"

"I *really* don't know. That crazy ol' man came bustin' in an' started shootin'." Shady glanced round at T.J., but T.J. just smiled at him, so he turned back toward me. "And they high-tailed it out the back window. They're out there somewhere, probably waiting for you, or him," he said, twitching his head in T.J.'s direction before continuing, "to stick your head out. Then they'll blow it off."

I stared at him. He glared back defiantly. He was telling the truth, I had no doubt. But I did doubt that they were still out there. Knowing Duvon, he would have been more interested in saving his own skin than trying to rescue his boss; they were long gone.

I nodded, then said, "Okay, I believe you. So now the question is... Where are the Iranians, Shady? Where are they hiding out?"

"You're too late, Starke. I heard them talking. Whatever it is they're planning to do, they're planning to do it today."

I heard Bob gasp, but somehow, what Shady had just told us didn't surprise me. They'd already been here at least two weeks. The longer they waited...

I stared at him. "Shady, if you're shitting me..." He wasn't; I could tell. "Where are they?"

He hesitated for a minute, staring at the cutters, then said, "They're out at the ammunition dump, at least they were."

The ammunition dump? What the hell... Oh shit! That's not good.

"You're talking about the old Army plant at Enterprise South, right?"

He nodded warily toward me.

The Volunteer Army Munitions plant was located on the north side of the city. For years it had manufactured munitions in aid of the WWII war effort. It closed many years ago and is now a virtual wilderness that covers more than six thousand acres; a dozen square miles. Volkswagen has since built a plant on the east side of what once was a vast industrial complex, and so has Amazon and several other large companies, but what remains is... a jungle.

"Tell me exactly where they are and how to get there." I was getting more impatient. I wanted out of there.

"I can't tell you exactly... Whoa, stop, I ain't kiddin'. I think I can show you on a map. It was Duvon who found the hidey-hole for 'em. If you know anything about that place, you'll know I'm tellin' you the truth. It's a friggin' wilderness, right?"

"But you've been there?"

"Yeah, once. But I don't rememb... *Nooo, stop!* Oh jeez, Harry. No more. Please take them cutters off my finger. I'll tell you what I know; I swear."

I nodded, unhooked the beak, and put them down on the table. I opened my briefcase, grabbed my iPad, and flipped the tablet's lock screen. I opened Google Maps, pulled up the Ammo Plant, changed the view to satellite, and the display updated to an aerial view of the site from several thousand feet up. I could see the site was bounded to the west and south by Hickory Valley Road, to the north by Highway 58—though driving along those roads, you'd never know it—and to the east by both the Volkswagen plant and the Amazon Fulfillment Center. The undeveloped areas, some five thousand acres by my reckoning, looked to be a place where nightmares are born, a vast, heavily forested, virtually uncharted wilderness.

I zoomed in and could see that the forest was interlaced with a maze of narrow roads and hundreds of long-abandoned works and buildings.

Son-of-a-bitch, I thought. *Duvon knew what he was about; he picked this spot with care.*

I turned the iPad so Shady could see it.

"Turn his hand loose," I said to Bob, then to Shady, "Show me."

"Can you make it bigger?"

I zoomed in a little more.

Gingerly he lifted his left hand, still dripping blood, and pointed to a spot on the map.

"There!"

He had pointed to, as close as I could figure anyway, a row of what appeared to be five identical structures, all in ruins. How big they were, I couldn't tell. I zoomed in some more.

"There?" I asked, pointing to the image where the row of structures was located.

He nodded, then said, "Yeah, but that's not it, not exactly. There are several more buildings in an' around that area, but they're hidden by the trees."

I zoomed in again. Too much. The image dissolved into a mess of pixels. I shook my head and zoomed out again.

"So, how do I find the right one?"

He shrugged, stuck the bloody stump of his finger into his mouth, and sucked gently on it.

I reached across him and grabbed the cutters, then looked up at Bob. He closed his eyes and shook his head, but he grabbed Shady's arm and pulled it down, away from his mouth.

"NO!" Shady screeched. "I told you. I told you all I know. I swear. Don't do it, Harry. Please... don't... not again... please." The muscles in his face were twitching, and suddenly I felt sorry for him. But I had no choice. I looked up at Bob and nodded. He grimaced and forced Shady's ring finger open. I set the cutters around it. And, yeah, even as I did it, I knew I didn't have it in me to slice off another of his fingers. But I couldn't let him know that. I applied a little pressure.

"*STOP!* That's where they are. I swear to God, Harry. Please don't cut me no more. I can't tell you anythin' else... I can't... I can't." He was shuddering all over, like he was freezing. I felt like shit, and I could tell that Bob did too. T.J.? He couldn't have cared less. I looked Shady in the eye. He was in bad shape. I removed the cutters.

"How are they planning to transport the bomb?"

"I... I... dunno for sure. Oh jeez; give me a minute, will you?"

"We don't have a minute. Now tell me."

He sucked in a deep breath, then said, "They have three vehicles that I know of: a Ford Ranger pickup, a Ford Expedition, and a Dodge Durango. It's not that heavy, the bomb, maybe sixty, seventy pounds, I suppose. I saw one of 'em haulin' it around."

I nodded and said to Bob, "Cut him loose."

He did, and Shady heaved a sigh of relief, then grabbing his injured hand, he held it tight against his chest. The bleeding had subsided to a slow drip.

"We need to get this piece of shit to a hospital," I said. "Maybe they can reattach his finger... It's somewhere over there, on the floor... There it is."

I reached down and picked it up, grabbed some paper towels from the table, wrapped it up, and put it in his lap.

"Hold that hand up in the air," I told him. "The bleeding's almost stopped. I'm going to get you some help."

Then I called Kate, told her where to pick him up, and that I'd call her later.

"Harry," she yelled down the phone, "what have you done to him? Why can't you take him? Where the hell are you going?"

"Too many questions, Kate, and I don't have time to answer them. The clock's ticking. Like I said, come and get Shady; he needs his finger fixed. I'll call you later." And I hung up.

"Let's go," I said, then to Shady, "You stay put. Kate's on her way. She'll get you to a doctor. I mean it. Don't move. If you do..."

"I'm gonna get you, Starke. I'm gonna hurt you so bad..."

"Yeah, yeah. Hold that hand up. Kate Gazzara will be here soon."

I turned to Bob and T.J. and said, "Let's go before she gets here."

Chapter Eleven

"Harry, we have to call Parker," Bob said as I drove the Range Rover out onto Amnicola, turned right, and hit the gas. "This is simply too big for us to handle." Jeez, was he agitated! "We now know for sure that they have a bomb, and..."

"There's no time, Bob!"

"No time? No friggin' time? What the hell are you thinking? There're only three of us. How the hell are we going to find them in that hell hole? We need help. And what the hell are we going to do with the damn bomb if we find it?"

"I've been thinking about that. I think I might have a plan..."

"You *might* have a plan? Are you friggin' crazy? This ain't a damn movie. Who the hell d'you think you are, Tom Cruise? You can't try to defuse it. You'll blow us all to hell. Get real, for God's sake..." Bob paused to think, then said, "I'm calling Parker, and Kate, and Whitey; and you can go to hell, Harry Starke."

I grinned at him as I said, "Good luck with that. How long d'you think it will take for them to get their shit together, let alone... Ah, go ahead. What can it hurt?"

I almost laughed out loud when I heard Parker's voice mail, "Leave a message. I'll get back to you."

"Parker, you need to call me... or Harry. It's urgent."

He called the sheriff's department and asked for Jordan White, but then soon hung up, shaking his head.

"Why'd you hang up?" I asked him.

He shook his head again. "He's in Knoxville, at a convention. How could he do that, leave town knowing what he knows?"

"You could have asked for Crabtree," I said. Jason Crabtree was Jordan's chief deputy.

I slowed as we passed by the PD on Amnicola, then hit the gas again, heading for Highway 153.

"Call Kate," I said. "You have her cell number."

He did, but we must have passed her unnoticed, because when she answered, she told him she'd just entered the marshalling yards and had already spotted Shady walking toward the road.

I reached over and grabbed the phone out of his hand.

"Kate," I said, "you need to listen to me and don't interrupt."

By the time I finished explaining what was going on, I was already on Highway 153 and heading for Highway 58. She kept quiet the whole time, but when I did finally finish, she let fly.

She called me every name she could think of, told me to hold off and let her people handle it, swore at me, called me more names, and then quieted down and asked for directions. I gave them to her as best I could, but I knew even then that we were on our own, at least for a while. Hell, *I* didn't know where we were going, much less was I able to direct her to the location. In the end, I told her I'd wait until SWAT arrived. Yeah, I knew I was lying, but it couldn't be helped. I had to get her off the phone. Driving fast and one-handed in heavy traffic wasn't the best plan. I handed the phone back to Bob. He took it. I could see him out of the corner of my eye. He was indeed troubled, slowly shaking his head. I think I knew exactly how he felt because I didn't feel so hot myself.

We drove on in silence for a few minutes, then Bob said, "You're in big trouble; you know that, right?"

"Hell, I'm always in trouble. Why especially now?"

"You can't go around cutting folk's fingers off, not these days. Kate will lock you up, Harry. She'll have to, and if Shady doesn't sue your ass... Well, you could go down for what you did back there."

I shrugged and, staring straight ahead, said, "I needed to get him to talk. I had to get the truth, too."

"What you did was torture. You know how people feel about that these days. They won't let you get away with it."

"You either, I would imagine. You held him."

"Yeah, but I didn't think you'd go through with it. What the hell were you thinking?"

I said nothing; the question wasn't worth answering.

I drove on, remembering what Shady had said.

"If he was lying, I'll—" I said.

"You'll do nothing," Bob interrupted me. "He'll be locked up and you won't be able to get to him."

"Yeah, well, I guess this is one of those cases where the end justifies the means. Now shut the hell up. I need to concentrate."

I turned off Highway 153 and headed north, blew through a dozen red lights, then reached the fire department at the junction to Highway 58 where I turned right onto Hickory Valley Road. I'd made the eight-mile trip in a record seven minutes. *Now all I have to do is find... What? Jeez, what a frigging nightmare.*

I was pumped, adrenalin coursing through my body. I was driving too fast, so I slowed to thirty, then twenty-five, then... *There! This is it.*

I didn't know if it was or not, but I had a hunch, so I turned left onto... what? It wasn't what I'd call a road. It might have been one once, but now I had to drive slowly. I continued for maybe twenty yards, the undergrowth on either side brushing the sides of the car, until I could go no further. The way was blocked by a gate, rusty with age.

"You think Kate can find this track?" I asked without looking at either of them. "Fat chance, I'd say." Neither of them answered.

The gate was locked but not with a chain. A huge, rusty padlock was linked through hasps at the right side of the gate.

"How the hell do we get through that?" I asked.

"I dunno," Bob said, "but this ain't the right road. There's been nobody come this way in years."

He was right. *Shit! Damn it all to hell.*

I jammed the shifter into reverse, turned in my seat so I could see out the back of the car, and stomped on the gas. The car lurched back as I fought the wheel, trying to keep it on the narrow track. Fortunately, I didn't have to reverse far before I was back out on Hickory Valley Road.

"What now?" Bob asked.

"We try the next opening, is what," I said, ramming the shifter into drive.

The next opening was no more than fifty yards on. I turned left again and was once more faced with a tree-lined one-time road, but this one was slightly wider, and again, I came face-to-face with an old iron gate.

"*Son-of-a-bitch! Damn it all to hell!*" I yelled, hitting the brake and slamming the shifter into reverse.

"*Wait! Stop!*" Bob shouted. "It's open. Look!"

I looked. It wasn't open, it stretched across the track from one rusty steel post to another, but he was right, there was no chain and no lock, nothing holding the gate to the right-side post.

I didn't bother to get out and open it. I shifted the car into drive, set the front bumper against the gate, and pushed forward, forcing the gate to swing open with a squeal from its rusty hinges. I'd pushed too hard. The gate hit the stop and bounced back, slamming into the front left fender. *Damn it. That sounded expensive.*

I slowly drove on for maybe another hundred yards until I finally arrived at a crossroad, if you could call it that.

I stopped the car and said, "T.J., I need my iPad."

Opening my briefcase, he took it out and handed it to me. I pulled up the screenshot of the area that I'd taken earlier and studied it. It wasn't easy, but I thought I had it figured out. At least I hoped I did. The road, track, whatever we were still on, was just to the left of the five ruined structures. "We're close," I whispered. Why I was whispering, God only knew. The sound of the engine would have been enough to warn anyone who might be listening that they had company.

"We need to turn right," Bob said. So I did.

"Maybe we..." I started to say, but paused to study the area for a moment, then continued, "Aha! That's the spot, I think; there, see? Through the trees. D'you see those concrete buildings?" I slowed the Rover almost to a stop.

"There's a spot back there a little way where we can hide the car." I reversed maybe fifty yards, then turned left onto what once must have been the concrete floor of a small building. It was almost completely overgrown, and I figured it was as good a place as any. I parked the car under the trees where I hoped it wouldn't be seen.

"Okay," I said, turning in my seat so that all three of us could see the screenshot. "Here's where we are. The road continues on and bears to the right, here," I said, pointing at the image on the screen, then continued, "around these old structures. There's a large building here, almost hidden by trees, and though you can't see it on this thing, it's right about here." Again, I pointed. "There's open ground to the front and what looks like a pathway around the back. It appears to be the only habitable building out of the six; it has to be the one." I paused and stared at the image. "There could be more hidden structures, but we won't know until..." I paused again, thinking, *Until what? We stick our friggin' necks out is what!*

"Okay, we know there are at least six of these guys. And we can be sure they're not going to go down easy."

I paused, turned so I could look into the back seat, and said, "T.J., last chance. Some of us, maybe all of us, could get killed. You don't have to do this. You can stay here in the car, yeah?"

"Are you nuts? Hell no, Harry. I'm in this with you... You took me in when... Ah bull. I'm better able to do this kinda shit than either of you. Two tours in Nam, remember? Yeah, yeah, I know you were a Marine, Bob. What the hell? Semper fi! That make you feel good? Now, can we get on with it?"

I nodded. I didn't feel good about it, but if he was willing to risk it, so was I.

I pointed to a spot on the iPad and said, "They must be in here, in the building we can't see. We'll cross the road here," again I pointed before continuing, "then separate. Bob, you and T.J. will go left and follow the road, staying under cover of the trees, all the way around the end of the row of structures to the back of the building, here. I'll advance between these two structures and go into the trees here. That will bring me to the edge of the open ground somewhere around here where I can cover this side of the building. I'll wait for a signal from you guys to let me know that you're in place, and then we'll hit them from both sides, yeah?"

"Yeah," Bob said. "And just how do you suggest that I send a signal without letting 'em know we're there? I don't do coyote."

"Send me a text, for God's sake. My phone will ding. I'll know you're there. Send it, count to ten, then hit 'em, hard. Okay?"

They both grinned.

"A friggin' text?" Bob asked. "Are you kidding me? I like it. Bet you couldn't do that in Nam, T.J."

"Check your weapons," I said, dryly. "And let's do it."

* * *

"This is beyond crazy," Bob said as we crept closer to the edge of the line of trees. "Shit like this doesn't happen in real life. Harry, I feel like friggin' Rambo."

"Ha, ha, ha," T.J. chuckled. "I never realized how much I missed the life. This sure does bring back memories. You want to swap that

AR15 for my VP9? I could do some real damage with that." That last bit he said to Bob, but Bob simply glared at him.

"Shut the hell up, both of you," I whispered. "Concentrate. We cross the road, then I go that way." I pointed through a narrow gap in the trees. "You guys follow me, then we'll separate and you'll both head that direction, and stay the hell out of sight. You got that?"

They both nodded, T.J. grinning like an idiot; Bob, not so much.

I took a deep breath, glanced down at my own AR15, and then, for God's sake, I looked both ways like there might be traffic coming—my mom taught me that when I was a kid—damn, did I feel stupid or what?

Stupid or not, I stepped out of the trees and, head down, doubled over at the waist, ran across the road into the trees on the far side. Bob and T.J. followed, all of us dropping flat among the underbrush.

I listened. All was quiet. *So far, so good.*

"Okay," I whispered. "Go." I nodded and waved my arm in the direction they needed to proceed.

They scrambled to their feet and crept off through the trees and undergrowth. I watched until they were out of sight, then I moved out myself.

My short trek took no more than a couple of minutes. I made it to the ruined blockhouses, if that's what they were, without incident, then dodged in between the two at the east end where I flattened myself against the concrete wall. I listened, took a deep breath, then hurried across a crumbling footpath and into the cover of the trees beyond. I figured a sharp turn to the left would leave me facing the objective. I turned and slowly moved forward, trying not to step on anything that might give me away.

I reached the edge of the clearing and stopped, taking cover behind the trunk of an old giant oak tree. I looked out across the open ground and figured that I was at least fifty yards away from my objective, an eight-second sprint for me at best.

Too far! I thought, looking for somewhere closer; there was nothing.

I checked out the building itself. A covered porch ran its entire length, so obviously I was looking at the front of building. There were two vehicles parked to one side close to the footpath I'd just crossed: a Ford Ranger pickup and a Dodge Durango SUV. The nearest, the Dodge, was perhaps sixty yards from my position. *No Ford Expedition,* I thought. *Unless... Jeez, I hope to God we aren't too late. Not much I can do about it; at least not right now, but we gotta get this done, and quickly. If they've moved it, or God forbid, they've already deployed it... Where the hell are they?*

I shook my head, settling down to watch and wait for Bob's signal. It never came.

Chapter Twelve

I was just about to give up waiting and go see what had happened to Bob and T.J. when I heard the rattle of suppressed gunfire on the far side of the building. Only then did I see the muzzle flashes and hear more gunfire, this time from inside the building. *Son-of-a-bitch! So much for...*

I was taken completely by surprise, and as I found out some time later, so were the three men who came running out from the front of the building. All three were armed: two had pistols of some sort; the other one who was in the lead had what looked like an Uzi machine pistol. They stopped running. The guy in front—obviously the leader —looked wildly around, made up his mind, and ran toward the vehicles; the other two ran after him. I hoisted my AR15 to my shoulder. *Disable those freaking vehicles... now!*

I dropped to one knee, peered through the holographic sight, and fired. The driver-side front tire of the Durango exploded with a bang. Next, I took out the front tire of the Ford, then its rear, and then I switched back and took out the rear tire of the Durango. They weren't going anywhere.

All of that took less than five seconds, but it was enough for the three terrorists to realize what was happening. One, the guy with the Uzi, took cover behind the Ranger, the other two behind the Dodge. I smiled. *You should have kept running, you stupid sons o' bitches.*

I could just see the guy behind the Ranger peeking through the window of the passenger-side door. I scanned the Durango for the other two. Looking under the chassis, I caught sight of two pairs of feet and knees. They were crouched down. I took aim at the one to the right, but before I could fire, there was a crackle of automatic gunfire and bullets slammed into the trunk of the tree I was stationed behind, tearing off huge shards of razor-sharp wood. The guy behind the Ranger had made me.

I flung myself to the ground and lying flat on my belly to make my profile as small as possible, I took aim. He must have fired over the bed of the truck. I had the AR15 loaded with .556 Greentip Nato rounds, so as quick as I could pull the trigger, I stitched a row of holes along the bed of the truck from one end to the other. I heard him yelp. How bad he was hit, I didn't know, nor did I care, at least not then. I turned my attention back to the two men hunkered down behind the Dodge. I still hadn't heard from them, and I didn't want to. I peered through the sight, picked a spot midway up the rear door that was in line with a pair of feet, took a deep breath, slowly let it out, then gently squeezed the trigger. The rifle bucked hard against my shoulder. From where I was, I couldn't see the hole the bullet made in the Dodge, but I didn't need to. The feet on the far side took half a step back and the guy collapsed. I swung the rifle slightly to the left, looking for the second pair of feet. They were gone. *Oh shit. Where the hell did he go?*

I knew I had to get him. If that Expedition was parked anywhere near, it was possible that the second guy could be the driver. Then I saw him, beyond the north end of the building, moving fast with a pistol in his right hand. He was at least a hundred yards away and weaving like a fish in a pond. I followed him through the holographic sight, waited until he dodged left, then squeezed the trigger. The bullet pierced his low-center mass; he staggered but didn't go down.

He continued running. I hit him again, and then again. That last shot did it. The bullet must have punched through his heart, because he crumpled and fell face-first into the dirt. *Damned Greentips, they must have gone through and through.*

I lowered the rifle and again checked the building. All was quiet, which could have either been a good or bad thing. We had either prevailed or I had lost both my guys.

A second or two later, a grinning T.J. Bron appeared on the porch, VP9 in hand.

"Hey, Harry," he shouted. "You're late for the party. We have this place locked down: one dead and one prisoner. You comin'?"

Yeah, I was coming, and they had some explaining to do. What the hell had happened?

"Is it clear?" I shouted at T.J. as I ran across the clearing.

"You betcha. We got these two, and the other three high-tailed it out of here. C'mon!"

"Did you see an Expedition parked out back? You didn't? Shit! Where the hell is it?"

"The Expedition," T.J. said as I mounted the steps to the porch, "is a big, tough vehicle, Harry. You think that's where they have the bomb?"

"I hope to hell not. If it is, it's not here, which means..."

"We're too late," Bob finished for me.

"It could be behind one of the sheds," I said with a sinking feeling that it wasn't.

"Harry! Look out!"

I didn't need to be told twice. I immediately realized my mistake. I threw myself sideways, hit the porch wall, and landed flat on my back on the wooden floor. I didn't see T.J. fire his weapon, but as I rolled, I saw the terrorist who must have been the guy behind the Ford Ranger spin, jerking under the impacts of three hollow points from T.J.'s VP9 as the bullets slammed into his upper body.

He grinned down at me and said, "You're welcome. Damn, that felt good. Just like old times."

So now I owe my life not just to Bob but to T.J. as well. I must be getting slow, losing my edge.

I nodded to T.J. and grabbed the hand he was holding out, allowing him to haul me to my feet.

"Thanks, buddy," I said as I slapped him on the shoulder.

"Bob," I said, turning my attention to him. "You want to tell me what happened to the signal you were supposed to send?"

He frowned and glanced wryly sideways at T.J., and I got the message. The man was a loose cannon. I was going to have to rein him in before he killed someone. *Bit late for that, Harry,* I thought. *He already has!*

I nodded, let it go for the time being, and said, "What about the live one?"

"Don't know. I smacked him over the head with this," Bob said as he waved the Sig .45, then slipped it into its holster under his arm. "He's unconscious..." I heard someone groan through the open door. "Well, he was," Bob said with wide a grin. "Why don't we check him out?"

Captain Majid Hammad, late of the IRGC—I say late not because he was dead, but because his career with said terrorist force was now officially over. Anyway, he was on his knees, trying to get up. Blood was streaming from a deep cut just above his right ear.

"You need to get that seen to," Bob said, smiling down at him.

"May you rot in hell, American pig," he replied and then rolled over until he was sitting upright on the floor.

Bob laughed and said, "Not me, fella. It's you that's going to hell... But you guys don't believe that, do you? Something about seventy-five virgins, right? Wow, that's hilarious. They, whoever they are, sure did a head job on you guys."

"That's enough, Bob," I said. "We don't have time to play. Get him a chair."

He did and we seated the man on it, next to a table upon which were the remains of some sort of meal. Whatever it was, it looked disgusting.

"So," I said, "talk to me. I need to know what sort of bomb you have, where it is, and what the target is."

He laughed, blood running down his face into his mouth, and then spat the bloody mixture at me. The blood spattered onto my vest. T.J. stepped forward, his hand raised. I held up my hand; he stopped and stepped back. I said again, "Talk to me."

"My name is Captain Majid Hammad—"

"We don't give a rat's ass what the hell your name is," T.J. interrupted him. "Tell us about the bomb. *Now!*"

Again, the laugh. "Of course," he said. "It will be my pleasure." His eyes were bright, his lips curled in an arrogant smirk.

The frigging sonofabitch is enjoying himself.

"It is one of your own. What you called a SADM, a tactical nuclear weapon. It was one of many you once had in your arsenal that was intended to be used by your filthy inferior forces during your so-called Cold War with the Soviets. Now we have it. It is not a big bomb," he said and shrugged, then curled his lips into a sneer before continuing, "not like the ones you used to kill hundreds of thousands of innocent Japanese children, but big enough for our purposes: just one-half kiloton, so I understand, and I really don't understa..."

Bob stepped forward and slapped his face hard enough to cut off the flow of words.

"You're playing for time, you piece o' shit. Tell us the damned target, NOW!" He slapped him again. This time he split his lip, and it began to bleed profusely.

"You are too late, my filthy friends," Hammad said as he glanced down at his watch. "By now the bomb is armed. It is ticking, tick tock, tick tock, counting down to your Armageddon. Soon you American pigs will know what it is for thousands of your people to die in an instant."

I happened to glance at the table. There were two sets of car keys on it, but only two sets. One with a Dodge tag, the other a Ford. In my peripheral vision, I caught the rapid blinking of Hammad's eyes. I looked out through the window. I could see the Dodge parked off to one side and the Ford Ranger a little farther on.

"It's in the Expedition, right?" I asked Hammad. He said nothing, but I could tell I was right.

"So, now I want to know the target," I said, tapping the table with the tip of the AR15. "You'll tell me, or I'll shoot your kneecap."

"Ha! You think you scare me? You don't. I was trained by the best in the world. I will tell you, American pig excrement, but I will tell you only because there is nothing you can do to stop us. By now, Babak will have deployed the weapon. Destiny is at hand."

"Okay, so you say. *Where... is... it?*"

He cocked his head to one side, smiled grimly up at me, and said, "It is at your TVA!"

"Sequoya? Yeah! That's what we figured..." Then I saw the look in his eyes and stopped talking.

"Not Sequoya," he snarled, and then he smiled, a huge smile, exposing two rows of perfect teeth, white, glistening. "TVA... on Broad Street... downtown Chattanooga."

Holy shit! Holy freakin' shit! I should have guessed. It's too friggin' easy. I gulped and stared down at him. "The underpass?" I whispered.

"The underpass!" he agreed, leaning back in his chair and folding his arms, the evil smile splitting his face from ear-to-ear.

Chapter Thirteen

I was stunned, and not just because of the target but also because it had never occurred to me. It actually made more sense than the nuclear plant. It's a relatively soft target, the TVA. Security downtown was almost non-existent, and a nuclear explosion there would do ten times more structural damage, not to mention the massive number of casualties, than bombing the relatively isolated nuclear plant.

The TVA operations center in downtown Chattanooga is a huge complex of office buildings, but in reality, it is little more than a giant super computer that controls more than sixteen thousand miles of the National Grid. If that goes down, and it will, well... there's no telling the chaos it will create. *Screw the freakin' National Grid,* I thought. *What about the casualties? Thousands of them.*

"You sick sonofabitch," T.J. snarled at him and again took a step forward, and again I held up my hand to stop him, never taking my eyes off Hammad's face.

"How long?" I asked him in a grim, quiet voice. "How long do we have?"

He sneered up at me and shook his head as he said, "Not long enough, my filthy friend." Again, he glanced down at his watch. "Not long enough," he repeated, and then closed his eyes. "And now that I have completed my mission, you may kill me. I will be a martyr and lauded throughout my country as a hero of the Islamic Republic." He spread his arms wide and said, "Do it. Do it now. I am ready. Malak al-Maut came to me last night in a dream and told me to ready myself. It is time. Do it now, American pig."

"Malak al-Maut?" Bob asked. "Who the hell is that?"

"He's the Muslim angel of death," I said. *These bastards are on a suicide mission.*

"I have no problem with that," T.J. said, leveling his pistol. "Go to your virgins; may they all be sheep." And then he shot him between the eyes.

I was taken by surprise, but I didn't give a shit. The smarmy bastard had it coming.

I thought for a minute, then headed for the door.

"I need to make a call," I said. "I'll be back."

I went outside and no, I didn't call Parker or anyone else in law enforcement. I figured that if I did, they'd try to shut me down, and if Hammad was to be believed—and I was sure that he was—there was no point; we were probably out of time or close to it. No, I called an old friend of mine and prayed that he'd answer. Fortunately, he was where I figured he would be at that time of day, eating lunch.

I told him what I was doing and what I needed. At first, he didn't believe me, but I must have gotten through to him because he eventually agreed and told me he'd be waiting for me. So, everything was all set up, but I had to move fast, and I hoped to hell I hadn't figured it wrong or was too late. Either way, if I had... Well, it wasn't worth thinking about; there was nothing else I could do.

I went back inside. "Stay here," I told them. "Clean this place up before they get here." I was referring to whatever law enforcement agency might be on the way, and then I ran out into the sunlight.

"Hey, stop," Bob shouted after me. "Where the hell are you going? Never mind. I can guess. Wait for me."

"Not friggin' likely. I told you. I have a plan. Maybe there's still time. If not, well, you'll be safe here. No sense in both of us dying."

As I ran to the Range Rover, I thought about calling Amanda but there was no point, no time for her to... and anyway, she was probably safe enough up there on the mountain.

Fireball, say one hundred yards across, maybe a little more, but not much, I thought as I climbed into the Rover and slammed the door.

Blast radius, a quarter of a mile—I hit the starter button—*enough to flatten downtown from West Main almost to Riverside Drive.*

I punched the address of the TVA building into the Rover's GPS system, reversed out from under the trees, and headed through the damned jungle back to Hickory Valley Road as fast as I dared on the crappy road.

I turned south and glanced at the GPS. *Oh hell. Twenty minutes... way too long. I'm not going to make it... But wait! Baboo, or whatever the hell his name is, will want to make sure he has enough time to get away, right? Maybe, just maybe. Maybe... if he left just before we arrived... and he wouldn't be in a hurry... but then there's the traffic... No, he'd take his time; he wouldn't want to risk getting pulled over. Twenty... minutes... Say twenty-five. If he left thirty minutes ago... Shit, he's already there. All I have is what's left on the timer. Why didn't I make that sonofabitch tell me exactly how long?*

I turned on my headlights and hazard lights and pushed the car south on Hickory Valley Road, breaking every speed limit and then some. I ran every light, red or green. Boy, did I piss some people off! Fortunately, I didn't see a single cop. *It's true what they say,* I mused. *There's never one...* I hauled on the wheel and slewed left off Hickory Valley onto Bonny Oaks Drive and floored the pedal. I know I hit ninety in places on that two-lane roadway.

Again, I didn't stop for a single red light. I reached the junction with I-75, dodged around the line waiting at the red light, sped over the on-ramp, and headed south on the interstate. In places, I posted a hundred and twenty miles an hour. I slowed only when I approached the I-75/I-24 split, drove onto the hard shoulder, shoved my hand down on the horn, kept it there, and screamed onto I-24, barely missing a semi heading west from Atlanta. I could see the big rig in my rearview mirror; it was rocking like crazy.

I floored the gas pedal, weaving from lane to lane, sometimes taking the hard shoulder, passed through the Ridge Cut, and then the split onto Highway 27, past the Market Street exit, all the way to the Main Street off-ramp toward downtown. From there it was just four blocks to the TVA complex and the underpass. I'd made that sixteen-mile run in twelve minutes. Unbelievable? Not possible, right? Oh yeah. Well, I did it.

The underpass beneath the TVA building—actually, there are two of them, each linking huge buildings on either side of the road, and each four stories high, including the road—happens to be a continuation of Broad Street. There's limited parking on either side of the road beneath the underpasses and the buildings. *Jeez, can you believe that? And no security other than whatever there is inside the complex?* I figured that's where he'd plant the bomb, under a damn building.

I drove slowly east through both underpasses, then made a U-turn and drove through again, this time going west. There was no sign of the Expedition, but there was a large dumpster—painted bright pink, for God's sake—set on two parking spaces on the east-bound side of the road, under the west-side underpass. *That has to be it. Has to be. Please God, it must be.* It was.

I made another illegal U-turn and parked the Rover at the west end of the dumpster, nose to steel. The frigging thing was huge. I exited the car and climbed up onto the hood to peer over the edge. And there it was, nestled among the garbage. Babak must have wanted rid of it. He'd made no attempt to hide it; it looked to me as if he'd just slung it over the side. *So much for handling the friggin' thing carefully.*

I climbed up onto the side of the dumpster and then clambered down inside. I grabbed the huge backpack by its straps. It was round, not like a ball but like it held a twenty-five-gallon drum, and made from heavy, green canvas that had seen better days. I lifted it... *Sixty pounds did they say? It's all of that and then some.*

I dragged the thing to the side of the dumpster and turned it over. There was a canvas flap on the side; it had fallen open, revealing a small, raised—no more than a half-inch—metal box-like attachment. It had once been painted green, but there was little paint left, just bare metal, dull, gray. The outer face of the box had a small window and through it I could see small red numbers, and they were moving, counting down. I was looking at the timer. *Oh shit. Twenty-seven minutes and thirty-three seconds, thirty-two, thirty-one. Damn, I must have missed Babak by only a few minutes. Shit! There's no way I can turn this thing off; can't get into it because those are tamper-proof screws. Jeez, I wouldn't know what to do if I could. Okay, Harry. Time for plan A. Get this mother out of here and let's go.*

I pushed the backpack up the dumpster wall and over the edge. I heard it drop onto the Range Rover's hood and closed my eyes, covered my ears with my hands, and waited for the big bang. Nothing! And then I felt pretty stupid. Much good my evasive action would have done me if it had gone off. I would have gone up in the center of the fireball along with all of the TVA buildings and half of downtown Chattanooga.

I hoisted myself up and out of the dumpster, falling hard onto the hood of the Rover next to the backpack. That thing had put a hell of a dent in it.

I jumped down, hauled the pack off the hood, and slung it onto the back seat, taking one more look at the timer: twenty-six minutes and fifty-four seconds. *Friggin' hell, I gotta move!*

I jumped in behind the wheel, hit the starter, and punched the address into the GPS. *Eighteen minutes. You gotta be kiddin' me!*

I backed up a few yards and swerved out into the traffic, clipping the rear fender of a Jeep, and as I headed back toward Main Street and the Highway 27 on-ramp, I hit the Bluetooth and shouted, "Call Jimmy Little!"

Chapter Fourteen

"Calling Jimmy Little."

It was one of the most irritating voices I'd ever heard. At least it was until I heard him answer.

"Harry, where the hell are you?"

"I'm coming up on Highway 27."

"How long?"

"GPS tells me... seventeen minutes. I think there's about twenty-four left on the timer, maybe a few seconds more."

"Oh shit, Harry. That's cutting it awful thin."

"Tell me about it. Can we make it?"

"Pedal to the metal, Harry. I'll have the gate open and be waiting for you on the tarmac with the engine running."

"Okay. Look for me in..." I closed my eyes momentarily, said a quick and silent prayer, then told him, "Ten minutes."

"That ain't gonna happen, Harry. You'll kill yourself."

"I'll make it; I have to. Just be there ready to go when I arrive."

"You got it."

I disconnected the call and pressed the Bluetooth again saying, "Call Kate Gazzara."

"Calling Kate Gazzara, mobile."

"Harry? Oh, thank God. Shady told me what's going on. Where are you?"

"I'm on Highway 27 heading for the airport. Listen, I'm almost out of time. This thing is running and I can't stop it. I can't get into it and I daren't try to force it. That might trigger it. I have less than twenty-four minutes to get it somewhere safe and get rid of it. There's a flooded quarry just to the north of the airport. My friend Jimmy Little runs a small skydiving business out of an old hangar located on the west side of the airport on Jubilee Drive. He's waiting for me right now. He has a Piper Navajo we can use to haul this thing over the quarry and dump it in four hundred and fifty feet of water."

"Harry—"

"Kate," I interrupted her, "stop talking. I have to drive. If I wreck... I need your help, so just shut up and listen, okay?"

She didn't answer.

"It's a little more than eight miles from where I am now—fourteen or fifteen minutes in normal traffic. I can do it in ten if I'm not stopped, maybe even less if I had an escort, but there's no time for that. I need you to broadcast the word to all law enforcement agencies that I'm not to be stopped and need to be allowed through.

"Jimmy said he can get off the ground in three minutes, but it'll take a couple of minutes to get it loaded into the plane. That's fifteen; it will take maybe five more minutes to get to the quarry, and that includes enough time to tip the thing out of the plane. That will leave maybe three minutes on the clock, which should be just enough time for it to sink to the bottom of the lake before it explodes."

I hit the horn. "Get out of the freakin' way you, you..." I yelled at the back of a rickety old Ford as I swerved around him. The driver flipped me the bird; I didn't respond.

"With four hundred and fifty feet of water on top of it," I continued talking to Kate, "the blast should be contained, minimal I hope. Now don't argue with me. I gotta keep this damn car on the road and moving as fast as possible. Just put the word out, okay? I'll talk to you later." *I hope,* I thought as I hung up.

I swerved right off I-24 onto South Terrace, made a hard left through a red light at McBrien, and then accelerated hard toward Brainerd Road. I had no idea if I was taking the best route, but this was the path showing on the GPS, so it was the way I was going.

At Brainerd, I ran into heavy traffic. No, I ran into a jam; traffic was at a standstill. I hit the brakes and screeched to a stop just a couple of feet from the car in front of me. Then I banged the wheel in frustration and looked around wildly. Some damned clown had pulled up too close behind me. I was blocked in and couldn't go forward or backward more than a couple of feet in either direction.

I looked at my GPS. I was a few yards south of the Krispy Kreme... *I wonder...* No, I didn't, I didn't have time.

I slammed the big SUV into drive and hit the gas. The Rover jumped the few feet that separated it from the car in front—a Honda Pilot—I shoved and then winced as I watched the Rover's hood crumple. The Honda jerked forward and hit the rear of the car in front of it, ramming it forward. It wasn't much, just enough for me to back up and turn left across the oncoming traffic. I rocketed across Brainerd and was clipped on my passenger-side rear fender by the front end of an oncoming pickup truck—the driver waving and screaming at me... boy, if he only knew—and then I squealed into the Krispy Kreme parking lot.

I punched the gas and must have hit forty as I raced through the parking lot. At the rear of the lot, I could see a chain-link fence. I braced myself, stomped the gas pedal to the floor, and smashed right through it into the backyard of a private house that bordered the grounds of the Krispy Kreme. I shot past the side of the house and out onto what I knew to be Belaire Drive. I swerved left and accelerated, traveling north on Belaire for maybe five hundred yards to a three-way stop where I turned right and headed back toward Brainerd Road.

When I reached Brainerd with my lights on and hazards flashing,

I hit the horn and didn't even slow at the stop sign. I just prayed like hell that the big SUV had enough weight to make it through the oncoming traffic. It did. Fortunately, I didn't hit anything.

I turned left onto Brainerd and, weaving in and out of the traffic, ran the final half a mile to Jubilee Drive where I found the traffic blocked again. This time though, and much to my relief, it was the oncoming traffic that was stopped, by a cop no less, and he was waving me into the turn.

I was almost there but frighteningly behind schedule. I figured I'd lost at least a couple of minutes making the detour. I glanced at the dashboard clock and calculated that I now had less than eight minutes to dump the bomb and get out of the way.

I hit seventy-five along Jubilee toward the Wilson Air Center. And boy was I glad to see another cop car blocking Jubilee at the entrance. That cop too, out in front, waving me through the gate.

True to Jimmy's word, the big gates to the airfield were open and the Piper Navajo was waiting on the taxiway, its engine running. Jimmy was inside but leaning out of the jump door, which had been removed, waving his arms like a maniac. I floored the gas, howled through the gates, slammed on the brakes, and slid to a stop almost directly beside the jump door, so close in fact that I had to back up to make sure the tail of the aircraft was clear.

I leaped out of the car, grabbed the fat, bulky backpack by its straps, and hauled it to the jump door where Jimmy grabbed it and hauled it inside.

He held out a hand. I grabbed it. He pulled me inside, pushed me to one side, and headed for the cockpit, leaving me standing next to the wide-open jump door.

"Best strap in, Harry. This is going to be a little hairy. If you fall out, I'll have a big problem." *You and me both. Jeez!*

"Hey, Harry," he yelled. "We got it made. They closed the airport for us. We get to use the runway." *Oh, that makes me feel a whole lot better.*

"Listen," he yelled back to me as he opened up the engine and the aircraft began to move, "I'll haul this thing into the air, then make a slight left turn over the lake. We'll be no higher than a couple hundred feet. I'll keep her slow as I can, but we'll still be moving faster than eighty knots. When it's time, I'll hit the jump button. See that green light above your head? When you see that come on, you have to kick that mother out of my aircraft, yeah?"

"Yeah!" I yelled back at him. "I got it. Hurry up and get this thing in the air; we're almost out of time!"

He opened the throttle and the aircraft picked up speed. We were still on the taxiway, so I took a quick look at the timer: four minutes and twenty-nine seconds. *Oh shit, are we cutting it close, or what?*

Jimmy turned the Piper left and then left again onto the runway, opening the throttle the rest of the way. The Piper seemed to set back on her two rear wheels and then leaped forward. Slowly the speed built up, and then we were off the ground, moving fast but not fast enough. I looked again at the timer: three minutes and seven seconds. *This is not good.* "Friggin' hell, Jimmy. Move it, for God's sake," I yelled. He didn't answer; I felt the plane begin to bank to the left.

"Hey, Harry," I heard him yell. "You ready back there? We're almost over the lake. Watch for the green light."

I did, and after what felt like fifteen minutes had passed, though it could only have been fifteen seconds, the light came on accompanied by a frantic Jimmy yelling, "Go, go, go! Get that mother out of here."

I slapped the quick-release buckle of my harness, stood, and nearly fell out of the jump door as the aircraft rocked in the turbulence. I dropped down onto my ass and with both feet, I kicked out hard at the backpack. It rolled to the door, and out it rolled... only it didn't fall. One of its straps had gotten hooked onto what I learned later was part of the jump door assembly.

I grabbed the strap and tugged on it. The damn thing was a frigging great lump of lead. I couldn't move it. *Oh shit! What now? What...* "I need a knife, knife, knife; I need a freakin' knife," I stuttered to myself, panicking as I tried to reach into my pants pocket. Found it! It got stuck in the lining. Trembling like a damned leaf, I finally jerked the knife free and, for once, was ever so grateful for the switchblade feature. Even so, I almost dropped the damn thing in my hurry to get it open, and the whole time I could see that damned red counter clicking away the seconds.

"Hey!" Jimmy yelled from up front. "You done yet? I can't go around again. Hang on, I'm going to bank her a little."

A little? He almost rolled the damn thing. The damn jump door yawned before me like the gates of hell, and then the plane righted itself.

"You gotta do it now, Harry! We're almost out of the pocket."

Screw you, you dopey bastard. You think I'm not tryin'?

I finally managed to get the knife open and slashed at the webbed strap. The impact felt like I'd broken my wrist; it was that tough. Would you believe it took three more strokes before the webbing parted and the bomb dropped away? As it dropped, I caught one more glimpse of the timer: two minutes and five seconds.

"Go, Jimmy! Get us the hell out of here!" I yelled at the top of my voice.

I reared back and braced myself against the seat frame next to the jump door as Jimmy hauled the Piper into another tight left turn. And once again, I almost slid out of the open door. For a moment, I swung there with my feet hanging over the edge of the doorframe. I had the horrible feeling that I was about to head downward after the bomb, and yes, I could still see the backpack as it tumbled through the air until it finally vanished with just a tiny splash some two hundred or more feet below. It was done. There was nothing more I could do. It was now in God's hands.

Jimmy righted the aircraft and turned north, then made a slow left turn to the west. I could now see the lake through the open doorway about a mile away.

I looked at my watch. I figured we had about a minute to spare

before the thing blew. The minute ticked by, and then another...
What the hell?

And then she blew. It was the most ethereal event I have ever witnessed. There was no big bang. The plane rocked a little in the updraft from the city, but nothing more.

However, almost as if in slow motion, the surface at the southeast end of the lake, the deepest end, mushroomed upward like a huge upturned bowl, and then the surface broke open with a gigantic spout of water shooting five hundred or more feet into the air as the quarry appeared to empty itself. I swear, even from that distance, I could see the rock walls almost to the bottom of the pit. For several seconds, the great column of water seemed to hang, frozen, glistening in the sunlight, and then it fell, cascading back into its rocky home. For ten minutes more, Jimmy circled the quarry. Its surface was a wild, bubbling, steaming cauldron: the water was boiling, literally. It was then that I began to wonder about fallout. I'd figured that because of the depth of the quarry and the steep rock walls, the blast would be contained, and it had been. But fallout? Somehow, I'd gotten it into my head that there would be none. How? I don't know, but when I saw all of that steam... *Well, I guess I'll find out soon enough.*

I carefully walked forward and leaned into the cockpit. "Hey. You okay?" I asked.

"Oh yeah. That was some show you put on, Harry. You wanna circle around again and take a closer look?"

I hesitated, then said, "Better not... Ah! Why the hell not? It's not often we get to explode a nuclear bomb."

Jimmy smiled and then said, "Come on up, take a seat and strap in. I have a feeling it's gonna get bumpy."

I did as he said, then he took the Piper up to three thousand feet and slowly circled the lake. It was a cauldron of boiling water, a column of steam rising maybe five hundred feet before dispersing in the breeze. The bedrock had to be molten, thousands of degrees. I glanced across at the great bulk of Lookout Mountain, and I wondered... *Oh my God, I have to get her off the mountain.*

I took out my cell phone and called Amanda.

She answered immediately. "What the hell is going on, Harry?" she yelled. "Did you have anything to do with what's going on down there?"

"Er, sort of, but I can't explain right now..."

"What did you say? What's all that noise? I can barely hear you."

I shouted, "I said 'sort of.' Listen, I can't hear you either. I'm in a small aircraft. The noise you're hearing is the engine and the wind from the open jump door."

"Oh my God. What have you done this time?"

"Nothing... well, something, but I'll explain later. Amanda, you have to get off the mountain. I want you to leave now, *right now*, and take West Brow to Trenton, book into a motel, and I'll meet you there. *Do not*, under any circumstances, take Scenic Highway. Stay on the west side of the mountain. Will you do that for me?"

She wanted to argue and ask questions, but the noise inside the Piper was prohibitive. I made her shut up and listen to me, then I made her promise to do as I asked. She finally agreed, but I could tell that she was anything but happy; no, she was mad as hell, the more so because I wouldn't explain to her why I asked her to take a specific route to Trenton. I didn't want to scare her.

"Let's get back, Jimmy," I said. "I'm feeling kinda sick..." I looked again at the still-boiling surface of the lake... *Jeez! If it doesn't cool down soon, it'll boil itself dry.*

"Hey, Jimmy. Can you imagine if that thing had gone off downtown?" I shouted it at him as he turned back toward the airport.

He shook his head, tightening his lips until they went white. "I can't. I don't want to. I have a wife and kids down there."

"Me too," I said. "Me too."

Chapter Fifteen

Jimmy circled the Piper around to land from the east. From almost a thousand feet, I could see that we were in for a hell of a reception. Wilson Air Center was alive with flashing red, white, and blue lights. There must have been at least a hundred emergency vehicles scattered over the property and along Jubilee Drive. I looked at Jimmy and sighed, then shook my head.

He grinned at me. "You're something friggin' else, Harry. How the hell you managed to pull that off... Well, I hope you're ready to face an adoring press."

I wasn't, and I didn't. Even before the Navajo had slowed and stopped, Kate Gazzara was already there waiting. She'd arrived as the Piper taxied to the hangar. Somehow, she managed to get me away, but not to go home. I had a lot of explaining to do.

I grabbed my briefcase from the back seat of the Rover and then walked away from it, Jimmy at my side. I couldn't help but to turn and look at it. It was a wreck. I turned to Jimmy and asked him if he'd mind arranging for the dealership to pick it up. He said he would take care of it, so I then allowed Kate to drive me to the PD for the debriefing.

They were all there waiting for me: The mayor, Greg Parker, Whitey, Chief Johnston, at least another dozen members of high-ranking law enforcement—including Deputy Chief Hinkle—and half of the county and city commissioners. There were agents from the local offices of the FBI, ATF, and the TBI. Finally, there were two assholes from Homeland Security and an assistant director of the NSA, but they didn't arrive until later that evening, along with God only knew who else and, of course, Bob and T.J.

I can't tell you how many members of the press arrived, seemingly in shifts throughout the rest of the afternoon and most of the early evening, but Kate managed to keep them all at bay.

And so it began. They seated me at the center on one side of the table in the PD conference room, and then everyone else lined up around it, at least twenty of them, and they fired questions at me almost nonstop. I was grilled in shifts until something happened that turned my world upside down and inside out. But I'm getting a little ahead of myself.

Before I was hauled into the meeting, I did get a couple of minutes to talk to my crew.

As you'll remember, I'd left Bob and T.J. at the Ammunition Plant, ostensibly to "clean up the mess." Their idea of cleanup was to simply drag Hammad's body out of the building and into the woods so they could claim that he was a victim of the gunfight. When I asked them how I was supposed to explain how I knew what the target was, Bob handed me a tattered Chattanooga guidebook.

"I found this in one of the rooms," he said, unable to look me in the eye. "Take a look at the centerpiece."

It was a double-page map; someone had used a red ballpoint to draw a circle around the downtown TVA building and scribble " 2PM" at the top-right corner.

"Oh, come *on*, Bob." I looked skeptically at him. "D'you really think anyone's going to buy this or that we're going to get away with it?" I asked. He shrugged and looked at T.J., who simply smiled, turned, and walked into the rest rooms.

"Okay," Bob whispered. "So, I found the book out there. Yeah, I drew the circle on it and wrote in the time. What was I supposed to do? T.J. murdered him, for God's sake."

I didn't answer. He was right. I told him to get out of there, and that I would handle it.

As it happened, miracle of miracles, they did buy it. In fact, apart from a cursory glance at it, no one, with the single exception of Chief Johnston, expressed any interest in the map at all. But again, I'm getting ahead of myself.

I thanked Kate for her help and said goodbye. For a moment, she stood in front of me, staring into my eyes, and then she stepped forward, put her hands on my arms, kissed me gently on the lips, and stepped back from me.

"No," she said, her voice almost a whisper. "Thank you." She then turned and walked away, leaving me to stare after her. I watched her go, then went into the meeting.

It began a little before three-thirty. An hour later, one of Chief Johnston's aides came hurrying into the room with an urgent message for me to call Kate. She couldn't call me because I'd turned off my iPhone when I took my seat at the table.

I apologized to the assembly, told them I had to make the call, and as I did, they all waited, staring at me.

Chapter Sixteen

"Harry. It's Kate. There's been an accident. Amanda is at the hospital in the emergency room at Erlanger. They couldn't get through to you, so they called me. I'm here at the hospital now. Please get here as quickly as you can."

"*What?*" I shouted as I jumped to my feet. "What happened? Is Amanda all right? The baby! What about the baby?"

"I don't know, Harry. I'm not family. They won't tell me anything. You need to come. Right now!"

"Where the hell d'you think you're going?" Arnold Brightwell, the assistant deputy director of the NSA, shouted as he sprang to his feet when I had pushed back my chair and jumped up before heading toward the door.

"My wife's had an accident. She's in the hospital. I'm going to her."

"The hell you are," Brightwell said. "We're not done with you... yet." And then he saw the look on my face and sat down again without saying another word.

I stopped at the head of the table to address Johnston and said, "Chief, I need a ride to Erlanger... can you..."

"Yes, of course. I'll have someone meet you out front... and, Harry, good luck, my friend. Let me know how she is, please."

I nodded, turned, and pushed out through the door.

I don't remember the drive to the hospital. I was in a daze when the cop dropped me at the emergency room door. Fortunately, Kate was out front and waiting for me.

She took my arm. "This way, Harry," she said and steered me through the maze of corridors. "Go on in." Then she turned me loose and gave me a gentle push. "I'll call August for you, and I'll be waiting here in case you need anything, anything at all."

I nodded and went inside the room.

"Yes? Who are you?" the nurse asked. She was black, beautiful, and obviously in charge.

"I'm Harry Starke, her husband. How is she?"

"You'll need to talk to the doctor. Please... sit down. I'll tell him you're here." And she left me alone with my wife.

Oh my God, I thought as I stood beside the bed and looked down at her. I was appalled, frightened... No, I was scared shitless. Now I understood my vision.

She was unconscious, her arms at her sides, an IV in her right wrist. Her face was a mass of cuts and bruises, and the top of her head and even her ears were swathed in bandages. The baby bump under the cover looked huge. *So close, so... close.*

"Ah, Mr. Starke," a voice behind me said. "I'm Dr. Cartwright. I'll be looking after Mrs. Starke... and I'll have help from several other doctors."

"Is she going to be all right?" I spoke quietly to the doctor without taking my eyes off her face.

He shrugged. I saw him out of my peripheral vision.

"She's... well, we're going to have to take the baby. They're preparing the operating room now. We did X-rays. It... she... wasn't injured and the heart is beating strongly, so it shouldn't be too difficult. She was only days away... I'm sorry, Mr. Starke. I really don't know what else to tell you, not yet."

"Can I sit with her until..."

"Of course. Do you need anything, a bottle of water, coffee, or..."

"No, no thank you. If you could just leave... Now please... No! Wait. You said 'she.'"

"Yes. The baby is a little girl."

He didn't say another word. He left, closing the door behind him. I pulled a chair up to the bedside, sat down, and took her small hand in both of mine. I now know and understand what the phrase "I felt empty" means. That's a gross understatement. To feel what I felt that afternoon is to feel as if your guts have been ripped out. My head was aching, a cold, unnatural ache the likes of which I'd never before known, and my brain... The room was spinning as if I'd been on a forty-eight-hour binge... *Forty-eight hours?* I looked at my watch. That's when it had begun, just a little more than forty-eight hours ago. *Sheesh, is that all?* It seemed longer, somehow.

I gazed down at her, my Amanda. Odd thoughts—fears, anger, regrets, memories—swirled around inside my head, a mad, kaleidoscopic vortex, an unreal phantasm like nothing I'd ever experienced before. And I was frightened, more frightened than I'd ever been.

I stared at her poor injured face, the closed eyes blackened, surrounded by deep blue-black bruises, lips swollen and cut in several places, cheeks a mass of cuts, at least a dozen of them, some deep, some superficial.

"Oh, you poor baby," I whispered. I kissed the tips of her fingers.

"Hey," I whispered, can you hear me?" Nothing, not a twitch.

"Mandy." Oh, how she hated being called that. "I'm here. We're going to have a little girl..." And at that point, I choked up. I just sat there and held her hand, tears rolling down my cheeks.

And then my mood suddenly changed and I was overwhelmed by a wave of white-hot anger. Had I not been in that hospital room, I would have smashed something, but somehow I managed to keep control of myself.

And then they came and took her away, and I became consumed with the idea that I'd never again see her alive.

I followed the gurney all the way to the operating room door. It closed in my face, and I knew it symbolized the end of an era. Whether she lived or died, my life would never be the same.

I, that is we, sat in the corridor outside the operating room. August and Rose had arrived some thirty minutes after Kate called them. I guess we must have been there for more than an hour before they came out of the OR: The doctor I'd spoken to earlier accompanied by a nurse carrying a bundle wrapped in a pink blanket.

"Mr. Starke?" the nurse asked.

I nodded and stood up. She placed the baby in my arms. I looked down at the tiny pink face, then at the nurse.

"It's a girl," she said, her face... unsmiling. I looked at the doctor.

"Yes, I know. My wife?" I asked.

"She's in an induced coma," Cartright said. "The blow to the side of her head fractured her skull and... Well, she suffered severe trauma to her brain. We induced the coma to allow time for the swelling to subside. She's comfortable. That's all I can tell you, at least for now."

"How long before you know anything? Can I see her?"

"The answer to the first question is that I don't know. It could be a couple of days, weeks... maybe. I can't say. The answer to your second question is no, not right now. She's in recovery and will go from there to the ICU. Maybe tonight, say nine o'clock. Then once we get her stabilized, you can come and go as you please; family too. Friends? You can make a list and give it to the charge nurse in the ICU."

I nodded, thanked him, and then turned to Rose and handed the baby to her. "I can't do this right now, Rose," I said, shaking my head. "I'm not prepared... There are things I need to do." I looked at my father and asked, "You and Rose, you'll take care of her?"

"Of course," Rose said, but it was the look on August's face that set me back.

"Do you know who's responsible, Harry?" he asked.

I shook my head and said, "No, not yet, not for sure, but I have a good idea."

"Go get 'em, Son. We'll look after the baby."

"What shall we call her?" Rose asked.

I shook my head and said, "I don't know. We never discussed names. Amanda wanted to... I don't know. Just call her Baby for now, okay?"

Rose nodded, cuddled Baby, and kissed her.

I turned away, not sure of my feelings, and I still didn't know what exactly had happened to Amanda. I found Kate seated in a small waiting room just a few yards away along the corridor.

"Kate, I need you to come with me, please." She followed me to one of the waiting rooms.

"Coffee?" I asked, shoving a five-dollar bill into the machine.

"Sure, why not. How is she? How's the baby?"

The coffee was... not what I was used to, but it was hot, wet, and black.

"She'll live, I think... I hope. The baby's fine, a girl."

We sat down, side by side. The chairs were hard, uncomfortable. *Why? People suffer enough in this place without having to deal with uncomfortable seating.*

"What happened, Kate?" I asked, quietly.

We were both leaning with our elbows resting on our knees, paper cups cradled in our hands, staring at the floor.

"Someone ran her off the road as she was driving down the mountain on Scenic Highway."

"Scenic Highway? What the hell was she doing there? She wasn't supposed to take that route. I told her to go west to Trenton, and that I'd meet her there. I needed to keep the mountain between her and the fallou... the steam from the lake."

"Come on, Harry. This is Amanda we're talking about. If she was watching the news, she'd know what was happening and was probably on her way to be with you at the PD."

I nodded. It made sense.

"Go on."

"It must have happened soon after you landed. There's a spot on the right just east of Cravens Terrace as you're coming down the mountain, a paved pull-off where there are no guardrails. It's part of someone's back yard. There was a witness in the car following her. She, it was a woman, a Jennifer Johnston, claims she saw a black SUV drive out of Cravens Terrace at high speed and slam into Amanda, forcing her off the road.

"Johnston said she saw the vehicle as she approached Cravens Terrace. It was parked ten or fifteen yards up the road. Whoever was driving it must have been waiting for Amanda, because, so Johnston claims, the second Amanda's blue Jaguar passed it, the black SUV lurched out and across the road, hitting Amanda's driver-side rear fender. It knocked the car sideways but not off the road. Johnston saw the SUV pull up alongside Amanda and smash into her driver-side door, forcing her car off the road, into the pull-off, and then... down the mountain into the trees.

"Johnston's a good witness, Harry. There's no doubt about what happened. There's black paint all along the side of Amanda's Jaguar. The witness is also certain that it was done on purpose. The driver of the SUV hit her two times before Amanda lost control. I'd say that the perp picked his spot with care. When Amanda's Jaguar went off the road, it veered across the pull-off, smashed through the end of a roadside wooden fence, and went careening over the edge where it collided with a tree, rolled, and landed on a fallen tree. A broken limb went through the windshield. That's what caused her injuries. It ripped through the airbag and slammed into the side of her head. The first responders had to cut her out of the vehicle... Harry, she's lucky to be alive."

"Did the witness get a look at the driver of the SUV?"

"Johnston said there were two men in the SUV, but from where she was, she couldn't see their faces."

"Two, huh? Sounds like it could be Duvon James and Marquis Lewis. I need to go talk to Shady. Can you set it up? Are you up for it?"

"You're... You want to leave... What about Amanda? Don't you need to stay here in case... she wakes up?"

"She's not going to wake up anytime soon, maybe never. She's in good hands. Let's go."

"Oh please, Harry. Don't talk like that. Of course she'll wake up. She'll be fine."

"You don't know that. Even the doctors aren't prepared to commit to her ever waking up... You should see her face, Kate..." And then I almost lost it, and Kate could tell, because she grabbed my arm in both of her hands and squeezed.

"It will be okay," she whispered. "You're right. Let's go." So we did.

Chapter Seventeen

I sat in the passenger seat of Kate's unmarked cruiser and stared out through the side window. If I saw anything during the drive to Amnicola, I don't remember it.

I must have had another of my sixth sense moments, because what I do remember is seeing myself sitting beside Amanda as she drove down Scenic Highway. I saw it all. First, the black roof of the SUV parked on Cravens Terrace, and I tried to warn her. I shouted at her, but she didn't seem to hear me. She just smiled and drove on. I looked frantically back through the rear window and saw the SUV come racing out onto the highway. I watched as it slammed into her fender, heard the smash of glass as the rear window shattered under the impact, and then I saw it. Through the open window of the black SUV was the grinning face of Duvon James as he pulled alongside and smashed into the side of Amanda's car... and then I saw no more until I was standing beside her bed, looking down at her sweet, broken face, and I knew... deep down I knew it was him, and I knew he was going to pay the ultimate price for it.

Kate took me through the PD offices to the interview rooms, and we stood together in front of a one-way mirror. She must have made a call on the drive over, but I didn't hear her do it. Shady was waiting for us, seated at the table, and shackled hand, foot, and waist. His hands were chained to a steel ring welded to the top of the steel table.

"I'm going to have to sit in with you," she said, "and everything said in there will be recorded on video. Do you understand, Harry?"

I nodded.

"And we'll be watched."

"Let's get on with it," I said.

She unlocked the door and stepped inside; I followed her through the doorway.

"Well, well, will you look at what just crawled in? Harry 'the butcher' Starke and Lieutenant 'the slut' Gazzara."

I almost went over the table after him, but Kate grabbed my arm and held me back. Shady laughed, a nasty, gurgling cackle.

"Don't let him get to you, Harry," she said in a low voice. "It's what he wants."

I knew that, but I just wanted to strangle the bastard.

"How you like that four-piece suit?" I asked, using the prison term for his suit of chains. "And how's the hand, Shady? Hurt does it? I fu... I hope so." That wiped the smile off his face.

His left hand was heavily bandaged. The look he gave me was filled with hate.

"Were they able to reattach the finger, Shady?" I wasn't concerned if they had or not; it was just said as a jab at him. "By the look on your face, I'd say not."

He leaned forward, rested his elbows on the table, and cradled the steel ring to which his chains were secured in his good hand.

"My lawyer tells me you're going to be charged with aggravated assault for what you did to me. You'll do time, Harry. I'm gonna make sure of it."

"You think? I don't. In fact, I expect to receive the keys to a grateful city. How about you? Oh wait, I know. The only key you're likely to see is the one that locks your cell door."

He laughed, didn't seem to be bothered by the prospect of a long stretch in prison.

"Tell me, Harry. How's that good lookin' wife of yours? I always figured she must be one hell of a fine lay."

"You sonofabitch," I said, rising to my feet, my hand resting on the steel tabletop. "You couldn't get me, so you decided to get my wife and unborn child instead."

"Oh, nooo," he said, his head tilted to one side. "Did something nasty happen to the lady... but maybe I shouldn't call her a lady. I did hear one time that she likes it big and bla... Whoa, Harry!"

I almost had him by the throat and would have if Kate hadn't grabbed me. I slowly lowered myself back onto my chair.

"I told you, Starke," he snarled. "I told you I'd make you pay for this." He twisted his bandaged hand upright, straining at the chains.

"And you did. It was Duvon and his buddy, right?"

"You think I'll tell you a damned thing, you arrogant piece o' shit? I hope your blonde bitch and whatever piece of garbage she was carryin' inside her died in the flames. You got what you deserved and..." He smiled nastily up at me before continuing, "I ain't done with you yet."

I leaned forward, linking the fingers of both hands together in front of me on the tabletop, and to avoid being heard in the video, I whispered just loud enough for him to hear me, "Yes, Shady, you're right. You're not done with me. You just confessed to the attempted murder of my wife and her nine-month-old fetus. You're going down for that. It's a state rap, so that probably means you'll go to Bledsoe, in Pikeville."

I leaned back in my chair and smiled at him, benignly, I hoped.

"That ain't gonna happen, Starke," he said, easily. "An' even if it did, all I'd get is five, maybe ten, but I'd be out in three. You know that. But as I already said, it ain't gonna happen." He was still smiling, still cocky.

"Ah," I said, airily, "such stuff as dreams are made of..." I leaned forward again and whispered, "You'll never get out, Shady... not alive."

"Screw you," he said. Then he looked up at the camera and shouted, "Get me the hell out of here; this sonofabitch is crazy as hell."

I leaned back again, and we waited, but no one came. Just as I knew they wouldn't. Oh, they were watching: Kate's boss, Henry Finkle, and maybe even the chief.

"Scary, ain't it, Shady?" I said as I leaned forward. "Even in here, you can't get help. Think what it will be like when you're in Bledsoe and someone sticks a shiv in your guts, rips them open, and your intestines fall out around your feet. No, Shady, I'm not done with you."

Shady laughed out loud.

I stood up and stared down at him, then made a motion to the camera, and just that fast the lock clicked before the steel door swung open and the chief walked in.

"You two done having fun?" Johnston asked. "Harry, you get what you needed?"

"I did. Did you?"

"Sure did." He stepped up to the table, released the catch that held Shady's wrist restraints to the table, and hauled him to his feet.

"Lester Arthur Tree," he began. *Arthur? You have to be kidding me.*

"I'm charging you with the attempted murder of Amanda Starke and... Well, Amanda Starke. You have the right to an attorney..."

And he continued droning on until it was done. Nothing the chief said seemed to faze Shady, not even a little. He just stood there and stared at me with that evil little smirk of his smeared across his face.

When Johnston finished, Shady exercised his right to an attorney. The chief told him he could either make the call himself or that he could have someone do it for him. He elected to do it himself.

"You think I'll ever get to Bledsoe, you stupid piece o' shit?" he snarled at me. "I already talked to your buddy, Agent Parker." He chuckled. "He offered me a deal. I get immunity and witness protection in return for spilling my guts about the Iranians. And you know what, Starke? I'm gonna grab it with both friggin' hands. How d'you like that, you stupid shithead? And remember I told you I wasn't finished with you? Well, I ain't. One of these days, Starke, when you ain't expectin' it, I'll be there, in the dark, waitin'... Hahahahaha!"

Why wasn't I surprised? It wouldn't be the first time it had happened to me.

How did I like it? That was one thing he'd never know. In truth, I was barely holding it together. My wife was lying in a hospital, unconscious, and he was the one who put her there, and it appeared as though he was going to get away with it. If I hadn't checked my weapon at the door, I would probably have ended it right then and there. Instead, I simply smiled at him and said, "We'll see, Shady; we'll see."

But deep down I knew that he'd beaten me once again. Many things I might once have been, but I was never a murderer... Or was I? Maybe I was!

I nodded to the chief, and then he signaled for the corrections officer to take Shady away.

And that was the last I saw of him... until, but that's another story, and I still had Duvon James to find.

Chapter Eighteen

The hunt for Duvon James and his partner Marquis Lewis began that very same evening. At first, Kate insisted that I shouldn't be alone, but I needed to be by myself for what had to be done. So I called Uber and arranged for a car to pick me up. I left the PD that evening with nothing but my thoughts.

I called the hospital from the car. There had been no change in Amanda's status. Next, I called August and checked on the baby; she was doing fine... Funny thing was that I had no desire to see her, not then. I told him I'd check with them in the morning and that I was going home to try and get some sleep. It wasn't exactly a lie: I was going home, but not to sleep.

My first thought was to tell the Uber driver to take Ochs Highway instead of Scenic Highway. I told myself I didn't want to see the spot where Amanda had been forced off the road, but then... Well, I changed my mind. I knew I had to face it sometime, and it would be better if it was done sooner rather than later.

We reached the spot—I knew it well, as would anybody who traveled the road regularly—and I had him turn onto Cravens Terrace and park the car, then I walked back down the road to where the Jaguar had careened off the roadway.

The wreckage of the fence had been cleared away, but the yellow and black tapes were still there, waving and fluttering in the breeze. I ducked under them, stepped to the edge of the pull-off, and gazed down the slope. Amanda's car had been removed, but it was evident that something terrible had happened there.

Dozens of trees, most of them saplings, had either been uprooted and thrown aside or were stumps, shattered spears of white wood, sharp...

I stood there, my hands in my pants pockets, staring down at the broken landscape for... how long? I have no idea. In my mind, I could visualize the series of events as the accident unfolded, and I knew how terrified Amanda must have been as the car smashed through the fence and... Eventually, the Uber driver came looking for me, and I reluctantly turned away from the scene and walked with him back to his car.

He dropped me off at my... our home on East Brow Road and left me standing there by the gate. I searched my pants pockets for my keys and would have laughed had I not felt so damned lousy and ridiculous. All I had in my pockets was my iPhone. The rest of my essential belongings were in the Range Rover, and unlike most sensible folks, I didn't have a spare key to the house hidden away outside where "no one could find it."

I clambered over the wall, picked up a rock, and walked around the house to the back door, then smashed one of the glass panes, reached inside, and turned the lock. I punched the code into the security keypad and headed straight for the shower, only stopping to pour myself half a pint of Laphroaig.

The house was silent, unnaturally so. I walked into our bedroom half-expecting to find Amanda lying there asleep, but then I wondered if I'd ever see her there again. I tried to put the awful thought out of my head, but it wouldn't leave.

I stripped, went to the shower, turned it on cold, and stepped inside; the glass of Laphroaig forgotten on the bathroom vanity. The shock of the cold water did little to alleviate my black mood... but thinking about it, I realized it wasn't so much black as it was... what? I felt... disassociated, empty... and cold, oh so cold inside.

I dressed—jeans, T-shirt, and sneakers—grabbed the glass of Laphroaig and my cell phone from the bathroom, and went out onto the patio.

I stood, phone in one hand and glass in the other, and gazed down over the city, a glittering carpet of dazzling colors, but I remember nothing of it... Except for the column of steam rising from the lake, I didn't see anything.

I don't know how long I stood there, occasionally raising the glass to sip the fiery liquid, but it must have been a while, because when my cell phone rang, I noticed the glass was empty.

I looked at the screen: Kate.

"Hey," I said.

"Where are you? Are you okay?"

"Yeah, I'm fine. I'm at home."

"D'you... Do you want some company? I could..."

"No, Kate. Not tonight. I need to be alone. I have some thinking to do."

"Well... Okay then. Harry, please call me if you need anything. I can't imagine how you must be feel..."

I lowered the phone, stared out over the city, and disconnected. I tried to think. One thing was for sure. I needed some help, but I didn't want it from my own people. I couldn't face them, not then, and especially not Tim; he loved Amanda almost as much as I do.

I set my glass down on the patio wall, hit the speed dial, and called Benny Hinkle. It was Laura who answered.

"Hey, I need to talk to Benny."

"Oh my God, Harry! I heard about Am..."

I closed my eyes tightly shut and disconnected. If this was how it was going to be, I couldn't handle it.

The phone rang. I looked at the screen and answered it.

"Benny?"

"Yeah, Harry. Look, I'm sorry..."

"Shut up, Benny," I said, tiredly. "I don't want to talk about it, any of it, okay?"

"Sure. I unnerstand. What can I do for you?"

"I need to find Duvon James."

He was silent for a minute, then said, "Okay. I'll see what I can do. It may take a while. Talk to you later!"

I nodded to myself, pressed the speed dial again, and called someone I hadn't spoken to in more than two years, Sol Wise.

Solomon Wise runs a one-man private investigation agency out of a one-room office on Rossville Boulevard. He's a twitchy little guy, weird, wiry, and... tenacious. A man who isn't averse to skirting the law to get what he needs, and he's good. The few times I'd hired him in the past, he'd always come through for me, and that's what I needed now.

"Hey, Sol," I said when he picked up. "It's Harry Starke." I tried to sound upbeat.

"Harry? Oh my God. I've been watching the news. What the hell have you been doing?"

I sighed. I should have expected it.

"That's not what I want to talk about, Sol, so can we leave it?"

"Well, sure. I just..."

"Yeah, I know. Listen. I need your help. You free for the next couple of days?"

"Er, no. Not really. I have..."

"I don't care what you have, Sol. I need help and I need it now, tonight. I'll double your fee. Now, are you in or are you out?"

"In. What do you need, Harry?"

"I'm looking for someone: Duvon James. He's here somewhere if he hasn't already run, and if he has, I want to know where. Got it?"

"Yes, I know him. In fact, I saw him in the projects just a couple of days ago. Let me see what I can find out. I'll get back with you as soon as I know something."

Chapter Nineteen

I would have stayed home the next day, but I had things I had to do. But before I could get started, I had a couple of calls to make, first to the hospital and then to my family.

The call to hospital was... depressing. No news, which, so I'm told, is good news. Although, it sure as hell didn't seem like it. I told the charge nurse I'd be by later in the morning, and then I called Rose to check on Baby. She was doing fine, and I told Rose too that I'd be by later, but those were the only calls I made.

My first job that morning was to go and retrieve my briefcase and weapons from the wrecked Range Rover, which was by then in the shop at the dealership and deemed a lost cause, so I was told anyway. Fortunately, Jimmy Little had the good sense to have stored my guns in the steel case and then locked it.

I called my insurance company from the dealership and got the answer I needed: the dealership had already called them and sent photos of the damage. The result was that they'd totaled the car and said a check would be in the mail soon. I spent the next half an hour at the dealership replacing the loss.

They had several like models in stock, but I wasn't interested in spending another hour with a salesman, so I told the sales manager to pick one, any one, and he did. It was, of course, the most expensive one on the lot, but I was in no mood to argue with him, so I wrote a check and was done with it just as soon as I signed the papers. Well, not quite. I had them remove the gun case from the wreck and install it in the new car. And then I stopped by the hospital to see Amanda.

It was my first visit since I left her the previous evening. She looked no better than she had then; in fact, she looked worse. The bruises had deepened and... I don't want to talk about it. I stayed with her for a little while, then I had a word with Dr. Cartwright who told me there had been no change in her condition, and I left. Next stop: I went to see my daughter.

August wasn't there; he had a court date. However, my stepmother, Rose, was... I should probably tell you about Rose.

Rose is twenty years younger than my father, which makes her just three years older than me. She's a very beautiful woman: tall, blonde, perfect skin, perfect figure. People who don't know her would tell you that she's the quintessential "trophy wife." Actually, she's not. She's a very caring individual and loves my old man dearly. I, in turn, love her for it. And never once, not to her, my father, or any of our friends, have I referred to her as "stepmother."

So now Rose was a grandmother, a role she seemed more than willing to take on. I found the two of them out on the terrace overlooking the tenth fairway. She'd been shopping... No, I'm not going to go into that, but I swear she must have emptied the store.

Baby was fine. Rose wanted to know if I'd decided what we were going to name her. I told her I hadn't and that at the moment, I didn't want to think about it.

I did spend some time alone with her though. Rose handed her to me and left the room. I sat there feeling kinda stupid, but the feeling didn't last long, not when I looked down into her mother's jade-green eyes. I fell in love all over again, and suddenly I knew exactly what I wanted to name her.

Rose returned some twenty minutes later, and I handed my daughter to her.

"I have to go," I said.

"When will you be back? Can you come to dinner tonight?"

"I don't know. I..." No, I couldn't tell her about the manhunt that was underway. "I'll call you later." I turned to leave. "Oh, and by the way," I said as if it was an afterthought, "her name is Jade."

Chapter Twenty

It was almost noon when I left Rose and... Jade.

My phone rang constantly all through the morning, afternoon, and evening: calls from the media, Greg Parker, Kate, Chief Johnston, the Sheriff's Department, and all the members of my staff. Jacque and Bob each called at least a half-dozen times and left a message following every unanswered call. I deleted them and ignored all of the calls except one, the last one from Sol Wise, which I took.

"Hey, Sol. What've you got?"

"He's holed up in a trailer with a girlfriend, out in the county just off Bates Road."

"Fantastic. How did you find him so quickly?"

"Ha! It wasn't difficult. He's a dealer, right? Let's say I put a little pressure on one of his customers, and it wasn't too hard to find the trailer when I got here."

"Thanks, Sol. I owe you, man. Is he there now?"

"Yeah, he is, but I'm not sure about the girlfriend. I haven't seen her, not at all."

"What about his buddy Marquis Lewis? Is he there too?"

"No. If he's around, I haven't seen him."

"The address?"

"I'm not sure exactly. There's nothing on the mailbox. I have the address for one of the places a little farther down the road. That should get you here. Ready?"

He read it to me as I scribbled it into my iPad. It wasn't an area I was too familiar with, but I did know Bates Road.

"I think I know where you are. Hold on. I'll punch it into the GPS... Okay, got it. Can you wait for me? I'm less than twenty-five minutes away."

"Sure. Come on."

I took it fairly easy, the drive over there. But all the way, my mind was churning. Now that I had him, what was I going to do with him?

I was almost there when I pulled over and went around to the back of the Rover. I opened the tailgate, then the gun case. Aside from the two AR15s and the Colt revolver Bob was so fond of, there was also a Berretta 70 and a Glock 43. I swapped the VP9 for the Glock, checked the load, made sure there was one in the chamber, slipped it into my waistband, and then grabbed a couple more items from the gun case and flipped them over the backrest onto the rear seat. That done, I closed the case and the hatch and then resumed driving. A few minutes later, I pulled up behind Sol's old Honda Civic and cut my lights.

He exited the Civic and slipped into the passenger seat beside me.

"Over there," he said, pointing into the darkness to the left.

At first, I could see nothing, but then I saw the outlines of a long, single-wide trailer silhouetted against the darkening sky and of a dim light glowing in a small curtained window.

"How far?" I asked.

"Twenty, twenty-five yards at most. It's not as far as it looks in the dark. You might be better off waiting until daylight."

"Probably. What about the girlfriend? Have you seen her since you called me?"

"No, I haven't seen her, but she could be in there. I don't know."

I took a deep breath. *If she's in there with him, I have a big problem. I wonder...* I glanced sideways at Sol. It was something I'd already thought about, and I didn't like it, but...

"Sol," I said. "How'd you feel about going in there with me?"

He turned, looked at me, and smiled—he reminded me of a snake about to strike.

"That depends... on what you're planning to do and what you're willing to pay."

"I'm going to kill him," I said, lightly, "but I don't want to hurt the girl. I want you to make sure she's contained and that she doesn't see us, especially me. It's worth a grand. You up for it?"

"Twenty-five hundred," he said without hesitating or even blinking.

I nodded and said, "Done."

I reached over into the back seat and grabbed the two ski masks.

"Are you carrying?" I asked.

He nodded, flipped his jacket aside, and revealed what looked like a Glock 17 in a holster on his belt.

"Okay," I said, handing him one of the ski masks, "put this on. When we get inside, we don't speak, not a word. Signals only. Understand?"

"Yes, sir."

"Okay then, we go in together. Use the flashlight in your phone. If she's in there, use these when we grab and subdue them." I handed him four cable ties.

"Not a friggin' word, Sol. If you speak, we're going to have to kill them both, and I don't want that."

As it happened, we didn't have that problem.

Weapons in hand, we crept through the dark to the side of the trailer. Sol was right; it wasn't far. Up close, I could see the flickering light of the TV through the curtains.

I signaled Sol to stay close, then I crept up the three steps onto a small wooden deck in front of the door with Sol following close behind. I tried the door knob, expecting it to be locked. It wasn't, and right then I knew that what I was about to do was meant to be. The knob turned easily, and I pushed the door open. It didn't make even the slightest squeak. Now with the door open, I could hear the TV; someone was watching *The Voice*.

I eased my way toward what I assumed to be the living room and peered inside. And there he was, lying on a sofa in front of the TV, asleep and snoring.

I rushed across the room and jammed the muzzle of the Glock into his open mouth. He woke with a start, his hands flailing, and then clamped his teeth down on the gun. I pushed it down his throat and he started to gag, but then lay still and stared up at me, wide-eyed, terrified.

I turned and nodded to Sol who dressed in black and wearing the ski mask, looked like some sort of Ninja. Any other time it would have been comical, but not then.

He nodded back and, gun in hand, eased past me to the bedrooms. He returned a minute later, shaking his head. *So, she's away. That's good, very good.*

On the trek up to the trailer, I'd decided I wouldn't kill him. Rather, I'd blow out his knees and maybe his elbows too, but now that I had him, I wasn't sure I was capable of doing either.

I turned to face Sol, or rather his mask, and said, "You can get out of here."

Duvon gurgled around the gun barrel. Sol nodded, turned, and left without saying a word.

I took the gun from Duvon's mouth, stepped away, and pulled the ski mask off my head.

"You!" he gasped. "Starke? How? Oh shit! You gotta listen to me, man; it was an accident. I didn't mean to kill 'er. I swear. Shady tole me to scare 'er, 'urt 'er, is all. You, you can't..."

He started to bring up his hands, both fists half-clenched. I thought at first that he was telling me not to shoot, but then I saw the two barrels, one above the other, almost hidden in his right hand. He must have had it stuffed among the cushions. I was lucky I'd let him go and stepped away. If I hadn't, he would have shot me in the side with a .45 Derringer.

I watched, mesmerized, as the gun came up, and then my instincts kicked in. The first shot must have shattered his sternum, the second... right beside it, and he slammed back down onto the sofa, the tiny gun falling from his limp fingers.

"Thank you, Duvon, for making it easy for me." I said it aloud, but he didn't hear me. He was already dead. He didn't bleed hardly at all, just a small trickle from the entry wound of the first shot. Neither of the two shots went through the body. He must have died almost instantly; when the heart stops, so does the bleeding.

I had to move fast. If the girlfriend came back... I shoved the Glock into my waistband, grabbed the Derringer and shoved it into my pants pocket, and then hauled him up off the sofa and onto my shoulder. I struggled through the narrow confines of the trailer, out onto the deck, and almost lost him there as I staggered down the three steps. It was then that I wished I hadn't sent Sol home, because Duvon was no lightweight. Fortunately though, it was all downhill to where the car was parked.

"Oh crap!" I said out loud when I saw the oncoming lights. I dropped the body and ducked down behind the Rover. *Damn it all to hell. I should have parked off the damn road. If anyone remembers seeing it...*

And then I remembered, it's no good worrying about things you can't change. I waited until the car had passed, the road dark and quiet again before opening the tailgate and hauling Duvon up and in. Two minutes later I was driving back into the city. I glanced at the clock on the dash. It was almost nine o'clock.

Despite a couple of mishaps, the operation had gone well so far. If the girlfriend came home, she'd find him gone. The place was a shithole, so she was unlikely to find anything amiss, and even if she reported him missing... *No one will give a shit!*

I'd been fantasizing all day about how I would get rid of the body. I tell you, no matter what you read or see on TV, it's not easy, especially at night in the darkness. I'd had an idea but dismissed it early on. It was... impractical, not to mention bizarre, but now... it was the *only* solution I could think of.

I pulled off the road into a field and hoped I was out of sight from any passing traffic. Then I called Jimmy Little.

I mentioned before that Jimmy Little was an old friend, and he was, but it went deeper than that. Jimmy's dad and mine were also close friends. They were both broke back then. Jimmy's dad never made it back from Vietnam. My dad made it big as an attorney specializing in tort law in general and big pharma in particular. So our friendship goes back to a time I can't even remember. We virtually grew up together, Jimmy, me, and... Henry, my younger brother, whose death Shady Tree was, at least in part, responsible for, but that, as they say, is another story.

I explained to Jimmy what I had in mind. He let me finish, then asked, "You killed him?" He sounded incredulous.

"It was self-defense," I said, somewhat recalcitrantly.

"Oh yeah. Sure it was. Try telling that to a jury."

"Hey, you going to help me or not?"

"Of course. How d'you want to play it?"

I explained what I had in mind, and he laughed saying, "Only you could come up with a crazy scheme like that, Harry. Let's do it."

"I'm on Apison Pike," I said. "About twenty minutes from the Air Center. What d'you think?"

"That will work. It should be pretty quiet here. I'm still at the airport... Harry, it's not going to be so easy this time. The feds have impounded the Navajo, so I'll have to use my backup, the old Cessna 206."

"If you think it will work, yeah, okay. What are you going to tell Chattanooga Air Traffic Control?"

"If they ask, which they won't, I'll tell 'em I'm doing an instrument check."

I nodded, even though I was by myself and he couldn't see it.

"So, how long?" he asked.

"Like I said, twenty minutes or so."

"Okay. Call me when you get close, and I'll let you through the gates. You can drive right into the hangar and park out of sight."

"Terrific. Hey, d'you by any chance have an old tow chain, or..."

"Jeez, Harry. I dunno. I'll look."

"Okay then, twenty minutes."

The drive to Jubilee was uneventful, and I called him just as I was about to turn off Brainerd Road.

The hangar doors were open wide enough for me to drive straight in, which I did and then cut the engine. Jimmy rolled the hangar door closed, and we got to work.

I opened the tailgate, and together, we hauled Duvon's body out. It fell to the floor with a dull thud. Wrapping him up in the chain wasn't easy. Jimmy sat him up—fortunately, Duvon hadn't been dead long enough for rigor to have set in—and I wrapped the chain around Duvon's torso, then Jimmy placed him flat on his back and lifted his legs while I looped the chain around them several times and then fastened it.

"That should do it," he said. "Now, let's get him into the Cessna." We did that but with some difficulty; the chain made the body not only heavier but also hard to handle.

Jimmy rolled back the hangar doors, started the Cessna's engine, and taxied out onto the tarmac. I waited until the Cessna was clear and then closed the doors. I didn't want anyone to catch a glimpse of the Range Rover while we were gone.

I climbed in through the jump door—as before, the door itself had been removed; easy in, easy out, I suppose—scrambled over Duvon's body, and strapped myself in.

I heard Jimmy calling the tower, asking for permission to take off. It was granted without question, so within minutes, we were in the air and heading north so that I could already see the lake.

The water was still gently bubbling, simmering is the word I think, and I was pretty certain that it would continue to do so for at least the next couple of days; God only knows what the nuclear explosion had done to the bedrock underneath the lake.

I smiled to myself. There would be no body to find or internal gases to bring it to the surface. A couple of hours in that cauldron, especially deep down at the bottom—now you know why I needed the chain—and there would be nothing left but bones... and possibly his shirt and pants.

"Low as you can, Jimmy," I shouted over the noise of the engine and the open jump door, "and go slow."

"Jeez, Harry. Any lower and we'll be swimming."

"Not in that soup." I smiled to myself. We were so low that I could feel the heat.

Oh Yeah... One, two... three. Out you go!

I rolled the body out of the aircraft and watched as it tumbled through the air... and then with barely a splash, it was gone.

Welcome to hell, Duvon, biblically and literally.

"Take us home, Jimmy."

The Cessna gained altitude, circling to the west over the crest of Lookout Mountain—I could see the lights of home.

Home? I thought. *I wonder if it will ever be the same.*

We landed and made it back to the hangar without incident. I hugged my friend, and we parted company, never to speak of what we'd done: it never happened.

* * *

Thirty minutes later, I was at the hospital seated beside Amanda's bed and holding her hand. I leaned in and gently kissed her bruised lips. Her eyelids didn't even flutter.

"Hey," I whispered. "If you can hear me, and I pray to God that you can, I just wanted you to know that I got him. It was Duvon who ran you off the road. I got him. It's over."

But I knew deep down that it wasn't—Shady would still have to be dealt with, sometime, whenever—but what the hell.

"Oh, and there's one more thing: the baby. I named her Jade after the color of your eyes. I hope that's okay."

Again, there was no reaction, nothing. I sat there for a few minutes more, staring at her poor injured face, and then I left; I had to.

* * *

I drove home that night thinking about the events of the past couple of days. On the whole, I was satisfied with what I'd done. I really didn't intend to kill Duvon and wouldn't have but for the Derringer. I'd have turned him in to Kate and let the law deal with him. Then there was Shady. I knew he'd never forget or quit, and that meant I had to deal with him. When, how, where? Who the hell knew? I didn't. It was something I'd have to deal with another day. For now, I have a child to look after and... My wife...

The End

Aftermath

The Harry Starke Novels Book 14

Chapter 1

Saturday, February 10, 2018

Lewis Walker was tired... No, he was worn out. It was close to midnight, and he'd been driving almost non-stop for close to fourteen hours; he was just about done in. His eyelids felt like lead.

He turned the air conditioner up as high as it would go and, for a moment or two, reveled in the icy blast.

Ridiculous, he thought. *It's friggin' February, for God's sake. I never signed up for this kind of shit.* He looked at the dashboard clock. *Geez, another hour, maybe. Hell. I gotta take a break.*

He reached for his iPhone, looked down at it, selected Maps, and began to tap in a search for the nearest truck stop.

He'd typed in the first three letters when there was a terrific bang on the driver's side, and the truck veered to the right onto the hard shoulder. Out of the corner of his eye, he saw a small black SUV tilted over onto its driver's side wheels, heading at high speed onto the median where it flipped and rolled.

Oh, shit—shit, shit. This ain't happenin'. Walker stamped on the brakes and fought the wheel as the heavily loaded box van slid along the crash barrier and finally came to rest, the diesel engine still running.

He shifted into neutral and glanced at his side mirrors: to the right he could see only the torn metal of the van hard up against the steel barrier. In the left mirror, the road to the rear was clear; he could see nothing on the road in either direction except for the SUV a hundred yards back in the center of the median. It was on its roof and flames were already flickering under the engine compartment.

"SHIT!" he yelled, banging the steering wheel with his fists.

I gotta go see if they're hurt, get them out of there... He pushed open his door and started to exit the truck, hesitated, thinking hard. *I can't. Damn it! What the hell am I gonna do? I gotta get outa here. They catch me with this lot I'm done. Damn. DAMN!*

He pulled the door closed, slammed the gearshift into drive, stomped on the pedal and, with a shriek of tearing, grinding metal, he drove back out onto the road heading east up Monteagle Mountain toward Chattanooga.

A mile or so later, having heard no sirens, he began to breathe a little easier. *I gotta get off this friggin' highway...*

There was a ramp up ahead, just a couple of miles. He slowed the box van, turned right onto the ramp and then right again onto the two-lane highway. Where the hell he was going, he had no idea. One thing he did know was that he had to ditch the truck, but first, he had to take care of his load.

He turned into a roadside pull-in and opened the Maps app on his phone, tapped the screen, swiped it, swiped it again, tapped some more, then smiled. *Got it.*

He took a burner phone from the glove box, tapped in the number and waited.

"Yes. What is it? No names and be quick."

Damn! Friggin' Santy Claus himself. It just had to be him.

He explained the situation, told the voice on the line where he was, where he was going, and the GPS coordinates.

"The cargo, it's intact?"

"Yes."

"Good. The Huey will be there in... forty-five minutes. Stay the hell out of sight until then. Then transfer the cargo and burn the truck. Make sure you leave nothing that can identify you. Understand?" He didn't wait for an answer. He hung up.

Lewis shook his head, exasperated, then grinned. *Okay, asshole.*

And that's how it went, except he had one more thing to do. Lewis removed the chip from the phone and tossed it into the undergrowth at the side of the pull-in. He tossed the phone itself into a creek some two miles on as he drove the box van to the designated location. He parked in what, at some time in the not too distant past, must have been a gravel pit. *Perfect,* he thought. *Couldn't have picked it better.*

He exited the truck, found a comfortable spot under a tree, lit up a smoke and settled down to wait for the helicopter. It arrived right on time. The cargo was duly transferred from the van to the chopper, and the van was set ablaze. Lewis grinned down from the open door. The van was an inferno. What could go wrong?

The TBI, Tennessee Bureau of Investigation, arrested Lewis a week later and charged him with a litany of offenses including two counts of vehicular homicide and leaving the scene of an accident.

Chapter 2

May 22, 2018 – Midnight

I t was a beautiful evening that twenty-second day of May. It was late, getting on for midnight, and I was driving home from the hospital, on Lookout Mountain's Scenic Highway. The moon was full, the sky a vast field of stars, the city lights below and to the east a glittering blanket of jewels. The great Tennessee River, an immense ribbon of liquid silver, meandered eastward into the distance—past the cooling towers of the Sequoya Nuclear plant that had played such a huge part in my life over the past several days—until it finally disappeared beyond the horizon. It was a spectacular panorama unlike any other on the planet, and I saw none of it... Well, I saw it, but it didn't register; that day in May had been one of the worst of my life.

Thirty minutes earlier I'd been sitting beside Amanda's bed, holding her hand. I was in a state of... Hell, I've no idea. All I knew was that my best friend, my beautiful wife was lying in a coma from which she might never awake. I'd stroked her sweet face and gently kissed her bruised lips.

Her eyelids didn't even flutter.

"Hey," I whispered. "If you can hear me, and I pray to God that you can, I want you to know, I got him. It was Duvon who ran you off the road. I got him. He's dead. It's over."

But I knew deep down it wasn't—Shady would still have to be dealt with, sometime.

"Oh, and there's one more thing, sweetheart: the baby. She's safe and beautiful. The doctors delivered her after the accident. I named her Jade, after the color of your eyes. I hope that's okay."

Again, there was no reaction, nothing. I sat there for a few minutes more, staring at her poor injured face, and then I left. I had to.

* * *

And so I drove home that night, thinking of the events of the past several days, and that day in particular. On the whole, I was well satisfied with what I'd done. It wouldn't be an overstatement to say that I'd saved the city of Chattanooga from total nuclear destruction. I was a hero, damn it—a reluctant hero for sure—but man, did I ever pay the price for it.

I didn't intend to kill Duvon James, and wouldn't have, but for the Derringer. I'd have turned him over to Kate—that's Kate Gazzara, a cop and my ex-partner—and let the law deal with him.

Then there was Shady, aka Lester Tree, bad guy extraordinaire, and my nemesis. He was gone, for now at least, into the Federal Witness Protection Program, but I knew he'd never forget, or quit, and that meant that sooner or later I had to confront him. When, how, where? Who the hell knew? I didn't: it was something I'd have to figure out another day. For now, I had a child to look after and...my wife.

* * *

I arrived at my home on East Brow Road atop Lookout Mountain at a little after midnight. The house was dark, cold, bleak, as was my mood. *If I lose Amanda... Goddammit.* I shuddered at the thought. *I suppose I should call my father... Nope, can't. Can't think... Jade? Later, tomorrow. Can't do it today... I don't think I could handle it. Right now, I need a frickin' drink.*

I poured myself what had to be a half-pint of Laphroaig in a tumbler and topped it off with ice cubes, grabbed the now half-empty bottle by the neck, then stepped out onto the patio.

I placed the bottle on a table beside a lounger and sat down. I cradled the brimming glass in both hands, put it to my lips and... sucked. The level of the liquid in the tumbler dropped by a third. I swallowed—no, I gulped—almost choked as more than three ounces of the fiery liquid hit the back of my throat and seared my gullet on its way south and into my bloodstream.

I coughed, coughed again, and again, then took a deep breath, wiped my eyes, closed them and lay back, the heavy glass still in my hands. Ten minutes later, it was empty, and I refilled it. My head should already have been swimming, and that was just where I wanted to be. I wanted to forget, but I couldn't: my head remained clear...and so did the memories and, Amanda... *Why? Why did she do it? I told her to... to; dammit, I told her to take the back road...*

I closed my eyes, shook my head, sat up, stood, stepped across the patio, skirting the edge of the pool, to the wall, sat down on it, and stared unseeing into the distance. The moon had moved on, westward. The river had darkened, but the lights of the city were still spectacular, but I only know that because they always are.

I must have sat there for an hour or more before I finally rose and went back to the lounger, my glass long-since empty, but I didn't refill it; I couldn't, the damned bottle was empty. I could have fetched more from the house, but I couldn't be bothered and besides, I wasn't enjoying it. The funny thing was though, I'd just swilled down a fifth of single malt scotch and didn't even have a buzz on.

So, I lay back and closed my eyes, thinking, remembering...mostly about my wife, Amanda, and the past three years. But also the events of the past five weeks that led up to that night, that moment...images of the bomb, tumbling downward, end over end into the water, the explosion, the waterspout, the faces of the people that had died during the hunt for the bomb... And, later that evening, Duvon's body, twisting and turning in the air as it tumbled from the aircraft into the same lake I'd dropped the bomb. *Yeah, finally that son of a bitch was going to meet his maker, and it was downhill all the way. Welcome to the gates of Hell, Duvon...* But the one image I couldn't get out of my head was that of Amanda lying there, silent, pale, unresponsive...

It was at that point I must have fallen asleep, because the next thing I knew, someone was shaking my arm.

"Harry... *Harry*, wake up."

* * *

What the hell? Ooowuh, oh shit, my head is coming apart. Oh, dear God...

I guess that fifth of Laphroaig hit me harder than I thought. I had a splitting headache... No, my head felt like that damn bomb had exploded inside it. I struggled to sit up, tried to hide my eyes from the sun with one hand and push myself upright with the other.

"*Kate?*" I said, shading my eyes, looking up at her, trying to bring her face into focus. "What the hell are you doing here? What time is it? Geez, I need a drink."

"It's almost eleven. Jacque called me. She's been trying to reach you. You're not answering your phone or texts. God, what a mess you are. You need a drink? The hell you do. Looks like you had more than enough last night."

"*Naw*. Hell, no. Not that. Coffee, I need coffee... Eleven o'clock in the morning? Damn. That's never happened to me before."

She stood over me like a damned statue, a beautiful statue, feet apart, hands on hips, face serious, eyes staring down at me. *Oh shit, is she ever pissed.*

I stood, staggered sideways, a little. She put out a hand to steady me. I waved it away, took a half-step forward, and again I almost went down. This time I allowed her to help.

She steered me into the house, the bedroom, pushed me down onto the bed, knelt down and grabbed my shoe.

"You need a shower in the worst way, Harry."

"Hey, *hey*," I said, gently pushing her away. "Don't do that. I can do it. Go make some coffee...*please?*"

And she did.

Twenty minutes later I was showered, dressed comfortably in jeans and a tee and feeling half-human again and heading for the kitchen and, I hoped, a half-gallon of Dark Italian Roast. Bless her, Kate had outdone herself. Not only was there a full carafe of the good stuff waiting but also breakfast in the form of a monster chopped egg sandwich. *How the hell did she do that? I looked last night: no bread in the house.*

She must have read my mind. "I found it in the freezer. Thank God for the microwave. Eat. You'll feel better."

"I already feel better," I said, grabbing a pint coffee mug from the cupboard. "Coffee is what I need. The sandwich is a bonus. Thanks."

"So sit," she said. "Talk to me."

"Oh shit, Kate," I said, sitting down at the table. "About what?"

"About what the hell happened to you last night... No, I don't want to know how you pulled it off, but the national press does. They are at your office and right outside, on Brow Road. They want to interview you, Harry. You're a hero."

"The hell I am... Oh wow, that hurts." I put my hand to my aching head. "I can't do it, Kate. I just can't. Get rid of 'em, will you?"

"Hah, you've got to be kidding. They're not going away, *ev-er!*"

"Then you've got to get me the hell out of here. I've got to go to Amanda...and I haven't talked to Dad...and I need to see Jade—"

"Jade? Who the hell? Oh, I see. The baby. Of course. Whew."

She thought for a minute, then said, "Where is she?"

"Jade? With August and Rose, at their house."

"Okay. So I already checked on Amanda. There's no change... Oh, Harry, I'm so sorry, but no change is not bad, right?"

I glared across the table at her.

"I know, I know, but she's hanging in there, and she will. She's tough. You're right, though, you need to get out of here, and you can't go to the hospital. They'll find you there. So, we go to August. His property is gated—"

"Uh, yeah. So's this one, but the press is here anyway."

"How are you on your feet? Can you walk?"

"Oh, for God's sake, Kate. I only had a couple of drinks—" I caught the look. It wasn't pleasant. "Yeah, I can walk just fine...but I dunno. I can't get her out of my head. The way...she is."

"I know, and I understand, but you have to pull yourself together. If not for Amanda, for the baby. Get a frickin' grip, Harry. This is not like you."

I stared at her; she stared back, defiantly, waiting.

I broke first, something that never would have happened if...

"Okay," I said. "You win. What's the plan?"

"You're not going to like it."

"Tell me."

And she did, and she was right. I didn't like it.

There are three rear doors to my house. Two of them—the patio door in the living room and the kitchen door that also provides access to the patio—could be seen by anyone looking over the perimeter wall on East Brow. The third door is in the basement, in my office. It opens onto a much smaller, lower patio and the trees and shrubland on the mountainside, and it can't be seen, from anywhere. Unfortunately, the terrain is steep, rocky, and densely forested.

From that basement door to Scenic Highway below is about seven hundred feet, almost straight down through the forest, and that's what she wanted me to do; hike down the damned mountain. But that wasn't all. I then had to hike north another five or six hundred feet to a pull-off on the highway where she'd pick me up. *In my condition? Are you freaking kidding me?*

"I guess I'd better put on another shirt," I said. "It's pretty wild country out there." *Geez, is that ever an understatement?*

Despite the heat outside—it was in the eighties—I also donned a heavy leather jacket which I hoped would provide some protection from the blackthorn and brambles and such, and ten minutes later I was heading out the door and down the mountain.

Fifty minutes later—yeah, it took that long—I scrambled into the passenger side of her unmarked cruiser. I was exhausted, filthy from head to toe, and so thirsty I could have emptied that freakin' lake I dropped the bomb into.

Holy shit! That's it. I've had enough. I can't do this anymore. I'm done, this time for good. I gotta get away.

Yes, I was in a pretty black mood, but things were about to change, and not for the better.

Chapter 3

May 23, 2018 – Noon

We rode the rest of the way down the mountain in silence. Not because I wasn't in the mood for conversation or because I had nothing to say. The enormity of the events of the past several weeks was overwhelming, hard to grasp.

The tires of the big car squealed as she negotiated the tight bend at the foot of the mountain, jerking me out of my reverie as she merged smoothly into the traffic on Lee Highway.

I don't recall exactly what I was thinking, but I do remember asking her what the plan was.

"Riverview! Your dad's place, you said."

I glanced at her, shook my head, then said, "No, I don't think so. Not right now. I need to talk to Jacque and Bob first."

She didn't look at me, but I saw the muscles of her jaw tighten. "I don't know how you think we can pull that off," she said. "The press are all over Georgia Avenue for several blocks. We had to send traffic units. It's a mess."

I thought for a minute. "Okay, Riverview it is. I'll have them come there."

I slipped my phone out of my pocket and pushed the speed dial for Jacque Hale, my business partner and personal assistant.

"Hey..."

"Oh m'God," she almost shouted. "Where d'hell are you? We bin outa our minds wid worry."

Black as my mood was, I couldn't help but smile. Jacque is Jamaican, but she'd lost her accent sometime back when she was in school except, that is, when she gets excited, and boy was she excited.

"I went home... Look, we need to talk. I'm on my way to August's house. You and Bob come on over soon as you can. Okay?"

"But—"

"No buts. Quit whatever you're doing and get over there. I'll be waiting." I disconnected before she could answer.

August and Rose were in the sitting room; Jade, my daughter, was in a bassinet in their bedroom, my first stop after I said hello... No, it wasn't quite that simple. Rose, tears streaming down her cheeks, grabbed hold of me and wouldn't let go. When she did finally turn me loose, August took a step forward and offered me his hand. I shook my head and grinned, my father never was one to show his emotions, and that day he was no different except... well, he seemed a little more distant than usual. I thought little of it, though; I was too wrapped up in myself, but I did take his hand and shake it.

"Well done, son," he said, looking me right in the eye. "I'm proud of you."

I nodded, let go of his hand and grabbed him, pulled him in close, and whispered in his ear, "Thanks, you old goat. I love you too." I felt him nod, slightly, and I smiled and turned him loose.

I left Kate with August. Rose went to make hot tea, and I went to see my daughter. She was asleep, and I didn't have the heart to wake her, so I simply sat on the edge of the bed and watched her, my brain a maelstrom of disconnected thoughts and emotions. I must have sat there thinking about life—mine, Amanda's, Jade's—and the future and what it might hold until Rose knocked gently on the open door and informed me that everyone was there.

I nodded, absently, and she left me alone again. I took a couple of minutes more, then stood, leaned over the bassinet, and kissed my daughter gently on the forehead. She stirred in her sleep, threw up her arms, tiny fists up and ready for a fight. I smiled, *Just like your stupid father... Yeah, but no more.*

They were all scattered around the great room, seated, holding or sipping cups of hot tea, staring up at me.

"What?" I asked, but before anyone could answer, I shook my head. "No, don't go there. I'm not in the mood. Read about it in the papers for God's sake or watch TV. They *always* get it right."

"So why are we here?" Bob asked.

Bob Ryan is my other business partner. He's also my lead investigator. He's worked for me almost since day one, when I first opened the agency. Now he's a twenty-five percent shareholder in the company. Jacque also has twenty-five percent. Bob's a year older than I am, a big man, six feet two and 240 pounds of solid muscle with a wry sense of humor. He, like me, is also an ex-cop— Chicago PD. He's also an ex-marine... At least, I thought he was. He's a quiet man, dedicated, but deadly: not someone you want to screw around with.

"As I told Jacque," I began, "we need to talk." I paused, looking at each of them. They waited. I shook my head and said, "I'm not coming back."

"What?" Jacque asked, her brow furrowed. "I'm not understandin'."

I started pacing. "It's simple enough. I'm not coming back. I quit. It's all yours, yours and Bob's. Run with it."

"Harry," August said, "this is not the time for this kind of thinking. You're upset, and rightly so, but you *must* give it some time. Don't fly off the handle and do something you'll regret."

I looked at him, shook my head, smiled at him, then said, "Regret? You say *regret*? Hah! I already have way too many of those. If only... No, Dad. This is something I should have done a long time ago... If I had—well, I didn't, so we won't go there. Look, it was never supposed to be like this... this... Do you have any idea what I—" I looked at Bob, shook my head, and said, "Sorry, Bob, what we just went through? I, that is we, killed almost a dozen men these last couple of days. I dumped Duvon James' body into that radioactive cauldron, for God's sake. Who does stuff like that? Come *on, tell me.* No comment? Then I'll tell you: Nobody... Nobody!"

I looked at Kate, then at my father, and then continued, "When I left the PD, I thought I had it made: a nice easy life doing what I do best, what I love, investigations. I had a good book of business: attorneys, corporate clients, banks, and that's what I wanted, what I thought it was going to be all about, and for a while it was."

I looked at Kate and continued. "Then here you come, Kate," I said, bitterly.

She looked stunned, opened her mouth to speak, but I held up my hand.

"No, don't say anything. You—okay, you and the chief—dragged me into one impossible criminal case after another. That was *not* what I wanted, but even that would have been okay, except that people started getting hurt, my people... Remember Calaway Jones, Kate? I almost died, remember? That never would have happened if you hadn't...sent me after Harper. And that's when I ran into Lester Tree, again, which wouldn't have been so bad except for the fact that I ruined his entire operation, and the SOB has dogged me ever since. Now I'm to spend the rest of my days looking over my shoulder, waiting for him to appear, and one day he will."

I paused, took a breath and said, "Then, Kate, when I needed you, you turned your back on me. Yeah, I'm talking about Jim Wallace. Well, no more. I'm done with it. Right now, all I can think about is Amanda...and Jade, and what's going to happen to them. I swear to God... Well, I'll never put either of them through anything like this again."

"Harry," Bob said, his elbows on his knees, hands cradling his glass, looking up at me. "We don't want it. Not without you. It's your company. Without you, there is no company, not one I want a part of anyway. So please, take some time, think it over. It will get better. It always does. And don't worry about Tree. I'll take care of him."

I had to smile, just a little, at that. Bob's always had my back... Yeah, he's killed for me. And I had no doubt he'd do it again. Only I wasn't about to let him, but I nodded anyway.

"Harry." The voice was soft, gentle. It was Rose. "You can't do this. You have a dozen people working for you, relying on you for their livelihood. Tim, think about Tim. He loves you, Harry. He's a puppy. He couldn't function without you." She looked at Jacquie, shook her head, looked down at the carpet, silent.

"Rose's right, Harry," August said. "You have responsibilities. You can't just quit."

I opened my mouth to speak, but he raised a hand, stopped me, and continued.

"And, for the record," he said, looking first at Kate, then at me, "none of the events of the past several years are Kate's fault. You made your own damn choices, now live with them. What you're contemplating is weak. I can't believe you're even considering it. I—" He paused, stared at me across the table. "Do you have any idea what life would have been like if you hadn't done what you did? Today, right now, Hamilton County would be a radioactive wasteland. Yes, I understand how you feel, to some extent, but to throw up your hands and quit?" He shook his head, stood, looked at me for a long moment, then turned away and left the room.

Ah, for God's sake...

I followed him to the door. "Okay, Dad, I get it. Come on back. I'll... I'll think about it." *I'll think about it. Yeah, and that's all I'll do.*

At the time, I meant what I said: I was done with it, and there was nothing anyone could say or do to make me change my mind. But life, cruel mistress that she is, has a way of sideswiping me, always has, and that time it took her less than ten minutes to turn me upside down.

I looked around at the rest of the group. They were all staring at me.

"What?" I asked, angrily.

No one spoke. Jacque's face had drained of its color. Bob was slowly shaking his head, his lips clamped together. Rose... her face a mask, held my gaze then turned her head away. Only Kate seemed unperturbed by it all. I waited several minutes, hoping August would return; he didn't.

That's not like him...

"Okay, Rose," I said. "Something's happened. What is it? What's going on?"

She turned and looked at me. "It's not for me to say," she said, quietly. "I think you should ask your father."

There was something about the look she was giving me. I nodded. "Okay, I will." And I did.

I found him in his study... Hmm, I should tell you about my dad.

My father, August Starke, is a lawyer, one of the best in the country. He specializes in tort, which is an upmarket way of saying "personal injury." His ads run on most local stations almost every day; and that damn jingle, geez, it embarrasses the hell out of me. My father is a showman, wealthy almost beyond comprehension. He's a billionaire.

He's sixty-eight years old and cuts an imposing figure. He's an inch taller than me, silver-haired, lean, toned, works out every other morning, is sickeningly healthy, and carries not a pound of extra fat. He's also the most competitive man I've ever met. He's a tiger in the courtroom and on the golf course. He gets more pleasure out of winning ten bucks on the greens than he does in winning a multi-million-dollar class action. August Starke is an enigma, even to me.

He has a brain like a computer and is the only man I know that can carry two trains of thought at the same time, an ability that had served him well, in his personal and private life.

He's been married twice; first to my mother, and now to Rose... Rose is also an enigma. She's twenty years younger than August, just three years older than me. She's a very beautiful woman: tall, blond, perfect skin, perfect figure. To those who don't know her well, she's the quintessential "trophy wife," but that's not her at all. In reality, she's a very caring individual and loves my old man dearly. I, in turn, love her for it.

Anyway, as I said, I found him in his study. He was standing at the window overlooking the sixth fairway. I stepped over to the window and stood beside him. He didn't turn his head.

"I suppose Rose told you, then?" he said.

"She told me nothing. Talk to me August."

For a moment he didn't speak. Neither did I. I simply waited.

"It's Joseph," he said, quietly. "He's gone."

"What do you mean, he's gone? He's dead?"

Joseph, Uncle Joe, is my father's younger brother, and he's... Oh hell, he's what they call a "special needs" person. His mental capacity is that of a seven-year-old. No, he wasn't born like that. At six months he developed an infection and the doctor gave him penicillin. Unfortunately, he was allergic to it and it fried his brain. Today, he's fifty-six and lives in a facility that caters to his needs.

"Not dead," August said. "Abducted. Someone picked him up at the nursing home two days ago and didn't return him. He's missing."

I was stunned. I stared at him. He continued to gaze out of the window.

"How the hell did they get him out, and why didn't you tell me?" I asked.

He turned and looked at me, a slight smile on his lips. "Why didn't I tell you? How was I supposed to do that? You've been rather busy."

Yeah, my old man could do sarcasm. It served him well in court, but it washed over me.

Anyway, he was right, and I didn't say anything. I just nodded, and he turned again to stare out the window.

"He said he was you," August said, quietly.

"What? What are you talking about?"

"You asked how someone got him out. The man who picked him up said he was you."

"You're kidding, right?"

He shook his head.

"So, he was kidnapped. That's what you're telling me. Have you told the police?"

He gave me a withering look. "What do you think? Of course I have, but with what's been going on these last few days—"

"Do you have any idea why...or who?"

"No."

"And the kidnapper has not been in touch?"

Again, he gifted me with a sarcastic look, but he said nothing.

I put a hand on his shoulder. "Okay, Dad. I'm on it, with everything I have. I'll find him, I promise. Let's go back and talk to the others." And that's what we did.

Chapter 4

May 23, 2018 1pm

"**K**ate," I said glaring at her as I reentered the living room, followed by my father. "Did you know about this? Because if you did—"

"Know about what?" she interrupted me.

"She didn't," August said. "No one but Rose knows."

"But you said you'd informed the pol—"

"And I did." Now it was August that interrupted me. "And I also told you that they had more to worry about than a missing mental patient."

Geez, he's never called him that before.

"Joe?" Kate asked. "Joe's missing? How? What happened?"

"Someone purporting to be Harry checked him out of the facility two days ago," August said. "We've heard nothing of him since."

"Harry?" Kate asked. "The person who took him said he was Harry?"

"That's right," August said.

"I don't get it," she said, shaking her head. "Why Harry?"

"I asked myself the same question," I said, sitting down next to Jacque. "I don't know."

"Just one person, right?" Bob asked as he flipped through the screens on his phone. "Okay. Do you have a description of the man?"

"Yes, I have a description," August said, "for what it's worth. Tall, medium build, in his early forties with either dark or light brown hair... Oh, and he was wearing glasses. That's it."

"Signature?" Bob asked.

"Harry Starke."

"And no ransom demand, at least not yet?" Bob said.

"No, and it's been two days," I said. "If they were after money, we'd have heard by now, so it's personal. Whoever took him has a grudge, either against me or maybe even you, August. If it's me—"

"How about Shady?" Jacque asked.

I shook my head. "No, two days ago he was already in custody." I thought for a minute. "There are plenty of people I can think of that might have reason to go after me, but I can't think of a one that would take Joe. Not many people know about him... He has no family other than you and me, Dad. What cases are you working? Can you think of anything, anyone?"

August thought for a minute, then shook his head and said, "Nothing sensitive: three class action suits that have been running for almost three years, two against big pharma—birth control and one for mesothelioma. Between them, I'm representing more than seven hundred clients... Aside from those, I have several local corporate clients, and I took on a wrongful death suit for Jack Martin, whom I think you know. That's about it. Nothing of any importance, other than those."

I did know Jack. He was a member of the country club. He wasn't exactly a friend of mine, but he was one of August's inner circle. I'd played golf with him on several occasions. I liked him well enough.

"What bothers me most," I said, "is that we've heard nothing from the people who took him."

"Not yet, we haven't," Bob said, "but we will. It's either a straight ransom for money or it's personal... payback, maybe. I'd say we'll know very shortly. Whoever has him won't want to be saddled with a... Well, you know what I mean."

I did know what he meant, and so did everyone else in the room. We all knew what he was implying. It had been more than forty-eight hours since they took him: poor old Joe, bless him, was as good as dead.

Kate nodded, then said, "It's already been too long. We need to move, and quickly. How do you want to proceed, Harry?"

"We start at the nursing home. They'll have security cameras, right?" I asked.

"I would imagine that they do," August said.

"I'm on it," Bob said as he stood.

"No," I said. "Wait. I'll come with you. August, this doesn't sound like Big Pharma. So if this has nothing to do with the class action suits, could it be the wrongful death suit?"

He thought for a moment, then shook his head. "It could, I suppose," August said, "but I doubt it. Although..."

"Talk to me, August," I said. "Who and what are you dealing with?"

"I'm suing a company in Atlanta. Christmas Security Concepts, known as CSC. It's a private security agency."

At the mention of the name, Bob turned and looked at him, his eyes narrowed. *He knows them. Good.*

"So what happened?" I asked.

"Three months ago, on an evening in February, Jack Martin's mother and father were returning home from Nashville when they were run off the road by a truck. The driver of the truck, Lewis Walker, left the scene, just left them there to die. They burned to death. The truck, a Ford E350 box van, turned out to be stolen. Walker dumped it in an abandoned gravel pit on top of the mountain and torched it. Walker works for CSC. I'm suing the company with Walker as a codefendant. That's it. It's not complicated."

"What do we know about Walker?" Bob asked. "And if he burned the truck, how did they catch him? At the scene, or what?"

"Not at the scene. They might not have caught him at all, but he made a mistake. The sheriff called in the TBI—Tennessee Bureau of Investigation. They processed the scene. They figured someone must have picked him up, and that he had to wait because they found two cigarette butts under a tree some fifty yards from the burned-out van. Walker, it turns out, is ex-military. His DNA is on record."

"Well, that's a break," I said. "We'll need to talk to him."

"Why?" Jacque asked. "We don't yet know if the case has anything to do with Joe's abduction."

"You're right, Jacque, we don't, but it's the only lead we have, so that's where we'll start... Okay, I need you to get with Tim and have him research CSC and Walker. I want everything, and I mean everything, he can find."

I looked at Kate. "How about you? You in?"

She gave me a look that would have frozen a waterfall. "You sure you want me?"

I sighed. "You know I do. I didn't mean any of that crap, and I'm sorry. I was just venting. So, are you in?"

"Of course you meant it, but yes. It's Joe. What do you want me to do?"

"Find out where Lewis Walker is being held. If he's at the sheriff's department, we're screwed."

"He's not," August said. "He made bail. He's been out almost three months."

"You're kidding," Kate said. "Two counts of vehicular homicide? How much was his bail?"

"His attorney, Ham Cronin, was able to get it down to half-a-million," August said. "CSC stood surety for it. He was out the same day and gone the next."

"Cronin? Hamilton Cronin from Atlanta?" I asked, already knowing the answer.

"That's the one."

"Geez, he has one hell of a reputation," I said, shaking my head, "and it's not good. From what I've heard, he's a rare piece of work, almost as crooked as the clients he represents."

"And Walker skipped?" Kate asked.

August nodded.

"So, CSC is out a half-million in bail money," I said, more to myself than to anyone else. "That's interesting. I wonder if it was part of their plan. Sounds like a write-off to me, to get him out of the way. How's the case going, August?"

"They're denying any liability, claiming Walker was acting alone. Unfortunately, now he's gone so we can't question him."

"You say he wasn't acting alone," I said. "How do you know?"

"He couldn't have been. There's no doubt he was driving the van that he torched. His DNA puts him at the scene, so someone must have picked him up. But it's not just that. It had been raining earlier that evening, and there was only one set of tire tracks into the gravel pit; those belonged to the van. Secondly, the TBI determined that the van was carrying a load when it went into the pit—they figured that out from the depth of the tire tracks—but the burned-out carcass was empty. There was no sign of the load, and no other tracks in or out, which means..." He paused and shook his head. "Which makes one wonder how they got Walker and the cargo out of there... They think it could only have been done by a helicopter. I'd say he's long gone, out of the country."

"Maybe, but we need to find him. Jacque, that's another job for Tim. Have him get on it right away."

She nodded and jotted in her notebook.

"Kate, this is officially a missing persons case. Can you get it assigned to you?"

She nodded. "I'll talk to the chief, and Carpenter. She won't like it, but it shouldn't be a problem."

"Carpenter?" I asked.

"Lieutenant Judy Carpenter. Missing Persons is her department."

I nodded, then said, "So, unless we hear from the kidnappers, we don't have much to work with. But as we all know, time is of the essence in cases like this, so we have to do what we can with what we have. Right now, until we find out differently, that's Walker and CSC." I paused to see if there were any more questions.

"Okay, everyone," I said, rising to my feet. "Let's get to it. Kate, I'll talk to you later. Jacque, call me as soon as you have something. Bob, you're with me. Dad, I can't go to the office, so I need a place where I can work, and I need access to a computer."

"You can use my office, and you can stay here for as long as you like. You can have one of the guest rooms. Rose?"

She nodded. "He can have the suite. I'll see that it's prepared."

"Thank you, Rose," I said. "Bob, let's talk."

Chapter 5

May 23, 2018 2:30pm

I took Bob back to my father's office, closed the door and we sat down; me at the computer, Bob in an easy chair by the window.

I searched the internet for CSC.

"Hah," I said, "it's just as I figured, Bob. CSC is a private military company headquartered in Atlanta, Georgia, founded by Nicholas Christmas in March 2009. It seems that Nick is running his own little private army."

"That's right. He is."

"You know this Nicholas Christmas then?"

"Oh yes, I know him," Bob said. "I had several dealings with him when I was in Afghanistan. He's a piece of work, smart but about as crooked as you'll find. I couldn't prove it at the time, but I knew he was dealing drugs, and I'm betting that's what was in that van—"

"Wait," I interrupted him. "*You* couldn't prove it? What does that mean? You were a Marine..." I caught the look in his eyes and paused, then I got it. "You were *not* a Marine?"

He grinned at me but said nothing.

"I had Tim do extensive background checks on you. You were a

Marine. You served for twelve years. You were a captain..." I let it die, watching his face. He was still smiling.

"What? All these years you've led me to believe... Just what the hell were you then?" I asked, shaking my head, dumbfounded.

"You know what they say," he said, laughing. "I could tell you, but then I'd have to kill you."

"Oh, for Pete's sake. Get over yourself. What the hell were you doing all those years?"

Now he was serious. "I can't tell you, Harry. What I did is covered by the Espionage Act."

"So, you weren't a Marine, then you must have... You were either NSA or CIA." And there it was, that telltale twitch of his left eye. "Holy Mary, you were CIA."

The smile was gone. He didn't answer. He simply shrugged.

I nodded, grimly, and said, quietly, "I don't give a crap for the Espionage Act. I want to know everything you know about Christmas and his operation. I need to know because if he had anything to do with Joe's disappearance, I have to go after him. You know that."

He nodded. "I do, but you can't. The man is running a private army for God's sake. You can't go up against that."

I stared at him, unblinking.

He sighed. "Okay, so you can't, but you will." He shook his head and then continued. "Nick Christmas was an Army Ranger, one of the best... Harry, the Navy SEALs are the glamor boys of the Special Forces. The Rangers get very little press and no glory. They are equally as well-trained as the SEALs, in some cases even better. Christmas is one of those cases. Between 2004 and 2008, he and his team—there were six of them—did three tours in Afghanistan, all of them in Helmand Province.

"It was during those three tours that I got to know him. He was part of MICO, the Rangers Military Intelligence Company. I was—" He shook his head and continued. "He and his team were highly trained Army Rangers operating independently as forward observers in the vicinity of Lashkar Gah, the capital of Helmand Province. This was just before the Afghan presidential elections, and before the Marines launched Operation Khanjar. His job was to provide us with actionable intel. And he was damn good at it, mainly because sometime in 2005, he had the great good fortune to make contact with a minor Afghan warlord known only by the code name Lazarus, a name given to him by Christmas himself. He never revealed his real name."

I grabbed a couple of water bottles out of the small refrigerator in August's office, handed one to Bob, kept the other for myself, and nodded for him to continue.

"So, over a period of almost three years, Christmas was able to build a mutually beneficial relationship between himself and Lazarus. During that period, Lazarus provided Christmas with a great deal of excellent intel, for which he was well-paid. What we didn't know was that it was a two-way street: Nick was supplying Lazarus with information that gave him an edge over his rivals and kept him safe from us and the Afghan Security Force. Nick was, in fact, playing for both sides. His team became our number one source, and as such he was allowed to do pretty much as he pleased, just so long as he kept on delivering. And he did, right up until he was discharged. I know because I was directly involved in analyzing and disseminating his intel."

He paused, thought for a moment, then continued.

"What we didn't know at the time was that Christmas was also buying heroin from Lazarus, and he and his buddy, Sergeant Johnson were smuggling it back into the United States and selling it to a distributor in Atlanta. At first, the quantities were quite small, but Nick reinvested the proceeds. By the time he received his discharge, he'd made a pile of money. He used that money to start his company, his own private army. As I said, I could never prove any of that, but I knew."

I sat back in my father's leather chair, unable to believe what I was hearing. The man had been with me almost from the beginning.

I trusted him, treated him like a brother. I'd even handed him twenty-five percent of my company.

"You know what, Bob?" I said. "You're really something. You sit there telling me all this..." I shook my head. "You came to me in 2008 with a documented employment history. It was a total fabrication, a lie."

"Not a lie, exactly, more a necessary fabrication."

"Was any of it true?"

He didn't answer. *A necessary fabrication? What the hell does that mean?*

And then it hit me, and I couldn't believe it.

"No! *No!* You son of a bitch. You're still working for them, the CIA!"

He looked away, then back at me. "In a way, yeah. I'm still on the rolls, not active, but yeah."

I stared at him, my stomach churning. I felt like I was about to throw up.

"All these years," I said, bitterly, "you've been lying to me, Bob. Geez, I always knew you were a piece of work. Always thought you were a borderline sociopath, but now I can understand why it's so easy for you to kill. Bob, never...*never* did I think you'd betray me."

"Damn it, Harry," he said, angrily. "Back the hell off. Do you think I had a choice? I didn't. I haven't betrayed you. I worked every hour you paid me for, and I've always had your back, and I always will. I tried to quit. Yeah, I freakin' did, but they wouldn't let me. I had to take what they offered. Yeah, they can call me back whenever they want, but they haven't, not yet. They've left me the hell alone. And besides, I was able to stay in touch with my contacts...and friends, which has worked damn well for you in the past. Get over it, Harry, or fire me. Whichever suits you." And with that, he stood and turned to leave.

"Sit the hell back down, Bob."

He took another step toward the door, then turned and glared at me across the desk.

"Sit down," I said, quietly.

He sat, then said, "Don't ask. I've already told you more than I should."

"I have to. I need to know what I'm up against."

He glared at me, then seemed to relax a little and said, "What we're up against."

I nodded. "Yeah, that. What we're up against. How well do you know him?"

"Christmas? I don't think anybody really knows him. I met him—oh, I don't know—probably a couple of dozen times. I've been in the field with him and his team twice. He's tough... You don't get to be a captain in the Rangers unless you are. On the surface, he's likable, sort of, for a sociopath." He paused, looked at me wryly, then continued. "Charming, I suppose would be a better word. I got along with him well enough." He stared at the desktop, then looked up at me. "He's a killer, Harry, a stone-cold killer."

"Kinda like you," I said, without humor.

"Screw you, Harry."

I didn't answer. I just stared across the desk at him and waited. Then he said, "I know that he's a killer because I've seen him in action. I spent three days in the mountains north of Gereshk with him and his team. We ran into an ambush. It wasn't a big thing; there couldn't have been more than a dozen of them. Nick deployed his men, and they quickly mopped them up. It was all over in less than fifteen minutes... Yeah, they're that good. Unfortunately, the Taliban left three wounded fighters behind. Our boy Nick popped all three, one after the other, quick as he could pull the trigger. If I'd known what he was about, I would have stopped him, but it happened too quickly." He looked down at the desk for a moment with a frown on his face.

"The bastard enjoyed it," he continued. "I could tell. And I know that wasn't the first time, or the last. I asked him, 'What the hell did you do that for?' He just smiled—no, not smiled—he laughed, and said, 'the only good Afghan is...' well, you know."

He looked at me, seriously. "So, Harry. Where do we go from here, now that you know what I am?"

Yeah, where the hell do we go from here? I thought. *I don't know if I'll ever trust you again. Ten friggin' years you've been lying to me... I don't know. What would Amanda say? She'd... I can't even think about her right now. Get a fricking grip, Harry.*

I shook my head, trying to rid myself of...what? I had no idea. My brain felt like it was full of concrete. Then I made up my mind.

I looked at him and said, "I have an uncle to find. Are you in? If so, the past is the past. It always was." But even as I said it, I had a hard time believing it.

He nodded. "Good enough. Yeah, I'm in. You know that. You have a plan?"

"It's coming together," I said, thoughtfully. "Your knowing Christmas might work for us. In the meantime, let's go see if the Sisters of Grace have some video footage we can look at."

Chapter 6

May 23, 2018 5pm

Sisters of Grace
    Located in a somewhat remote area of Hixson northeast of Highway 153, Sisters of Grace was a small Benedictine convent, and they ran one of the oldest and well-thought of nursing homes in the area. Joe had been living there for most of his adult life. As I said, he was a happy person, living in a small world all his own where everyone he met was his friend. He loved to paint, and he was good at it. I have one of his pieces hanging in my office.

Bob and I didn't talk much on the ride over to Sisters that day. What little conversation we did have was strained. Yep, it was going to take some getting used to, knowing that Bob was CIA, active or not, but I'd get there. Anyway, I spent most of the trip remembering the times—and there had been plenty of them—when Bob had saved my ass, and Kate's, and it was only a couple of years ago when he'd saved Amanda's life, at the cost of a bullet to his own shoulder.

It was almost five in the afternoon when we arrived, and as I pulled in through the gates, I glanced sideways at him. He was sitting like a damn statue, upright, stiff, obviously feeling uncomfortable.

"Hey," I said, as I parked the car and turned off the engine. "I think I may owe you an—"

"You owe me nothing, Harry. I'm the one at fault, and I'm sorry for it. But know this: if I could have done things differently, I would have. So—"

I nodded, grabbed his arm and squeezed it. "Forget it, buddy. You've been there for me and mine; you always have. As far as I'm concerned, it's forgotten. Let's do this, okay?"

Forgotten? Not hardly. That was going to take a while, if ever. CIA? Sheesh!

"Geez, Harry, you're one hard-to-read son of a bitch. If I didn't know better, I'd say you were some kind of—"

Whatever he was about to say, he didn't. Instead, he said, "Yeah, let's do it."

I was quite familiar with the Sisters complex. I'd visited Joe, not often, but several times over the years. It had been a while since the last time. *A while? It's been almost a year.*

The business office was just beyond the main entrance, in the Narthex, what I would have normally called the lobby. I tapped on the sliding glass window and was rewarded with a bright smile from a young lady seated at a desk on the far side of the office. She stood and came to the window, slid it open.

"Good afternoon. I'm Sister Victoria. How can I help you?" The soft voice had a slight Irish lilt. The smile was infectious; she was beautiful. *Sister? I thought they all wore those coverings on their head... those habits.*

"My name is Harry Starke. I'm a private inv—"

Her face fell. "Oh my," she interrupted me. "You must be here about Joseph. I'm so sorry, Mr. Starke. Let me get someone who can help you."

She picked up the desk phone, dialed a two-digit number, and waited, the handset to her ear, looking at me.

"Sister, it's Vicky. I have Mr. Harry Starke and one of his associates here. Can you come? Thank you. I'll tell him."

She returned to the window and said, "Sister Julia, our administrator, will be with you shortly. If you'd like to take a seat..." She gestured through the glass at a wooden bench set against the far wall. We sat. I felt like a schoolboy waiting to see the principal. Fortunately, we didn't have to wait long.

Sister Julia was not what I was expecting.

She seemed to appear out of nowhere. I don't know exactly what I expected, but it certainly wasn't what would have passed for a corporate CEO. She was wearing a modest, light gray business suit over a white blouse that was buttoned almost to her chin. The skirt was cut just below the knee. She wore her hair tied back in a bun. The only giveaway that she was a member of the order was the large wooden cross that hung around her neck almost to her waist.

"Mr. Starke," she said, holding out her hand, as she walked quickly toward us. "I'm Sister Mary Julia, you can call me Sister Julia. It's easier and less confusing. We're all named Mary here."

We stood and I shook her hand. Her grip was gentle but firm. I introduced Bob.

"I'm so sorry about what happened to Joseph. The poor young woman who signed him out is devastated. It's not all her fault though. She doesn't know you and the man who came for him had a driver's license in your name. What can I do to help?"

"Well," I said. "I'd like to talk to her, if possible, and I was hoping you might have security footage we could look at."

"You can, and we do, although the police officers already have it. Well, no matter. Please follow me."

She led the way along the corridor to a large office where several more—none of them were wearing habits, but I guess they also were sisters—were seemingly hard at work.

"This is our administrative office," Sister Julia said. "What you need is over here."

We followed her to a desk beside a bank of filing cabinets where yet another sister was working at a computer; her fingers were flying over the keyboard as if her life depended on it.

"A minute, if you please, Sister Frances," Sister Julia said, interrupting the flow.

She looked up, smiled and stood. "Of course."

"This is Sister Mary Frances, Mr. Starke," Sister Julia said. "It was she who signed Joseph out. Sister, this is Mr. Harry Starke and his associate Mr. Ryan. They'd like to talk to you about Joseph."

Then Julia turned to me, offered her hand, and said, "It's been nice to meet you, Mr. Starke, but this place doesn't run itself; I have lots of work to do, so I need to get back to it. If there's anything else I can do to help, please don't hesitate to call me."

I thanked her, shook her hand, and said goodbye, and then turned to Sister Frances.

The smile was gone, replaced by a frown. "Of course," Sister Frances said, her arms folded, "but I must apologize. I should have been more diligent, but the man was so charming, and he had identification. I wouldn't have—"

"It's okay, Sister," I said. "You did what you were supposed to do. You couldn't have known he was an imposter. The thing is though, Joe knows me. He might have gone happily with a stranger, but I think he would have said something."

She looked away and said, "Well, I did think he looked a little apprehensive, but the man put his arm around Joseph's shoulder and said—and I remember exactly—he said, 'Hiya JoJo, you ready to go get some ice cream?' And that's all it took. Joseph was chattering away to him as they headed outside."

"Yes, that would do it," I said. "He loves ice cream."

I thought for a minute, then said, "Can you describe the man who took him? Did you notice anything unusual about him: scars, tattoos, jewelry, anything?"

"No, nothing like that. He was like you in some ways, maybe not quite as tall, but he looked about your age, similar build. He was charming, affable, all smiles, glasses, not much else. Oh, yes, he was wearing tan pants, a black polo shirt, and a ball cap. It was a black one, had a red bill with a big letter A on the front. Atlanta Braves, I think."

"Yes, that sounds right," Bob said. "Would you recognize him if you saw him again, Sister?"

"Yes, I think so."

I nodded. "So, can we see the video footage please?" I had a feeling it wasn't going to be useful, and I was right.

I already knew that security there was not all it should have been, but the folks who ran the place, though not short of funding, liked to spend their cash where they figured it did the most good and didn't consider security a priority. Yes, they had a fair number of CCTV cameras placed at strategic points around the facility, but most of them were in place to keep a watchful eye on their guests, as they like to call them. Still, there were several actual security cameras on the property: one in the lobby—yeah, I know, but it's easier to say lobby than Narthex —and three outside; one at the front of the building set high on a light pole, one on the right side, and another at the rear of the building. *Thank you for that anyway, dear Sisters.*

The cameras at the rear and right side captured nothing. The one in the lobby was in the office, set high—too high—on the opposite wall with its field of view directed through the glass sliding window.

The camera captured the suspect all right, but as I said, it was set too high. The man kept his face lowered so that the camera only picked up the cap and his chin, which was in shadow under the bill of the cap, and several seconds when he signed the release.

"May I suggest, Sister," I said, shaking my head in frustration, "that you have the camera repositioned somewhere off to one side and lower so that it gets a better view of the people at the window."

I had her stop the video several times, but I saw nothing helpful other than the ring on the man's right hand.

"The video is useless for facial recognition, Bob," I said. "But look at the ring."

The sister chimed in. "Oh yes, I forgot. It's a college ring, isn't it?"

"No," Bob said. "It looks like an Army Ranger's ring. They all wear them."

"Yes," I said. "That's what it is, but the stone... shouldn't it be red? This one is black, and that looks like lettering, initials, perhaps."

He stared at it, then nodded and said, "You're right. It's been reworked, but it's fuzzy... I don't think that's lettering, Harry. We need to turn Tim loose on it. Maybe he can enhance the image. I doubt he can do anything with the face. Can we look at the exterior footage please, Sister?"

She tapped the keyboard a couple times and then rolled her seat away so we could see the screen. The images of the suspect coming and going were good quality, clear and sharp, but he knew what he was doing; not once did the camera get a good shot of his face. The vehicle was a late model, black Chevrolet Suburban. Unfortunately, the windows were heavily tinted, and the license plate was muddy, the details obscured; most of them.

"Stop," I said, and she stopped the video.

"Can you enlarge that part?" I said, pointing to the license plate. She could.

"That's a Georgia plate," Bob said. "Fulton County. You can just make out the O and the N, see?"

"Yes, I see," I said. "But there are a dozen counties in Georgia that end in ON. It could be any one of them, or none of them."

"I have a twenty-dollar bill that says it's Fulton. You wanna take the bet?"

I grinned at him. "Atlanta, huh?"

He nodded. "That's what I think."

I nodded. "You may be right, but that"—I pointed at the enlarged image—"is useless. No, keep your money. I'll keep mine."

"So, all we have is the ring, then?" Bob asked, staring at the screen.

I nodded, slowly, also staring at the screen. I had a feeling I was missing something.

"Go back to where they leave the building please, Sister," I said, "and then run it in slow motion."

We, the three of us, watched intently as the scene played out.

He had his arm around Joe's shoulder, his head down as if he was talking to him—which he may well have been—as he escorted Joe to the passenger side of the Suburban, which was facing the convent entrance. Then, at the last moment, the man lifted his head and reached for the door handle, and I spotted something that looked like a smudge on the car window.

"Stop," I said. "Now, enlarge it... There, now stop." *Gotcha, you bastard.*

"There." I pointed to the passenger door window. "See it? It's not clear, but it's the reflection of his face in the window." I looked at Bob. He leaned in closer and squinted.

"You're really reaching, Harry. I see it, but I can't make out any details."

"*You* can't, but when Tim's done with it, you will. I'll need copies please, Sister."

She burned the footage from all five cameras to DVDs. I took them from her, thanked her, and asked her to call me if she remembered anything that might be helpful, and then we left.

"What do you think, Bob? Do you recognize the man on the video footage?" What I was really asking was if it was Nick Christmas or not.

Bob hesitated. We'd worked together long enough I was sure he knew what I meant.

"I don't know," he said. "He looks familiar, but it's not Christmas. He wouldn't get that personally involved."

Bob dropped me off at my father's house in Riverview some thirty minutes later. I left him with the DVDs and instructions to turn them over to Tim the following morning.

Me? I was tired and hungry, but more than anything else I needed to go to the hospital to visit Amanda. How I was going to make that happen, I had no idea; the press was everywhere. Fortunately, Kate arrived a short while after I did. Problem solved.

I spent a few minutes with August and Rose while I ate a

pimento cheese sandwich, and then I went in to see my daughter.

She was awake. I picked her up, sat down on the edge of the bed, and held her close.

"Don't squeeze her too hard, Harry," Rose said, smiling, whispering. "She needs to be able to breathe."

"Hey," I said, "I didn't hear you come in."

"I'm sorry," she whispered. "I didn't mean to interrupt. I just wanted to make sure you were all right."

"You're not interrupting, Rose. Come, sit."

She sat down on the edge of the bed beside me, pulled the blanket away from the baby's face with a finger, looked lovingly at her, then sighed and said, "Oh dear, Harry. What are we going to do? First Amanda and now Joe. It's horrible, all of it. Your father's almost out of his mind with worry... about all of you. I've never seen him like this before."

I handed Jade to her, and said, "I know. He doesn't say much. He internalizes everything. I'll talk to him. Not now, tomorrow, maybe even this evening, I promise."

She took the baby from me and held her, cheek to cheek.

"Thank you, Harry. He loves you more than you'll ever know."

"Oh, I know," I said, rising to my feet. "Look, Kate's agreed to take me to the hospital, so I need to go. Can we get together later?"

She nodded. I leaned in and kissed Jade on the forehead. She opened her eyes wide, and I swear she smiled up at me. *Yes, Jade is the right name.*

I looked down at Rose. Her eyes were watering.

"Hey," I whispered. "It will be okay. I promise."

Then I leaned in close and kissed *her* on the forehead. Then I turned and left, my brain churning. I had the certain feeling I'd just made a promise I wouldn't be able to keep.

Kate was waiting when I returned from the bedroom.

"You ready to go?" she asked.

I nodded, then said to August, "I don't know what time I'll be back, but you and Rose need to sleep. Don't wait up for me."

Chapter 7

May 23, 8pm

Erlanger Hospital

"I talked to Chief Johnston," Kate said as we walked to her car. "He's okay with me taking over the missing person case, so I'm in, officially."

"Good," I said, absently. My mind was miles away. I was thinking about Amanda.

"How did it go at the nursing home?" Kate asked as she pushed the starter button.

"Well enough, I suppose. Maybe better than I expected. Kate, this not being able to go to the office is getting to be a real pain in the ass. I need to be able to communicate with my people, especially Tim and Jacque, and..." I was going to say Bob, but then I remembered, and I didn't.

We traveled almost a mile before Kate finally said, "Well, are you going to tell me?"

I wasn't sure if I should tell her or not, but I did.

"I learned something today." I shook my head and said, still not really believing it myself, "Bob's CIA."

For a moment, it didn't register. Then she glanced quickly sideways at me, and said, "*What?* What are you saying? He's a spook? He can't be... You're kidding, right?"

"I wish, but no. He was never a Marine. That was a cover. I'm not even sure he was ever a cop; I didn't get that far. He was twelve years with them, mostly in Afghanistan. Hell, Kate, what happened I still don't know. What I do know, at least according to him, is that he's still on the books; inactive, but still CIA."

I waited for her to say something; she said nothing.

"Comments?" I asked.

"What the hell am I supposed to say? I dated the SOB. He never said a word. What are you—how are you going to handle it?"

"I don't... know. What can I do? He's had my back, and yours, ever since I hired him. Hell, Kate, he's my right hand, my best friend. He owns a fourth of my company. The problem is—no, the question is—can I trust him?"

"He's never let you down, Harry—has he?"

"No, never."

"So there's your answer. You can trust him, I think, at least as far as you and your business are concerned."

I sighed, nodded, and said, "It's not like I have a choice, is it?"

She didn't answer. She turned left off East 3rd onto Central and then left again into the Erlanger complex, but instead of taking me to the main entrance, Kate dropped me off on the top floor of the hospital multi-story parking garage. It was a ploy to avoid the press that I was sure would be lying in wait for me, somewhere.

I told her to go home, but she insisted on staying with me. She parked the car, and we took the elevator down to the first floor and from there navigated the corridors to the ICU waiting area where I checked in and was told to go on through. Kate said she'd be in the waiting room.

I stood beside Amanda's bed, took her hand, looked down at her and felt like I was about to throw up. The top of her head down to her earlobes was swathed in bandages. Her eyes, closed, were surrounded by deep, blue-black bruises; her lips cut and swollen; her cheeks and jaw were bruised and covered in cuts, some deep, some little more than scratches.

As far as I could tell, she hadn't moved since I'd left that morning. The tubes had been removed, but she was still receiving medication through an IV.

"Good evening, Mr. Starke."

I turned. "Hello, Dr. Cartwright. How is she?"

Cartwright, a heavy-set man in his mid-forties, pushed his hands deeper into the pockets of his scrubs. "Not much change, I'm afraid. I still have her in an induced coma, and I'll keep her that way for at least another three days, maybe longer, depending upon how the brain swelling responds." He paused, shook his head, and then continued, "She also has three fractured ribs, but they're nothing compared to her head injury. She was lucky, Mr. Starke, very lucky. Another inch to the right and that tree limb would have taken her head off."

"So she's going to be all right, then?"

He looked sideways at me, tilted his head and said, "Will she live, do you mean? Yes."

"What about—"

"Her facial injuries?" he asked, interrupting me.

"That wasn't what—"

"Most of them should heal without scarring," he said again interrupting me. "This one"—he pointed to it— "and this one...I'm not sure, so I've asked Dr. Rohm to look at her."

"I was going to ask about permanent brain damage, Doctor."

"Yes, I know you were." He sighed, shook his head slightly, then said, "Only the good Lord knows that, Mr. Starke. We've done all we can. It's up to her now. Look, I'm sorry, but I have to go. I have other patients. You can stay as long as you like, of course. If you need me, you can contact my nurse. I know you won't, but I do hope you have a good evening." And then he turned and left the room.

I pulled up a chair and sat down, close to the bed, took Amanda's hand in both of mine, put her fingertips to my lips, and closed my eyes. I don't remember much about the next several hours, just a vague recollection of nurses coming and going. I finally woke up to someone gently shaking my shoulder. I was still in my chair but sprawled across the bed, my head on Amanda's chest, though she was unaware of it.

"Mr. Starke," someone whispered.

I came to with a start, looked up into a pair of deep blue eyes. I sat up.

"I'm—"

"It's all right, Mr. Starke," she said. "I just need to take some blood. It won't take but a minute, then I'll leave you alone."

I looked at Amanda. She hadn't moved. I nodded absently, rose to my feet, and stepped away from the bed. I looked at my watch. It was ten after two. *Oh my God, Kate! What the hell was I thinking?*

I waited until the nurse was done poking needles into Amanda's arm, and then I kissed my wife gently on the lips, told her I'd be back soon—I don't know if she heard me or not—and I left. I went to the waiting room: bless her, Kate was still there, asleep in a chair. I shook her gently. She woke with a gasp and stared up at me wide-eyed.

"What time it?"

"It's after two. I'm sorry. I fell asleep too. Look, go on home. I'll call Uber."

"No, Harry. I'll take—"

"*No!*" I said. "You need to go home. I can manage. Now go, please." And she did, though reluctantly.

I had the Uber driver drop me off at my father's house on Riverview. The lights were on and, yes, he was waiting up for me.

"Hey," I said. "You should be in bed."

"I was, but I couldn't sleep. How's Amanda?"

"The same," I said, sitting down on the couch beside him. "No change. I talked to her doctor. He said she'll make it, but he didn't seem too optimistic about her future. God, she's a mess, Dad... No word from the kidnapper yet?"

He was leaning forward, head down, elbows on his knees, cradling a cup of coffee in both hands.

"No."

I put my hand on his shoulder and squeezed it, gently, but said nothing.

"It will soon be light," he said, without looking up. "You should go to bed. Try to get some sleep."

He was right. The events of the past several days had left me drained, and right then, I was really beginning to feel it. My body was aching all over, but all I wanted to do was sit and talk. And that's what we did.

No, I'm not going to bore you with our reminiscing. Let's just say we both managed to depress ourselves to the point where we had to quit and call it a night. It was almost four when I finally fell onto the bed.

Chapter 8

May 24, 9am

Riverview
        I awoke with a start; sunlight was streaming in through the window. Bleary-eyed, I rolled over onto my side and grabbed my phone: it was ten after nine. *Oh shit. Damn it all to...*

I rolled onto my back, closed my eyes, and tried to orient myself. It was no good. My mind was refusing to cooperate. *I gotta get a shower.*

I rolled off the bed, realized I was still fully dressed, groaned, sat down on the edge of the bed and slowly began to remove my clothes. I was so stiff, I was barely able to reach my feet. With no little effort, I managed to drag my socks off and stand up. Every muscle in my body protested. I guess the rigors of the past several days had finally caught up with me. I also realized I hadn't worked out in more than a week... *Yeah, and it's not going to happen again any time soon, either.*

I was just about to head for the shower when I heard a gentle knock on the door.

"Hold on. Just give me a minute."

"It's me, Harry," Rose said on the other side of the closed door." I just wanted to make sure you're all right. I have coffee and bagels."

"Oh, okay, that's terrific, thanks, just what I need. I'll get a quick shower and be right there. Fifteen minutes, Rose, that okay?"

"Yes, of course. You'll find toothpaste, toothbrush, and an electric razor in the drawer to the left. When you're done, look in the closet. August went to the pro shop and bought clothes for you."

"Oh, you can't be serious. That's... Good old dad. I was wondering what the heck I was going to wear today. I'll be just a few minutes, Rose."

"Let me have your dirties, and I'll see that they're laundered."

"I love you, Rose."

She laughed, and I hit the bathroom; two minutes later the scalding water hit me. It was so hot it almost took my skin off, and I reveled in it, but not for as long as I would have liked; tempus was fugiting.

I dried off, cleaned my teeth and ran my fingers through my hair; the razor, I didn't bother with. I was already feeling better.

I felt even better when I went to the closet. August had provided everything, and then some: underwear, three pairs of slacks, shirts—all of them white—socks, even a pair of Golfstreet shoes.

August and Rose were waiting for me in the breakfast room. I went straight to the coffee pot, poured myself a huge mug and sat down at the table between them.

"How's Amanda?" Rose asked.

I shook my head and shrugged.

"No change," I said. "Have you heard anything, August?"

He shook his head and stared down into his cup, "No. It's been almost seventy-two hours; I'm beginning to think we won't. That maybe it's not connected to me, us, after all."

"You're the only relative Joe has," I said. "We'll hear from them, even if it's only to demand money, but I'm betting it is connected... Dad, I have a problem. I can't work, not hiding away like this. I need to be able to communicate with my team. I can't do it efficiently by phone and email. If it's okay with you and Rose, I propose to bring them here, well, some of them: Tim and Jacque, Bob, and maybe TJ. For how long, I've no idea: days, maybe weeks. And Tim will need to bring some equipment. You okay with that?"

"Of course," August said, "but I have a computer he can use..." He caught the look on my face.

"Oh, I see," he said.

As bad as the situation was, I had to smile at the thought of Tim trying to work with my dad's circa 2010 PC.

"He'll need some extra room then," August said. "How about the sunroom, will that do?"

I thought about it, then shook my head and said, "I don't think so: too much light. How about the basement, the gym? That's really dark, even during the day."

He nodded.

"Not the gym," Rose said. "Maria is coming today. It's her day to clean. I'll have her work on the storage room down there. We have two trestle tables, and EPB's network equipment is in there too."

She was talking about the Electric Power Board, one of the largest providers of electrical power in the country. and lately, with internet speeds of 1.0 Gig and up, the fastest fiber optic network supplier too, earning Chattanooga the sobriquet Gig City.

"That will work," I said. "I'll call Jacque and have her put things in motion, but first I need to talk to Tim and let him know what he'll need." *That was a stupid statement. Nobody but Tim knows what he needs, and not even him most of the time.*

"Just give me a couple of minutes," I said. I made the call to Tim and told him to get started putting enough equipment together for an extended stay at Riverview, and that got me wondering how long it would be before press cottoned on to where I was hiding out. *Not very long, I bet.*

Next, I called Jacque and gave her the heads up. Hers was a different situation; she had a full-time staff to keep organized, and there wasn't enough room for all of them at Riverview. Still, it didn't seem to bother her, and she said she'd be with me within the hour. And she was.

Tim arrived an hour after Jacque. His company van loaded to capacity: four fifty-inch monitors, two 5-GPU tower servers, and a whole heap of crap I didn't even know he had, let alone used.

He parked his van outside the basement door, opened its doors, grabbed one of the towers and then, staggering under the weight, he came inside, grinning like a fool.

I just looked at him and shook my head. He never ceased to amaze me.

For those of you who don't, you should know that Tim Clarke runs my IT department. He's the quintessential geek. He's worked for me since before he dropped out of college when he was seventeen. He's tall, skinny, weighs less than 150 pounds, wears glasses, is twenty-seven years old and looks sixteen. I found him in an internet café, just one small step ahead of the law. He was a hacker back then, and still is when he needs to be. I love that boy like a son, but he scares the hell out of me sometimes. You have no idea—I have no idea —exactly what he's capable of, but he is, without a doubt, the most useful and effective member of my staff.

He set the server down on one of the two tables and said, "Hey, Chief. Where's my space?"

"You're in it," I said.

He grinned, shoved his glasses further up the bridge of his nose with a forefinger and said, "Cool. How's Mrs. Starke? She feeling better?"

Tim loved Amanda almost as much as I did, and she, in turn, had a real soft spot for him, and he knew it and played it for all it was worth.

"Not so good, Tim. It's too soon."

"Geez... she's going to be all right though?"

"I hope so. Listen, get yourself organized ASAP and let me know when you're up and running. In the meantime, if you need me, I'll be upstairs in August's office. It's just on the right. Okay?"

"Harry, wait," he said. "Listen, I'm worried about you. Has anyone checked you for radiation?"

I thought about it and decided they hadn't.

"Not that I know of... Oh, you want to do it, right?"

He nodded, frowning.

"Well, you can't, not right now. I—"

He shook his head. "Harry. I need to do it now. That stuff can kill you—"

"Maybe later. Come see me when you're done."

"Mr. Star—"

"I said later, Tim. Now stop bothering me and get your shit together. Were you able to do anything with those images, the ring and the guy that checked Joe out of the nursing home? Bob gave them to you? Where is Bob, by the way?"

"Yes, I was. Yes, he did. He's on his way here now, I think."

"Okay. When can I see them, the photos?"

"You should already have them. I emailed them to you. Didn't you check?"

"No," I said, "I haven't had time. How about CSC and Christmas?"

"I was working on that when you called. I'll get to it again as soon as I get set up."

I nodded and turned to leave.

"Harry, wait. If you won't let me check you out, will you at least take these?"

He took a small plastic bottle from his pocket, opened it, and shook two blue capsules into his hand and offered them to me.

I looked warily at them. "What are they?"

"Prussian Blue. If you have been poisoned, they will help."

"Look, I feel great—not sick, not tired, not... Oh, what the hell."

I took them from him. "Okay. I need water. I'll take them when I get upstairs."

And with that, I left him to it. I was just about to go up the stairs out of the basement when I glanced back; he was already hauling in the second tower. *I guess his desire to check my radiation levels are forgotten, at least for the moment.*

I continued on up the stairs to the powder room and flushed the pills. Yeah, I know, but needs must.

Jacque, bless her, had brought my laptop from the office so I was able to download the images. I did, and I opened them with a certain amount of enthusiasm that quickly turned into disappointment. The image quality was pretty bad. The photo of the ring was fuzzy; the hand was moving when the footage was taken, and the security camera was old, analog, and basic. Tim had tried to enhance it, and he'd succeeded, to a point. I was eighty percent sure it was indeed a US Army Ranger ring. I could just make out the lettering around the outer edge, but the usual red stone emblazoned with 75th had been replaced with a black stone, possibly onyx, with what looked like a central diamond. I'd not seen one like it before.

The image of the reflection in the car window was hardly any better. It too was fuzzy and, yes, I was frustrated. *Maybe Bob... He should be here by now, damn it.*

I picked up my phone and called him.

"I'm outside the front door, Harry."

Rose let him in, and he joined us in the breakfast room.

He greeted August and Rose, looked coolly at me, then nodded.

"Hey," I said. "There's coffee over there. Grab a cup and then come and look at these images."

"No word from the kidnappers?" he asked.

"No."

"So what's the plan, then?"

"See this," I said, pointing to the image of the ring. "What do you make of it?"

He stared at it for a minute, then said, "It looks like a Ranger ring, but unlike any I've ever seen."

"You saw nothing like it in Afghanistan?"

"I just said so, didn't I? If I had, I would have told you."

"What's wrong, Bob?"

"Not a damn thing," he said. "You're going to question everything I say from now on, is that it?"

August and Rose got up and left us alone.

"*No!* Of course not. That was just... just a response... Now wait a minute." I interrupted myself. "I have enough frickin' problems without having to put up with stupid crap from you. I told you yesterday, I'm over it. Now you get over it, and let's concentrate on the job at hand."

He glared at me for a long minute, then nodded, "Okay."

I also nodded and then turned again to the computer screen and the image of the ring.

"So it's a custom job?" I asked.

He shrugged. "It's definitely a Ranger ring, but its significance... I don't know."

I flipped the screen to the image of the reflection.

"What do you think?" I asked. "You said he looked familiar."

He shook his head. "I don't know. It's hard to tell."

"Bob," I stared at the image. "Could this guy be active military?"

He shrugged again. "He could, but I doubt it. The military isn't into kidnapping civilians, especially not—"

"Yeah, I get it," I said interrupting him. "So, if not military, a contractor then, CSC? Christmas is ex-Rangers and a contractor."

"He is, but we know nothing of what he's doing now."

"We will," I said, "as soon as Tim gets his sh—gets his stuff together."

"Yes, well, I have *stuff* I need to do back at the office, so that's where I'll be. Give me a call if anything happens."

I nodded, absently. I was still staring at the image in the car window when he left.

Finally, I gave it up. There was nothing more to be done until Tim was able to work his magic. I was at a dead end, so I went to find August and Rose. I found them in the kitchen, and we sat together and talked, boy how we talked. Talk about life flashing before your eyes.

Around eleven, I followed Rose into their bedroom where Jade was hanging out, watched while she changed her, intending to grab a few quality moments with her myself when she was finished.

It was while I was with Rose and Jade, at eleven-forty-four, that August got the call. No, I didn't hear it, not first-hand anyway.

August walked into the bedroom just as I was about to take Jade from Rose.

"They just called," he said. "They said that if I don't drop the case, they'll kill Joe. That was it. That was all they said."

I looked at him. His face was white. I put my hand on his arm. "Take it easy," I said. "Now we know. Now we have something to go on. Was it a man?"

"I couldn't tell. The voice was electronically altered."

I closed my eyes for a moment, thinking. "Damn!" I said, more to myself than to August. "I hope Tim got it."

Fortunately, Tim was ahead of the game and was already monitoring all incoming calls.

What the caller actually said was, "If you want to see your brother again, stay the hell away from Lewis Walker."

Tim had a voiceprint and said it was indeed a man's voice: he would know, I guess. Me? If it was, I couldn't tell. August was right: the voice sounded like something out of one of those old movies. The call—with no caller ID—lasted exactly six seconds; too short for Tim to trace.

"Any idea where it might have originated?" I asked.

Tim shook his head. "Sorry." *Yeah, me too.*

"Why Walker, August?" I asked. "It makes no sense."

"Actually, it does. Walker is the whole case. Without him, it's all circumstantial. Cronin, Christmas' attorney, maintains that CSC is clean, that Walker was working alone. Without Walker, if we can't find him, or if he's dead, I can't make the case against CSC."

Tim nodded, and said, "I get that, but now we know different. Somebody abducted Joe, and now we know why; to put pressure on you. We also know, because of the connection to Walker, that Christmas is behind it. Isn't that enough?"

"No, Tim," August said. "Unless you can tie that call, or even the voice, to a person, it's all circumstantial; it means nothing... Well, it means something, but only to us."

"I think Walker's dead," I said. "It's what I would do if I was Christmas. If Walker is that important, I'd have put him away the minute the system turned him loose. Yeah, he's dead, for sure."

"I don't think so," August said. "But let's say you're right, in which case, why take Joe?"

He had me there.

"There's only one way to find out. I need to talk to Christmas, and quickly. Every hour we lose is critical, but first I need to talk to Tim, and I need to get Bob back here."

Chapter 9

May 24, Afternoon

Riverview
        I went to the basement and found Tim sitting in front of four huge monitors—two over two—banging away at one of three keyboards. He was wearing earbuds and oblivious to everything other than the stream of data scrolling down one of the screens.

I stood behind him and tapped him gently on the shoulder. If he felt it, he didn't show it. I tapped again, a little harder.

"*Wait*, please." Not for a second did he take his eyes off the screen. So, I waited... and I waited.

Finally, I pulled one of the earbuds out. He swung around, reaching over his shoulder, trying to locate the missing bud.

"*Harry!* I knew you were there, but I couldn't stop what I was trying to—" He shook his head, frustrated. "You wouldn't understand."

"Try me," I said.

"I was, as they say on Star Trek, running a Level One diagnostic. I was making sure everything is running as it should."

Star Trek. I stared down at him. *Are you kidding?*

"Well?" I asked.

He nodded, did his thing with his glasses, and grinned up at me.

"I'm ready, Captain, to explore strange new worlds..." He caught the look I was giving him. "Er, sorry. What do you need Cap—I mean, Harry."

I rolled my eyes. "I need information: Nicholas Christmas and his company, CSC. When can I have it?"

"Well, let me think." He grabbed the glasses from his face and a microfiber cloth from the table, polished them vigorously, threw down the cloth, rammed the glasses back in place and poked them with a forefinger. "A couple of hours?" he asked, tentatively.

"You have one hour. I'll be back with Bob and Kate at two-thirty, and you'd better have something for me."

He frowned, squinted. I thought for a minute he was going to burst into tears, but he didn't. Instead, he grinned up at me and said, "Aye, Captain."

I shook my head and left him banging away at the keys and twittering to himself, "He wants the impossible, Geordi."

I didn't know who Geordi was, but I suspected he had something to do with the Enterprise. *Oh well, 'that's gotta be worth a couple of pages in someone's book.'* I smiled at the thought. *Tim would be proud of me.* I continued up the stairs to August's office where I made the call to Bob and asked him to join me.

I also called Kate because, one: I needed to know if there had been any developments with the missing person case. There hadn't. Two: I asked her to also join me at Riverview because she needed to know what was going on and... well, I hate having to repeat myself.

Next, I went to see Jacque.

Jacque had taken over August's office but not his vintage computer. That, she'd moved temporarily to a credenza off to one side of the room. She was seated in August's great leather desk chair —the damn thing is even bigger than mine—her phone to her ear. She looked up at me, smiled, held up a finger and mouthed, "give me one minute."

I nodded and turned to leave. She tapped sharply on the desk and pointed to the chair in front of it.

I smiled at her and sat down. She continued her call for what could only have been twenty or thirty seconds, then set her phone on the desk and looked across it at me.

"So," she said. "I see from the look that you want to talk. You've been like a bear with a sore tooth since I got here. What's up?"

"Oh, not a thing," I said, sarcastically.

"There you go," she said, leaning forward and putting her forearms on the desk, her hands clasped together. "Like a bear..." She paused, tilted her head to one side, then nodded and smiled at me.

"Look, Harry," she said. "What you did was unbelievable. You saved us all. How you did it—how you held it together—I don't know. And then Amanda getting hurt. If it was Wendy, I'd be out of my mind. And now there's Joseph kidnapped. What else is there? What else *could* there be?"

"Thanks, Jacque. Yeah, I do have a lot on my mind." *And now I have to tell you about Bob.*

"So you wan' to unload? Talk to me."

There it was, the Jamaican accent.

"It's Bob."

She sat up straight. "What about him?"

I hesitated. Was I doing the right thing? Did it really matter? *Ah, the hell with it. If I don't tell her, I'm as bad as Bob, keeping it a secret all this time.*

"He's CIA, Jacque. Always has been."

Her eyes widened, Her mouth opened and then shut again.

"Apparently, they let him off active duty back in 2006, but they never removed him from the books. He's inactive, but still CIA."

"How'd you find dis out?" she asked, very quietly.

"He told me, yesterday. He didn't seem to think it was a big deal. But it is: not the fact that he's CIA though. It's that he didn't tell us. He didn't tell *me*."

"And you did a background check on him, right?"

"Yes, of course."

"And?"

"Nothing... well, nothing about the CIA. I asked him why not, and he said it was a need-to-know thing, covered by the Espionage Act."

"Tell me this, Harry: Would you have hired him if you'd known?"

I thought for a minute, then nodded. "Yes, I would have."

She leaned back in her chair, smiling, her arms high, hands palm up, like Buddha. "So it's okay then; no foul. He's still Bob Ryan. Yes, he's got a murky past, but he worked for the government, not the Mafia, so what's your beef?"

"Well, he—" I stopped, stared at her, and then I realized she was right, and I nodded.

"You're right, Jacque. You always are. Thank you."

And that was the end of it, at least as far as I was concerned.

I looked at my watch, it was one-fifteen.

"They'll be here soon, Kate and Bob," I said. "I'll need you to join us downstairs."

She nodded. "No problem."

"There are some folding chairs in the sunroom, let's grab a couple and head on down." And we did.

They arrived together at a little after two; Kate had called Bob and arranged to pick him up, and they didn't look happy. In fact, I got the distinct impression that they'd been arguing. That being so, I decided to put it to bed once and for all.

"Okay, you two," I said, "outside. We need to talk."

I led the way out onto the patio and pointed to a round, teak table and chairs. "Take a seat."

We sat, and I continued, "Okay, we don't have time to fool around like this, so I'll make it short. We, the three of us, have a problem, and we have to solve it... now."

I looked at each of them in turn. Bob sat back in his chair, his arms folded, his expression blank. Kate stared stoically back at me but said nothing.

"Bob," I continued, "I've done a lot of thinking these last twenty-four hours, and I think I understand why you weren't forthcoming about your past. I don't like it, but what's done is done. You haven't changed; you are who you are, what you are, and I love you like a brother, so I'm over it. Kate, we all have to work together, so you need to get over it too."

She glanced sideways at him. Her face softened. She looked back at me with just the hint of a smile and nodded.

"Bob?" I asked.

He shrugged. "As far as I'm concerned, there never was a problem. Now, is that it? Can we go back to work?"

Just like that? I wonder...

"We can," I said. "Let's go talk to Tim."

Jacque had arranged the seating in a half-circle with Tim's computers at the center and was already seated next to him. He'd spun his chair around and was sitting with his back to his monitors, flipping through screens on his iPad. He was, as usual, lost in a world of his own.

"Hey, Tim," I laid a hand on his shoulder, to get his attention. "You in there?"

He turned, looked up, grinned at me and nodded.

"Good," I said. "What do you have? I need to know everything there is to know about Christmas, CSC and their operations."

He stared down at the iPad, scratched his ear, then said, thoughtfully, "The last couple years are pretty murky... Okay, this is what I have so far. Nicholas James Christmas was born in Clarksville, Tennessee, on October 7, 1974, the son of Theresa and Jordan Wesley Christmas, a U.S. Army major. He grew up in Clarksville and graduated from the Clarksville Academy, a private prep school, in 1992. He attended the University of Georgia on an ROTC scholarship and graduated in 1996 in the top five percent of his class. Then he was commissioned into the United States Army as a

2nd Lieutenant in 1997 and was immediately recruited into Military Intelligence.

"He applied to become a Ranger a year later and was accepted into Ranger School at Fort Benning, GA, in January 1999 where he specialized in counterintelligence. On graduating from Ranger School, he was promoted to 1st Lieutenant and deployed to Beirut.

"In October 2001, right after 911, he was promoted to captain and was with the Iraq invasion force in March 2003. He was in Iraq for nine months and then in November 2004, he was deployed to Afghanistan where he did three tours, almost back-to-back, three years in all. He resigned his commission within three months after returning home from his third tour in March 2008. He founded CSC a year later in March 2009."

Tim took a drink of water from his Star Trek water bottle. Then he continued reading from his iPad.

"Okay, so on to CSC, and this is where it gets murky. It was a tough one. What little information I could find about Christmas Security Concepts—CSC—is buried deep." He paused, looked up at me, scratched the top of his head with one finger, then continued.

"CSC Incorporated, from what I was able to find, is a small, covert private military company that provides security services to the United States federal government on a contractual basis. The corporate offices are in Atlanta... well, Marietta, actually. But they have a satellite location. It appears to be a training facility of some sort—in the Copperhill, Tennessee area with access to Martin Campbell Field—where they keep a Huey helicopter and a Beech 90 King Air jump plane."

"Copperhill?" I asked. "There's nothing there but a few hundred people. Why there?"

"Just that," Bob said. "It's remote, desolate country. Ideal for training purposes and... other activities."

"Other activities?" I said. "You're talking drugs, trafficking, smuggling?"

He shrugged. "To say the least. You can't do any of that crap in Atlanta."

I nodded. "Maybe that's where they're keeping Walker or Joe."

"Could be," Bob said. "Can you pull it up, Tim?"

He could, so he spun his seat to face the monitors, and in just a few seconds, we were looking at a satellite view of the area.

"That's Campbell Field, there," Tim said, pointing.

"What's all that mess there, to the left?" Kate said.

"All of that area was once dedicated to copper mining," Tim said. "What you're seeing—the lakes—is called Gypsum Pond, all part of the devastation the mining caused. I'm thinking that, right there, is the CSC compound." Tim pointed to what looked like a collection of prefabricated buildings just to the south of three fairly large lakes and west of the south end of the airfield.

He leaned back in his chair, adjusted the position of his glasses, then said, "See? There's a dirt road leading from the complex to the airfield."

"Hmm, interesting," I said. "Can you enlarge it? I'd like to see what they have there."

He did, and I could see there were six buildings in all, each having a steel roof.

"I wonder, how big an area do they own?" I said. "Surely it's not just the compound."

The compound, and that's surely what it was, was surrounded by what looked like a steel security fence with light poles set at regular intervals. At night, the place would be ablaze with light. *I bet there are cameras on those poles.*

"If they're training mercenaries," Bob said, "I'd say they use the entire area around and including the lakes, from the road east of the airport to... hell, who knows? It has to be at least five or six square miles, most of it forested."

"What else could they be doing?" I said. "That's quite a facility. That one building looks to be big enough to house a small army." I sighed and shook my head. "Go on, Tim. What else did you find?"

"Yes, sir! Okay. So, since 2009 when the company was founded, the group has provided services to the CIA."

I couldn't help but glance sideways at Bob. If he saw the look, he ignored it.

"I could find very little information about the company staffing," Tim continued. "The numbers—payroll, social security, and so on—are unavailable, classified. I stopped short of hacking into... Well, if that's what you want..." He paused, expectantly.

I said nothing.

"Okay then," he said. "So, as far as I can tell, I'd say there are less than fifty official employees and maybe as many more off the books. Soldiers of fortune, I guess you'd call them. Most of them seem to be deployed: here in the U.S. and in Afghanistan and Iraq."

He paused and grinned at me. "You wanna know how I know that?" He pushed his glasses further up the bridge of his nose.

I glanced over at Kate. She nodded.

"Tell us, Tim," I said.

"I followed the money, well, some of it—which wasn't easy, I can tell you—some of it I couldn't... Well I can, but it's all buried in off-shore accounts, shell companies, you know. It will take a little time. So, anyway, I was, however, able to get a handle on his immediate senior staff. They're all former Army Rangers.

"They are: ex-Sergeant Henry 'Hank' Johnson, ex-Sergeant Jessica Roark, John 'Johnny' Pascal, James 'Bunny' Hare, Herman 'Herm' Garcia, and"—he paused, for effect—"ex-Corporal Lewis Walker."

Bob spoke up. "I'd say that's his entire team from Afghanistan. I met Johnson maybe a half dozen times, and Roark three times, no four. She's one tough b—cookie."

"Ex-Sergeant Johnson is an enigma," Tim said. "His title is now Executive Vice President and, from all accounts he's Christmas' second in command, but take a look at this photo of him." He put it up on one of the screens. "The man's a hulk, a brute. He was discharged from the army a year later after Christmas in November

2010 and joined his former CO at CSC where he is now VP of Field Operations."

"Yeah," Bob said, "That's Hank all right. I always figured the two were strange bedfellows. Christmas was an intelligent, well-educated military officer, and he talked to him as if he was his equal. Johnson, on the other hand, was less well-educated but was a street smart, dedicated soldier of fortune. I'd say he's Nick's fixer."

Tim nodded, and continued, "In February 2009, after conducting more than fifty interviews, Christmas hired Julia Stein, a somewhat gifted accountant. She was then thirty-two and held two master's degrees in finance and banking. As far as I can tell, she's clean: no criminal record, no debts, nor even a parking ticket."

Tim nodded, looked up at me, and said, "That's all I have right now. If you want, I can dig into Johnson and the rest of the team, but it will—"

"No, Tim," I said, interrupting him. "Not now anyway. What I need you to do is upgrade the security system here and at the office, and I need it done right away. Get hold of—oh hell, you know that better than I do. Just do it, okay?"

"I'll get right on it," Tim said. "Budget?"

"Since when did you care about such things? Just do it."

He grinned at me. I shook my head, then glanced at my watch; it was almost two-thirty.

"Okay," I said. "Bob, you and I will go visit Christmas, now, this afternoon. It's what, a hundred miles to Marietta? It's a straight shot on I-75. We can be there in ninety minutes, say by five anyway. The rest of you, get some rest. Who knows what tomorrow will bring?"

"What if he's not there?" Jacque asked.

I looked at Bob, quizzically.

He nodded. "You have his number, Tim?" he asked.

Tim gave it to him, and he punched it into his phone, then put it on speaker. It rang a couple of times before being answered. The voice was female.

"CSC. How can I help you?"

"Tell Nick that his old buddy Bob Ryan is on the phone."

The other end of the line was silent and stayed that way for at least a couple of minutes, then, "Well, well, now ain't that a blast from the past? How are you, Bob?"

"Oh, you know how it is, Nick. Listen, I need to see you this afternoon. I have a proposition for you. I'll be there by five-thirty. You gonna be there?"

"Yeah, but what's the rush? Wouldn't tomorrow be—"

"For you, maybe, but not for me. It has to be today."

"So what is it you want, Bob?"

"Not over the phone, Nick. You know how it is, probably better than most."

There was a long pause. We could hear him breathing, then, "Okay. Five-thirty. I'll be waiting." He disconnected, and the room was quiet.

"You ready, then?" Bob asked.

"Yes," I said. "Almost but give me just a minute."

I went upstairs to my room, swilled water over my face, dried off, then I slipped into my shoulder holster, then put on a dark green, lightweight golf jacket. I checked my VP9 then slipped it into the holster under my arm. My backup, a tiny Sig P938 in a sticky holster, I slid into my waistband at the small of my back. I love that little gun, a tiny replica of the classic, .45 Colt 1911. In fact, I have two of them. The one I carry as a backup and a second that, on rare occasions, I carry in an ankle holster, but not that day.

Now I was ready to go.

Chapter 10

May 24, 6pm

Marietta, GA

We were late, not by much, but enough to make me more than a little antsy. We turned off the Interstate, right onto Marietta Parkway and then right again onto Kennestone Circle where we found CSC housed in a large warehouse with offices facing the street.

We parked in front of the main entrance, sat for a moment discussing strategy—of which we really didn't have any—and then went inside where we found a sliding glass window. Beyond the window, seated at a desk, was an incongruously big man with a shaved head.

"Hello, Hank," Bob said, through a talk-through hole. "Long time no see."

The man looked up from what he was doing and smiled... Ha, it was more snarl than smile, eyes half closed, and tight lips over two rows of teeth a barracuda would have been proud of.

"Bob Ryan, no less," the giant said, rising to his feet. "Nick said you were coming. Hold tight, I'll let you through."

He pushed a button under the sliding window. There were two

loud clunks as the bolts from inside of the steel door slid back and hit their stops.

"Come on through. He's waiting for you."

He was indeed waiting for us, and he didn't look pleased about it.

He was standing just inside his open office door.

"Bob, my old friend," he said, holding out his hand. He sounded affable, but there was an edge to his voice. "How the hell are you?" he asked, not waiting for an answer. "Come on in. What have you been up to? It's been what, ten years?"

Christmas was a tall, slim man, maybe six-one, with dark brown hair and a neatly trimmed beard and mustache. He was wearing a dark blue business suit that must cost every penny of five grand with a white shirt and a red and black striped tie. His office was plush: a huge walnut desk, bookcase behind it, two leather Chesterfield chairs in front, and some obviously expensive artwork on the walls. The suit and the office seemed more the accouterments of a banker than that of a soldier of fortune.

"Nick," Bob said, with a quick, single nod as he gripped his hand. There was nothing friendly about it. "Yes, ten years, give or take. You're looking well."

"Thank you," Christmas said, as he looked at me. "Who's your friend?"

Why do I get the distinct impression that you already know? I thought.

"Harry Starke, Nick Christmas," Bob said, never taking his eyes off Christmas.

Christmas narrowed his eyes, tilted his head a little to one side, then nodded slowly and said, "Holy cow. *The* Harry Starke? The Harry Starke that only two days ago saved Chattanooga from nuclear destruction? Lord! I *am* honored."

The son of a bitch is mocking me.

He offered me his hand. I almost ignored it, but then I thought better of it and took it. His fingers closed on mine like a steel vise. If I'd been expecting it... well, I wasn't, and I stared into a pair of taunt-

eyes as he increased the pressure. It hurt like hell, but I

ing, icy blue eyes as he increased the pressure. It hurt like hell, but I gave no sign of it.

"That's enough, Nick," Bob said. "You've nothing to prove."

The pressure slackened, enough for me to be able to return the compliment, and I did. He didn't give an inch, but the smile turned humorless, and I knew I'd taken him by surprise. Oh yeah, I know, it was childish, but I enjoyed the hell out of the look in his eye. I turned him loose.

"Not bad, Harry," he said, flexing his fingers. "Not bad at all. You're obviously a man to be reckoned with." This time the tone was one of contempt.

"Okay," he said, brightly. "Please sit down. What can I do for you? Oh, forgive me: would you like something to drink? Scotch, perhaps?" he asked looking at me and smirking.

Bob and I shook our heads and sat down, side by side in the two Chesterfields. They were so low, I could barely see over the edge of his desk. So, no sooner had my rear end settled into the leather than I stood up again.

"What?" Christmas asked, grinning.

"You know what," I said, grabbing a straight-backed dining chair from the rear of the room and setting it down to the right of the Chesterfield I'd just vacated. I sat down, nodded, and said, "Now, can we get on with it?"

Before we could, however, Bob also decided his chair was too low, and he stood up and looked around. Unfortunately, there were no more chairs.

Christmas leaned forward, picked up his desk phone, tapped the screen and said, "Dana. Would you please bring my guest a chair? Thank you." He leaned back, and again made with the smile.

Dana brought the chair, and Bob sat down. "Okay, Nick," he said. "You've had your fun. Now stop playing stupid games. We've come a long way."

"Ah, Bob. You haven't changed at all. Still the brusque, no-nonsense company man. Are you still with them, by the way?"

"No, I'm Harry's partner, but you knew that, right?"

Nick nodded.

Bob looked around the office, and said, "You've done well for yourself, Nick. The security business must be treating you well."

"I can't complain," he said, his smile broadening. "Business is good. What's to complain about?"

"Yeah," Bob said. "You always were one lucky son of a bitch. Now you have your own private army, so I heard."

"What do you want, Ryan? You said it wouldn't wait until tomorrow. So tell me."

He leaned forward, placed his elbows on the desk, clasped his hands together, and did his best to be sincere. I wasn't convinced, but it was then that I noticed the ring on the middle finger of his left hand.

"Nice ring," I said. "Army Rangers, I think, but a little unusual. Custom?"

His eyes narrowed as he frowned. He looked down at the back of his hand, balled his fingers into a fist, the ring on top. The large diamond sparkled darkly. He placed the fist into the palm of his other hand and screwed it back and forth as if polishing the ring; he wasn't. The gesture was pure threat.

"Yes, custom. A gift."

"Do all of your men have them?"

"Several do. Why do you ask?"

"Oh," I said, feigning surprise. "No reason. It was just a thought."

And then something totally unexpected happened; something inside me snapped. I don't know if it was because of what was going on with Amanda and Joe, but whatever it was, I suddenly realized I was done pussy-footing around.

I leaned forward, looked him right in the eyes, and said, "No! The hell it was just a thought. Five days ago, one of your thugs kidnapped my uncle Joseph. I know he was one of yours because he was wearing an identical ring. Then you called my father and told him to drop the case against your company or you'd kill Joe. I want to know where the hell he is, and I want to know right now, you self-satisfied, preening, arrogant son of a bitch."

I reached inside my jacket, pulled my VP9 from its holster, stood, walked around the desk and slammed the muzzle of the gun down hard on his knee.

"Now, you piece o' shit," I said snarling. "Where is he? Tell me or I'll put you on sticks for the rest of your life."

That's all it took, right? Wrong. He simply leaned back in his chair and smiled up at me.

"Harry," he said, quietly. "I have no idea what you're talking about. I made no such call, and I don't have your uncle. Now, put that thing away before you hurt someone."

I saw red. I took a half-step sideways and slammed the barrel of the heavy gun against the side of his head. He fell sideways out of the chair and lay wide-eyed on his back, both hands to his head, blood streaming through his fingers.

"For God's sake, Harry," Bob yelled as he jumped to his feet. "What the hell do you think you're doing?"

He came around the desk like Tony Gonzales; he was flying. He hit me with his shoulder, and the next thing I knew, I slammed backward into the bookcase. I went down like a sack of garbage. And then I was up again, boiling mad and swinging.

"You son of a bitch, Ryan."

"*Hey!*" Bob yelled as the VP9 missed his ear by less than an inch. "Hey—hey! Calm down, Harry. For God's sake stop."

I stopped, one hand on the desk, breathing heavily, the other gripping the VP9 at my side.

"Step, back, Harry," Bob said, quietly.

"You dumb shit," I said, as I staggered around the desk toward him. "I almost frickin' shot you."

"No, you didn't. If that's what you intended, you would have. Now calm down, damn it. Look what you've done."

I looked. Christmas was lying on his back, groaning, blood seeping through his fingers onto the carpet.

Dana rushed into the room. "What's going on? Oh my God. You've killed him." She grabbed the desk phone.

Bob took it gently from her.

"It's okay," he said to her. "Nick is okay. He's just hurt a little, is all."

"Get out, Dana, I'm fine," Christmas said, using the edge of the desk to pull himself to his feet.

"Do you want me to call an ambulance?" she asked.

"Hell no. I told you, I'm fine. Now go and leave me alone. These two *gentlemen* are leaving."

She left, closing the door behind her.

Christmas sat down at his desk. He pulled open a drawer and removed a fistful of paper napkins from a box and held them to his ear, which was still bleeding. Then he reached under his desk and did something we couldn't see, but I could guess what it was; he'd called for help.

"You," he said, looking at me. "Do you have any idea what you've just done, or who and what you did it to? I don't know where your frickin' uncle is; I don't have him. But I do know where to find you, Starke. You're screwed; you too, Ryan. Now get the hell out of my office, both of you, before my men arrive and throw you out."

I took a deep breath, then said, "You're lying, Christmas. I know you are. Now, I'll make you the same deal you offered my father: turn Joe loose or I'll kill you."

I heard the door open behind me. I never took my eyes off Christmas, who held up his hand, and said, "Take it easy, Hank These two are just leaving, show them out."

"Hell, Boss," the giant said. "You're bleedin', man. These sons-a-bitches—"

"It's okay," Christmas said, interrupting him. "I'm okay. Just show them out and see that they leave the premises."

"Hey, dickhead," the giant said to me. "You going to put that thing away, or do you want me to take it away from you?"

Aftermath

I turned to face him. I was boiling; not good. "Do it," I said, pointing the VP9 at his right knee, my finger on the trigger.

"Whoa," Bob said, stepping between us. "That's enough, both of you. Harry, we've got to get the hell out of here. Johnson, you stand still, right where you are, or I'll bust that shiny head. Nick, this ain't over. You can't pull your kind o' shit in this country. You turn the man loose, or by God..." And he grabbed my arm and hauled me out of the office.

"What the hell was that about, Harry?" he asked, as he closed the car door. "Those people are killers. You can't treat them that way."

I punched the starter button, with way more force than I needed, slammed the gear shift into drive, and squealed the tires out of the complex out onto Kennestone Circle, heading for the Interstate.

By the time we hit the on-ramp, I'd calmed down, just a little.

"Bob, I can't keep doing this shit... I need to go and see Amanda. Before I do, though, I'll drop you off at Riverview. We're going to have to resolve this thing, and quickly. I'll have Rose make up a bed on the couch. You can have my room."

"Oh, don't talk shit, Harry. I'll take the couch."

Chapter 11

Friday, May 25, Early

Riverview
Bob did indeed sleep on the couch that night, but he didn't get to it until well after midnight. He was on the couch watching TV when I returned from the hospital.

Amanda? No change. I don't think she'd even moved since the last time I'd seen her. I didn't stay long; there wasn't any point. I talked to one of the nurses, but she could tell me nothing... or maybe she just wouldn't. I didn't know. So finally, I stood, leaned over the bed and gently kissed her lips, then looked at her face. It was beautiful—badly damaged, and expressionless, but beautiful just the same. The only encouraging sign was that she was breathing steadily, on her own.

I have to say, I was more than a little pleased to find Bob still awake: I needed someone to talk to, and talk we did. We sat together, reminiscing about the past... No, not the events of the past week. I wasn't ready for that, not yet. And we did a little drinking... No, not a lot, just a couple, more for something to do with our hands than... well, you get the idea.

Talking together about nothing and everything was something

Bob and I had never done before. Why, I don't know. It was just something we never did. That night, however, I learned a lot about Bob and, if I'm truthful, myself too. It didn't take long for me to figure out that Bob never really was who I thought he was; it was as if I was getting to know a whole new person.

I always knew he was smart... Well, smartass might be a better way to describe him, but he was more than that, way more. I don't know whether or not he was glad to drop the pretense, but I soon realized I was talking to a highly intelligent, highly trained CIA officer, not the rough and tumble, hard-charging ex-cop I'd always thought him to be.

It was inevitable then, that the conversation turned to the present situation: first Nick Christmas and then my missing uncle.

"You do know that they have Joe, don't you, Bob?" I asked.

"It's possible," he said.

I shook my head. "No. Christmas has him. I'm sure of it. I'm also just about convinced that he's at the facility up there in the mountains, and if he is, I'm going to get him."

"If he's there, sure. If he's not; what then?"

"I don't know," I said, "and right now my brain feels like concrete..." I thought for a minute, then said, "There's nothing we can do until morning, so I'm going to turn in. You sure you want to sleep on the couch?"

"I'll be fine. Go to bed, Harry. Get some sleep. We'll talk in the morning."

I nodded and left him, staring out of the window.

* * *

I woke early the following morning... No, that's not quite true: I rose early the following morning—at just after five-thirty—having slept very little. I decided to forgo my morning run and made coffee and bagels instead. I filled a couple of mugs, stuck half a toasted, buttered bagel between my teeth, and went into the lounge where Bob was still asleep.

"Hey," I said. "Wake up. I've brought coffee."

He didn't move, not even the flicker of an eyelid. I set the mugs down on the coffee table and gave him a poke with my finger.

"Hey, wake up."

"Geez, Harry," he said, blearily. "Don't you ever sleep? You put sugar in that?"

"You don't take sugar."

He blinked up at me, swung his feet off the couch and sat up.

"Don't ever ask me to do that again," he said. "I had maybe five minutes; the couch is too damn short. Yeah, yeah, I know. It never was meant for sleeping, right?"

"You're full of it, you know that?" I asked. "I came in here twice during the night to check on you; you were out cold both times."

He cut me a weird look over the rim of his mug, and said, "Well, the coffee's good anyway. How long have you been up?"

"Most of the night, thinking."

"So, you been thinking, huh? What did you come up with? Do we have a plan?"

It was a question I'd asked myself many times during the night, and the truth was, I didn't. One thing I knew for sure, though.

"We need to go in there and get Joe out," I said.

"We don't even know if he's there. Hell, we don't even know for sure that Christmas has him."

"True," I said, "but I think he does have him, and that facility up at Copperhill is where I'd hide him, if it were me. Look, we won't know, not until we go and look." I paused for a second.

He sipped on his coffee and looked at me expectantly.

I checked my watch. "It's almost seven. There's no point in doing this now. We need to wait for the others. Go get yourself cleaned up, and then we'll have breakfast. You can use my shower. When you're done, you'll find underwear and golf shirts in the closet. You'll find them a little tight, but they should work for you; I wear my shirts loose. They're all new. August bought them for me from the club."

He looked at me skeptically. "You can't be serious. I'm twice the man you are."

"Don't you wish," I said. "Go on, get out of here. You're stinking up the place."

Chapter 12

Friday, May 25, Morning

Riverview
Kate was the first to arrive, then Jacque and Tim arrived together. Jacque had given him a ride home; having left his van at the back of the house. By the time they, Jacque and Tim, had arrived it was almost nine, and I was pacing the kitchen floor.

"You need to calm down," Bob said.

Calm down? Me? The man's on his third cup of coffee.

"Don't you look at me like dat," Jacque said, dumping her heavy bag and laptop on the kitchen table. "I can't just up and leave the office any time I want, you know."

I sighed, nodded, and told everyone to grab coffee, bagels, whatever, and get downstairs. I'd be with them just as soon as I'd said good morning to Jade.

Yes, I know what you're thinking: why hadn't I done that earlier? Because Rose, God love her, had warned me in no uncertain terms that I couldn't. She wanted the baby to sleep uninterrupted.

So, at nine-fifteen, she finally allowed me to enter the bedroom and hold my daughter. That was something I'd not yet gotten used to, and I couldn't help but wonder if I ever would.

After a while, Rose came in to check on us.

"You look like you're holding a basket of eggs," she said. "Here, let me."

She took the baby from me, and I received my first practical instruction on parenting. Did I learn a lot? Hell no, and I have to admit I was glad to hand Jade over to her grandmother, kiss her on the nose—the baby, not Rose—and make my way back to the kitchen.

Amanda, what are you doing to me? Please get well!

I grabbed my fourth cup of coffee and headed downstairs to join the others. Tim was already banging away at the keyboard. The top two monitors were both showing the area of wilderness surrounding Gypsum Pond Campbell Field. One was a wide satellite view of the entire six square miles, it's dirt tracks, forested areas, the three lakes, the airfield, and the compound. The second monitor was showing a closeup of the compound. The detail was amazing.

"I know that's not Google Maps," I said. "You've tapped into a direct feed, right?"

"Oh yeah," Tim said, enthusiastically. "Well, not quite. What you're seeing is a recording I made fifteen minutes, or so, ago. The satellite designated EIO209C passes just to the west every ninety minutes. It's in optimum position for less than ten minutes, so what you're seeing is already old news. We'll get another update in... sixty-eight minutes."

I stepped closer, studied the compound, looking for details, for anything that might give me a hint as to what was going on there. But there was little to see, other than several vehicles parked close to the biggest of the six buildings, including a black SUV, a pickup truck, a Jeep Wrangler, and a box van.

"What do you think, Bob?" I asked. "Can it be done?'

"It can, but it won't be easy. They won't know we're coming, so we'll have the element of surprise, but see those boxes on the light poles? Those are cameras. If I know Nick, they cover every inch of the compound. That area outside the fence; it's a hundred feet of open ground all around the fence. There's no way to cross it without being seen." He paused, thought for a minute, then said, "Brute force might be the answer, but it would be dangerous."

"Brute force?" I asked. "What are you thinking?"

"See this track here?" He stepped up, pointed to a spot on the monitor screen. "We can access it here." Again, he pointed. "From there it's a straight run to the gate. We'd need a heavy vehicle to smash through the gate, but it could be done."

I stared at the screen, picturing what Bob was suggesting in my mind.

"Can you zoom in tighter, Tim?" I asked.

He tapped the keyboard. The gate grew larger, and I shook my head.

"It would take a tank to get through that; the fence too. No, we'll have to think of something else."

I stared some more. It didn't get any better. I sighed, shook my head again, and said, "ease out a little please, Tim. Whoa. Stop. Right there. What's that? Go back in a little."

I was looking at what I thought might be a drainage ditch at the rear of the row of buildings. It wasn't. It was just a shallow depression.

"It's time for the satellite to make another pass. I can give you some real-time footage."

"Oh shit. Look, there... and there. Zoom in, Tim. Shit, those are armed men. They must be guards. They're heading for the fence. They... yes, they're patrolling the perimeter. How come we haven't seen that before?"

"I'd say because they're on a schedule," Bob said.

"Harry," Tim said, looking sheepish. "Before we go any farther, there's something you should know. I did a little research when I got home last night. Everything you're looking at, the entire area, is government property. Department of Defense, to be precise."

"Oh hell," Bob said. "That complicates matters. How the hell did Nick get access to that, I wonder?"

"It makes no difference," I said. "We have to do this no matter who owns the damned property."

"True," Bob said, "but it means the security up there will be even more sophisticated than we first thought."

I shrugged. "Probably. It looks tough, I agree."

I really didn't see that it made much difference. We were planning a raid on a secure property, sure, but the said property was being used for criminal activities. I hoped, and at that point, the only way I could prove that was to find Joe and get him out. If he wasn't there, then yes, my team and I, if we were caught, would be in deep trouble. But thinking back to those days, I really didn't have a choice. As I said before, we had to do it. Well, I did. The others were under no obligation, not then.

"So what's the plan then?" Kate asked. "Are we going in balls to the wall, or do you have something else in mind?"

We? I don't think so!

I stared at the sea of wilderness. It looked daunting... No, it looked frickin' impossible.

"I'm working on it," I said, more to myself than to anybody else. "I'm working on it," I mused, quietly.

"So, work out loud," Bob said. "You never know, we might be able to provide a little input."

I turned and grinned at him. "Always the blunt one, you are. Okay, so—" At that point, the image froze. The two guards weren't moving.

"What the hell?" I said, turning to Tim.

"We've lost the feed from the satellite; it's passed on and won't be back for another ninety minutes. It's okay though. I recorded it, so I can run what we have on a loop, just give me a minute to set it up." He tapped at the keyboard, then looked up at me and said, "Here you go." He tapped a single key, and the images again lit up both screens.

"Tim," I said. "I need you to record each pass throughout the day.

I need to know what's going on up there. And I especially need to know the guard's schedule, if they're on one."

"Gotcha. I'll set that up."

"Great, thanks."

I stepped in as close to the screen as I could, then backed off again, my eyes unfocused.

"Geez," I said. "That's the way to get a headache in a hurry. Okay, so I'm still not sure exactly what that depression here is." I pointed to it. "How deep is it, I wonder? There's no way to tell."

"Yes, there is," Tim said. "Not right now though. This afternoon, say around five o'clock, I might be able to give you some idea. It won't be precise of course, but it will give you a clue."

"You can?" Jacque asked. "And how might you do that?"

Oh no. Now we'll never shut him up.

"Well," Tim said, rising enthusiastically to the occasion, "the depression is almost due east of the compound; the sun sets in the west, so..."

"You'll be able to tell by the density of the shadow," I finished for him.

"Well, yeah, but it's not quite that easy, but in principle, yes. That's basically it."

"You're thinking that if it's deep enough," Kate said, thoughtfully, "we can use it to—"

"Get close enough without being seen to effect a breach in the fence," I finished for her.

"Oh hell, Harry," Bob said, derisively. "You've been watching too many movies. Real life ain't like that. I wish to hell it was."

"You think?" I asked, smiling to myself. I hadn't watched a movie of any kind in more than a year.

I stepped away from Tim's desk and the monitors, sat down, and stared up at them.

"Those cameras," I mused, out loud. "Are they fixed, do you think?"

Tim tapped the keyboard, and the image zoomed so fast it made my head spin. It blurred, stabilized, backed out, refocused on one post and the camera thereon, and we watched. The image was still too small. If the camera was moving, I couldn't tell... not at first, then I blinked, closed my eyes and opened them again. It had moved, at least I thought it had.

"It's programmed, right, Tim?"

"Looks like it. Yeppy. See? It's moving."

We watched. My eyes were straining to see. It didn't look like it was moving to me.

"Come on, Tim," I said. "Talk to me. What are you seeing?"

"It's moving all right, and quite quickly. I make the arc to be about forty-five degrees, maybe fifty. It's taking fifty-five seconds to complete its rotation, each way."

"Oh shit," Bob growled, "Fifty-five seconds? That's no damn good."

"If it's all we have—"

"It's just enough to get us caught," Bob said, interrupting me.

I nodded. "Then we'll just have to be *really* careful," I said, mocking him.

"So that's your plan, then?' he asked. "You're out of your frickin' mind."

"Do you have a better idea?" I asked.

"Yeah, I like bustin' through the gate a whole lot better, or maybe even the fence."

"Now who's been watching too many movies?" I asked, smiling at him.

"Harry," he said. "I'm with you, you know that, but for God's sake... we need a plan, a real, workable plan."

"Like I said," I replied. "Do you have any ideas?"

He stared up at the screen, then, shook his head.

"Okay, then," I said. "We wait until this afternoon, until Tim can give us an idea exactly how deep that depression might be."

I looked around at the group. Most of them had said little, but all had listened intently.

"Okay," I said. "There's little more we can do for now, not until we know the guards' schedule and if the depression is a viable option. If it is, you and I'll go in tonight, Bob, late, around midnight. Any questions, anybody?"

"I do," Kate said. "I'm going with you."

"No!" I said, and I held up my hand to stop her from saying anything. "We'll discuss it later."

She opened her mouth to speak, but I stopped her before she could. "I said, later. Now, if that's it, I'm going to spend a little time with my wife."

I checked my watch. It was just after eleven-thirty.

"I don't want any of you going to the office. Take the rest of the day off. You can stay here. Rose is providing lunch. Get some rest. We'll resume at three o'clock."

I turned to Kate. "I know, but you can't, so drop it. Would you mind taking me to the hospital, please? You can drop me off, and I'll get an Uber to bring me back."

The look she gave me would have frozen a polar bear, but she nodded, and I followed her up the stairs and out to the cars. And there, wouldn't you know it, we found my old friend and Amanda's colleague from Channel 7, Charlie "Pitbull" Grove.

"Hey, Harry," he yelled over the gate. "You took some running down. How about an exclusive, old buddy."

"Charlie, you piece o' shit," I said. "Get the hell away from here and don't tell anyone you know where I am. If you do..." I left the threat unstated.

He looked mortally wounded. Maybe I was a little too hard on him. He was, after all, not as bad as some of the kids the other channels have running around with mikes in their hands.

"But, Harry—"

"No buts, Charlie." But then a thought entered my mind... *Hey, Harry, you could do a whole lot worse than Charlie. At least you can trust him not to bend your words.*

"Look, Charlie, tell you what: I will give you an exclusive, but here's the deal. Right now, I'm up to my eyes in... something. Let me get through it, and we'll sit down and talk. I'll give you all the time you need... well, within reason, but you've got to keep my location to yourself. Deal?"

He thought about it for a minute, then nodded and said, "Deal, but I need for you to throw me a bone."

I was about to stop him, but...

He held up his hand and said, "No, no, no, Harry. Hear me out. I need to know about Amanda. We're all worried sick about her. How is she, Harry?"

I sighed, nodded, and said, "Okay, here's what I know, and it's not much.

I spent the next couple of minutes bringing him up to date—the short version of what had happened—off camera, of course. I left him with a promise that I would call him. He left looking decidedly pleased with himself.

* * *

I spent the rest of the morning sitting beside Amanda's bed holding her hand, whispering promises I knew I'd probably not be able to keep—but I meant them at the time—and leaving out any mention of what I'd now gotten myself involved in.

What bothered me most about it all was that I made the same promises to myself only a couple of days earlier. *So much for good intentions. Oh well, as Scarlett would say, tomorrow is another day... if I'm lucky.*

Amanda? As far as I could tell, there had been no change. She looked much the same except that the bruises were not quite so dark, and the cuts—held together with butterfly strips—didn't look quite so red. She looked very peaceful, beautiful, and the next thing I knew I was up, on my feet, and out of the room. I was frickin' devastated.

And here I am doing it all again.

I had barely made it through the door into the corridor when I bumped into Dr. Cartwright.

"Hello, Mr. Starke. I was hoping to see you. The front desk told me you were here. You want to know how she is, I suppose. Well, I have some good news for you. First, her condition is stable and improving. We ran an MRI earlier this morning, and the swelling on the right side of her brain is receding quite nicely. I'm going to keep her as-is for the next forty-eight hours and then reassess the situation. If all goes well, and she continues to make progress, I should be able to bring her out of the coma on..." He thought for a moment, then said, "Let's try for Tuesday the 29th. So there, I hope that helps you to feel a little better."

Doc, you have no frickin' idea. You just lifted the Market Street bridge off of my shoulders.

I was so overwhelmed by the good news, I couldn't find the words to thank him. Instead, I grabbed his hand in both of mine and squeezed. I swear the poor man winced.

"Thanks, Doctor," I whispered, barely loud enough for him to hear, then I let go of his hand and, head down, I turned and reentered Amanda's room, sat down beside her, put my face on her stomach and... yeah, I cried. Yeah, that's what I did. I couldn't help it, and you know what, I don't give a damn what you think.

I stayed with her for another hour, then I upped and left to share the good news with August and Rose and... Jade.

* * *

It was just after two-thirty that afternoon when the Uber driver dropped me at the gate. I found August in his office, lately vacated by Jacque. He was hunting and pecking on his old desktop PC.

"Harry," he said, looking up as I entered the room. "How is she, son?"

"She's doing fine... Look, where's Rose. I'd like her to hear it too."

"She's in the bedroom, I think, with the baby. Shall we go and see?"

He stood, and I followed him to their master suite where Rose was seated on the bed holding Jade in her arms. She looked, no they looked... lovely together, like they were mother and daughter. I looked at my father, and I could tell he was moved by the scene, but my dear old dad never was one for sentimentalities, not like me, that's for sure.

"Rose," he said, "Harry has good news."

She looked up at me expectantly. I squatted beside her and held out my arms. She handed the baby to me, and I was gifted with a look from Jade's amazing green eyes and... yes, she smiled up at me. Well, I thought she did. Rose told me later it was just gas that made her look like that... but I still wasn't so sure.

While I held Jade, I told Rose and August what the doctor had said.

Much as I wanted to stay with my daughter, I couldn't; I had a lot to do, and quickly if we were going to pull off what I had in mind that evening. So, reluctantly, I handed her back to Rose and headed down to the basement.

Chapter 13

Friday, May 25, 3pm

Riverview
    I checked in with Rose, then headed down to join the others. They were already there and waiting for me when I arrived in the basement: Tim, Kate, Jacque, and Bob.

"Hey, Harry," Tim said as I took my seat. "Did you see Amanda? How is she?"

"She's doing great, Tim. Dr. Cartwright said he hopes to bring her out of the coma on Tuesday, so she's going to make it."

That statement set off a round of conversation that I won't bore you with. Suffice it to say, the mood in the room, including mine, lifted tremendously.

"Okay," I said, finally, "we have work to do. Let's get to it. Before we do, though, Tim, what have you done about upgrading the security?"

"I need to check, but Jack Thomas should be at the office on Georgia Avenue right now. He's scheduled to come here to Riverview tomorrow and your home on Lookout Mountain on Monday."

"Monday's no good, Tim. I need the house done tomorrow. He'll need to split his crew. Tell him I'll pay for the overtime, but make sure he gets it done. Now, let's talk about Copperhill. Bob, what are your thoughts?"

The mood turned serious. Bob thought for a minute, then said, "You sure you want to do this, Harry? We could have the local sheriff go in instead of us."

"That's not an option," I said. "He'd need to get search warrants, and we have no probable cause. Besides, it would take days, and we don't have that kind of time. We can do it."

I thought for a minute, tapped the tabletop with my fingers, then looked and continued, "Look, they won't be expecting us, so we'll have that advantage. If all goes well, we'll be in and out in less than fifteen minutes."

Bob looked at me, skeptically. "Harry you have no idea what we'll be up against, what these people are capable of. They're ex-Rangers, for God's sake."

"Yes, but how many could there be? Tim says most of Christmas' assets are deployed. Look, I'm not planning on starting a war. I've had enough of that to last me the rest of my days. So," I said, "we go in, we grab Joe if he's there, and we get out. It shouldn't be too difficult."

"Harry," Bob said, shaking his head. "You can't be serious. Just the two of us, you and me? We don't have the manpower."

"Three," Kate said. "I'm in."

"The hell you are—"

"Shut up, Harry," she said. "I said I'm in. Joe is my case. I'm in. No arguments."

I shook my head, frustrated. Hell no, more than that. I was scared; I didn't want to put Kate at risk, but knowing her as I did—

"What's the matter, Harry," she asked, with a mocking smile on her lips. "It's easy, right? You just said so. In and out in fifteen minutes, you said. You did mean that, didn't you?"

"Whew," I sighed. "Okay, but you'll do as you're damn well told, capiche?"

She nodded, still smiling. Oh yeah, I knew that look, and right then I knew I was wasting my time arguing with her.

"Geez," Bob said. "That's all we need. Okay, but we still don't have enough—"

"How about T.J.?" Kate asked

"Oh no," Jacque said. "Not him, he's crazy, looney toons."

"Kate's right," Bob said. "And so are you, Jacque. Crazy? For sure, but he's just the kind of crazy we need for a job like this. And there's nobody else, so we don't have a choice."

"Perhaps we don't," I said, "but he does. Look, I'll talk to him. If he agrees, he's in." *Ha, that's a joke. He'll agree all right. Jacque is right: the man's a loon.*

"Okay," I said, "if we count T.J. in, that's four—"

"Five," Tim interrupted me.

"Six," Jacque said.

"Oh no, no, no, no," I said. "That's not happening. Tim, you couldn't fight your way out of a wet paper bag, and you..." I paused and glared at Jacque. "Not one chance in hell, young lady."

"Okay," Tim said. "I didn't say I was going into the compound, but you guys can't go in either, not blind. You don't know the territory and—"

"And you do?" I interrupted him. "*No!*"

He grinned happily up at me, stood, and said, "If you'll give me a minute, please?"

Then he went to the door and out to where his van was parked. He opened the rear door of the van, clambered inside, and then backed out again dragging a large and obviously heavy metal case and, using both hands, hauled it inside.

He set it down on the floor and unsnapped the three metal latches, opened the lid, stood upright, and stepped back so that we all could see what was inside.

"Holy crap," I said, looking down at the biggest damn drone I'd ever seen outside of the military. "How the hell much did that cost me? You did it again, you little... I told you to ask before you go spending my money."

He shrugged. "Well, it's a... it's a hexacopter. It's not the most expensive one on the market—the entire package was less than ten thousand—but it does have reasonably good optics. I chose this model because of its extended flight time. I added a couple of upgrades, modified the power supply, basically trading payload for power and endurance. I also added a double gimbal assembly, two extra cameras —night vision and infrared—and I have four extra sets of batteries and one or two other bits and pieces."

I glared at him.

"We had to have one, Harry," he said, plaintively. "And you know only too well, you get what you pay for. This unit is the absolute best choice for what you do—or might do. No self-respecting agency should be without one. Should they?"

I stared at him in wonder. Sometimes the boy was beyond even my comprehension. How many times had I wanted to chastise him? I'd lost count, but it never happened. All it took was a look from those soft, puppy dog eyes and I was lost. But those eyes... Oh, they were so misleading: Tim was a wolf and as crafty as a fox, and my agency was his own personal hen house. That being so, he got away with not quite murder, but close enough. I just shook my head, exasperated.

He got the message, smiled and said, "Good, you see what I mean, right? So I'll be there, in the van, flying the drone. I'll be your eye in the sky. You *will* have to be in and out quickly though. Even with the upgrade, even with *my* upgrades, this baby is good for only about fifty-five minutes of flight time before I have to recharge the batteries or change them."

I looked at Bob, questioningly. He smiled and nodded.

"Okay, you're in, but—" I began.

"An' what about me?" Jacque asked, in full Jamaican mode. "I can help Tim and—"

"Okay, okay," I said, "but only in the van with Tim." *It ain't gonna happen. I'll have to figure out a way to keep her out of it. But keep her out of it I will.*

"Jacque, I need you to call T.J.," I said, "and have him join us."

She nodded, smiling, and headed back up the stairs to make the call. T.J. arrived thirty minutes later.

T.J. Bron is something of an enigma. Only a few months ago, he was on the streets, homeless, and ready to do away with himself. But while he was preparing to off himself, he stumbled upon the body of a young woman in an alley at the rear of the Sorbonne.

Kate was the investigating officer. What she saw in him... ah, who knows. Whatever it was, she took him under her wing and brought him to me. Turns out he's a war hero, a highly decorated Vietnam vet —two tours, the first beginning in 1968 and then again in 1972—an ex-Marine down on his luck...

Nope, luck had nothing to do with it. He was the victim of a shady bank officer who accused him of stealing from the bank: he didn't do it. He did some time, and it ruined him. He lost everything: wife, kids, home. He has a degree in accounting, and at the time, I happened to be looking for a financial investigator. Bearing in mind the man's military record, including his earning of a Silver Star and two Purple Hearts, I figured I could take a chance and hire him. So I did. Jacque found him a place to live, and here we are.

At sixty-eight, T.J. is way older than the rest of my team. However, he's also in way better shape than any of them, perhaps with the exception of Bob and, on a good day, me; this being due to a rigorous workout regimen he started the day Jacque took him in hand and that still continues.

T.J. is six feet, 190 pounds, with white hair and a heavily lined, deeply tanned face. What I didn't know when I hired him was that he's crazy... No, I don't mean he's insane, far from it, but he is absolutely fearless, has a wicked taste for violence, and will kill without hesitation, as I found out only in the last couple of days or so. So yes, I had my doubts about involving him, but I also knew he would be highly pissed off if I didn't.

While we were waiting for him, I spent some time alone, thinking about what I needed to do, trying to formulate a plan. The problem was, as Tim had so rightly pointed out, we didn't know the property or the surrounding terrain. In the end, I decided to keep it simple and go for the direct approach.

So, when T.J. arrived at around four-thirty, we, the six of us, were seated together in a circle around a small card table in the basement. I told him to grab a chair and join us.

"T.J.," I said, "when I hired you, it was never my plan to involve you in what can only be called black ops, but—"

"Yeah?" he said, leaning forward on his chair, his elbows on his knees, his hands clasped together in front of him. He was wearing a black Tee, jeans and Nike sneakers. He was also carrying the VP9 I'd given to him only days before in a holster on his right hip. He looked like an aging gangster, but looks, as they say, can be deceptive.

Anyway, I had his attention.

"Jacque's told you what's happened, to my uncle Joe, right?"

"She did. Someone grabbed him. So, we gonna go get him?"

And there it was. I knew I didn't even need to ask the question, T.J. was in.

"We are, if he's there. We think we know who has him, but where on the property we're not sure. So, we'll just have to cross that bridge when and if we need to."

"Harry," Kate said, quietly. "We have to keep it clean. If we go in there, there can be no killing."

"I told you, Kate: I'm not looking to start a war. All I want is to get Joe out. That's all I want, okay?"

She didn't look okay, but she nodded, and I continued.

"Tim, bring up the satellite images please."

He swiveled his seat to face his array, and we waited while he tapped the keyboard until we had a bird's eye view of the Gypsum Pond area on one of the big monitors.

"Okay, this is the latest recording, right?" I asked.

"Yes," Tim said, checking the time stamp. "It's thirteen minutes ago."

"What about the depression? Any idea how deep it might be?"

"Not really. It's still early, but eighteen inches, maybe two feet. I'll know better when the satellite makes its next pass, in about seventy-five minutes."

Damn, I thought. *It's not deep enough... Sheesh, it will have to be; it's all we've got!*

I looked at my watch, then said, "So, around six o'clock?"

He nodded.

I thought for a minute, then said, "We have to make preparations, so we have to make a decision, now. We'll go tonight, late. I want to be there no earlier than midnight. Tim, you'll take your van and the drone. You can fly that thing, right?"

"Oh... yeah!" He grinned and poked at his glasses.

"At night?"

"Yeppy!"

I shook my head, amazed, and continued, "I'll take Bob, Kate, and T.J. to this point here." I pointed with a pool cue. "Then we'll take this track and park here, in the trees. It's about as close as we can get to the depression without being seen by the cameras, about a hundred feet. There's a camera on the corner, here." I pointed. "We wait for it to make its sweep and turn in the other direction. At that exact moment, we make a run for the depression. We should be able to make it before the camera reverses its sweep. If the depression is deep enough, we should be okay."

I paused, stared at the screen, and then said, "Tim, you'll park somewhere on the road in this area here, out of sight, but somewhere where you can fly that thing."

"Wait," Tim said. "You'll all have body cams and earbuds, so we can see and hear everything you do, and I can communicate with you."

"We?" I said. "You said we."

"Yes," he said. "Me and Jacque. I'm going to need her to monitor the body cams while I fly the drone."

Oh hell, there goes that idea!

I glanced at Jacque. She smiled sweetly at me. *Damn!*

"I'm thinking," I said, "that if we can get to this point here, we can—"

"Okay," Bob interrupted me. "We make it to the trench, then we can what?"

"We blow the fence and head for this building, here. I figure from the vehicles parked outside that it might be the office. We subdue the occupants—there's no point in expecting them to talk. Then... we look for Joe. We grab him and get out of there."

"And that's your plan?" Bob asked, skeptically.

"It is," I snapped, and immediately regretted it. "Look, I don't know what's there any more than you do. We don't have the time or the wherewithal to do a proper recon. We're going to have to play it as we find it. If you have a better idea, I'd like to hear it."

He shook his head. "Nope."

"Okay, I said. "It's now five-thirty-five. We'll meet back here at eight. In the meantime, we'll get something to eat—I think Rose has made sandwiches. Tim, you and Jacque get everything you need together and make sure it's all working, especially the drone. Bob, we'll need weapons, body armor and something to blow the fence. That means a trip to the office. You and Kate can handle that, right?"

He nodded.

"Good," I continued. "There are some half-pound packs of C-4 in the gun room. A couple should be enough... make it four, just in case. T.J., you'll stay here with me. Any questions, anybody? No? Good. Let's go eat."

Chapter 14

Saturday, May 26, 12:05am

Copperhill

By eight o'clock that evening, we were all back together in the basement. By ten, all was ready, except that we still had to get into the body armor.

Bob and Kate had returned loaded with gear, including four Sig Sauer M400 AR15s. *I'm not too sure about letting T.J. loose with one of those*, I thought, *but what the hell... finish what you start, right?*

They also brought just about every handgun we owned and enough ammunition to start a small war. Bob never did anything by halves.

I donned my lightweight, Tactical Scorpion vest—ceramic plates front and back—my VP9 in a holster on my right hip along with three extra mags, plus two more for AR, Tim's body cam and earbuds, and I was ready to go.

I looked at my companions: Bob and Kate's faces were devoid of expression; T.J., however, was grinning. He looked like a frickin' crocodile about to devour a duck. *Oh hell*, I thought, *I really don't know about this.*

I turned to Tim. "You ready, son?"

He looked pale, but he nodded.

"Jacque, you sure about this?"

She also nodded, a determined look on her face.

"Kate... you're sure you want to do this?"

She nodded, grimly, looking like a real badass in her tactical gear and with an AR tucked under her arm.

"Okay," I said, turning to the already open door where Bob had parked his Hummer alongside Tim's van. "Let's go."

* * *

We arrived at the first waypoint on Highway 64 at eleven-fifty and turned left onto what must have once been a mine access road. It was still in good condition, which meant it was still in use, probably by CSC. We would leave Tim and Jacque parked just off the road under cover of some trees, and we waited while Tim opened the rear doors of his van, readied the drone, checked all of the monitors to make sure we were all in communication, and then he launched the drone. I was surprised by how quiet it was. The six lifters whispered as the machine left the ground and rose quickly until I could no longer see it.

I watched Tim as he operated the controls. He looked up at me, a huge smile lighting up his face, then he gave me a thumbs up, climbed back into the van and closed the doors.

"Sound and video check, please," I heard Tim say through the earbuds.

One by one, we checked in, then Tim said, "Okay, you're fit to go. I have video feed from the drone. You want to see?"

"Yes, but we don't have time—fifty-five minutes, didn't you say?"

"Right. You should go. The drone should be over the compound in three minutes. Harry, let me know when you're in position. Well, you don't really need to. I'll be able to see you, but—"

"I'll check in, Tim," I said, dryly, interrupting him.

Five minutes later, we were out of the Hummer and lying prone under the trees at the edge of the open space in front of the compound and... damn it, I couldn't see the depression. Which really wasn't surprising, because Tim had estimated it to be two feet deep at best, and some six feet wide.

"Tim, are you receiving me?" I whispered.

"Yup, and I see all four of your heat signatures. I can also see a lot of signatures in three of the six buildings. I estimate at least sixty, maybe seventy occupants, most of them in the big building."

"Holy cow," Bob said. "Are you serious?"

"I am. Are you still a go?"

I looked sideways at them; they all three nodded. Bob and Kate were grim. T.J. had his teeth bared, his eyes half-closed; it was a look of total concentration. *Geez, he's a scary looking bastard.*

"Yeah, we're still a go," I said. "Where the hell is that trench?"

"It's to your right. You should be able to see the corner light post from where you are. Can you?"

"Yes, I see it."

"Okay, you need to head for that. I timed the camera. It's on a fifty-second sweep cycle, a little less than I'd hoped, but you can make it. On my mark. Get ready... Okay, go, go, go."

And we upped, and we ran. It was the longest hundred and sixty feet of my life, but we made it, just in time.

I threw myself into the trench—it was indeed about six feet wide but a little deeper than Tim's estimate, maybe thirty inches; maybe a little less, but better than I'd hoped. Kate landed on top of me, Bob a dozen feet further back, and T.J., wouldn't you know it, was fifteen feet closer to the fence than I was.

"Okay, okay," I heard Tim in my ear. "I see you. Get down, *now!* Okay, it's swinging back again. What's the plan now?"

"Tim, and the rest of you," I said, "listen up. Tim, I need you to watch the camera. Give me the word, and I'll make a run for the light post. If I can get there without being seen, I should be out of the camera's sightline. I'll set a charge and bring the post down; the camera and the fence will come down with it, I hope. We'll head for the nearest building and gain access. Then hell, who knows? T.J., for God's sake, no shooting unless..." *Oh, hell. What's the use?*

"T.J.," I said. "You hear me? Answer me, damn it."

"Take it easy, boss. I hear you. No shooting unless... Don't worry, I got it, and your back."

It wasn't much, but I had to live with it.

"Okay, Tim," I said. "What about the guards?"

"I don't see any. You ready, Harry? On my mark... *Go!*"

I jumped out of the trench and ran for the post and dropped to the floor at its base. It was round, made of steel, hollow, I hoped, and the fence—horizontal steel bars with thick steel wire net between them—was anchored to it on both sides. Beyond that, maybe seventy-five feet away was the nearest of the six buildings. It still figured it might be an office, but the side and rear that I could see had no windows or doors.

I looked at the light pole, shook my head, and wondered, *Geez, it's too fricking big. A half-pound might not be enough. Better use two.*

"*Harry!*" Tim yelled in my ear. "*Get down.* Someone's just exited the building and is coming toward you."

Holy shit! There was no cover. What could I do? I dropped flat on my face, my hand on my VP9, and I lay still, waited, and watched.

He came into sight, walking slowly. He was wearing combat camo and carrying what looked like an assault rifle. *One of the guards.*

I eased the VP9 out of its holster, took a deep breath, and steeled myself for what I was sure was about to come: it didn't. He stopped, stood for a moment, looked around, let the rifle hang from its sling, and lit a cigarette, and then turned and slowly walked back out of sight. *Whew!*

I lay still for several moments, barely breathing. Then I rolled over onto my back, slipped the VP9 into its holster, and removed two half-pound slabs of C-4 from the pockets of the jacket I was wearing over my vest, and set them to the base of the pole. I wired them together with an electronic detonator and waited for Tim to give me the word. A couple of minutes later, I was back in the trench with the others.

"Ready?" I asked, looking round at them. They all nodded. "Tim, how many are there inside that building?"

"Four, that I can see."

"Right," I said. "The fence comes down, and we hit that building, hard. Got it?"

They had. I took a deep breath.

I pushed the trigger and the world ended, or so it seemed at the time, so loud was the explosion the ground shook. In fact, what happened was: the two packs of C-4 sheared the pole at its base, bringing it down along with the camera and at least fifty feet of steel fence. *Hmm, a half-pound would have been plenty after all.*

"*Let's go!*" I shouted and jumped to my feet, running as hard as I could go for the front of the building. I covered the distance in no more than ten seconds, maybe less. Even so, I barely made it before the door opened. I slammed into it without stopping, blasting it wide open, smashing it into the two guards that were about to exit.

I careened on through the doorway, almost falling over one of the guards; Bob was right on my ass, followed by... No, not T.J., by Kate.

"*Drop your weapons!*" I shouted at the two men still on their feet, my AR at the ready. They were taken completely by surprise. For a few seconds, they stood as if they were frozen, then their weapons clattered onto the concrete floor.

"*Good,*" I was still shouting. "*Now, get down, on the floor, quickly, and stay still, all of you.*" And, slowly, the two men, never taking their eyes off me, lowered themselves to join the other two. *Sheesh, so far so good.*

"Bob," I said, "strap 'em up. Kate, you and T.J. head for that next building and see what you can find, and for God's sake be careful, especially you." I glared at T.J.; he grinned back at me, and they took off.

"Tim, give Kate and T.J. a heads-up, okay?"

He said he would, and I heard him giving them directions.

Aftermath

"There are four people in there. Wait, wait... T.J., two just exited at the front and are heading your way, running. *Watch out. They're almost on top of you.*"

I waited, listening. Neither T.J. nor Kate answered. Then I heard a volley of automatic fire, followed by the steady pop-pop-pop of an AR15 and the heavier bam-bam-bam of a handgun.

"Oh shit, Kate. What's happening. Answer me damn it."

"It's okay," she came back. "We have it under control. They're both down."

"Oh shit," I yelled. "Are they dead?"

"No. Not yet anyway. T.J. clipped one in the arm; he went down. He's yelling like an idiot, the guard is, not T.J. The other guy fell over him and hit his head. He's out cold. We're about to enter the building. You all okay?"

I told her I was, and then while I kept our four guards at gunpoint, Bob strapped them up with heavy cable ties. That done, I sat on the desk and looked down at them.

"Harry," Tim said. "You have twenty minutes more before I have to recall the drone. How much longer are you going to be?"

"Hell, I don't know. Do what you gotta do, Tim. We'll cope."

I turned my attention to the guards.

"Which one of you is in charge?" I asked.

No one answered.

I sighed, shook my head, and said, "Okay, if that's the way you want to play it. I'll ask one more time. If I don't get an answer, one of you will lose your balls. Now, who's in charge?"

"He is." It was the smallest of the four who answered.

"You?" I said, leaning forward. "You're holding a friend of mine, a man, an older man with special needs. I want him. Where is he?"

"I don't know."

I slammed the barrel of the AR15 down on his knee cap as hard as I could. I heard the cap crack, and he howled like a wolf in the night, and then he passed out. *Damn!*

"Now," I said, quietly. "Who wants to go next? Come on, one of you, answer me. I don't have all night."

I looked at the small guy, the one who'd given up his boss.

"You," I said, "where is he?"

"He—there ain't—"

I slammed the gun down on his knee. I almost missed; clipped the side of it.

"Ow, oh God. Oh, ow."

I shoved the muzzle of the gun hard into his package.

"Oof! Screw you."

I nodded, removed the mag from the AR, cleared the chamber, reinserted the mag and slowly eased back the bolt until it cocked and locked, and let it slam back into position, loading a new round into the chamber.

Again, I stabbed the muzzle into his package, my finger on the trigger, and I looked into his eyes, my eyebrows raised; the question was plain enough.

"Go to hell!"

I nodded, looked him in the eye and said, "The magic number is three," and I began to count: "One... two..."

He closed his eyes and, for a moment, I thought he was going to tough it out, but he didn't.

"He's in the next building. There's a room at the back."

"Kate, can you hear me. Joe's in your building—in a room at the back."

"Okay, I hear you."

"Okay, we're heading your way," I said.

I looked down at my four prisoners. They weren't going anywhere.

"Let's go," I said to Bob, and I ducked out of the door; Bob followed.

"Harry," Tim said in my ear. "Someone needs to take a look in that big building. There are a lot of heat signatures."

"Okay, but we have to get Joe out of here first."

By the time we arrived, Kate had already found Joe. They had him locked in a small—no tiny—room at the back of the second building. T.J. had overpowered the third guard, and Kate had smashed the flimsy lock with the butt of her AR.

The main door into the building was wide open, and T.J. was just inside holding three guards at gunpoint. Two of them, a guy with a knot on his head the size of an egg, and a young woman aged about twenty-five, were on the floor with their hands strapped together behind their backs. A third man was lying against the wall in a corner of the room. His face the color of dirty rice, he was holding his arm, trying to stop the blood leaking out between his fingers. An Israeli Tavor assault rifle lay on a table close to where T.J. was standing, along with another fully automatic rifle, two 10mm Glock 29s, a Glock 17, and a Glock 43, which I assumed must belong to the woman.

I left Bob with T.J. and joined Kate in the back room where she was trying to sooth an extremely upset Joe. He was shaking like a leaf and tears were streaming down his cheeks.

"Harry," he yelled and jumped to his feet and flung his arms around my neck. "They were mean to me, Harry. They said they were going to do bad things to me. They said they were going to cut my pecker off. You won't let them cut it off, will you, Harry?" he sobbed.

"Hush, Joe," I said, holding him tight. "I'm here now. No one's going to hurt you, I promise. Now calm down. We're going to get you out of here."

"I'm scared, Harry. Please don't let them cut me."

"I won't let them cut you. Now let's get out of here."

I let go of him, turned him around, put my arm around his shoulder, and steered him out into the larger room.

"It was him," Joe said, pointing to the guard lying in the corner. "He was going to cut my pecker off. He said so, lots of times."

"It's okay, Joe," I said. "He's not going to cut anybody. Now look,

I need for you to help me. I need for you to do exactly what I tell you. Will you do that for me?"

He nodded, tearfully.

"Listen to me very carefully. T.J. here, is going to take you to my car where you and he will wait for me, okay?"

"No, no, no, Harry. I want you to stay with me, pleeease!"

"Joe, listen to me. I'll only be a couple of minutes, but I have to do this. You're safe now. Go with T.J. to the car. I think there's some candy in the glove box."

At that, he brightened up a little but was still reluctant to leave me.

T.J., however, much to my surprise, took his hand and said, "C'mon, Joe. Let's get that candy before the others steal it all."

And that was all it took. T.J. led him off into the night.

"Harry," Kate said. "Over there."

I looked at where she was pointing. The building was bigger than I'd first thought, maybe fifty by thirty. On the far side, two rows of trestle tables, two of which were piled high with plastic-wrapped packages. On the second row of tables were several dozen plastic trays, two sets of scales, and a small wrapping machine. We were in a damned illegal drug factory.

"Shit," Bob said, "I knew it. That son of a bitch is importing drugs for distribution. I'm gonna frickin' burn it—"

"No," I said, interrupting him. "We'll leave it for the law."

"The law," he almost exploded. "This is government property, remember? No, Harry, this is my call. Get the hell out of here and let me do what I gotta do."

I hesitated. *Aw, what the hell do I care?* I thought. *If we leave it... who knows what will happen to it. If they were able to get the word out that we were here, Christmas' men might already be on their way.*

"Okay, do it. There's a fuel tank with a pump on it outside, to the left, between the two buildings. Make sure you get them safely out first." I nodded at the three guards. "We'll go and see what the hell they're up to in that other building."

So I left him to it, and Kate and I exited the building and headed north toward what looked like a small, commercial chicken rearing house.

The main door was at the center of the building. It was locked; a padlock through a hasp on the outside. From what I could see, I figured it was there more to keep people in, rather than out. One hard kick and the hasp tore out of the frame.

We stepped back, guns at the ready, and waited: nothing. I stepped forward and cautiously eased the door outward and open. I held my breath, listened, still nothing, then: *Was that a whimper?*

Yes, that's what it was.

We stepped inside, and I got the shock of my life. In both directions, the far wall was lined with cages. There had to be at least fifty of them. The interior was lit with a string of tungsten light bulbs, each about twenty feet apart, that stretched all the way down the center of the building from one end to the other. In the dim light, it was just possible to see that some of the cages were occupied: mostly women of varying ages, some Asian, some Hispanic, some as young as eight or ten. I didn't count them, but I estimated there were at least fifty, with room enough for three times that number.

And then they started to shout and scream.

"Oh, my, God," Kate whispered. "What the hell is this place?"

"Looks like they're into trafficking as well as drugs," I said. "Now we don't have a choice. We have to call the authorities. Go stop Bob from firing that building."

But it was too late, just as she stepped out of the door, there was a loud whoosh and then an explosion as the windows blew out of the building.

"Tim," I said. "You there?"

"I'm here, Harry. I had to pull the drone. It was running out of power. What do you need?"

"I need you to give us time to get clear, then call the local sheriff's department and get them up here. There are at least fifty women and kids caged in that main building. Use a burner phone, and don't for

God's sake let 'em know who we are. Understand? Good. Have T.J. and Joe got there yet? They have? Good. Wrap things up and make ready to get out of there. Give us fifteen minutes. If we're not there by then, make the call, and go. No ifs or buts. You make the call. You understand?"

"But, Harry—"

"Damn it, Tim. Do as you're frickin' told, just once, will you?"

He said he would, and I went after Kate. I found them together, standing over the three prisoners. Bob had dragged them out into the open—watching the building burn.

"Hey," I said. "Get a grip. This ain't the 4th of July. Bob, those three are okay, so let's go check on the four guards in the first building and then get the hell out of here."

Tim was still waiting for us when we arrived. I should have kicked his ass for disobeying me, but he hit me with those big puppy dog eyes, and I didn't have the heart. Besides, we needed to get out of there, and fast, and we did, making it back to Riverview without incident.

Chapter 15

May 26, 3am

Riverview
As I said, we made the journey back to Riverview without incident. Joe fell asleep in the back of the car. He didn't wake until I eased him out of the car; that was at just after three o'clock that morning.

We'd been on the road for maybe thirty minutes when I suddenly had a thought, *I haven't seen any first responders... Hell, I haven't even heard any sirens...*

"Bob," I said. "Stop the car. I need to talk to Tim."

He pulled the Hummer off the road; Tim pulled in behind us.

I exited the vehicle and walked back to the van, signaling for him to roll down the window.

"You didn't make the call, did you?" I asked.

"Call? What call—"

"911," I said, interrupting him, shaking my head. "Make it now, airhead. Do it now, and then toss the phone."

"What was that about?" Bob asked, shifting into drive.

"Just Tim being Tim," I said.

* * *

August and Rose were at the front door, waiting. No, I'm not going into the reunion, or August's effusive stream of thanks and appreciation to my team and me. Let's just say it was something of a tearjerker. Even T.J. looked a little affected. Anyway, some fifteen minutes after we arrived, Rose had him, Joe, tucked safely in bed in one of the spare rooms.

The rest of us? We arranged to meet at nine the following morning and, with the exception of T.J., who hit the couch, they all went home; Bob providing transport for Kate.

Me? Rose wouldn't let me visit Jade, so I too went to bed, but sleep didn't come easy. Once again, the demons of the night haunted the dark corners of my bedroom. Sleep did come, eventually, but it was restless, fraught with dreams, not quite nightmares, but disturbing, nonetheless.

I woke the following morning, at just after seven, feeling like I'd just run a marathon. I lay there for a minute, staring at the ceiling, breathing deeply, hoping... what? Damned if I could remember, so I rolled out of bed and went out through the sliding glass doors, straight to the pool, dived in and swam laps for the next twenty minutes. Ten more minutes and a quick shower later, I was feeling better than I had for more than a week. We had Joe back, and Amanda was improving. But something I couldn't quite get a grip on was niggling inside my head.

Rose was already up and about, and so was Joe.

I sat down at the kitchen table, and Rose handed me a huge mug of steaming coffee. August was nowhere to be seen. Joe, seemingly without a care in the world, was calmly eating a bowl of cereal.

I sat quietly for a minute, enjoying that first cup of the day, when I remembered that T.J. was in the living room

I poured coffee and took it to him. He wasn't there; his clothes were. *What the hell?*

"Hey, Harry. Hope you slept as well as I did."

I turned and stared at him.

He was coming in through the door wearing a towel wrapped around his waist, another in his hands toweling at his head. *Geez, the man's built like a weightlifter.*

"So," he said. "I hope you don't mind. I heard you in the kitchen, so I grabbed a shower in your bathroom, and boy did I need it. I was stinkin', Harry. Listen, I got to go get a change of clothes. I'll be back by nine, all right?"

I nodded, realized I was still holding his coffee, and said, "Sure. You want this before you go?"

"Oh yeah. Gimme."

He took it from me and swallowed half of it in a single gulp, then set the mug on the coffee table, dropping the towel from around his waist. You can believe me when I tell you he really was well built. *Time I wasn't here.*

"Okay, T.J., I'll see you back here at nine. Wait a minute—what's that?"

He looked down at his genitals. "What the hell do you think it is?"

"Damn it, T.J., not your dick, you idiot, that cut on your thigh?"

"Oh, that. It's nothing."

"It doesn't look like nothing to me. It looks like a damn bullet crease. Were you hit?"

"I told you. It's nothing. Just a clip, is all. That damned guard got lucky, or not, before I put him down. I never even felt it. I washed it good and soused it with Neosporin. It'll be gone in a couple of days... And talkin' about the guard I shot, you'll note that I did as you asked. I didn't kill him. I should have, but I didn't. Ah, you worry too much, Harry. Now get outa here and let me get dressed."

"You should have told me," I said, but I did as he asked and headed back to the kitchen and more coffee... and eggs and bacon... and toast.

I ate the breakfast and decided to spend what little time was left before the team arrived out on the patio where I could think. I hadn't been there more than ten minutes when August appeared.

"Harry, do you mind if I join you?"

"No, not at all."

He sat down on the bench beside me, put his hand on my knee and, for a moment, said nothing; he just sat and stared at the pool. Me? I just let him be.

"Harry," he said, finally. "You know I can never thank you enough for what you did."

"Stop it, Dad. It's not necessary." Dad? I didn't call him that very often, but somehow it just seemed right.

He squeezed my knee. "Yes, it is, but I know how you are, and I won't embarrass you further. Just know that... I love you, son."

Now that was a rare one and a huge surprise. August wasn't one for endearments.

"I know," I said. "I love you too. Okay, now that we've gotten that out of the way, I can tell there's something on your mind. What is it?"

He was silent for a minute, then said, "It's not over, is it?"

I knew exactly what he meant. "No, probably not."

"So, where do we go from here?"

"We sit tight, and wait," I said. "We have what we wanted. Christmas doesn't, and he's lost his bargaining chip. You haven't dropped the suit and, if I know you, you won't. So, he'll figure out some other way to apply pressure. And there's something else: last night, we destroyed several million dollars' worth of drugs. You can bet he'll be looking for payback for that too... It's not over."

"So that's it? We just sit around and wait."

I nodded. "That's all we can do. It's his move."

We sat for several minutes more, discussing hypothetical scenarios and even more hypothetical options. Yes, it was a waste of time, but I think it helped my father; not a lot, but some.

It was at that point Joe decided to join us.

"Hi Harry," he said, parking himself happily down beside his brother.

"Hi Joe," I replied. "How are you feeling today?"

"I feel good, Harry. And thank you for not letting that man cut off my pecker."

Oh shit, now that's really funny. Just look at August's face.

"You're welcome, Joe," I said.

I couldn't help but smile. August, however, wasn't smiling at all. He was aghast.

"Would you like to explain?" he asked.

And I did.

"Oh, my God," he said, quietly. "What are we dealing with?"

"Good question," I said. "I think we'll know soon enough."

"Augi," Joe said. "I want to see my friends. Can I go home, please?"

$$* * *$$

"Those guys were not Rangers, Harry," Bob said.

It was already after ten in the morning and we, the six of us, had been discussing the events of the previous evening for more than an hour.

"It was too easy," Bob continued. "They gave up too easily. Rangers never give up, not while they're still breathing."

"If they weren't Rangers, then what?" I asked.

"I'd say they were new recruits." He paused, then continued, "Probably ex-military. Army, maybe, but not special forces, and certainly not Rangers. And there were only what, seven of them? I always figured Nick was into drugs, but trafficking, that's something I wouldn't have thought he would do." He paused, thought for a minute, then said, "I wonder if that's what Walker was carrying in that box van. If it was, he's sure getting cocky in his old age, is our Nick."

"Okay, that aside, you know the man," I said. "What do you think his next move will be?"

He didn't need to think about it; he already had.

"With Joe now out of his clutches," he said, "Christmas has lost his leverage, so now he has only one option: he has to go after the principal, August. The only way to stop August is to kill him, and Nick won't hesitate to do just that. I'd say he'll come after us, hard, in force, and not with recruits. We can expect the real deal, and sooner rather than later."

I looked around the group. With one exception the expressions on their faces were serious. The exception? I don't need to tell you. T.J. was sitting comfortably, leaning back in his chair, arms folded, a half-smile on his lips.

I can't let them do this, I thought. *Someone's going to die, and I can't let it be one of them.*

"Okay," I said, in a tone that I hoped brooked no arguments. "You guys go home. It's over for you... No, don't. I've seen enough death these last couple of years. I'm not going to lose any of you. Go. I said go... *Now!*"

They didn't move, not one of them. All five of them just continued to sit there, staring at me, unblinking. *Ahhh shit!*

"Come on, guys," I said, softly. "You know I can't let you do this."

"It don't look like you have much say in it, boss," T.J. said. "I know that I, for one, am in it to the end. I owe you, but that aside, I ain't had this much fun since I left Nam."

"These are not gang-bangers we'll be dealing with," I said. "Christmas will send professional soldiers, Army Rangers, for God's sake. We can't fight that kind of power. There aren't enough of us, and we're not trained for it. You could die, all of you."

I paused, waited for someone to say something. No one did.

"T.J.?" I asked.

"Like I told you, boss. I'm stayin'."

"Kate?" I asked, already knowing the answer.

She merely nodded.

I sighed. "Bob?"

"You need to ask?"

"No," I said, quietly. "Jacque?"

"Yes. You know it."

I looked at Tim. He grinned back at me, pushed his glasses further up the bridge of his nose, and nodded enthusiastically.

"I can't let you do it, Tim," I said.

"Ah, but you have to. You need me," he said. "Information is your best weapon, without it, you're blind. You can try and keep me out, but you know I rarely ever take any notice of anything you say. You've told me so yourself, many times. So, you might as well give it up. Like it or not, I'm in."

I looked at each one of them in turn. I couldn't believe that these people would so willingly put their lives on the line for me. Suddenly, I was more choked up than I had ever been, even at Amanda's bedside. *Oh crap. What the hell do I do now?*

I pursed my lips, trying not to show any emotion, then said in a voice that I know must have betrayed me, "So, that's it then, you're sure?"

They all nodded.

I nodded, bit my bottom lip, sucked on it, closed my eyes, thought, made up my mind and said, "Okay then. Now we wait. The ball is now, as they say, in Nick Christmas' court. We can't do anything until we know which way he'll jump."

"We can't do that, Harry," Bob said. "If I know Nick, he'll come in quick and hot, no warning."

"Bob," I said. "I hope to hell you're wrong."

Fortunately, he was. At noon precisely, just as we all sat down to eat lunch, August's phone began to vibrate on the tabletop.

He picked it up, looked at the screen, then at me and said, "No caller ID."

"Answer it. Put it on speaker. Tim, go do your thing. I want to know who it is and where he is."

Tim jumped up and ran to the stairs. August answered the phone.

"Hello."

"Well played, August, or should I say Harry?" the voice was heavily distorted.

Nobody said a word, we all waited.

"Cat got your tongue, August?"

"What do you want, Christmas?" August asked.

"Christmas? What are you talking about? No, I don't want Christmas. What I do want is for you to drop the lawsuit against CSC... Oh, that Christmas. Hahaha. You think this is Nick. He has nothing to do with this. Think again, August."

"No, you think again, whoever you are," August said. "I will not drop the suit."

"Oh, now that's really too bad. I was hoping we could end this thing amicably, but it seems you're not willing to cooperate. Well, I'd like you to take a minute and think about it, and to reconsider. You can't win, August. You can die for what you think is right, and so can your loved ones, but you can't win. I will win. I always do."

"Go to hell," August said.

"Now that really wasn't nice, August. Do you have me on speaker? Yes, of course you do. How's your wife doing, Harry? She's in Erlanger, I believe. Room 3007, as I recall."

My blood ran cold.

"Harry?" he said. "Are you there? Haha, yes, of course you are. I do hope she's feeling better. *August*," the voice hardened, "drop it. Do it today. You have twenty-four hours. If you don't, a lot of people are going to get hurt. And you? Well, that won't matter, because you won't be around to settle the suit, much less take it to trial."

The phone went dead.

The room was quiet. We all just sat there, staring at the silent phone on the table.

"So," I said, finally breaking the silence. "Now we know. Bob, you think that was Christmas, or are we dealing with someone else, someone he's working for?"

"It was him all right," Bob said. "He was just covering his ass.

Harry, we're in serious trouble. He just threatened your entire family. August, I know you don't—"

"Forget it, Bob," August said.

Bob nodded and looked at me.

I shook my head, resignedly. Bob just shrugged.

It was at that moment that Tim came bounding into the room, "Hey, y'all, I got him, but it will do you no good. It was a burner. When he hung up, I lost it. He must have removed and destroyed the chip. Harry, he was less than a quarter mile away on Hixson Pike."

I was stunned, but on thinking about it, I wasn't really surprised. If it were me, that's exactly what I would have done: fear is a great motivator.

"I don't suppose there's any point going after him, is there?" Kate said, then answered her own question. "No, I suppose not. We don't even know what we're looking for. He's long gone."

"So, what do we do now?" Jacque sounded worried.

"You do what Harry said," August said, "and go home. You heard what Christmas—if that's who it was—said. People will die."

"Yeah," T.J. said, "they sure as hell will."

"Not on my account," August said.

"So, you'll drop it, then?" I asked.

He glared at me. "No!"

I shook my head. "Okay, August's right. It's over. Go home. Now!"

No one moved.

"Oh, for God's sake, people," I said. "This isn't a game. We cannot, can't possibly go up against a small frickin' professional army. I'll get August, Rose and the baby out of here, out of the country, right now, today. August, call the airport and have Tom ready the plane, then you and Rose—"

"Stop it, Harry," August said, quietly. "I'm not running, not this time. Rose and the baby, yes, but I'm staying to see this thing through."

Or not, I thought.

"I'll call Tom and tell him Rose and the baby will be there within the hour, but that's it."

"Oh no," Rose said. "If you're staying, so am I."

"*No!*" August snapped, in a voice that brooked no argument. "You have to take the baby to safety."

She looked miserable, and I thought for a minute she was going to argue, but she didn't.

"But where will we go?" she asked.

"Calypso Cay. I'll call Leo and tell him you're coming. Now go and get ready. I want you out of here as soon as possible."

He paused, watched her go, and then turned to me and said, "Now you, Harry."

"Forget it," I said. "I'm staying."

"Yeah, don't even think about it, August," Bob said. "I'm staying too. What's the plan?"

"*Stop!*" August was livid. "What about Amanda? Have you forgotten about her? What if they decide to go after her?"

Oh, God... Yes, in the heat of the moment, I had forgotten about her. *Oh shit, How could I... What the hell do I do now?*

"Put me through to Chief Johnston, please, Kelly."

I looked at Kate. "What the hell are you doing?" I asked her.

She held up her hand. I waited, listening, as she continued.

"Chief, it's me, Gazzara. I need you to put a round-the-clock guard on... Stop, Chief. Give me a fricking minute and I'll tell you. What? Yes, at Erlanger, Harry's wife. Two officers at all times, twenty-four-seven until further notice. Yes, yes, I know, damn it. Harry will pay the overtime. Here, you want to talk to him? No... No... Yes, she's in danger... Right, room 3007. No, Chief, I can't explain, not now. I don't have time. Look, just do it, damn it... Okay... No, I shouldn't, sorry. Later? Yes, I will. I promise."

She looked sheepishly across the kitchen table at me, smiled and said, "Well, after that I guess I just kissed my career goodbye. Two officers are on their way to Erlanger now. Ten minutes, no more."

I didn't know what to say. I just looked at her stunned. She smiled at me, raised her eyebrows, and cocked her head to one side, but she didn't speak. I didn't either, but she knew.

I put my elbows on the table, my head in my hands, and I prayed, something I didn't do very often.

"Okay," Bob said, interrupting my thoughts. "That's Amanda, Rose, and Jade safe. Now what?"

I looked up and said, "Beats me. I need a break. I need to think. In the meantime, I'm open to ideas."

And I rose from the table and went outside, sat down on a bench poolside, and tried to clear my head. It didn't happen.

I need to see Amanda. Can't... But I might not ever get to again. Bullshit, Harry. Course you will.

Chapter 16

May 26, Noon

Riverview
   When I returned to the kitchen some fifteen minutes later, I immediately noticed that T.J. was missing.

"Where'd T.J. go?" I asked as I resumed my seat.

"Don't know," Jacque said. "He said he had something he needed to do, and that he'd be back. He didn't say when."

I nodded. "No problem. Maybe he won't come back. I wish he wouldn't. No, no I don't. He's right, we need him."

I paused and thought for a minute. "Okay, so does anyone have anything to say?"

They didn't, so I continued, "Jacque, the first thing we need to do is close the office. Call and tell them all to go home, indefinitely. Don't tell them why. Just tell them also that you'll pay everyone for the time off. Call it extra—no, call it bonus vacation time."

Jacque jotted on her tablet and then nodded at me.

"Look," I said, "I figure there's no point in trying to hide from this. It would be a waste of time and accomplish nothing. We have to face this thing head-on, but not here. That would be disastrous."

"Harry," Kate said. "Don't you think we should bring in the

authorities and let them handle it? They're way better equipped than we are, and—"

"Handle what?" I asked, irritably; she'd ruined my train of thought. "What would you tell them, Kate? Even we don't know that?"

"But the people up there at Copperhill—"

"We weren't there, remember? And we were on government property, and how would we explain the wounded—"

"Harry," Tim raised his hand.

"*What?*" I snapped at him. "Geez, sorry, Tim. What?"

"They weren't there either," Tim said.

"What? What are you talking about?"

"The wounded, the women. Sorry, Harry. I would have told you before, but I got kinda sidetracked."

He looked at Jacque and shrugged. She nodded like she was telling him to go ahead.

"See," he said. "I had my police scanner on. It's something I like to do. Listen in, you know. Sometimes you hear interesting—"

"For God's sake, Tim," I said, "Stop rambling and get on with it."

"The sheriff's officers didn't find anything. By the time the first responders arrived, it was more than ninety minutes after we left—and that was my fault," he said, looking at me. "I forgot to call... Well, anyway, by the time they got there, the fire was out—nothing left but a pile of ashes, most of that already blown away—you must have used a lot of gas, Bob—and there was no one there... just two guards, which means they must have taken the women and kids away... some-where... in that box van, I guess."

He caught the look I was giving him and hurriedly continued, "Anyway, they were all gone, all but the two guards in the office. They told the officers the fire was an accident, and that everything was under control, so they left, the officers did. Those folks up there are pretty laid back. I heard one deputy say they'd check in with the owners—I guess that would be CSC—and they left. Sorry."

"You knew all this, Jacque?" I asked, stunned that she hadn't told me. "Why didn't you tell me?"

"I told him not to tell you," she said. "You already have too much on your mind, and I didn't think it would matter anyway, and it doesn't. Not now." She stared at me, defiantly.

"Okay, then," I said, shaking my head, "I guess that answers that question, right, Kate?"

She shook her head, then said, "I guess, but something doesn't add up. We'll deal with that later. Just get on with it."

I nodded. "As I said, we need to face this thing head-on. He, Christmas, won't be expecting that. But not here. I have a cabin in the mountains, north Georgia. That's where we'll go."

Sheesh, I thought *I haven't been up there since...* Well, that's a whole nother story.

"And do what?" Bob asked. "I thought you said you wanted to face him head-on. How the hell will he know where we are?"

"Tim?" I asked.

He grinned and said, "Cell phone tracking."

"He's too smart for that," Bob said. "He won't fall for it."

"Yes, he will, if you turn 'em off. He'll think you don't know that they can still be tracked. I betcha he'll go for it... Wait a minute... He was here, or someone was, at least they were on Hixson Pike... Why? He could have made that call from Atlanta."

He jumped up and ran out of the house. *What the hell?*

He returned almost immediately, a huge grin splitting his face. He held up a small black box between his finger and thumb.

"GPS tracker," he said, "on the Hummer. I didn't look, but I bet the other vehicles have them too. Christmas could have had a lackey stick the trackers on the cars any time we weren't with the vehicles. So if we turn the phones off, but leave the trackers, they'll know where we are. Easy peasy."

"It makes sense," Bob said. "It's exactly what I would have done."

I nodded, slowly, and sat for a minute, thinking, my head full of all kinds of garbage, then I looked up and said, "Okay, let's get moving. We need to get out of here. Where the hell is T.J.?"

And that's when he walked in followed by two of the roughest, ugliest, scruffiest individuals I have ever seen outside of a soup kitchen, which is exactly where he'd found them.

Chapter 17

Saturday, May 26, 1:30pm

Planning the Coup.

"T.J.?" I looked at him quizzically through narrowed eyes. "You want to explain what these two are doing here?"

"No prob', chief. I figured we need some extra help. This is it. Monty, Chuck, say hello to Harry Starke."

I stared at him, then at the two men; they both grinned back at me and said "Hi."

I grabbed him by the arm. "Come with me. You two stay here while I sort this out."

I walked him out of the door into the foyer, turned him around, and said, "Are you out of your cotton-pickin' mind? Where did you find them, at the homeless shelter?"

"Well, seein' as you guessed, yessir, that's where they came from, only I didn't find them. I already knew where they were. They're old friends, buddies from Nam. They don't come any better'n them. I told 'em you'd make it worth their while. When I told 'em what was happenin', they jumped at it. I told them you'd tip 'em a couple of hundred for a couple of days. That was okay, right?"

I was speechless. No, I was dumbfounded.

"No, T.J., it's not going to happen. Geez, the small guy, Monty is his name? He must be seventy-five years old."

"Seventy-two," he said. "That's gunnery sergeant Montgomery Fowler. He did three tours in Nam; won a Silver Star, a Bronze Star, and two Purple Hearts. You were sayin'?"

I stared at him. I didn't know what to say.

"T.J.," I said, shaking my head. "The big black guy can barely walk."

"Staff Sergeant Charles Wilson Massey, Chuck to his friends—of which I'm proud to say I'm one—is seventy-one. He also did three tours. He was a sniper credited with sixty-two kills, confirmed, but it was more like ninety. He took one to the shin; has a prosthetic leg. They don't come any better than him either. Oh, he also has a Bronze Star and two Purple Hearts. These men are soldiers, Harry, real soldiers, and they want to help. Let 'em."

"T.J.," I said, "you can't just pull people off the streets and—"

"Why not, Harry?" he said, with a sly smile. "You did when you took me in."

My jaw dropped. He had me there.

"Don't look a gift horse in the mouth, Harry. These two guys—they're about at the end of their time. They need something to live for. Look, I told them you were good for a couple of hundred each, but I know you better than that. You'll see them right, I know you will. Give 'em a chance. You won't regret it."

Geez, I thought, shaking my head. *If they're anything like you, I'll regret it for the rest of my days.*

I nodded, sighed, and said, "Okay." I paused, then said, "Why are *you* doing this, T.J.?"

"I owe you, man. You took me in when I was down and out. This is payback, well some anyway. Nothing I can do for you would be enough. Now, cut the crap and let's go tell 'em."

It wasn't that I'd forgotten what they looked like, but when we rejoined them in the kitchen, I took a second, long look at them. They looked like they'd just crawled out of a landfill, and they were both seated at the table eating what was left of an apple pie they'd obviously found in the fridge.

"You got coffee, boss?" the big guy, Chuck, asked.

"In the machine," I said. "Help yourselves."

"Can't. Don't know how to work it."

That, I could understand. It was a new model with all the bells and whistles—cappuccino, foam, you name it—and it had taken some figuring out, even for me. I made them a mug each.

"You guys have any idea what you're getting yourselves into?" I asked.

They looked at each other, then at T.J., then smiled up at me and nodded.

"We're goin' to war, right?" Chuck asked.

I closed my eyes, and said, "What did you tell them, T.J.?"

"Pretty much everything, I guess. Had to, didn't I?"

I sighed, resignedly, and said, "Grab your cups. I'll introduce you to the team. Oh, and you'll need some clothes."

"Already got 'em," Monty said. "T.J. took us by Walmart. We got shirts, camo pants, and jackets. We just need to change, is all."

"Great. Okay, you can wash up in here—there are towels in the drawer, there, and then you can change in the living room. Show them where and then bring them on down when they're done, T.J. I'll go warn the others."

And that's exactly what I did; the three old soldiers joined us a few minutes later. Cleaned up, though, and with a change of clothes, they didn't look too bad. I introduced them to the rest of the team.

"Oh shit," Bob said. "This is all we need. Harry."

"It's okay," I said. "These guys can carry their weight." *Sheesh*, I thought. *I sure as hell hope they can.*

"This is not happening," Kate's face was livid. "Harry, this is crazy. We don't know who they are, anything about them."

"That sounds familiar to me, Kate," T.J. said. "I seem to recall you saying something similar when you picked me up out of the gutter. I can vouch for these two. I've known them for almost fifty years. That good enough for you?"

She didn't answer him. She just nodded.

"Hello, Chuck, Monty. I'm Jacque, Harry's partner. This is Bob Ryan, and the kid is Tim. Welcome aboard. I, for one, am glad you're here." She looked at the rest of us, defiantly.

"Now, Harry," she continued. "Can we get on with it? Will you please tell us what the plan is?"

And that was basically all there was to it. Fifteen minutes later, the two men had been integrated into the team and were acting like they belonged there.

The plan? Well, I did have one, sort of. It wasn't much, but I figured it was better than nothing.

Rose and the baby were already in the air heading for Puerto Rico, so that was taken care of. August would be going wherever I went so I could keep him safe. Amanda was under guard at the hospital. I would have liked to go see her, *maybe for the last time,* I remember thinking, but that was out of the question; the clock was ticking. We had to get out of the city, and fast.

My plan was to go to my cabin in the Northwest Georgia mountains—actually, it's more than just a cabin, but I'll get to that later. It's located northwest of New Hope in the Cohutta Wilderness area, on a bald knob just about as far away from civilization as I could get. That was by design, though it turned into something of a white elephant. My idea when I bought the place had been to use it as a getaway... Yeah, it was one of those wilderness homes and the getaways? In the six years I'd owned the place, I'd been up there only three times. *What a waste of $350K.*

One thing I'd made sure of, though, the place was self-sufficient. It had its own rainwater tank, solar panels, and a damn great gas-driven generator. Over the years, I'd made sure the place was kept in good repair. I had a couple of guys I trusted go up there several times a year to maintain it and keep the area around the house clear from encroaching undergrowth.

Well, that was what I hoped, but I hadn't seen the place since the senator and I... Well, that's another story too, and one I won't go into here, and it was more than three years ago. What condition the place was currently in—what I was likely to find when we left Riverview that day—I had no idea.

So by the time the introductions were over, it was already pushing two o'clock in the afternoon. I wanted out of there, but there was still too much to do.

"We'll take Bob's Hummer. That okay, Bob?"

He nodded.

"Thanks—" I was going to continue, but T.J. interrupted me.

"I'll take the boys in my pickup," he said.

The old, blue 1968 Chevy C-10 was a classic with a 327 V-8 backed by a four-speed manual transmission. It had cost him a bundle, and he was still paying for it. It was the ideal vehicle to navigate the tracks and trails where we were headed, but I wondered why he was so keen to risk his baby. I didn't learn that until later, but I'm getting ahead of myself.

"Well," I said, "if you're sure."

"I'm sure," he looked at his buddies and grinned; they grinned back at him.

I have a feeling, I thought, *that I'm going to regret this too.*

"Okay, so that's the transpor—"

"I'm gonna need to take the van," Tim said.

"There's no way," I said. "It wouldn't make it up the mountain."

"Well, I got stuff in it I gotta have."

"What stuff?" I asked.

"Stuff—you know—stuff."

I didn't know, and I didn't want to.

"There's no room for a bunch of electronics and gizmos," I said. "You can take your laptop. That's all you need, right? And don't forget to put that GPS tracker back where you found it."

"*Nooo,*" he all but howled. "We need the drone, and I have a bunch of cameras I need to bring. There might be something else. I don't know. I need to think about it some more."

"Get it together, Tim," I said, quietly. "And do it quickly. I don't have time for your nonsense."

He snorted once, rose from his seat, and started rooting through the pile of—I'm going to call it crap—he'd hauled into the basement less than two days ago, muttering loudly to himself.

"I said quietly, Tim."

He turned and glared at me. I almost smiled, but I didn't. The boy needed some discipline.

I turned to Bob and said, "We need to arm those two and ourselves. What do we have left in the gun room? How much C-4 is there?"

Now you may be wondering what I was doing with C-4. It's easy enough. I'd seized it from Lester Tree back in the day when he murdered my brother Henry. Well, he didn't do it himself, one of his henchmen did that. Anyway, I just never did turn it in. Now it was going to come in useful; it already had. *Tree,* I thought, *I'd forgotten about him.*

"I dunno, eight or ten pounds, maybe," Bob said. "Other than that, there's not a whole lot left: a couple a 12-gauge, an old Savage 30-06 bolt action rifle, and a couple of antique 1911 semi-autos. That's about it."

Crap, I thought. *Is that it? Add that to the four M400s and our puny handguns, and we were not only outnumbered, but we were also totally outgunned to boot.*

"Geez," I said, looking at the three amigos. "It's not much, but it will have to do."

They said not a word, just sat there smiling, like three all-knowing Godlets.

"Nothing to say?" I asked.

"I have what I need," Chuck said, looking up at me, still smiling.

"Me too," Monty said, also still smiling.

I looked at T.J. He shrugged and gifted me with one of those huge tight-lipped smiles.

Oh yeah, I'm going to regret it.

"Okay," I said to Bob, "go get everything you can lay your hands on: the C-4, detonators, ammo, everything. Take Kate with you. As soon as you get back, we'll leave. It's a good ninety-minute drive to the cabin, so I want to be away from here no later than 4pm... Oh, wait. You'd better grab my Spider. I hate that thing, but it saved my life last time I wore it." *Yeah, it sure as hell did. I took six from Calaway and lived to tell about it.*

I turned to Tim. He was still muttering quietly to himself, but the stack of what he wanted to take with him had been reduced to the drone case, two more aluminum cases, and a top-of-the-line Macbook. It was more than I wanted, but I had a feeling he wasn't about to give up any more of his toys.

Chapter 18

Saturday, May 26, 5:25pm

Cohutta Wilderness
I'd thought at first that my ninety-minute estimate was a bit ambitious, but fortunately, we'd had a dry spell. The forest roads and tracks were hard, though rough going, and we made it to the cabin with five minutes to spare.

"Oh, my God, Harry," Jacque said. "It's beautiful but so remote."

"Hah," Kate said, dryly. "That it is. A girl could scream her head off and no one would hear her."

She was right; they both were. The next nearest dwelling was at least a half-mile away. The cabin—that's not really a good description —was built in the early sixties by a reclusive millionaire. He died there. His body wasn't discovered for more than a month.

The place is a huge, elevated two-story log house built from pine logs twenty inches in diameter; big enough to stop a bullet. It was surrounded on all sides by an eight-foot-wide porch and sat on a poured, reinforced concrete basement. It even had a hot tub, as T.J., to his delight, quickly discovered. How the hell the original owner had gotten the materials up there to build it, I never asked. There are, however, companies that specialize in the construction of this type of wilderness home.

The first thing I did, when we arrived up there at just before five-thirty that afternoon, was check the inside of the house. What a frickin' mess. Unfinished meals on the kitchen table, sideboard, and sink drainer. Trash covered just about every inch of the floor; beds had been slept in and in disarray. There was no one present in the house, but it was obvious someone had been living there, and maybe still was.

I was even more astonished to find the pantry was well-stocked: no perishables, but enough canned foods and dehydrated survival meals, a lot of survival meals, to feed an army. I checked the freezer; it was crammed full of frozen meals. *What the hell's been going on?*

I had no idea, but I soon found there was more to come. By the time I gave it up inside the house and went back outside, Bob had parked the Hummer out of sight, around the back on the south side of the house overlooking the gorge. T.J. had parked his truck on the same side but under the porch, well out of sight, and close to the steel, basement door.

"Hey," I said to Bob in a low voice. "Someone's living in the house. There's trash everywhere."

"But there's no one here now, right?"

"I didn't see anyone," I said so only Bob could hear. Then I raised my voice and addressed the whole group. "Okay, listen up, people. Get the gear out of the vehicles and into the house, through here."

I unlocked the basement door and opened it. The interior was dark, smelled musty, damp even, and... gasoline? I turned on the lights, stepped inside, and got the shock of my life. The west wall was lined with weapons of all shapes and sizes, enough to start a small war.

"Geez," Bob said, looking over my shoulder. "Where the hell did you get this stuff?"

"I didn't. It's not mine. It must belong to the Thackers, Ricky and Bubba. They're a couple of good-old-boys I've known for years, trusted them. I pay them to maintain the place. What the hell is all this, I wonder?"

"Looks like a gift from the Gods, if you ask me," T.J. said, muscling his way through the door. "Wow, look at that, Chuck, a Barrett M107 .50 caliber rifle."

"Two of them," he said, enthusiastically, "and scopes. Geez, I wish I'd had one of them back in Nam. Makes my Ruger look like a peashooter."

I looked at the stash. I couldn't believe what I was seeing. On the west wall were three racks that between them held a collection of at least a hundred assorted firearms, ranging from the Barretts to an antique Remington to several Henry repeaters, AR15s; there was even an AK-47. Stacked against the north wall, under the stairs, were dozens of steel ammo cases. In the southeast corner were six one-hundred-gallon drums; one had a hand pump. *I guess that accounts for the smell of gas,* I thought.

"Just how well do you know these two 'good old boys'?" Bob asked.

"I met them years ago; handy-men. I had them do several small jobs for me. Seemed like a good idea to have them look after the house. I've met them maybe three times since."

"Looking at this stash, I'd say that maybe these guys are white supremacists, and they're squatting in your house, Harry," Bob said.

"Harry," Kate said, urgently. "Listen. Someone's coming."

I swung around, listened; she was right. I could hear an engine grinding away in the distance.

Chapter 19

Saturday, May 25th, 5:45pm

The Thackers

I pulled my gun, so did Bob, Kate, Chuck, and T.J. while Monty ran to the back of T.J.'s truck, opened the toolbox, and withdrew a 1960-era M16.

"*August, Tim, Jacque,* get inside the basement, now. Close the door and stay there. The rest of you spread out, but don't do anything unless I give the word. I don't want anybody killed... Not yet, anyway."

And we waited, silently: T.J. and Monty out of sight beyond the tree line; Kate, Bob, and Chuck were spread out around the house. Me? I sat at the bottom of the porch steps, looking down the trail, listening as the straining engine grew louder... And then it appeared, a battered old Ford F250 FWD jerking and rocking as it slowly dragged itself up the rutted trail.

I could see that there were three men in the front seat. I stood, took several steps forward, and leveled my VP9 at the driver.

"Stop!" I shouted. "Get out of the vehicle and down on the ground. *Do it. Now.*"

Both doors flew open. "Don't shoot, Mr. Starke. It's just me an' Bubba an' Otis."

Geez, it's the frickin' Thacker brothers.

The three men scrambled out of the cab and dropped flat on the ground, their legs and arms spread-eagled. *Hah, they've done that before.*

"Don't move," I said, walking toward them. "Stay right where you are. Bob, Kate, pat them down."

All three of them were carrying. Between them, they had two Colt Pythons, three .45 1911s of varying brands, and—I couldn't believe it—a .50 caliber Desert Eagle, one of the most powerful hand-guns on the planet.

"Sit up," I said.

Ricky and Bubba, I already knew. Otis, a small, skinny individual with lank, dirty blond hair, I didn't know—he was the one carrying the Eagle. *Geez, if he ever fired that thing, it would lift him off his feet.*

The Thacker brothers are identical twins, handsome, bearded, reminded me a little of Keanu Reeves, but where he's a very smart guy, these two were... not quite dumb, but certainly not so smart.

"Hey, you guys in the basement," I shouted. "It's okay, you can come on out."

I waited for them to join us, then said, "Okay! Talk to me, Ricky. What the hell have you been doing up here? I pay you to maintain the place, not live in it."

"An' that's zackly what we do," he said, nodding enthusiastically. "Maintain the place. We come up here maybe once a month and spend a couple days workin' around the place. It takes time, you know?"

"Bullshit, and no, I don't know. You've been living in my house. Explain."

He looked at the other two. Bubba shrugged. Otis didn't react.

"Okay, so look," Ricky said, earnestly. "You ain't been up here in more'n two years. An', well, it's quiet up here, nobody ever comes. So I, we, figured you wouldn't mind if we come an' stayed a piece, do a little huntin' an' shootin'. We ain't hurt nothin', an' we kept the place up, mostly."

I stared at him, lowered my weapon, waved at the others to indicate all was well, then said, "What about all this?" I asked, waving the VP9 at the small pile of unbelievable firepower. "And all of the weapons in the basement, and the food. How the hell long did you figure on squatting in my house?"

"It ain't like that, Mr. Starke. We were just layin' in some supplies." He paused, took a deep breath, then continued, "Okay, it's like this. See, we figure that, come the revolution, an' it surely is comin', Mr. Starke, and sooner than you might think, why..." He caught the look I was giving him and got back on point. "Well, we thought we'd, an' you too, Mr. Starke, better be prepared for the cattyclis... the cattyclis... Oh hell, what's the frickin' word?"

"Cataclysm," I said.

"Yeah, that," he said. "So we laid in a few things. See, we reckon that we can bring the girls up here an' hold for months. An', well that's it. We gotta be able to survive, right?"

I wanted to smile, but I didn't. I looked at my people. With the exception of Kate, they were all smiling.

"So what're you doin' here, Mr. Starke?" he asked, amicably. "You come for some fishin'? Huntin', maybe?"

"Fishing?" Bob asked. "Where the hell can you fish up here on top of a frickin' mountain?"

"There's a lake about a quarter-mile that way," I said.

"Get your stuff together, Ricky," I said, "and get out of here. You're fired."

"Oh, come on now, Mr. Starke. We ain't hurt nothin', an' besides, it'll take us hours to—"

"You'd best get started then. Get to it. Now."

"Oh man!" he said, "Okay, c'mon boys, do as the man says." And, grumbling among themselves, the three turned, picked up their weapons, climbed back into the truck, and drove around to the basement door.

Chapter 20

Saturday, May 26, 6pm

Cohutta **Wilderness**
I checked my watch. It was almost six. I figured we had maybe two, two-and-a-half hours of daylight remaining; we had a lot to do.

"Okay," I said, "they may not come, but I think they will. We need to prepare for the worst. There are six of us not counting August, Tim, and Jacque."

"I can—"

"No," I said, interrupting August. "You'll stay out of it. That's not up for discussion."

If looks could kill. Well, it's a good job they can't, because the look August gave me would have shriveled a Saguaro cactus. Fortunately, though, he took me at my word and said nothing.

"Now," I said, "to continue, I want firing stations at the front and both sides; the back shouldn't be a problem. The gorge is too steep—"

"Harry," Bob said, interrupting me, "you're forgetting these guys are Rangers. It's highly likely they'll do just that, the unexpected, and use scaling equipment."

I thought for a minute. He was right. In my mind's eye, I could see them scaling the gorge wall and come storming over the top.

"You're right," I said. "Stupid of me not to think of it. So, until we know what they're up to, let's have two at the front; that would be you and me, Bob. Chuck, you and T.J. take the back. Monty, you take the east end; Kate, you take the west end." I turned my head to look at Tim.

"You still up to it, son? If not—"

"I am. You need me to fly the drone, right? And communicate, as we did last night?"

Last night? Is that all it was?

"Yes, that's what I need. Can you do it without—"

"Getting my head shot off?" he asked, Interrupting me. "Sure can. All I need to do is launch it. I can set it out on the porch ready to go and fly it from in here. I'm just about ready. I'll monitor it on my laptop. You'll need the earbuds and, if you intend to go outside, the body cams."

I looked at Jacque. "You look after August, okay?" She nodded. "Oh, for God's sake," he muttered.

"And, Jacque, make sure that Glock is locked and loaded. If anyone comes in through the back door don't hesitate, shoot to kill." And I had no doubt that she would, and even less doubt that she could; I'd taught her to shoot myself.

"Okay, we'll think about the rest of those details later, when we get done outside," I said. "Right now, T.J.," I turned to him and said, "you and Monty take some of that C-4 and head north up the slope." I looked out of the window. Beyond the trees, the rocky mound that was the top of the mountain rose another thousand feet.

"If they do come," I said, thoughtfully, "I figure it will most likely be from that direction. So get yourselves up there into the trees and lay down some trip wires. There's nylon fishing line in the basement. Well," I said, thinking about the Thackers, "there'd better be. Try to cover the approaches through the trees from the north. Cover as much ground as you can. Okay, everyone, let's get to it."

I waited until they'd left, then said, "How about you, Chuck? I heard you say that you have a weapon, right?"

"I do, it's still in T.J.'s pickup, a Ruger Precision Rifle chambered for 6.5 Creedmoor. It's good, but I'd sure like to get my hands on one of them .50 cals downstairs."

"Go get you one," I said. "Tell Ricky I said so, and that he still owes for the mess." And he did.

"Kate," I said, "are you okay?"

"No, Harry, I'm not. I can't believe this is happening. Have we all gone mad?"

I smiled at her, put a hand on her arm, and said, "I know. It's crazy, but we didn't start this. We have no choice, at least I don't. But you still do."

"The hell I do. How would I leave?"

"You've got a point. I wish—"

"Eh, you know what they say about wishes. Don't worry, Harry. I'll do my bit. I just hope to hell no one gets killed."

"Me too, Kate. Me too."

* * *

"Hey, Mr. Starke!"

I was on the back porch overlooking the gorge. I'd returned to check on the Brothers Grimm, to see how much longer they were going to be. I wanted them out of there before the crap hit the fan.

"Yeah, what. Why are you still here?"

"It's seven-thirty. It'll be dark soon. It's too late for us to try to make it down the mountain. We could get ourselves killed. We'll stay till mornin' and—"

"You'll go now."

"No, sir. We will not. It ain't right. You cain't expect us to kill ourselves. We ain't gonna do it. What the hell are you guys doin' anyway? Looks like you're preparin' for a fight."

I pulled my VP9, but before I could point it at him, Bob laid a hand on my arm and said, "He's right, Harry. Let 'em stay."

I hadn't even heard him coming.

"I can't, Bob. If Christmas sends in his troops—"

"If he does," he said, interrupting me, "the extra firepower will come in handy."

"Oh, you've got to be kiddin' me. Those three? They're idiots playing some sort of survival game."

"No, we ain't," Ricky shouted. "We're ready, man. Who we talkin' about, the army? Let 'em come. Otis here can shoot the eye out of a squirrel at five hundred yards. Though you'd never be able to know it, not after it bin hit by one o' them fifty cals. It don't matter though. I ain't riskin' a ride down Old Baldy at night, no matter what you say."

I shrugged, turned away, and said, "Your choice, Ricky. I hope you live long enough to regret it."

"Hey wait. Where we gonna sleep?"

"Anywhere you like, so long as it's outside."

"Oh, ma-an."

I smiled and continued on into the house.

"Harry," Bob said, following me in. "If they're staying, that means the road will need to be... Okay, listen, I have an idea, so I'm going to see what I can do about it. I'll be back in as soon as I can."

And, without waiting for an answer, he ran down the stairs into the basement. What he had in mind, I had no idea. I had plenty on my own mind, and I needed to get on with it.

By eight that evening, we were all back together in the living room, with the exception of the Thackers and Otis. The work outside had been taken care of. We'd done as much as we could in the short time that we had. All we could do now was sit and wait.

And we did, and it was one of the worst experiences you can ever imagine. The lights inside the house were mostly off, all except for a small end table lamp in the living room; the windows were open so we could hear. Outside, there was still some light left but, other than the sounds of the night—the insects and the occasional call of an owl —all was quiet. We watched, and we listened. My mind began to wander, and then I remembered something.

"Bob, do we have any C-4 left?" I asked, thoughtfully.

"Yeah, we still have four half-pound packs."

"Good. Do you see that deep rut in the trail down there?" I pointed at it. "You hit that on our way up here, remember? So did Ricky. I saw him. There's no way to avoid it."

"Gotcha," he said grinning. "I'm on it."

"Wait," I said, placing a hand on his arm. "Is it close enough for you to wire it to a trigger?"

The grin grew wider. "Just about. I gotta go."

It took him about fifteen minutes to set the AID—two pounds of C-4 in an empty paint can buried in the center of the rut.

"Hey," he said when he returned. "I already booby-trapped the trail a ways back. I don't think anyone will make it past it, but if they do, I'm gonna be the one to trigger this thing, right?" He held it up for me to see.

I smiled, and said, "You got it, brother."

I settled down again with my back to the window... and then, some thirty minutes later, I heard it; the sound of an airplane engine, and it was approaching fast.

Chapter 21

Saturday, May 26, 7:30pm

The Battle of Cohutta Wilderness

"Shit! That sounds like Nick's King Air jump plane," Bob said."

My heart sank. I'd been expecting something, but...

I checked my watch. It was eight. "You were right, Tim," I whispered, though why I was whispering... No one was in earshot... yet!

"Just like I said," Tim said, grinning.

Does nothing ever bother that boy?

"Yeah, well," I said, "it matters little. It's what we wanted. I just wasn't expecting them quite so soon, is all. It's still quite light."

But that wasn't all, I could hear a powerful diesel engine hauling up the trail."

"Okay," I said, "August, Jacque, basement, now! Everyone else, weapons check."

"Harry," August said as he rose to his feet.

"Not now, Dad. Just do as I ask, please. Go with Jacque." And he did, though reluctantly.

I racked my VP9, reholstered it, hauled back on the bolt of my M400 and let it slam back, ramming a cartridge into the chamber.

"Vests," I said as I jumped up, went over to the couch where I'd dumped my Spider tactical vest, grabbed it, checked the ceramic plates in the sleeves, chest, and back and then climbed into it. I hadn't worn it since my fiasco with Calaway Jones. It still felt like I was wearing a straitjacket.

The sound of the engines grew louder. They were almost on us. Ready or not, we were out of time.

"How many jumpers can that thing carry, Bob?" I asked.

"Fifteen."

"Holy shit. I wonder what the hell is coming up the trail."

"Sounds big, whatever it is."

"Get ready everyone," I said, tersely. "Tim, get that thing into the air, and for God's sake keep your head down."

Tim didn't answer. He was seated on the floor with his back to the north wall, busy jiggling the controls. I watched him, shaking my head. He was like ice, concentrating, methodical, and then he began his commentary.

"We're at five hundred feet and climbing, six hundred, seven... one thousand. I see nothing... Wait, there's something moving on the trail. It looks like... It's a freaking Humvee..."

He was interrupted by the clatter of an automatic rifle somewhere back down the trail.

"Well, there goes that surprise," Bob said, with a sigh. "I figured it would tear up the cab of a pickup, and anyone inside it, but a Humvee? I doubt they even felt it. They'll feel this, though."

He held up the C-4 trigger for me to see and grinned.

The sound of the aircraft engine grew louder, so did the sound of the Humvee. I got up onto my knees and peered out of the window; I couldn't see the aircraft, but I figured it must be somewhere to the north, beyond the mountain.

"Tim," I said, "where's that pesky aircraft?"

"I can't see it... Wait, there it is. Maybe a mile away to the north, beyond the ridge. It's circling. I doubt you can see—"

BAM!

He was interrupted by the most terrific bang I'd ever heard. It had come from somewhere behind the house. *Oh shit! They are coming up the gorge.*

And then the door to the kitchen burst open and the three hillbillies rushed into the room, Ricky carrying an AR15, Bubba the AK47, and Otis had the second Barrett fitted with a scope the size of a beer barrel, and the Desert Eagle strapped to his right leg. Would you believe it? That rifle was bigger than he was, and the muzzle of the Eagle hung below his knee. It would have been funny if the situation hadn't been so serious.

"Weehooo," Ricky shouted at the top of his voice. "Otis done got him. He got that damn plane. You see that? Did you see *that?*"

"No, he didn't," Tim said. "I can still see it."

"No shit?" Ricky was outraged. "I know 'e did. You sure? Oh man. Sheeeit. Give 'im another one, Otis."

"Stop it, for God's sake," I shouted. "Shut the hell up, Ricky. I can't hear myself think."

"Quiet, damn it!" Bob shouted, then. "Watch now, Harry," Bob said, quietly, peering out of the window. "It's almost there..."

At that point, T.J., Chuck and Monty abandoned their firing positions at the rear and rushed into the room.

"What the hell was that?" T.J. shouted.

"It was Otis," Ricky, yelled, excitedly. "He shot the damn plane."

"*Quiet!* I need quiet, damn it," Bob shouted. "And get down."

Everybody, those that were still on their feet, dropped to their knees at the windows and we watched, and we waited, no one seemed to be breathing. Even Ricky managed to keep his mouth shut.

Slowly, the big armored vehicle lumbered out of the trees, rounded a slight bend in the trail.

"Wait for it," Bob whispered to himself. "Wait..."

The driver's side front wheel rose over a bump in the hard surface, then dipped down into the deep rut and...

Bob jerked his hand upward as he thumbed the button.

The explosion was ear-shattering, mind-rending. The vehicle

rose, almost in slow motion, so it seemed, twisting in the air, then flipped over onto its side and lay still, as dead as the dinosaurs that once roamed the forests of the Cohutta Wilderness.

Yes, the vehicle was finished, but its occupants? Not so much. The doors flew open and four men dressed in full combat gear, including helmets and body armor, clambered out onto the driver's side of the stricken vehicle.

I didn't wait. I opened fire with my semi-auto M400. I saw a single puff as one of my slugs slammed into the armored shoulder of one of the men, knocking him off the Humvee. He flipped over and disappeared down between the wheels, out of sight. The other three men quickly followed him and, taking cover behind the vehicle, began to return fire with fully automatic weapons. I ducked down out of sight, so did everyone else in the room.

Within seconds, every pane of glass in all four front windows was shattered, and great shards of wood, torn from the log walls outside, spun through the air like tiny spears; bullets whined in through the windows, slamming into the walls, smashing pictures, light fixtures, wall ornaments... The noise was unbelievable: it was as if the house was being torn apart by a tornado. And then, everything went quiet.

I waited, looked around at the others. Kate had her back to the wall, her knees to her chest, head down, hands over her ears, and so it was with just about everybody else; the exception being Tim. He too had his back to the wall, but he had his ears stuffed full of buds and, the idiot was still flying his drone.

"Everybody okay?" I asked.

They all indicated that they were, with Tim being the exception.

I rose up on my knees and peered out of the window, just in time to see two men run from behind the Humvee, heading east along the tree line, toward the west end of the house. I raised my AR, but I was too late: they were both cut down by a hail of automatic fire from the window in the next room at the west end of the house.

"Oh yeah," I heard Monty yell.

What the hell?

I leaned back on my haunches, looked sideways through the open bedroom door. I could see him on his knees at the window.

"Like ridin' a freakin' bike." He was excited. "Fifty freakin' years, man, an' I still got it."

I could see that both men outside were down; one lay still, the other on his back, writhing in pain, clutching his right thigh, blood seeping from his wounds. *So much for not killing anyone,* I thought, wryly. Then, inwardly, I shrugged. *So frickin' what. It was them or us.*

As I watched, Monty raised the old M16 to his shoulder and sighted through the optic, and I realized what he was about to do.

"No, Monty. I need him alive."

"Ah shit," he said, lowering the weapon.

I turned my attention back to the Humvee, just in time to see a third heavily armored man make a break for the trees.

Then, the world ended, or so I thought. There was an enormous explosion just to my right, and the running man was lifted at least two feet off the ground before he slammed face first onto the rocky floor.

The concussion from the blast almost knocked me over; it pounded the walls, ceiling, floor, and my eardrums, and everyone else's, including Otis', who was slammed backward and down onto the floor by the recoil of the big rifle. Had he been just a little less skinny, and had he been properly set up, he could probably have handled it. As it was, he banged the back of his head hard on the wooden floor.

"You crazy piece of shit," Kate yelled. She'd dropped her AR and had both hands to her right ear. "Ow! Oh, my God. He was three feet from my head. He's busted my eardrum. Damn."

I stood, walked to where Otis still lay on his back, groggily shaking his head, and I grabbed him by the front of his camo jacket and hauled him to his feet.

"You *ever* fire that thing inside the house again, and I'll stuff it up your ass and blow you inside out. You got that?"

He nodded, weakly, squirmed. "Yeah, yeah, I got it," he said gasping. "Not in the house."

I sure as hell hoped so. My ears were ringing. God only knew what Kate and the rest of the crew were going through. Gunfire, any caliber, in an enclosed area, like the one we were in, is bad enough, but a .50 cal... Why the hell do you think we wear ear protectors, even at an outdoor range? Geez, I have to laugh when I see the likes of Tom Cruise or Keanu Reeves banging away and not the slightest flinch. In the real world, it just isn't that way.

I changed the mag on my AR, looked out of the window. All was quiet. Two men down and still, one wounded, and another... somewhere behind the Humvee, I supposed.

"Where's the plane, Tim?" I asked.

No answer. He continued working the drone controls.

I flipped one of the buds out of his ear and asked again.

"Gone. It circled away to the north and disappeared behind the top of the mountain."

"Any jumpers?" T.J. asked.

"Not that I saw, but I can't hear it, so the plane is definitely gone."

"Must have dropped 'em beyond the knob," Chuck said.

"Yeah," Bob said. "If so, we can expect 'em to be here in thirty minutes, maybe less."

I nodded. "Right. Ricky, get that crazy bastard and his cannon out of here. Find a place for him outside the house where he can do no more harm, to us anyway. Chuck," I said turning to him, "you better do the same, but go west about fifty yards. There's a rocky outcrop that should work well for you."

I stepped over to where Kate was holding her ear. "How are you doing?"

She looked up at me. "My eardrum. I think it's busted. It's bleeding, look." She held out her hand. Her palm was covered in blood. "I can't hear out of it, Harry." Her face was white.

I squeezed her shoulder. There was nothing I could say to make her feel any better, so I said nothing. I returned to my place at the window and kneeled down again, staring up through the gathering darkness at the silhouette of the crest, outlined against a clear, purple sky, and I waited, and I watched. The only sound to be heard was the wounded soldier, groaning.

"Hey, Bob," I said, getting to my feet. "Come with me. We need to get him inside, make sure he doesn't bleed to death. T.J., Tim, the rest of you, keep watch for any signs of movement out there. I don't want us to get caught out in the open. T.J., keep an eye on that Humvee. If that guy is still alive, and he shows himself, take him out."

"You got it, boss."

I nodded. "Kate, how are you feeling?

She looked up at me and shook her head, grimacing in pain.

"Well, just try to take it easy," I said. "Let's go, Bob." I opened the front door, peered outside, nothing; all was quiet.

I turned and looked at Chuck, quizzically. He nodded, raised his AR to his shoulder, and aimed it at the Humvee.

We stepped cautiously out onto the porch and then headed down the front steps. The wounded soldier was some fifty yards away to the east.

I started to run toward him. I could hear Bob following me, close up.

We dropped to the ground next to him, one on either side. I checked his wound. A round had gone clean through his upper right thigh. The exit wound was quite small, so it must not have hit the bone. The wound was bleeding, but not enough for him to bleed out. *Lucky bastard*, I thought.

"Okay, son," I said. "We're going to get you inside. Hold tight."

"Screw you," he wheezed, breathlessly.

"Yeah, of course," I said, sarcastically. "Grab his arm, Bob."

He did, and together we hauled the man back to the house, through the living room, into the kitchen and then into the laundry room, and dumped him on the floor.

"You-you-you freakin' sons o' bitches," he whispered, his face, blackened with shoe polish, twisted with pain as he fought to get the words out. "You've no frickin' idea what's about to come down on you. You're all frickin' dead; you just don't know it."

Bob reached out, undid the man's helmet strap, and hauled it off his head.

"Well, well," Bob said. "Hello, Johnny. It's been a long time. Harry, say hello to Johnny Pascal. He's one of Nick's people. I met him, just once. He was with Nick in Kandahar. How is Nick, Johnny? Is he up there somewhere?"

"Screw you," Pascal said, between teeth that were clamped shut. "I've never seen you before in my life, an' I've never been to Afghanistan. An' who the hell is Nick?"

Bob laughed. "Yeah, right," he said. "How about I leave you here to bleed to death?" And he turned to walk out the door. I started to follow.

"Wait. You can't let me die. Please?"

We turned. "So, tell us what the plan is," I said, quietly.

"I don't know. No, honestly. They don't tell me anything. I'm just a peon. Yeah, I work for Nick, but I'm just one of the troops."

Bob looked at him, then said, "Makes sense, Harry. Nick always was a tight-lipped son of a bitch. You want me to patch him up?"

I stared at the wounded man, thinking. Not really, my mind was somewhere else—I was thinking about Amanda—but I nodded, and said, "Yeah, while it's quiet out there. No, on second thought, they could be here any minute. Let's get him down to the basement. Jacque can handle it. Strap his hands."

Jacque wasn't happy about it, but August said he'd help. She looked squeamishly at the man's blood-soaked pants, then made up her mind, steeled herself, reached into her pants pocket, took out a folding knife, opened it and set to work cutting his pants. I grinned at Bob, and we left them to it.

"See anything?" I asked the group as Bob closed the basement door.

"Nope," T.J. said.

"Tim?" I asked. No answer.

I sighed, stepped over to him and was about to yank one of his earbuds when he looked up at me.

"What?" he said, removing one of the buds.

"What's going out there?"

"I'm not sure. The plane has gone, and I'm not seeing any movement. I have the drone at five-thousand feet, and I'm sending it north, beyond the crest, to see if I can find anything. Wait... look, there." He pointed to a spot on the screen. "There they are. Those are heat signatures—one, two, three-four-five—I make twelve of them."

I knelt down beside him, squinted at the almost black screen. At first, I couldn't see anything, but then I could make out the small red dots moving slowly through the trees.

"I'm too high," he said. "I need to lose altitude. Then we'll be able to see better."

"Be careful, Tim. If they hear that thing—"

"They won't. It's almost silent... There, how's that?"

The red dots had turned into blobs, and he was right: there were twelve of them.

"How far, Tim? How long do we have?"

"It's hard to tell; too dark, but maybe..." He looked up at me. "Maybe a little more than a mile, say fifteen, twenty minutes at most."

"How much longer can you keep that thing in the air?" I asked.

He looked at a ticking timer in the corner of the screen, "Fourteen more minutes, then I need to change batteries."

"Get it back here and do it now. We need the eye. How long will it take?"

He thumbed the controls, the image on the screen tilted, blurred, then adjusted itself. Even I could tell it was moving fast.

"Get the case for me, Harry. Sorry, but I need to fly her."

Her? Geez, now it's a girl.

I opened the case. "Okay," I said. "Now what?"

"You should be able to see four sets of batteries. They're in packs of three. I need one of those, then I need you to go out onto the porch and grab the drone and bring it in here."

"You can't go outside to it?"

He looked up at me plaintively, and said, "It's not heavy."

And I got it. The boy was scared, and I didn't blame him, not one bit.

"Done," I said as I handed him the batteries, then stepped out onto the porch. Suddenly, it was there. I didn't even see it coming. With no more than a whisper, it settled gently at my feet, and the six propellers slowly wound down and stopped. I stooped and picked it up. It was huge: more than five feet in diameter. I had to turn it on its side to get it through the door. It took him maybe thirty seconds to change the battery pack.

"Okay," Tim said. "Go! Yell at me when you're clear."

I did as he asked, placed the drone gently down on the porch floor, stepped away, and shouted "Okay," and watched as the propellers began to spin. It lifted slowly, a couple of feet, and then it tilted slightly, and... like a giant dragonfly, was gone into the still darkening sky. I checked my watch. It was just after eight-thirty.

I returned to Tim's side and knelt down, "Do we have them?"

"Not yet... Where the hell are you?" he whispered to himself. "Ah, gotcha. There, see? Wait, I'll lose altitude. Okay, now. There!"

And there they were, twelve red blobs moving steadily up the north side of the knob.

"Oh hell," I said. "They'll be at the crest any minute."

"Lemme see," Bob said, and he came and stood behind me.

"We're out of time, Harry," he said. "Chuck, are you listening out there?"

He was; we all were, except Kate. She was seated with her back to the wall, her head back, her eyes closed.

"Yessir, loud and clear. They'll be on us any minute, right?"

"Right, so watch the crest. Anything moves up there, shoot to kill. Have you got the range?"

"I do. I make it nine-hundred-twenty yards, but whoever calibrated this scope didn't know what the hell he was doing, so it's a crapshoot if I hit anything, or not. I'll do my best though."

"Don't worry," Monty said, slamming a full mag into his M16. "He's jerkin' your chain. He won't miss."

I raised my own M400 and sighted through the scope at the ridgeline. It was tough to see anything in the darkness, but I adjusted the focus, and the dark line of the ridge against the now deep purple sky leapt sharply into focus. As far as I could tell, nothing was moving... and then... a tiny, black figure appeared, then another, and another.

Bam! Bam! Two shots from two Barretts, and one of the figures disappeared. I saw it happen, but... it was too quick. One second it was there, the next it was gone.

"Yay, Chucky," I heard Monty yell in my ear. "You got 'im, man."

"Like hell he did," a strange voice shouted in my ear. "That was me, damn it. I shot 'im." It was Otis somewhere outside and to the east.

"Like hell you did, you little shit," Chuck said.

"You dumbass son of a—" Otis started to reply, but I cut him off, both of them.

"Shut the hell up, both of you. This ain't a pissing match. Keep your freakin' eyes on that ridge and nail anything that moves."

Never for a second had I taken my eyes off the ridge. Not only had Chuck's victim disappeared—yes I figured it was him that had made the kill—so had the rest of them.

And then it began. Slowly at first, a single shot screamed in through the window and slammed into the wall on the far side of the room, and then another, and then all hell broke loose, and it seemed as if the room, all of the front rooms, were filled with hornets. I sat with my back to the wall under the window, my hands over my head, and I waited, praying. The noise was unbearable; I can only describe it as akin to the room being filled with the sound of shattering glass and thunder as the bullets hammered the interior log wall. Debris: glass, china, chunks of wood ripped from the walls flew in every direction.

Oh, they were good. I estimated that almost a hundred percent of the fire was entering the house through one window or another. There was nothing we could do but keep our heads down and wait.

I could hear Otis banging away outside, but what good he was doing who knew. I sincerely doubted that he was even getting their attention. Chuck? I heard nothing from him at all. I guessed he was biding his time.

Suddenly, there was a huge explosion up on the hillside, and then another. *The trip wires,* I thought.

And then it stopped. The sudden silence was... okay, I know it's cliché, but there's no other word for it, deafening.

"Tim," I said, "the C-4, did we get any of 'em?"

"Don't know. Can't tell. Don't think so!"

Damn!

I waited, we all did; no one moved. Several minutes passed... *This is frickin' crazy,* I thought. *We're waiting for them to come and get us. Gotta do something, now!*

I turned over onto my knees, slowly raised my head, inch-by-inch... and then there was a sharp crack of a suppressed weapon and a bullet slammed into the window sill. Three inches higher and I would have been dead. Well, it wasn't, and I wasn't.

I dropped back down again.

"Tim," I said. "What can you see?"

"They're coming, and fast. Harry, you gotta do something."

Do what? We were screwed, pinned down. All they had to do was keep us that way while they approached, then toss in a couple of grenades and we were done.

"Okay, people," I said, "listen up. They have us, or they will soon. Chuck, Otis, you gotta hold 'em while we get out of here. Kate, you're in bad shape, so you go join Jacque and August in the basement. Lock the door behind you. Keep them safe. Tim, can you keep that thing in the air a little longer?"

He nodded, but I could tell he was scared shitless.

"Okay, T.J., you and Monty stay here with Tim and keep him

safe. Ricky, Bubba, go to Otis and set up a firing position, but do not open fire until you hear from me, understand?"

They didn't reply, they just ran out of the back door. To Otis or to escape? I didn't know, nor did I care.

"Bob, you and me, out the back and go right. We'll set up with our backs to the gorge between here and Chuck. Ready? Let's do it."

Chapter 22

Saturday, May 26, 9pm

The Battle of Cohutta Wilderness Part 2

Five minutes later, we were back outside, in position, and waiting.

"Harry, Bob, Chuck," Tim said in my ear. "Five hundred yards northwest. Seven—no, eight men—nine, coming down the slope through the trees directly toward the house."

I turned to look. It was too dark. I could see nothing.

"Otis?" Tim said. "Can you hear me?"

"I can!"

"Yeah, me too," Ricky said. "I'm here with him. What do you have?"

"Four hundred yards to the northeast, three more, and they're closing, fast. Oh shit—"

He was cut off by a stream of automatic fire from one of the windows in the house, followed immediately by a second, much slower volley of fire from an M400, Monty's M16, and T.J.'s AR.

"Hang on, guys," I yelled as I jumped up and started to run. "I'm on my way. Bob, Chuck, keep your eyes open. Do what you can."

Bam! Chuck fired the big rifle, and I swear the ground shook under my feet. I took no notice. I ran for the house, bullets screaming by and kicking up spirts of dust and shards of rock around me. And then, just as I made the turn to my right toward the back of the house, something slammed into the center of my back and I went down, head first, like a sack of potatoes. I lay still for a second, my head ringing, my back feeling as if I'd been stomped on by an elephant.

It felt like every nerve in my body was on fire. What the hell had hit me, I'd no idea, not then. It wasn't until later, much later, that we figured it must have been a 5.56 NATO round.

I stumbled to my feet, staggered toward the back of the building, turned left and threw myself to the ground, and I lay there, gasping for breath.

"Harry," Bob yelled. "Talk to me. Are you okay? For God's sake, Harry..."

"Yeah, yeah, I'm okay, damn it. Concentrate on the enemy, not me, damn it."

"Well okay, then. Just so long—"

"I said I'm okay, okay? Just give me a minute to catch my breath."

I lay there for what seemed like an hour but could only have been a few seconds, and then I was up on my feet and running for the steps up onto the rear porch. I slammed the door open, ran inside and joined T.J., Monty, and Tim behind the front wall of the house. T.J. was on his knees, cool as ice, firing steadily into the darkness. Monty was firing quick, three-round bursts from the M16, at nothing I could see. Tim, bless him, had his back to the wall, his head down, his eyes glued to the screen, and was issuing a steady stream of fire directions to all three groups, inside the house, and out. The floor around the three of them was littered with expended brass cartridges.

"Boss," T.J. said. "You get hit?"

"Just a little, but the armor stopped it. I'm fine." *Like hell you are,* I thought.

I found a spot at one of the windows, dropped to my knees, peered out over the sill, and was rewarded by a half-dozen impacts as bullets slammed into the wood, inside the house and out. *Holy shit!*

But we were wearing them down.

Tim kept up a steady, excited report, not only of where they were, but also as they were hit, or at least stopped moving. Slowly, the fire from the hillside began to slow, until finally, it stopped. No, we hadn't got them all, far from it, but we'd done one hell of a lot of damage.

"I think they're regrouping," Tim said. "I make five down and seven on the move. They're converging. Seven of them, almost directly to the north—three hundred and fifty—now three-sixty yards out. Chuck, you should have a direct line of sight."

Bam! Bam!

"Looks, like, you got one of them, Chuck."

"No, he di'nt, damn it. I did," Otis yelled.

"*Otis*," I yelled. "Shut the hell up."

"Well, he di'nt. It was me."

I let it go. It wasn't worth the hassle.

"So six left, then, Tim?" I asked.

"Looks like it. Harry, I have twenty-nine minutes of flight time left."

Oh shit! We lose that drone, we're done for.

I thought for a minute, then said, "Bob, I'm coming back out. Wait for me." Then to the group in the house, "I'll be back."

"Okay, Arnold," T.J. quipped.

"Okay," I said to Bob. "Tim, are you listening?"

"I am."

"We can't get these guys from here. We need to circle around back. There's a trail through the trees, that way, down the track, past the Humvee, to the west. Bob and I will circle around and then come down the hill at them. Tim, can you see us?"

"I can. Be-be careful, guys."

"Okay, will do. We don't have much time, so let's go."

We headed west at a fast run, stooped over, heads down, rifles cradled in our arms, down the trail, past the Humvee—out of the corner of my eye I saw the body of the fourth occupant of the vehicle —for about a hundred yards. The damn trail was hard to find in the dark; we had to slow down, but eventually, there it was. We turned right through the trees and up the mountain. We ran for maybe five more minutes then swung right along the ridge, then right again for about fifty yards and stopped. I'd thought I was in good shape, but that run just about did me in.

"Tim, you still got us?"

"Yeah, but not for much longer. You have about seven minutes and then I'll have to pull the drone, or we'll lose it. Your targets are two hundred yards to your southeast. Go!"

And we did, and as we did, Tim guided us in, until, "That's it, guys. I'm pulling the drone. They're less than fifty yards dead ahead, go." Geez, that was the quickest seven minutes of my life.

And we looked sideways at each other, nodded, and we went.

Tim was right. We found them right where he said we would. Seven of them. We caught them completely by surprise. Dressed from head to toe in black, combat gear, armor, helmets, night vision, the works, they were spread out over maybe a hundred feet, in line abreast, their attention on the single light left burning in the house some three hundred and fifty yards away.

We separated, came at them from two different angles, and opened fire together, caught them in a semi-crossfire, pumping round after round into the group. I blasted through one thirty-round mag, stopped advancing, ejected it and slammed in another, dodged to my left and resumed my all-out charge. I saw wood, debris, blood, and flesh flying in all directions, and we cut them down... well, five of them.

I was still more than twenty yards from them when the first guy heard us, rolled onto his back and began to level his assault rifle. I managed to nail him in the face before he could pull the trigger. And then everything turned into a blur, a wild melee where time seemed to stand still. A second man went down under a hail of bullets from Bob's AR... and then I completely lost track of what was happening around me. I dropped to my knees, dumped the second empty mag and replaced it, emptied the new one, flung the weapon aside, jerked my VP9 from its holster and emptied it, all seventeen rounds, quicker than you could count.

And then... it was over. I jumped to my feet and ran forward, the empty mag falling away. I rammed in a full one, on the run: I didn't need it.

Two of the men jumped up and ran like rats into the night. The remaining five? Their body armor had stopped most of the hits, but all five lay dead, blood oozing from wounds to heads, necks, arms, and legs.

I skidded to a stop on the loose surface of the forest floor, three feet from one of the bodies, the VP9 hanging loosely in my right hand. I was doubled over, head almost between my knees, my left hand on my knee, taking my weight. I was so out of breath; my head was spinning. I truly thought my lungs had burst.

I don't think they got off more than a couple of dozen shots between them. Unfortunately, Bob collected two of them, center mass, right in the chest; thank God for ceramic plates.

I breathed hard for several more seconds, then pulled myself together. "Bob," I gasped, looking sideways at him. "You okay?"

"Geez, Harry, I think my chest is busted. Yeah, I'm good, I think. You okay?"

"Yeah. If I could just get my breath..."

"You're outa shape, buddy..."

"Harry," I heard Tim yell in my ear. "What the heck's happening up there? We heard the shooting. Are you guys okay?"

"Yeah, Tim," I said, exhausted. "We're fine. We cleaned 'em out. Well, two got away, but I don't think they'll bother us anymore. Sheesh, I'm winded. Give us a minute to catch our breath, and we're on our way."

It wasn't until several days later that, when I got to thinking about it, I realized that without Tim and his toy, we would all have died up there that day: me, Bob, August, Kate—all of us. As it was, well, we did okay. We all survived, though Kate's hearing would never be quite the same, and Chuck had lost the tip of his right ear. And... we had a prisoner. I was feeling pretty good, pleased with myself, as we headed down the rise toward the house. *It's over,* I thought. *Thank God for that.*

But it wasn't. No sooner had we climbed the steps to the front door and entered the house when, in the distance, we heard a sound that turned my blood to water—the steady whump, whump, whump of an approaching helicopter.

Chapter 23

Saturday, May 26, 9:50pm

The Battle of the Cohutta Wilderness Part 3
"Oh shit," Bob growled. "That has to be the damned Huey. Now we're in for it. Put that damned light out." Monty did, and Bob was right, we were in for it, and how.

T.J. jumped to his feet and ran out of the room, heading for the rear of the house. *Where the hell does he think he's going?* I wondered, Not that it mattered, we were screwed, of that I was sure.

The Huey came sweeping in fast and low from the northeast, twin spotlights piercing the darkness, sweeping back and forth over the forest, like a pair of glistening scissor blades, searching... It disappeared to the west, the noise of its engine and rotors diminishing as it circled away to the north, around the knob, then eastward, the spotlights dimming until they finally disappeared, and all was quiet again. But that didn't last for long. Minutes later it came roaring back along the gorge, lifted up and over the house, bathing the building in light from the two spotlights, rose up to perhaps two thousand feet, tilted to one side, slid northward, then it hovered over the crest of the mountain, turned slowly until its left side was facing the house...

"Get down, *now!*" Bob screamed.

Never had an order been issued and obeyed so fast. I threw myself down and lay tight up against the wall under the window: bad mistake.

No sooner was I down and safe beneath the window, so I thought, than the sill above me, and the twenty-inch diameter log supporting it, exploded in a shower of pulverized wood and bullets. I said before that I'd just experienced the longest seven minutes of my life. That burst of fire from what I now know to be a Gatling gun, AKA a Dillon minigun, was, without a doubt the longest three seconds. That damn thing was capable of firing three thousand 7.62 rounds a minute. Can you imagine that? That's a hundred and fifty rounds concentrated on a single spot. Now count slowly to three, and you might get some idea of what it must have been like.

Again and again, the mini-gun hurled its deadly firestorm at the house and, for the most part, the great logs held, but we all knew it couldn't last. Suddenly, the clamor of the big gun stopped, and the spotlights played over the house. *They must be checking to see if we're still alive,* I thought. *Tough shit, assholes. We are. All of us, I think.*

I looked around to see if that were true. *Oh yeah, at least for now.*

I ventured up onto my knees and peered over the remains of the window sill... just in time to see a streak of fire lance upward into the night sky from somewhere behind the house and hurtle toward the still hovering Huey. *Oh my God; it's a freaking missile.*

It hit the Huey just forward of the tail rotor and exploded, severing it from the fuselage. The tail rotor flipped over backward in a shower of fire and flaming debris. The main body of the machine jerked sideways, tilted nose down, began to spin, slowly at first, then quicker and quicker as it lost altitude. Finally, it slammed vertically, nose first, into the rocky knob, exploded spectacularly with a noise like a thunderclap, and settled into a burning, melting heap of twisted metal and... bodies too, I supposed.

"What the hell was that?" I asked.

"Looked like an RPG to me," Bob said, as the basement door flew open and Kate, followed by August and Jacque burst into the room.

"Oh, my God," Kate yelled. "What *was* that? Are they gone?"

"Harry," August rushed to me, "Are you hurt? Is anyone hurt?" I told him I was fine, though I'm pretty sure he didn't believe me.

Jacque? Bless her, she collapsed in the middle of the floor and burst into tears.

And then the kitchen door opened and T.J. sauntered in, grinning widely. "Hey, y'all," he said. "I'm... ba-ck. Everyone okay? Boy, I sure took that sucker out, did I not?" he asked, rubbing his hands together like he was washing them. Even his eyes were laughing.

I was stunned. "You crazy old bastard," I said. "What the hell was that?"

"That, boss, was an RPG 7. Cool huh? As soon as I heard they had a Huey, I er... acquired one? I had it in the toolbox on the back of my truck."

"You acquired one?" Bob asked. "Just exactly where did you 'acquire' it?"

"You can acquire anything, if you know where to look. Good thing I did, though, right?"

"Much as I hate to admit it, yeah," I said, "a real good thing." *He's gonna get us all locked up; I know he is.*

"Somebody must have seen that," Tim said, now on his knees gazing up at the dwindling flames. "There'll be cops all over the place any minute."

"I doubt it," I said. "We're too far from civilization, but even so we have to report it. There are bodies all over the hillside." I paused, counting to myself. "I make it nine, and one still alive in the basement." I looked at Jacque. She nodded.

I continued, "There's also the chopper crew, and three more at the Humvee... and there are still two mercenaries running around loose somewhere up there." I paused, thinking, trying to get a grip of the situation.

"We got lucky," I continued. "Thanks to T.J., but they'll be back. What do you reckon, Bob? You know the guy. Will they be back? And more to the point, do you think he was in that chopper?"

Blair Howard

"Not on your life; our Nick ain't one to get his hands dirty or put himself at risk if he doesn't need to. Will he send in new troops? If he has them, yeah, I'd say so. We just cost him a bunch of money and men. And he doesn't do anything by half measure."

"So," I looked at him and said, "what's the answer? Head of the snake?"

He nodded. "Yup, and ASAP, before he can regroup. Got to, Harry. It will never be over unless we cut it off. Let's do it."

I stared at him, then at T.J., Chuck, Monty. All three just stood there grinning back at me. *Three freakin' stooges...* I pushed the thought from my head. Without them, August would be dead. So would I and Kate and... *Oh, for Pete's sake. We still had work to do.*

"Okay," I said to Bob. "The Head of the Snake it is."

"What?" Kate asked. "What are you talking about? What's going on?"

"Nick Christmas," I said. "We have to finish it, once and for all. If we don't..." I let the inference hang, unfinished.

She nodded, and said, "I get it. When? How?"

"Oh no," I said, quietly, firmly. "Not this time. Bob and I will—"

"Don't forget me," T.J. said. "I just saved all our asses. I'm in."

I turned and glared at him; he grinned back at me. I was just about to set him straight when:

"Me too," Chuck said.

"An' me," Monty said.

"Yeah..." Ricky began.

"Not one frickin' chance in hell, Ricky," I growled. "You three are done. When we leave here, I never want to set eyes on any of you; that's *ne-ver!* You understand?"

"Aw, ma-an!" Ricky said, disgusted. "What you wanna be like that for? We done good, di'nt we? Aw, crap... C'mon, man."

"No. I've had a gutful of you and your crazy friends. Now sit the hell down and shut your face, before I shut it for you."

"Well, okay then," he said, dejectedly, and he sat down on a

308

three-legged stool, the only piece of furniture in the room that was still in one piece.

"As I said, we have to finish it, so Bob and I..." I looked at the Three Stooges, shook my head and continued, "and you three, will visit our friend in Marietta.

"And—" Tim began.

"Nope, not this time, Tim," I said, interrupting him.

"But you'll need the drone. I can stay in the van. I promise."

Oh, hell. He's right. Without him, we'd be going in blind.

"Those heat signatures; can it find them through roofs and walls?"

"Well, ye-ah."

"Okay then, but you stay in the van."

I looked at Bob, my eyebrows raised in question. He nodded. "When?" he asked, checking his watch. "We can't do it in daylight, not in the city, and we need to get out of here, and quickly."

"We need information first," I said, nodding in the direction of the basement door.

"I need for y'all to stay here for a few minutes," I said, to the group. "Bob and I have a little something we have to do in the basement."

Kate gave me a look that could have shredded a cat.

I shrugged it off. "Gotta be done," I said and turned and followed Bob down the stairs.

Chapter 24

Saturday, May 26, 10pm

Basement, Cohutta
Johnny Pascal was seated on the floor in a corner of the basement, his wrists and ankles strapped together with cable ties. Jacque had cut away his pant leg and dressed the wound with strips of towel. The dressing was clean and neat, showing only a spot of blood the size of a quarter. He looked... uncomfortable... Hmm, that doesn't quite cover it. He *was* uncomfortable, no doubt about it, but he was over the shock of the wound and was, or at least he looked as if he was, once again all Army Ranger.

Together we lifted him and sat him on an old dining chair, one of six that were stacked against the wall. Bob cut the ties that held his ankles, then fastened them to the legs of the chair.

"So," I said, lightly, pulling up a chair so I could sit down in front of him. "It's Johnny, right?"

He stared back at me, defiantly, but didn't answer.

I nodded, thoughtfully... at least it was supposed to look thoughtful, and said, "Gotcha. Not gonna talk, and I can understand that, but here's the thing, Johnny. I need information, and only you can provide it. Now, I'm not going to torture you."

"No," Bob said, stepping in front of me, "but I am."

It was typical good cop, bad cop stuff.

Bob gripped the man's thigh, screwed his thumb into the wound, and said, "Where, exactly is—"

Pascal howled in pain, cutting him off. I grabbed Bob's hand and pulled it away.

"Bob!" I said, sharply. "That's enough!"

He turned away and grinned down at me.

"So, now look, John," I said, amiably.

"*Screw you!*" he yelled at the top of his voice, cutting me off. "You think I don't know what you two are doing? You're like a couple o' stupid kids playin' a man's game. Go to hell. I ain't tellin' you nothing."

"A man's game?" Bob asked, derisively. "You and your team, you're nothing, Johnny. We wiped out your entire force of what, sixteen so-called Army Rangers, a Humvee, and a freakin' chopper, and all without losing a man. Just Harry, me, three decrepit old men, all of 'em on social security, four kids, and a woman police officer. Are you kidding me? Army Rangers, my ass. Pussy Patrol is what you are, or should I say were?"

"Like I said, screw you."

Bob looked at me askance.

I hesitated, just for a moment, then nodded and said, "Go ahead."

Bob turned and smiled at the man; it was a look of pure evil, something I'd seen only once before when I asked him if he'd killed Congressman Harper.

He turned and walked over to the workbench, prowled from one end to the other, picking up a tool here and there and then laying it down again, until he found one he liked.

He hefted it, looked at me, then at Pascal and smiled again. Pascal? He still had the same "screw you" look on his face, but that was about to change.

"Let me sit down, Harry," Bob said. I let him.

"Now then, Johnny," he said, leaning forward so that his face was close to Pascal's. "Here's how it's going to be."

He reached out with his free hand, grasped the ragged edge of the man's cut-off pant leg and, with a quick jerk, tore the front of his pants apart exposing a pair of dirty undershorts.

"Eww," Bob said. "That's disgusting. Don't you ever change your underwear?"

"Piss off," Pascal said, but he had to squeeze the words out; he was terrified.

"No," Bob said. "Last chance, Johnny." He waved the carpet knife in front of his face. "Where's Nick, and how many men does he have with him?"

"I'm tellin' ya, I don't know."

Pascal stared at the knife, mesmerized, and his whole demeanor changed, "Look, I dunno. I don't. I swear I don't."

Bob twisted in his seat, looked up at me, smiling, and said, "What do you think, Harry?"

"I don't believe him."

He turned again to face his prey. The man's face was the color of two-day-old oatmeal. Bob shook his head slowly, looked down at Pascal's crotch, and said, "I don't know if I want to touch that dirty thing, Harry."

He looked up into Pascal's eyes, and said, "Come on, Johnny. Don't make me get my hands dirty."

"I told ya, I don't know anything. They don't tell me shit. Please don't. *No!*" he yelled as Bob grabbed his shorts and ripped them away.

"My, my," Bob said. "Who's a big boy then?"

He leaned in closer. "Eww, smelly. Geez, you're frickin' filthy, disgusting."

He lifted Pascal's genitals, gently, using the point of the blade. Pascal flinched and reared back, almost tipping the chair onto its back.

"*I told ya,*" he yelled. "*I don't know shit. Aghhhh!*"

Aftermath

I winced as I saw the thin trickle of blood run down between Pascal's legs, onto the seat, and drip onto the floor.

"Oh, come *on*," Bob said, mocking him. "That was just a little nick, no pun intended. It couldn't have hurt *that* much. The next one, though, now that will hurt." He paused as if he'd had a sudden thought. Then said, "Are you married, Johnny? Girlfriend? I bet you like the ladies, right?"

Pascal didn't answer, he was shaking uncontrollably.

"Cat got your tongue? Maybe I can get that next, your tongue, that is. After I take ol' Petey here." He jiggled the knife, more blood ran down onto the floor, and then...

"Aw shit. Now look what you've done," he said, disgusted.

Shit was right, but I didn't need to look, I could smell it. Pascal was terrified; he'd lost control of both his bowels and bladder.

"Okay, Pascal. That's it. You're one filthy son of a bitch, and I've had enough. You're gonna tell me what I need to know, or I'm going to relieve you of your family jewels. Now, what's it to be?"

Pascal looked up at me, his eyes pleading. "I don't... I... I..." he tried to speak, but he couldn't get the words out. He lowered his chin to his chest and began to sob.

"Freakin' Ranger, my ass. Pussy. Okay then—" Bob said.

"Stop," I said, interrupting him.

"Get up, Bob. Let me."

"Shit, Harry. You don't have the balls for it. Although, maybe you do. You did cut that guy's little finger off last week. Have at it, my friend. You want this?" He offered me the carpet knife.

I shook my head. "No. I think he's ready to talk. If not, well, you can sit down again."

I faced Pascal and said, "How about we start over Johnny, a new leaf, so to speak, yes?"

"Yeah, okay," he whispered, but he didn't look at me.

"Where," I said, "is Nick Christmas, and how many men does he have with him? And it had better be the truth."

He was silent for a long time. I let him be, gave him time.

313

Finally, he looked up at me and said, "He has a barracks and offices in Marietta."

"You mean the warehouse, right?" I asked.

He nodded. "Yeah, but it's more than that. He keeps his men there, equipment: vehicles, weapons. He has an apartment on the upper floor; likes to keep an eye on the troops—his exact words. That's where he is, unless..."

"Unless what?" Bob asked.

"He goes out sometimes, to eat dinner, have a drink with Hank and Jess, but he never stays out late. He likes to—"

"Yeah," I said, "keep an eye on the troops. Jess?" I asked. "Who the hell is he?"

"Not he, she. Sergeant Roark, Jessica. They sometimes... you know."

"You know her?" I asked Bob.

"Yeah, she's a tough, good-looking broad, a ball buster. Yeah, I can see Nick and her—"

"Never mind," I said, interrupting him and turning again to Pascal.

"How many men?"

"That, I don't know, not for sure. Not so many now that this happened. He sent sixteen here, plus the chopper crew. Most of the rest are deployed. Sixteen, maybe twenty."

"Geez," I muttered to myself. That wasn't what I wanted to hear. I looked at Bob.

He shrugged, then said, "It's gotta be done, Harry."

I nodded and turned again to Pascal.

"Tell me about the warehouse, Johnny."

"It's located on—"

"I know all that," I said, interrupting him. "Tell me about the building, the interior, the layout—and don't leave anything out."

"Shit, I dunno. Okay, okay, gimme a minute to think... It's two stories front and back. The center from north to south is one story, thirty-five... forty feet at the ridge. The upper story on the back side is all weapons storage, includin' guns, ammo, explosives. There are barrack rooms, sleeping quarters, on the ground floor along the entire east side. The ground floor front is all offices. The upper floor is the captain's living quarters. The center section is where he keeps the vehicles. There's also a firing range in the basement and more storage. There're security cameras everywhere. That's all I know, honest."

He stopped talking, looked pathetic. Bob was right. Ranger he might once have been, but he'd grown old—I figured him to be at least forty-six—and soft. In another time and place, I might even have felt sorry, but the man had just tried to kill us all. Now, he was probably quite wealthy with a lot to lose. I wondered if it was an infectious disease. I sure as hell hoped it was, and that the rest of Christmas' crew was as badly infected as Pascal. But somehow, I knew that was a forlorn hope.

"Tell me about his men. Are they all ex-military... Rangers?"

"Some, but he's hired a lot o' recruits lately. They're good, or he wouldn't have hired 'em, but they ain't like us—"

"Hah," Bob laughed, interrupting him.

"Screw you." He would have continued, but seeing the look on Bob's face, thought better of it."

"We need to see a satellite view," Bob said.

"No, this time we'll use Google," I said. "You can drive the damn streets with that. We'll get a good look at the outside of the building without ever being there. Bob, I don't suppose you thought to bring suppressors?"

"Sure did. They're in the Hummer, ammo too."

He was talking about low-velocity rounds, subsonic. Without those, suppressors—most people like to call them silencers—firearms aren't silent at all. The high velocity round, as it leaves the barrel of the gun, breaks the sound barrier and creates a sonic boom, which is what you hear, what Kate heard when that damned Barrett burst her eardrum. Anyway, if you want to silence a weapon, you need subsonic ammunition—no sonic boom, just the explosion, which is suppressed. Fortunately, Bob had brought it.

"We need to get out of here," I said, checking my watch. "It's late, real late, and we have a long way to go. Let's go bring everyone up to speed."

"What about him?" Bob asked, nodding in Pascal's direction. "We can't leave him here. If he bleeds out—"

"We can. We have to. He won't."

I spent the next ten minutes explaining to the group exactly what I had in mind.

My plan, such as it was, was first to get August, Kate, and Jacque out of danger, then go back to Riverview where we—that's me, Bob, T.J., Monty, Chuck and, of course, Tim could grab a few hours rest before we headed to Marietta. Before that could happen, though, we needed to familiarize ourselves with the layout of the warehouse, and for that, we need Tim's array of monitors.

So, with all of that explained so that everyone understood, I made sure the three revolutionaries, the Thackers and Otis, were well on their way out. Then I turned to what was left of my exhausted little army.

"Jacque, you take August and go find a motel somewhere—I don't want to know where—and stay there until this is done. You go with them, Kate. I'm not risking you getting hurt any more than you already are. Stop in at a Walmart and buy burner phones and keep them close in case you need them. Do NOT call me. Tomorrow is Sunday. We're going in tomorrow evening. So wait until Monday morning and then go home. We'll be waiting for you." *And Lordy do I ever hope to hell we are.*

Kate didn't argue, and I wasn't too surprised. She'd seen and done enough. Now I had to make sure all of this didn't blow up in her face. If it got out that she was involved in any of it, she'd lose her job and probably her freedom too.

Chapter 25

Sunday, May 27

Riverview

It was after two-thirty in the morning when we arrived back at Riverview. I didn't know if Tim had been right or not when he'd said that somebody must have seen the helicopter crash. My first instinct was that I'd have to call it in soon—the house and ten acres of forest were registered to me—but that would be an admission that I'd been up there and involved, would lead to a whole lot of questions I didn't want to have to answer. Not that I was too worried: no law enforcement agency in the land could take one look at the carnage up there and deny that we acted in self-defense, but I had to protect August, Kate, and the rest of my team. My one hope was that the Thackers and Otis had got clean away. I didn't trust any one of them not to throw us under the bus.

Then there was Pascal to consider. I couldn't leave him up there bleeding... not for too long anyway, I figured an anonymous call to the local sheriff from a burner phone would solve that problem... I decided to give myself until midday and then make the call, which is what I did. I made the call and in just a couple of cryptic sentences informed the desk sergeant that I'd seen a helicopter go down, gave him the rough coordinates, then tossed the phone. As it turned out, I was worried about a problem that never arose.

We grabbed a few hours' sleep and then, after we'd downed several dozen eggs, two full pounds of bacon, two entire loaves of bread, and what had to have been a couple of gallons of coffee, we gathered around Tim's bank of monitors in the basement.

I would have liked to have gone to see Amanda, but that was out of the question, considering the situation I, that is we, were in. She would have to wait.

Just a couple of minutes after we'd finished breakfast, we, the six of us, were looking at two huge aerial views of Marietta—one wide, one close up—and two views of the surrounding streets, at street level; none of it in real time. We would have to wait another hour before that could happen. It turned out that we didn't have to.

Pascal had told the truth. There were at least a dozen security cameras, that we could see, and probably more inside. It wasn't going to be easy, that was for sure.

"Tim," I said, thinking out loud, "you remember when you hacked the camera system at Hartsfield-Jackson Airport in Atlanta?"

"Yeah, I do," he said, quickly. "I don't know about these, though, unless they belong to a government agency. Which is entirely possible, I suppose, seeing as—"

"Tim, please," I said interrupting him in full flow. "Just do it, or not."

He tapped at the keys for what seemed like an interminably long time, then whispered to himself, loud enough for all to hear, "Got it, yay!" And suddenly, instead of looking at the building from the street, we were looking out from it, at the street, from an angle high up near the roof. Tim swung around on his seat with a look of excitement on his face.

"DOD," he said, triumphantly, "Department of Defense." "Took some figuring out. I had to hack nine different agencies before I found the right one. I started with the FBI, then—okay, okay—watch this."

He tapped for several seconds more, and the image on the top right screen split into six different, smaller images, each providing a different view of the streets around the warehouse. I was dumbfounded. I had always said that Tim was the most valuable member of my staff and boy was he ever proving it that day.

"Want to see inside?"

He didn't wait for an answer. He tapped some more, and the views changed from exterior to interior, which was great, but not encouraging. There were, and I know because I counted them, sixteen vehicles parked down the center of the interior of the building, including four Humvees, two military trucks, the designations of which I didn't know—one even had a small helicopter on a trailer attached to it—and an assortment of smaller vehicles including three black Chevy Suburbans.

But what really got my attention was the number of people. I counted thirteen, but there could have been more, a lot more.

"Can you zoom in, Tim?" I asked.

"No, sir. They're all static, well not exactly static, but I can see only what the cameras are seeing. I have no control over them, sorry."

"How many cameras are there inside the building?"

"Twelve, on this system, but there could be more. If they've installed a system of their own, well, you won't know until—"

"Until they chop us down," Bob said.

I turned and looked at him. "How much of that C-4 do we have left?"

"Very little. Three half-pound packs. Why?"

"I'm hoping we won't have to use it, but I'm thinking doors. Three should be plenty. If we cut 'em up into four-ounce packs, that will give us six. How about detonators?"

"We have plenty."

I nodded. "Can I leave that to you, then?"

"You can."

"Tim," I turned back to him. "The drone, it can pick up heat signatures inside the building, right?"

"It can, but it can't differentiate between our people and his. Out in the open, up there in the forest, that didn't matter, but inside that warehouse, it's going to be tough. Still, it's better than going in blind, right?"

"I guess," I said, wryly.

"I can hover it over the building, say at five hundred feet. From that height, I'll be able to tell you how many live bodies are within, and where they are. Once you mingle with them, though, we're screwed."

"Okay," I said. "Give me a minute, please, everyone. I need to think." I stared at the interior images, had Tim flip back and forth between cameras. I was trying to get a feel for the layout.

"Okay, Tim," I said, finally. "We know that the offices are here, on the ground floor, and we know that Christmas's quarters are directly above them, or thereabouts. See, this balcony here?" I pointed to a spot on the screen. It was really nothing more than a steel walkway protected by an iron handrail. "I'm guessing that's where he's living. There are iron stairs that provide access here. Once inside the building, those stairs will be my objective. We won't know exactly where he is until you can provide us with pinpoint locations, so we won't worry about that now."

I paused, stared at the images, then said, "The real problem will be the people living here." Again, I pointed at the screen. "I count fourteen doors, so fourteen rooms. If they have allocated more than two to a room, and I'm betting it's probably four or more, we're talking a lot of potential firepower." I rubbed my hand on my chin, considering if I really wanted to say what I was thinking. I did.

"So," I continued, "T.J., Chuck, Monty; as soon as we gain access, you go for the barracks and, one way or another, you eliminate that threat."

I caught the looks on their faces; even T.J. looked serious.

"Eliminate the threat?" Bob asked. "Are you kidding? We don't even know how many there are."

"True," I agreed, "but we do have some idea. I counted thirteen, so we know there will be at least that many, but we also know that the bulk of his people are deployed elsewhere. Pascal topped the number at twenty, and these images would seem to confirm that. I'm thinking, at worst, we're looking at twenty-four, including Christmas and his girlfriend. Any comments?"

"Yeah," T.J. growled. "We're gonna go in there and kill twenty-four professional soldiers? Have you gone out of your freakin' mind, Harry? That's frickin' murder. And anyway, it can't be done," he said, shaking his head.

I didn't have a problem with that. In fact, I'd already persuaded myself the same thing. It couldn't be done, unless...

"You're right, T.J.," I said. "But they are not who we're after. All I want is Christmas."

"Then find a way to take him outside of his fortress," Bob said. "We know he goes out, occasionally. We wait, watch, and we grab him, bring him back here and bury him on a construction site."

"Occasionally," I said. "That's the operative word. We could wait for a week before he goes anywhere. And grabbing him in downtown Marietta? No! What I'm suggesting is a surgical strike. We hurt no one unless we have to. Okay people, look," I said. "It's not my intention that we go to war, but we do need to be prepared for the worst, and the unexpected. The target is Nick Christmas. No one else."

I got up and started pacing. "We go in quietly. Weapons suppressed, in the early hours of the morning, when everyone's asleep—"

"You hope," Bob muttered.

"Yeah, I hope. If not, well..." I shook my head, annoyed at the interruption, and continued. "T.J., you, Chuck and Monty will take up positions down the center, here, here, and here, and cover the barrack rooms. Bob and I will head straight for the stairs, here, and go after Christmas. With any luck, we can be in and out without even waking anyone else. If we do wake anyone, you guys will subdue everyone who sticks their nose out, without killing anyone unless you have to. We'll be going in late at night, so they won't be prepared. Even so, the chances are that we could have a fight on our hands. If we're lucky, we won't have to shoot anyone." *Sheesh, Harry, you should be so lucky!*

"So let me get this straight," Bob said, his voice dripping with sarcasm. "You think we're just going to walk in there and drag him out?" He shook his head in open disbelief.

"That's what I'd like to think," I replied. "Do you have a better idea? If so, let's hear it."

"Yeah, I do, I like the idea of waiting until he leaves the property and catching him out in the open, but you're right; that could take a month."

"If we do have to shoot..." I continued. "Well, you know the rules: center mass only. No fancy head, arm or leg shots. Even if you get lucky and make the hit, these are elite professional soldiers, so they'll probably still be able to shoot back. If you have to shoot, shoot to kill."

I looked at each of them in turn. No one looked happy, and I didn't blame them. Tim? I could see he was scared witless.

"It's okay, Tim," I said. "It will—we'll be fine."

I thought for a minute more, then said, "Look, guys, you don't have to do this, really. I don't expect anyone, including you, Tim, Bob, all of you to—"

"Oh, shut the hell up, Harry," Bob said, "and get on with it."

"If you're sure..."

"We're sure," Tim said. "Carry on, Harry."

I nodded and turned my attention away from the interior views and concentrated on the exterior views provided by Google. I had Tim drive the streets around the building, stopping here and there to view the entrances; there were six of them, including huge overhead doors at the north and south ends, both had small doors beside them. The entrance to the offices and, which I assumed also provided access to Christmas' living quarters, was on the west side. There were two more entrances on the east side.

"There," I said, pointing to the big door at the south end. "That end of the building is enclosed by a steel security compound. And see these dumpsters?" There were four of them, two on either side of the enclosure. "They'll provide cover from prying eyes in the street. We can park in this strip mall lot here. It's directly opposite, and you can operate the drone from there, right, Tim?"

He nodded, thoughtfully.

"We'll travel in two vehicles: Tim's van and Bob's Hummer. We'll leave here at one in the morning. That should put us in the parking lot no later than two-thirty. They'll all be sleeping. Any questions?"

There were none, so I ended the meeting, told everyone to make their preparations, then get some rest. Me? I called Uber and went to the hospital where I spent an hour talking to Amanda. If she heard me, she gave no indication, so I went home, set the alarm for eleven o'clock and lay down on the bed. I hoped "to sleep, perchance to dream."

Chapter 26

Monday, May 28, Midnight

I slept fitfully for maybe a couple of hours, and then I must have gone out like a light because the next thing I knew it was eleven o'clock and my iPhone was loudly playing "Don't Worry, Be Happy." *Oh yeah. That's what I'll do.*

I hauled myself off the bed and took a quick shower, dressed in black jeans, black tee, and black combat boots. I stood in front of the mirror and a me of more than three years ago stared dourly back. I hadn't dressed like that since I lost my brother Henry.

I checked my VP9, slid it into its holster on my right hip along with three extra mags; the body armor would have to wait until we arrived at our destination. It was way too bulky and heavy to travel in.

I went down to the basement where I found Bob, Tim, T.J. and his buddies ready and waiting for me.

"All is good?" I asked.

They all answered in the affirmative, except Tim.

"Tim?" I asked. "Are you okay? You sure you want to do this?"

"Yes, I'm sure. I was just going over my list, in my head, making sure I had everything. I do. I'm ready when you are."

I took a deep breath, nodded, and said, "Let's do it."

The drive to Marietta was uneventful and unusually quiet. I traveled with Bob in the Hummer along with the three amigos. Tim followed in his van.

We pulled into the strip mall parking lot at just after two o'clock that morning. All seemed quiet, but I felt decidedly uneasy when I looked around the lot. Our two vehicles were the only ones there, and I figured they'd attract the attention of the first police cruiser that happened by. That would be disastrous. How the hell we'd explain our presence, much less the arsenal we had inside the Hummer, I had no idea. No, it just wouldn't do. We couldn't afford to risk getting caught; we had to find another spot, and that posed our first setback. We had to find somewhere out of sight of the open streets, but it also had to be close to the warehouse.

"Drive around the block," I said to Bob.

He drove, we looked, and we saw nothing that even remotely looked like what we were looking for: a secluded spot within striking distance of the south end of the warehouse.

"Geez," I said. "This could be a deal breaker." Then I had a thought. "Go back to the mall, take the service road, and drive around the back."

At first I thought it was going to be a bust, that we'd have to take our chances and park in the lot, but then I spotted a large, yellow rental box van parked at the rear entrance to a furniture store which was adjacent to the rear entrance to a pizza restaurant—one of those all you can eat places. The pizza place was an end unit, and just a few yards beyond it and to one side was a large dumpster with just enough room to slide our two vehicles alongside. Provided no one looked too closely, they would be in the deep shadow of both the box van and the dumpster. The downside was that we were now more than a hundred yards from the warehouse security fence: most of it brightly lit open street.

This is not good, I thought. *We'll be exposed until we can get through the fence. If we get caught by the police—sheesh, I dunno. Well, I guess we'll just have to take our chances, and time's a wasting.*

"This will have to do," I said. "Park it, Bob."

He parked between the dumpster and the restaurant wall, and I exited the Hummer and went back to talk to Tim. He was already at work with his laptop.

"Harry," he said, obviously worried. "You can't do this from here. You'll be in full view of these two cameras. See, that one is covering the south end of the building." He pointed to the image on the screen. "And this one is covering the approaches from the street."

"Oh hell, now you tell me. You have access to them, right? Can you turn them off?"

"No. I told you. I can see what they see, but I can't control them. And even if I could turn them off, it would do you no good if they're being monitored—and you can bet that they are—it would set off every alarm in the place."

Damn it all to hell, I thought, furious with myself. *I should have thought of that.*

"So what the hell do we do, then?" I asked, more of myself than of Tim.

He thought for a minute, staring intently at the screen, flipping through the exterior from one to another, and then back again. He switched from the cameras to a satellite view of the building, studied it, then switched back to the cameras, flipped some more, then switched again to the satellite.

"There's a blind spot here, at the other end of the building." He pointed to the northeast corner. "As far as I can tell, there's no camera coverage between here and here. There's an open lot here, just across the street, behind the store. If you move the Hummer and park there, you'll be within thirty yards of the door at the south end, here. It's more exposed, but if you can get through the gate here, you'll be out of sight of the cameras and can access the building through this door here." He pointed to the rear entrance. "That door gives access to a passageway between the barrack rooms to the central vehicle storage area. The stairs to Christmas' living quarters are directly opposite. What do you think?"

I thought for a moment, then nodded, and said, "We don't have much choice, do we? What about you?"

"I can stay here. I won't launch until you tell me you're inside the fence. Make sure you're all in communication with each other and me."

I looked at him. "Tim, this is me. I'm not stupid."

He looked at me and grinned. "Just checking."

"What about the cameras inside? Can you pinpoint them for me?"

"Yup! There are two that you really need to watch out for, here and here. You'll have to take your chances, but if you move quickly, you can use the vehicles for cover. You'll be in view of either one of the cameras for just a second or two. If they're monitoring them, and they spot you, you're screwed. If they are just recording, you should be okay. Just keep your heads down—facial recognition has come a long way, so move fast."

I stared at him. "You're kidding, right?"

He shrugged. "No, sir, but it's two-thirty in the morning. I'd say they're all asleep."

"That's very reassuring, Tim. I'll be in touch," I said, slapped him on the shoulder and headed back to the Hummer.

It took a few minutes to explain the new plan, and then Bob drove around to the store at the northeast corner of the warehouse. It turned out to be an equipment rental store. Tim was right. How the hell we'd missed it the first go round I don't know. Probably because the frickin' alley to the side of the store was unlit, pitch black.

Bob eased the big vehicle down the alley and turned in behind the store. Perfect, we'd caught a break at last.

"Tim," I said, quietly. "Can you hear me?"

"I can. Check in please, everyone... Okay, comms are good. Are you in position?"

I told him we were, and he told me he was about to launch the drone.

"She's up, and I have you," Tim whispered a couple of minutes later. "All five signatures and—oh Lordy," I heard Tim whisper. "I see twelve hot bodies. Eight of them are static, in the barrack rooms, so they must be sleeping, but four of them are moving; two at ground level traveling from north to south in the center aisle. They're on the east side of those vehicles, between them and the barrack room walls; must be guards."

"Where are the other two?" Bob asked.

"One is in a room on the west side, also on the ground floor, I think; the image is not quite so bright. Would that be the offices? If so, then he's probably monitoring the security system. The other is also on the west side, but his signature is much brighter, so he must be on the upper floor, above the office, south end, midway between the front entrance and the end of the building. I'd bet that's Christmas, and he's awake."

There was a moment of silence, and then Tim continued, "There are two sleepers in a room at the north corner of the entrance passage, three more in a room at the southeast corner of the building, and another three in the room next to them, that's the eight, plus the four on the move, that's twelve in all. Harry, I have fifty-one minutes of flight time left. Oh gosh, what was that? I think someone's coming. I gotta go. I'll be back soon, I hope."

"Oh hell," T.J. said. "That's not good. Now what?"

"We hope he's okay, and we do what we came to do," I said. "Load up. Vests, weapons, suppressors, balaclavas. And, grab some of those cable ties and duct tape; we're going to need them. Bob, grab the bolt-cutters and let's get moving."

We exited the vehicle and donned our gear. I slipped into the heavy tactical vest, checked the VP9 once more, more out of habit than necessity, slipped my tiny Sig and two extra mags into my vest pocket, and I too grabbed some of the cable ties, stuffed them in a vest pocket.

"Hey," Tim said in my ear. "It's okay. It was just a couple of stray dogs. They really scared me. I thought I was... Okay, never mind. I see you, but what are you doing? What's the plan?"

"Okay," I said, "here it is. Listen up, everybody. I want to keep this as clean as possible: no shooting unless you absolutely have to. I don't want this to turn into a damned bloodbath. The target is Nick Christmas; that's it. No one else gets hurt unless it's absolutely necessary."

I paused, waited for comments. There were none, just nods all around, so I continued.

"Bob, give me the bolt cutters. You guys stay here out of sight while I go open the gate. Then when I give the signal, you follow me. Once we're inside the compound, we go south staying tight against the wall to the rear entrance. No noise, *none!* I'll handle the door lock. Bob, you and I will take care of the two guards in the main storage area first, then the one in the office. Y'all got it?"

They had, so I continued, "Tim, it's going to be on you to keep an eye out for any unexpected movement, especially in the barrack rooms, and for God's sake keep an eye on Christmas."

"Yessir!" he replied. He sounded a little breathless and, on thinking about it, who could blame him?

"When we go in," I continued, "we'll stay out of sight in the passageway. We wait until you give us the heads up, Tim, and then we subdue them.

"T.J.," I said, "you, Chuck and Monty will spread out and watch the barrack rooms. Anybody pokes their head out, you subdue 'em and strap 'em up. Don't shoot unless you absolutely have to. Above all, from the minute we leave this vehicle until we return, we keep our faces covered. If any one of us gets caught on camera, we're all screwed. Got it?"

They were excited, getting antsy, but they agreed.

"Okay," I continued. "We take the guy in the office down, and then we go for the stairs and find Christmas. Hopefully, we can take him by surprise."

"Question," Tim said.

"Go," I said.

"What do you intend to do with him when you get him?"

I looked at Bob. His face was a mask.

"Persuade him—"

"We're gonna dump him in that lake alongside Duvon James," Bob growled, interrupting me.

It wasn't exactly what I had in mind, and now that we'd reached the point of no return, I had serious doubts about terminating the man but... His stated intent was to kill August, and he'd already demonstrated that he fully intended to carry it through, so I really didn't have a choice.

"Oh," Tim said, "I see. You're going to... kill him?"

I ignored the question, and said, "Time to go. Cover your heads. Chuck, are you going to be able to keep up?"

He gave me a wry look. "Oh yeah!"

Chapter 27

Monday, May 28, 2:30am

Thirty-two Minutes

The padlock on the gate was a little tougher than I'd expected. The bolt cutters could have done with being a size bigger, but after a couple of attempts, the hasp finally gave with a crack that would have done credit to a .45 and left me breathing heavily. The thirty-five-year-old lock in the steel door wasn't the easy pick I'd thought it would be either. I must have fiddled with it for several minutes before Bob finally shoved me aside and grabbed the picks out of my hand.

"Oh, for God's sake," he growled. "Here, let me do it." I swear it took him less than thirty seconds. He shoved the door open and we slipped inside, into almost total darkness. The only light in the passageway leaked in indirectly from the central aisle. Chuck, the last man through the door, pulled it shut but didn't actually close it. We paused for a minute, listening. Somewhere, not far from where we were standing, I could hear footsteps and low voices talking together, and they were getting louder, closer.

"Tim," I whispered urgently. "Where are—"

"Maybe twenty-five feet and closing," he interrupted me.

"Move! Get out of the way," Bob said, ungently, shouldering me to the side. He moved silently, quickly, to the end of the passageway, stopped, and stood with his back against the wall, waiting.

They were both carrying automatic weapons. The instant the first guard appeared, Bob leaped forward, grabbed the barrel of his rifle, wrenched it out of hands, and in one sweeping movement, used it as a club to disarm the other guard.

They were taken completely by surprise, but they were well-trained and recovered in an instant, and they were good.

They'd obviously had advanced unarmed combat training because they attacked from both sides, knuckles advanced, kicking swinging, punching.

Bob, as big as he is, moved like a panther, crouched, dodging, ducking; they didn't land a single punch or kick, but he did. A single devastating knuckle punch to the throat and the first man went down on his knees, gasping for breath. The second backed off a little, composed himself, took two quick steps forward and... Bob side-stepped, turned slightly to his left, and landed a huge, roundhouse punch to the side of his head.

I was just about to leap into the fray, to go to his aid, when I suddenly realized he didn't need any help. I'd never really seen him in action before, other than the odd heavy-handed punch from which most mortals never got up. He was something to watch. He easily blocked every punch and kick, returning each with a devastating blow that carried his entire body weight. I'd studied Krav Maga, a little, but what Bob was doing was the real thing.

Krav Maga is a martial art first developed by the Israeli Defense Force to inflict as much pain and as quickly as possible on an attacker, often to the point of the attacker's death. Only once before had I seen it done better than Bob, and that was by Calaway Jones, who nearly ended my own life. It took a bullet to the head to stop her.

Anyway, that aside, it took Bob less than a minute to silently subdue the two guards. And another to strap them up and tape their

Aftermath

mouths. *Now for the one on the west side,* I thought. *And then it's Christmas time.*

We found the guard in the office sitting behind a desk, his feet up, supposedly watching a bank of six security monitors, only he wasn't; he was playing a game on his phone.

"Hey," I said.

His surprise was complete.

"Are you winning?" I asked, pleasantly.

He didn't answer. I don't think he could. His jaw dropped, and so did his phone, and he sat frozen in his seat, staring at us, wide-eyed. Slowly, he raised his hand, more in protest than surrender.

"Now you just sit still and be a good boy," Bob said, stepping around the desk.

I held him at gunpoint while Bob did a number on him with cable ties and duct tape. We left him lying on the floor behind the desk, but before we did, I jerked all of the power cables out of the wall sockets. The monitors went black, the computers stopped humming, and it was suddenly so quiet the silence was... I know, I know, but I'm going to say it anyway: it was deafening.

Now, Nicky boy, I thought, grimly. *It's your turn.*

There was now no need to worry about the security cameras, so we quickly and silently climbed the stairs and, just as we reached the balcony, Tim shouted, "Look out behind you."

But it was too late.

"Hey, Bob, and Harry is it?" a soft voice said. "Yes, I thought so. Nice to see you both."

Shit! I thought, resignedly. *It's Christmas. Why am I not surprised?*

I glanced sideways at Bob. He was smiling.

"Now," Christmas said. "Please put your weapons on the floor, that's it; nice and gentle. Kick them away. Now your backups, nice and slow, please."

I reached behind me and slid the P938 out of its holster, placed it on the floor, and kicked it away. Bob did the same with his M&P9.

"Awesome," Christmas said, lightly. "And now put your hands in the air. Good, now turn around, and uncover your heads and drop the masks. You won't need them anymore. Good... slowly... keep 'em up, keep 'em up. That's it. All righty, then."

He was standing just inside an open door, a dark silhouette against the bright lights within the room, a Glock 17 in his right hand. He held it loosely, casually, pointed slightly downward. *My groin or Bob's?* I thought, grimly.

"Well, well," he said. "Who would have thunk it, except for me, of course?" He was smiling, but there was nothing friendly about it: lots of teeth and half-closed eyes that glinted blackly.

"Do come on in," he said, and casually waving the Glock from side to side, he backed slowly into what appeared to be a large private office. We did as he asked and followed him inside.

"I must say, Bob, after all these years I was beginning to wonder about you, but you've still got it. I had no idea you were here until just a few seconds ago. I'd offer you a job, but what use would you be to me? You'll be dead."

"Screw you, Nick," Bob said, seemingly without a care in the world. "I don't work for criminals... or creeps."

"No," Nick said, tilting his head slightly to one side, tapping the barrel of the Glock gently against the outside of his leg, "you always were a true company man, but they did let you go, right? Anyway, after that mess on the mountain, I had an idea you'd be coming after me. It's what I'd do, so I was kind of expecting you. And you almost made it, and would have if I'd been just a little more trusting. See, I don't trust anyone; never have, not even my closest friends, and certainly not the people that work for me. They're all... well, not nice people, shall we say? So, it was a little late when I found out you were here, in the building, but not too late... It's never too late, as they say, is it? Anyway, thanks to a little extra technology, I did get to know you were coming for me. Here, take a look."

Have you ever noticed how so-called smart people like to hear themselves talk? Nick Christmas was no exception. Without taking his eyes off either of us, he reached behind him and turned the laptop on the table around so we could see it. The image was frozen, but it showed a still shot of the two of us halfway up the stairs.

"Surprised?" he asked. "You shouldn't be, especially you, Bob, being CIA. You know," he continued, conversationally, "back in the day, when I was... oooh... ten years old, I think I was, I was a Boy Scout. That was quite a learning experience, as you can imagine, but the one thing I learned that has stayed with me ever since, that helped my career more than anything else, was the true meaning of the Boy Scout motto. Do you happen to know what that is? You, Harry. Do you know?"

Of course I did, but I wasn't about to give him the satisfaction of joining him in his game.

"Be prepared," he said, thoughtfully. "Be prepared, that's what it is, and I am, *always!*" The word snapped out of his mouth, then he smiled again, and slowly shook his head, watching me through slitted eyes.

"And I was," he said, pleasantly. "Fortunately, I was awake. And who wouldn't be after they'd just lost several million dollars' worth of equipment, not to mention sixteen of my assets... including poor old Hank, and Johnny, although Johnny... he was, well, I won't go into that. Anyway, I was working on my laptop, and up popped the warning flag. I had you from the second you put your foot on the stairs: motion detectors, you see, there at the foot of the stairs and here in my office. You set off the silent alarm and started the cameras rolling. One can't be too careful in this business. Now, please sit down; talk to me."

Neither of us moved to sit.

"Oh well, suit yourselves. I hope you don't mind if I sit." He sat down on the corner of the desk, his left foot on the floor, his right hanging loose, the gun held comfortably on his lap.

"So, Harry Starke," he said, smiling humorlessly at me. "You're something else—stand still, Bob," he snarled, interrupting himself, "or I'll shoot your frickin' dick off."

Bob didn't answer. Christmas turned his attention back to me.

"I dread to think how much money in manpower and equipment you've cost me these last couple of days. Oh no, Harry," he said as if he'd had a sudden thought. "My people downstairs. You killed them all, right?"

Neither of us answered.

He nodded. "Of course you did. It's what I would do," he said, for the second time. "So sad. Nice bunch of kids. Never mind. There are plenty more where they came from. But it's such a damned nuisance, you know, all that training down the shitter and now I have to start over."

He shook his head in mock exasperation, then said, "Harry, what the hell is it with you and your daddy? I offered to pay that family off, a really generous chunk of change, but he advised them to turn it down, said they'd do better in court. But, of course, I couldn't allow that, now could I? I couldn't let him drag me into court; who the hell knows what the old goat might uncover. And I did try to persuade him, but he wouldn't give an inch. Now look where we are. He's about to lose a second son... and, well shit, it's all his fault. Where is he, by the way?"

He looked at me expectantly, then at Bob, then back at me and continued.

"Well, no problem. I'll find him. In the meantime, I need to deal with you guys."

We stared at him without speaking. My mind was churning. He was going to kill us both and, at that point, there was little I could do about it. The one advantage we had, if you could call it that, was we, Bob and I, were about ten feet apart. It would all depend on which one of us he went for first. I was betting it would be Bob.

"Okay," he said, twitching the barrel of the Glock, which was still lying in his lap. "As I see it, you guys are trespassing. You broke into my place of business, my home, and I caught you. You're both armed, and I'm in fear for my life so..."

We both saw it coming: the Glock began to rise and, just as he pulled the trigger, Bob dove to the left and I to the right, and even while I was in flight, I saw the puff as the bullet impacted Bob's vest.

I landed on my right side, rolling, reaching, scrambling for cover. I jerked the second Sig from my ankle holster as I rolled and snapped off two quick shots and I got lucky: the first shot missed and slammed into a photograph hanging on the wall; the second clipped his left hand ripping away his thumb. He howled with pain, staggered backward, the big Glock swinging in my direction as I continued rolling across the floor. And then I hit the wall and could roll no more. I jerked myself upright, my back against the wall. He disappeared behind the desk. I had no shot; Bob had no gun.

Me? I did something really stupid, something that, if it went wrong, if Bob didn't...

"*Bob!*" I yelled, and I flipped the Sig across the room to him. He reached up and snatched it out of the air.

I don't know if he saw me do it... I guess he couldn't have, but oh, he was quick, was Christmas, and he was good. His training took over. He stood up, flung himself to the left, shooting one-handed, aiming purely by instinct, thank God. If he'd taken his time and tried for a head shot, I'd be dead. But he didn't.

He managed to snap off two shots faster than you could blink. They slammed into my vest, center mass, less than two inches apart, just as he'd been trained to do.

Bob had also been trained that way. We all had, but Bob ignored his training. He waited, for just a split second, and went for the head.

The shot hit Christmas, whose attention was still on me, and the bullet entered his skull just forward of his right ear and angled slightly backward: the bullet ripped through his head and exited through his left ear and slammed into the wall, spraying blood, bone and brain matter across the room.

Bob collapsed, sat down on the floor with a thump, and lay there breathing heavily.

"Damn, that hurts," he said, softly, his hand on his vest just below his rib cage. "It feels like I've been kicked by a frickin' horse. That's three times in the last two days. Damn." He rolled over onto his side, facing me. "Hey," he said, worriedly. "Are you okay. You don't look so good. You hit?"

"Two to the chest. A horse, you say? More like being stomped on by an elephant."

"Yeah, right," he said, sarcastically, "a frickin' elephant. How the hell would you know?"

"Harry, Harry," I heard Tim in my ear. "What's happening? I heard shots."

"It's okay, Tim," I said. "Don't know about T.J. and the others, but we're both okay. Keep your eyes open for cops."

Bob turned and looked at what was left of Nick Christmas, shook his head, and said, "How do you like that, you sick son of a bitch. Payback for all of those women and children you defiled, and all of the poor bastards you murdered in Kandahar. Go rot in hell, where you belong."

I stared at him. *Where the hell did that come from?* I thought, but I wasn't about to find out, not then, at least.

"Well, Harry, old son," he said, lightly. "Problem solved, I guess, but we need to get outa here."

He groaned as he scrambled to his feet and offered me a hand up.

"Grab your mask and cover up," I said, wincing as the pain seared through my chest. "His troops downstairs must have heard the gunfire, and T.J. will—"

"I don't think so," Tim said, tentatively, into my ear. "I see eleven signatures, besides your own, and they're all bunched together in the center aisle across from the stairs where you are."

Bob grabbed Christmas' laptop, and we hurried out onto the balcony and looked down. And there they were. All eight of them were lying face down, in a row on the floor, bound and gagged, with T.J., Chuck, and Monty standing over them. *What the hell? How did they manage that?*

"You said no noise, right?" T.J. said when I asked what the hell had happened, after we'd rejoined them. "So I figured—that is we figured, that there was no point in takin' any chances. If anyone of 'em had realized something was wrong, we'd have had a fight on our hands. We knew from Tim that they were all dead to the world, so we made a preemptive strike. Well, it was more a preemptive wakeup call than a strike. It was just a matter of rounding 'em up. So we went room-to-room, and we got 'em all; no fuss, no noise; problem solved. Better this way, right?"

"Yeah, right," I said, sarcastically. But I had to agree that he was right: it's always better to solve potential problems before they arise.

And so I took out my pocket knife, opened it, wiped it clean, closed it again and showed it to the nearest prisoner, then I laid it on a nearby table, told them to stay where they were and count to one hundred. We left the gang of eight lying there as we slipped away into the night. It was ten after three in the morning.

Thirty-two minutes, I thought. *Seemed like a frickin' lifetime.*

Chapter 28

Aftermath

There's no describing the feelings I experienced that morning when I walked into August's home on Riverview and found him, Jacque, and Kate waiting for us. You'd be forgiven if you thought our reception was one of exuberance, but you'd be wrong. It was quite the opposite, in fact. Sure, they were relieved that we all made it home, for the most part unscathed, but after we'd told the tale, the stark reality of what we'd done over the past several days had descended upon us all like a giant wet blanket. There was nothing, nothing at all for us to rejoice about.

True, the threat to my father, Rose, and Amanda had been eliminated, but at what cost? And the repercussions? I didn't want to even think about what they might be. The reunion was somber, to say the least. Fortunately, it didn't last long. Such meetings can quickly deteriorate into maudlin gatherings of self-pity and doubt, and I wasn't about to let that happen.

So I sent Tim, Jacque, T.J., and his two buddies home.

Kate? As I said, she was there waiting for us, but she was hurting. The hearing loss in her right ear was almost complete. She'd stayed only to make sure we were all okay, and then she headed out to the

Aftermath

emergency room to get treatment. I offered to go with her, but she would have none of it. For some reason, she wanted to be alone. Yeah, yeah, I know. She blamed me for it, and for the whole dang mess. I understood, and I sure as hell intended to make it right if I could.

The news, though, when it came later that same day, was good: Kate's right tympanic membrane was indeed ruptured, but the doctor had assured her it would heal naturally, by itself, in two or three months.

I forwent my usual nightcap of Laphroaig, not because I didn't want it, but because August didn't have any. Oh, he had some good scotch, but I had to be in the mood for that. I wasn't, so I settled for a steaming hot mug of Dark Italian Roast, which he did have, though not in the blend I... But I digress.

It was almost four-thirty that morning when I finally flopped down on the bed. Even so, I woke early, at around seven. It was after all, "the big day." If all went well, Amanda would wake up and... and? What? Would she blame me for what had happened to her? I wouldn't blame her if she did. And what about the baby... What if she didn't like the name I'd given her? So many questions, so many fears. There was nothing I could do until she woke up. *Hell, I'll just have to wait and see.*

So I rose from a deep sleep that morning, groggy and with a head on me that felt like it was full of concrete. That, however, was not unusual. Usually, it's easily gotten rid of, a brisk five-mile run, and I feel like Rocky Balboa, on top of the world, but not that day. A run was out of the question: who the hell knew who I might encounter along the way? The press? Pitbull Charlie Grove? I couldn't and wouldn't face that, not yet.

So I settled for a long hot shower, and then I joined August in the kitchen.

"Good morning. What's the news?" I asked, nodding at the TV as I headed for the coffee machine.

"Not a word," he said over the rim of his cup. He was sitting at the kitchen table, his elbows on the tabletop, hands cradling the cup.

"You're kidding," I said.

He shook his head, and I sat down opposite him, and over the next ten minutes, drank two mugs of black coffee, ate a toasted onion bagel with cream cheese, and I felt like... I still felt like shit. And all the while I was watching the news. He was right. Nothing.

I checked the time. It was almost eight. I still had a couple of hours before I had to be at the hospital.

"Have you talked to Rose?"

"Yes, they're scheduled to land at nine-thirty. She'll bring Jade to the hospital. That okay?"

"Perfect," I said as I checked the TV for the umpteenth time. "I hope it won't be a wasted journey for them."

He looked sharply across the table at me. "I hear any more of that kind of talk, I'll slap you silly."

He wasn't joking, and I knew he wouldn't hesitate to try, but somehow it struck me as being quite funny, and it lightened my mood, a little.

"Yeah, right," I said, smiling at him. "That'll be the day."

In the background, I could hear Charlie Grove speaking on Channel 7 and turned to watch. The guy was, as always, full of himself and his own importance, but he had a way with words, and he could grab your attention, but not that day. The local news was all minutia with a couple shootings thrown in for good measure, but not a word about last night's adventure.

"What do you think?" I asked, nodding toward the TV.

"Something isn't right," he said. "I checked every station before you came in, there's nothing."

I got up, filled my coffee mug for the third time and then sat down again. I picked up the remote and flipped through the channels, expecting to see... what? I really wasn't sure, but something, surely, about what had happened the night before, right?

Wrong!

Not a word, either about Marietta or Gypsum Pond, not on any of the TV channels, including those in Atlanta, of which Marietta is a bedroom community. And that I found to be extremely disquieting.

We continued watching until it was time to leave, at which point I reluctantly picked up the remote and turned the TV off.

"Time to go?" August asked.

"Yes," I said, taking a deep breath. I was nervous, I mean *really* nervous. My head was full of what-ifs: what if she doesn't come out of it? What if her brain's damaged? What if she's lost her memory and doesn't recognize me? What if... she hates me? *Geez, Harry. Get a frickin' grip. She'll be fine!*

"Yes," I repeated. "Let's go."

We arrived at the hospital at precisely ten o'clock. We stopped in at the flower shop, and I grabbed a huge bunch of, hell, I dunno, flowers—August bought an arrangement of daisies—and then we made our way through the maze of corridors to the waiting area just a few short steps from room 3007. There I left August to wait; this was something I had to do by myself.

I crept as quietly as I could to the door and peeked around the corner. She was lying there, eyes closed, breathing normally. I turned away and went to the desk.

"Where's Dr. Cartwright?" I asked.

"He's just getting out of surgery," the nurse said. "He shouldn't be too much longer. Is there anything I can do for you?"

I shook my head, disappointed. "Is it okay if I go and sit with my wife? She's in 3007."

At that, the nurse looked up and smiled. There was something about that smile...

"Of course. Go right ahead. I'll send in Dr. Cartwright as soon as he arrives."

And so I wandered back to her room, put the flowers on the nightstand, dragged a chair up to her bedside, sat down, took her hand gently in both of mine, and gazed at her face.

The bruises had lightened a little, the cuts on her lips were beginning to heal, her eyes were the most beautiful... shade... of... *Oh my God, they're open. She's awake.*

I couldn't speak. I sat there staring at her, transfixed, like I was some kind of loon.

"Hey," she said, and she gently squeezed my hand. It was barely a whisper, and hoarse, but it was the most beautiful sound I'd ever heard.

"Hey yourself," I finally managed to say. "Where the hell have you been?"

She smiled, just a little. "I can't talk, Harry."

"Oh... no, no, no, don't even try. I'll talk for both of us, okay?"

Again, she gifted me with that tiny, but oh so lovely smile. Oh my God, was I ever on cloud nine?

"The... baby?" she asked.

"She's fine. Absolutely fine. Beautiful. She's a she. I mean she's a girl. Gorgeous. She is, gorgeous. Just like you, well, not really, but she has your eyes, and that's what I called her, Jade. Is that okay? If it's not, we can change it. But her eyes are the same color as yours." I knew I was babbling, but I couldn't stop.

"She's with Rose. They're on their way. August is in the waiting area. They'll be here in a minute. Jade and Rose and August."

She was smiling up at me, her eyes watering, lips trembling, and I—

Dr. Cartwright walked in and saved me from making an even bigger fool of myself.

"Came out of it all by herself. Clever girl, aren't you, my dear? I took her off the drugs last night, had the nurses keep an eye on her. She came to at ten after three this morning, perky as can be. Well, not so much, and I had her kept under light sedation. But now that you're here, no more need for that, I think. So, my dear. How are we feeling?"

Ten after three, are you kidding me? That's exactly the time when we left the warehouse in Marietta.

Aftermath

She didn't even try to answer. She just looked up at him and rewarded him with the same tiny smile she gave me.

He nodded. "Right then. I'll leave you to it. Please don't excite her, and don't stay too long. The more rest she gets, the sooner she'll be out of here. Hello, who's this?"

I turned and saw Rose holding the baby, August behind them, all three smiling hugely. Well, no, Jade wasn't smiling at all. She was asleep.

"Can she?" Rose asked Dr. Cartwright.

"I don't see why not. Here, let me get out of the way."

He did, and Rose handed Jade to me, and I laid her down in the crook of Amanda's arm and stepped back. Jade stirred slightly in her sleep, opened her eyes, sighed, and then closed them again.

It was at that moment when I knew exactly what I was going to do with the rest of my life.

Chapter 29

Four Days In May

D r. Cartwright released Amanda the following Saturday morning, June 2. The five days following her awakening were hectic. The press finally found me at Riverview, and my world became a nightmare: I was obliged to face them head-on.

I gave Charlie Grove his exclusive, but I limited it to the attempt on Amanda's life and her improving condition. It wasn't exactly what he'd been expecting, but Channel 7's viewers certainly appreciated it.

That done, I held a press conference the following day, a one-time thing, I hoped, and answered questions for more than an hour about the foiled nuclear attack on the city. Some I could answer, some I was prohibited from answering, and some I just had no idea what the hell they were talking about, so I ignored them. Even so, I spent those next five days almost constantly dodging the reporters and cameras, but one thing I learned for certain was that the situation couldn't continue as it was.

Having dealt as best I could with the press, I figured my next chore, if you can call it that, was to deal with Bob. No, I hadn't forgotten his perceived duplicity, nor would I until I had a full explanation. And so, early on Friday morning, the day before Amanda was due to come home, I headed downtown to my offices on Georgia Avenue.

Jacque, Tim, T.J., Bob and the rest of my team were more than a little enthusiastic in their welcoming me back. It was only then that I realized I hadn't been to the office and seen most of the team for more than three weeks. So, after thirty minutes of effusive conversation, I finally called a halt and asked Bob to join me in my office.

I had him take a seat opposite me, across the over-large coffee table that I used for less-than-formal meetings, and I put it to him.

"Bob," I said, quietly, "we have to talk. You know that, right?"

He'd been lounging comfortably in the corner of the sofa, but he sat up straight, narrowed his eyes, frowned and, for a minute, I thought he was going to get up and leave, but he didn't. He stared at me for a moment, then tilted his head to one side, looked away, and sighed.

"Okay, Harry," he said. "I guess you deserve some answers. Where would you like me to begin?"

I gave him a cockeyed look and said, "How about the beginning?"

He nodded, leaned forward, rested his elbows on his knees, and clasped his hands together in front of him and stared at them.

"I was twenty-two," he began, "academically gifted, so I was told, when I graduated college in 1993. I hadn't even left the campus when I was visited by—well, that I can't tell you. Let's just say this, as a result of that visit, I was recruited immediately into the CIA." He paused, looked up at me and smiled.

"Don't laugh, Harry," he said, "but I'd always been fascinated by James Bond and when the opportunity was offered... Ah, forget it." He shook his head and looked down at his hands.

"So anyway," he continued, "I spent my first year as a spook at Quantico before being transferred to the CIA's Office of Military Affairs; that was in '94. From then until I was 'deactivated' in 2005" —he made quotes with his fingers, then continued—"I was assigned to the Kabul Field office in Afghanistan where I had responsibility for coordinating CIA and DoD operational activities. When I was deactivated in 2005, after twelve years of service, I took a little time off and then spent the next two years as a cop in Chicago. I joined you in 2008, and that's it. The rest you know."

I stared hard at him and said, "Was coming here your idea or did someone put you up to it?"

He shook his head. "No, nothing like that. I hated being a cop, and I hated Chicago even more, especially the winters, so I came south. I needed a job. The PI thing fascinated me. So I did a little checking, found out that you were the best and, Bob's your uncle if you'll pardon the pun." He finally looked me right in the eye. "Look, Harry, I really am sorry. I should have been upfront with you, and I would have been if I could, but..." He shrugged. "I couldn't."

I nodded, slowly. I believed him. I had no reason not to.

"And you're still part of the CIA? What exactly is your status?"

"That's something else I can't answer, not because of any regulation, but because I simply don't know. I'm still on the rolls, but I'm—as I told you—deactivated."

"So you could be *reactivated?*"

He shrugged. "I suppose, but why would they?"

If he didn't know the answer to that, I sure as hell didn't. So, still not really satisfied, or happy, I accepted the situation and left it at that. Other than firing his ass, I really had no other choice, and besides, there was something amiss about the way the events of those four days had been covered up.

I wanted answers to a whole boatload of questions. And I was hoping Bob could help get them.

Some, after much digging and hacking, we managed to get. Some, not even a sniff. Here's what we were able to find out:

As you know, there had been nothing in the media about the happenings in Marietta that night, not then nor any time since. And it was more than a week before we found out why. Actually, it was Tim who first found out; Bob confirmed Tim's findings at a later date.

It simply never happened.

Someone at the highest levels of the government, in all probability the NSA, had clamped down on and cleaned the building before the word leaked out. And when I say "cleaned," I think that was probably the understatement of the decade.

But that wasn't what bothered me—well, it bothered me, but not to any great extent. We'd been careful, and I was certain they'd find nothing on the security system. I'd pulled the plug on that, remember? And we had the laptop. No, what bothered me was that someone had the power to erase that entire series of incidents, the whole four days, from reality, including the firefight on the mountain. That didn't make it to the media either, but even more scary was that they could effectively wipe away part of a man's existence. I'll explain that in a minute.

But going back to the warehouse: by six o'clock that morning, after we left, the word must have reached someone with decision-making authority, because a busload of—I'm going to say armed soldiers—arrived and locked the place down. By noon, the building was empty and abandoned. As I said, "cleaned."

What happened to Christmas' employees? We don't know. They disappeared, along with all of the vehicles, weapons, explosives, supplies, and every piece of paper and computer. Those assets already on assignment, including, so we think, Nick's girlfriend Jessica Roark, were quickly reassigned, absorbed, their identities changed.

Hank Johnson, we know, died during the fight on the mountain. What happened to the bodies, or Johnny Pascal, we never found out. Just as dawn was breaking that morning, several black helicopters were observed coming and going, to and from the site. What the sheriff found when he arrived later that afternoon, if he even bothered to respond to the call I made, I have no idea. He certainly didn't get in touch with me.

It was more than six months later when I returned to the cabin to find it gone, burned to the ground. Only the two stone chimneys and what once had been the basement remained to mark the spot. Fortunately, the cabin was insured.

Gypsum Pond? As you already know, Christmas cleaned that up himself.

Bob turned Nick Christmas' laptop over to Tim. Its contents were revealing, to say the least. Nick, so it seemed, had been a meticulous record keeper.

The women and children we'd discovered at Gypsum Pond were part of a slave and sex trafficking operation that Christmas and his crew had been running for almost a decade.

Lazarus, his Afghani partner, was never identified, but between them, over the years since Christmas had been discharged, they had imported more than seventy-four million dollars' worth of illegal drugs from Afghanistan, most of it heroin. His combined operations—not including his company's legitimate net earnings which were in excess of eighteen million dollars—Tim estimated to be more than one hundred million dollars, all of it missing without a trace.

I mentioned earlier that what bothered me most about the entire affair was that whoever was in charge of the cleanup operation had enough power to be able to effectively wipe away a man's life. I'll explain:

What happened to Christmas' body we never did find out. Bob, Tim, and I, we all tried to find out, through official channels—Tim, of course, went a little deeper than that—but as far as the government was concerned, he never existed. Well, not after 2008 when he was supposed to have been discharged. The official records stated that he died on August 25, 2008, while on active duty, the victim of an IED just outside of Kandahar, his body being cremated upon its return to the United States. We tried to reach his parents, but they had both passed several years earlier, and he had no siblings that we could find.

We, of course, knew different. The fact that more than ten years of his life had been completely expunged from the records as if he'd never existed, that really did bother me. And it raised a whole new set of questions the most pressing of which was... Why? Why was his slate wiped clean? Better yet: what was he really doing, and who for? Was it some obscure, clandestine government department? Or was it a breakaway faction of the DoD, Department of Defense, or some other covert, non-acronymic government agency operating to an agenda outside of and beyond its official mandate?

That, I think is the more likely answer. We always knew he'd been supplying security for the DoD, but I guess we'll never know.

Nick's laptop? It was dynamite, a ticking bomb. If it were ever to fall into the wrong hands, it would destroy us. I had Tim destroy it instead; problem solved.

But that still left me with more questions than answers, most of which would never be answered, including the most intriguing one of all: Who the hell had been pulling Nick Christmas' strings? I had no idea, but I knew damned well that whomever it was, he—maybe it was a she—sure as hell knew all about me.

Chapter 30

Finally

It was one of those balmy, late summer mornings in September. Amanda and I were lying side by side on loungers beside the pool. Jade was asleep in her stroller, and all seemed right with the world. It was the first time since Amanda had come home from the hospital that we were truly alone. The preceding three months had been hectic. We'd stayed at Riverview with August and Rose, until just two days earlier, that because Amanda had been pretty busted up and the healing was slow. Thus, she needed almost as much care and attention as did Jade.

Me? I was pretty damned useless and found it best to stay out of the way. What little time Amanda and I did have alone wasn't the time for talking, and the events leading up to her accident we'd never discussed, not until that morning and... Well, it was a long and very private conversation, most of which I'd rather keep to myself.

So, there we were, at our home on East Brow Road, enjoying the stunning view, the gentle rays, the warm breeze, and each other when suddenly she turned her head toward me and said, quietly, "I love you, Harry."

It wasn't so much what she said, more how she said it. Almost as a question.

"I love you too," I said cautiously.

She smiled and said, "But we need to talk."

"Oh-kay."

"That day, on the mountain, when Duvon ran me off the—"

"Amanda, hush," I said, interrupting her. "I'm so sorry..."

"No, please, don't be." She rose up on her elbow and turned toward me. "It was my fault. I was angry with you. I thought the round trip would take too long. I was within days of giving birth. Harry, I could have killed Jade."

"But you didn't." I also raised myself up and turned to face her. "And it wasn't your fault. Look, it's over. Duvon is gone, so's Shady. But you're right. We do need to talk, but not about that. Look, all this... this... stuff that's gone down, this crazy cycle of violence; it has to end. We have to get past it, move on, make a proper life for ourselves... for the three of us."

I sat up, swung my legs off the lounger, and turned to face her. I took her hand in mine and looked deep into her eyes. Some of the scars hadn't yet quite faded, some would always remain, but to me, she was more beautiful than ever.

"It's over," I said, quietly. "I'm going to resign, give up my half of the business—"

"You can't," she said, pulling her hand away. She stood up, folded her arms, lowered her head, and walked a small circle on the concrete patio. Then she stopped, looked at me, sat down again, face to face, and said, "Harry, you can't do that. I won't let you."

I smiled at her, took both her hands in mine, raised them to my lips, kissed her knuckles, then looked up at her and shook my head.

"What happened to you, my love, was to have been the final straw for my career as a private eye. But then Joe was kidnapped. I don't want to talk about it, but that really was the end, for me at least."

I was, of course, referring to the Christmas fiasco.

She twisted her hands out of mine and said, "Okay. Let's think about it. You're done, finished, no more Harry Starke Investigations. Now what? What are you going to do for the next forty years?"

Forty years? That's a bit optimistic.

"Enjoy life. You, Jade, more kids?" I said with a smirk.

"And just how long do you think it would be before you became bored with all that *enjoyment?*"

She tilted her head, narrowed her eyes, and looked into mine. "Come on. Tell me. How long?"

She had me there. Hell, my attention span for the mundane was that of a lemon.

"And there's another thing," she said, "several in fact." She grabbed my hands. "Harry, where do you think we'd be today if you weren't you? If you didn't do what you do so well? If you'd been off somewhere *enjoying life?* No, don't answer. I'll tell you." She turned and looked out over the patio wall at the city laid out below and nodded.

"All of that would be gone, Harry, and thousands of lives along with it, including all of your family and friends. This view that you, that we, love so much would be nothing but a nuclear wasteland. It's still there because you were doing what you do best, Harry.

As I followed her gaze, I was speechless. Such thoughts had never entered my head.

"But I'm not—"

"A hero? Yes, you are, and no buts. You know I'm right. This is your town, and mine, and now Jade's and all those other kids you'd like to have. Now shut the hell up and come kiss me."

I did. I shut up, and I kissed her. And then I had another thought: *How come she always gets the last word?*

* * *

Aftermath

At that very same moment, more than fourteen hundred miles away, on a beach on the eastern shores of the Dominican Republic, Lester "Shady" Tree, known locally as Sam Cooper, was enjoying a tall glass of iced rum and cola. He was in paradise, not wanting for anything. Life was good, except... *Harry Frickin' Starke!* he thought, savagely.

Backlash

The Harry Starke Novels Book 15

Prologue

September 2018

I t was one of those balmy, summer-like mornings in September. Amanda and I were lying side by side on loungers beside the pool. Jade was asleep in her stroller, and all seemed right with the world.

It was the first time since Amanda had come home from the hospital at the end of May that we were truly alone. The preceding three months had been hectic. We'd stayed at Riverview with August and Rose until just two days earlier, that because Amanda had been pretty busted up and the healing was slow. Thus, she needed almost as much care and attention as did Jade.

Me? I was pretty damned useless and found it best to stay out of the way. What little time Amanda and I did have alone wasn't the time for talking, and the events leading up to her accident... we'd never discussed them, not until that morning and... Well, it was a long and very private conversation, most of which I'd rather keep to myself.

So, there we were, at our home on East Brow Road, enjoying the

359

stunning view, the gentle rays, the warm breeze, and each other when suddenly she turned her head toward me and said quietly, "I love you, Harry."

It wasn't so much what she said, more how she said it. Almost as a question.

"I love you too," I said cautiously.

She smiled and said, "But we need to talk."

"Oh-kay."

"That day, on the mountain, when Duvon ran me—"

"Amanda, hush," I said, interrupting her. "I'm so sorry."

"No, please, don't be." She rose up on her elbow and turned toward me. "It was my fault. You told me to stay off Scenic Highway, but I was angry with you. And I thought the round trip would take too long. I was within days of giving birth... Harry, I could have killed Jade."

"But you didn't." I also raised myself up and turned to face her. "And it wasn't your fault. Look, it's over. Duvon is gone, so's Shady. But you're right. We do need to talk, but not about that. Look, all this... this... stuff that's gone down, this crazy cycle of violence that I've been living for the past eight years, or so. It has to end. We have to get past it. I have to. It's time to move on, to make a proper life for ourselves, for the three of us."

I sat up, swung my legs off the lounger, and turned to face her. I took her hand in mine and looked deep into her eyes. Some of the scars hadn't yet quite faded, some would always remain, but to me, she was more beautiful than ever.

"It's over," I said quietly. "I'm going to resign. I'll give up my half of the business—"

"You can't," she said, pulling her hand away. She stood up, folded her arms, lowered her head, and walked a small circle on the concrete patio. Then she stopped, looked down at me, and then sat down again, face to face, and said, "Harry, you can't do that. I won't let you."

I smiled at her, took both her hands in mine, raised them to my lips, kissed her knuckles, then looked up at her and shook my head.

"What happened to you, my love, was to have been the final straw for my career as a private eye. But then Joe was kidnapped. I don't want to talk about it, but that really was the end, for me at least."

Joe, Joseph, Uncle Joe, is my father's younger brother, and he's... Oh hell, he's what they call a "special needs" person. His mental capacity is that of a seven-year-old. No, he wasn't born like that. At six months he developed an infection and the doctor gave him penicillin. Unfortunately, he was allergic to it and it fried his brain. Today, he's fifty-six and lives in a facility that caters to all of his needs.

Uncle Joe was kidnapped by an enemy of mine, in what I now refer to as the Nicholas Christmas fiasco.

She twisted her hands out of mine and said, "Okay. Let's think about it. You're done, finished, no more Harry Starke Investigations. Now what? What are you going to do for the next forty years?"

Forty years? That's a bit optimistic.

"Enjoy life. You, Jade, more kids?" I said with a smirk.

"And just how long do you think it would be before you became bored with all that *enjoyment?*"

She tilted her head, narrowed her eyes, and looked into mine. "Come on. Tell me. How long?"

She had me there. Hell, my attention span for the mundane was that of a lemon.

"And there's another thing," she said, "several in fact." She grabbed my hands. "Harry, where do you think we'd be today if you weren't you? If you didn't do what you do so well? If you'd been off somewhere *enjoying* life? No, don't answer. I'll tell you." She turned and looked out over the patio wall at the city laid out below and nodded, then waved her hand at the panorama.

"All of that would be gone, Harry, and thousands of lives along with it, including all of your family and friends. This view that you, that we, love so much would be nothing but a nuclear wasteland. It's still there because you were doing what you do best, Harry."

As I followed her gaze, I was speechless. Such thoughts had never entered my head.

"But I'm not—"

"A hero? Yes, you are, and no buts. You know I'm right. This is your town, and mine, and now Jade's and all of those other kids you'd like to have. Now shut the hell up and come kiss me."

I did. I shut up, and I kissed her. And then I had another thought: *How come she always gets the last word?*

At that very same moment more than fourteen hundred miles away, on a beach on the eastern shores of the Dominican Republic, Lester "Shady" Tree, known locally as Sam Cooper, was enjoying a tall glass of iced rum and cola. He was in paradise, not wanting for anything. Life was good, except for... *Harry Frickin' Starke!* he thought, savagely.

Chapter One

Monday, June 25, 2019

It was just after nine o'clock in the evening one Monday in June of 2019. I was working... Well, I was sitting in my car watching the side entrance of a construction site off of Chestnut Street, only it wasn't a construction site. It should have been. There was plenty of equipment on site. The problem was, though, none of it had moved for more than a month.

One of those prefabricated mobile offices had been installed. The site had been cleared, the slab and foundations had been laid, and... that was it. Everything had come to a grinding halt; nothing was happening.

The site was shut down and had been for more than a month. The project, however, was still hemorrhaging money, which is why I was there.

I'd been there for hours, five hours, in fact, and I was bored. And hungry. And I was wondering what the hell I was doing there. I was also thinking about a conversation I'd had with Amanda, back in September, and wondering why the hell I'd allowed her to talk me out of quitting. Sitting alone outside a construction site for hours on end wasn't my idea of how a high-flying private investigator should be spending his evenings. But I'd made her a promise: no more dangerous jobs. Was it a promise I could keep? Hah! You know me... or do you?

My name's Harry Starke. I'm an ex-cop, but these days I run a successful private investigation agency in Chattanooga. I have a wife, Amanda, and a one-year-old daughter, Jade, whom I adore. Well, I adore both of them. Anyway, my life to date has been... for want of another word, chaotic: one hazardous case after another. I've lost count of the number of times members of my team have saved my life, including Amanda, who's killed for me, but that's another story.

Anyway, the reason I was watching the site that evening was because one of the investors, who shall be nameless, had hired me to find out what was happening to the money, his money... It's always about the money, isn't it?

I took the job because it seemed simple enough. Certainly not dangerous. I'd had T.J. take a look at the accounts and, sure enough, someone had been siphoning off large amounts of cash.

T.J.—whose full name is T.J. Bron—came to Starke Investigations by way of my friend and one-time partner, Kate Gazzara, a captain in the major crimes squad at the Chattanooga Police Department. She'd found him on the street, destitute, homeless and ready to end his life. He, in turn, about to commit his last act, had stumbled on the naked body of a young woman. Kate saw something in T.J. that nobody else did, and she brought him to me.

T.J. is... different... a Vietnam vet with an accounting degree who'd fallen on hard times. I'd taken him on when Ronnie Hall left me for greener pastures. T.J. is a man with a past. Not a criminal past, but a violent one, nonetheless. He's been put through the mill on more than one occasion. Today, aside from being great with numbers, he's also one tough son of a bitch. He's fiercely loyal and will kill at the drop of a hat. Not someone you should keep around, you might say? I'd say you're wrong. He, too, has saved my life, twice that I know of.

So, here's how T.J. had figured it out. One of the majority share-holders, a man by the name of Daniel Ruthman, who was also the general contractor in overall charge of construction, had, for months, been siphoning off funds. How? Well, as general contractor he made large payments to a number of subcontractors, most of which were registered to offshore companies owned by... you guessed it: Daniel Ruthman.

My team and I had been watching Ruthman for more than a week. He was using the onsite office as his headquarters, and he kept weird hours. Watching his comings and goings was a full-time job all by itself. My plan that night was to confront him, but he had yet to make an appearance. When he did, if he did, I was determined to find out what the hell was going on.

It was close on fifteen after nine when he finally showed up, and I could tell right away that something was wrong. He barely slowed his Range Rover as he turned off Chestnut and skidded to a stop in front of the gates. He jumped out of his vehicle, ran to the gate, unlocked the chain, pushed open the gate, then ran back to his car and drove through, all the time looking over his shoulder as if he was being chased. He made a beeline into his office and slammed the door shut. Something was obviously wrong,

I drove through the open gates, parked beside Ruthman's Range Rover, ran up the steps and tried to open the door. It was locked. I knocked three times and shouted that I just wanted to talk.

I heard the lock click, and the door opened a crack. I put my shoulder to it and pushed. The man swore. I pushed the door all the way open just in time to see him stagger backward, holding his nose in both hands.

"You broke my frickin' nose," he yelped. "Who the hell are you and what do you want? If you're here to rob me, you're wasting your time. I don't keep any money here."

"My name's Harry Starke," I replied. "And I'm not here to rob you. I'm a private investigator. I've been hired to find out why this site is shut down and where the money's gone. Most of it I already know. What I want to know is why."

"You don't have—"

He took one look at my face, and the grip of my Heckler and Koch VP9 half-hidden beneath my jacket, and decided it wasn't the way to go, and he was right. I was all out of patience and in no mood to fool around.

"Talk to me, Danny. I know about the phony safety issues. I also know about the companies you've been paying... well, not for the work they've done here, that's pretty obvious. I also know that, with a couple of exceptions, those companies are registered to you in the Caymans. You've been a naughty boy, Danny. Embezzlement is a felony. You're looking at ten years, federal. That means you'll serve every minute, unless... Now talk to me, before I make you."

He backed away and sat down at his desk under the window, swiveled his chair so that it faced me, looked up at me, and I swear he had tears in his eyes.

"Hell, come on, Danny," I said quietly. "I didn't hurt you that much. What the hell is wrong with you?"

"You don't understand," he replied.

He stopped talking, turned in his chair to look out of the window. He'd heard something. I'd heard it too: a car. I stepped to the window and looked out.

"You've gotten us both killed," he whimpered.

I could see a woman and a man in the car. I turned and looked at Ruthman. His face was white. He was trembling.

"What the hell's going on, Danny?"

"They're going to kill me, and you, too."

"The hell they are."

I took out my phone and called Jacque, my business partner and PA.

"Don't say a word," I said when she picked up. "I'm with

Ruthman and we have visitors. I'm going to put the phone down. You listen. If this thing goes sideways, call the cops."

I put the phone face down on a side table, stepped away and put my back against the wall.

The door opened and the woman, whom I recognized as Ruthman's ex-wife, stepped inside, followed by a man I instantly recognized... only I didn't. For a split second as he lumbered in out of the shadows, I thought it was Duvon James. And my heart almost stopped. Duvon was dead. I know because, a little more than a year earlier, I'd killed him and dumped his body in a four-hundred-foot-deep lake of boiling water.

Yes, I know how that sounds, but you had to be there.

Anyway, as the man stepped out of the shadows, though, I could see he bore no resemblance at all to Duvon. He must have been at least twenty, maybe thirty pounds heavier with arms nearly as thick as my waist. He was also a couple of inches taller than Duvon and, for Pete's sake, he had an 80's style mullet. He also had a baseball bat in his hand.

I could see that the ex-wife was... well, angry would be an understatement.

"Who the hell is this, Danny?" she snarled. "You hire yourself a bodyguard? I can't say as I blame you, you sneaky little son of a bitch. Take care of him, Rufus."

Mullet, or should I say Rufus—Rufus? What the hell kind of name is that?—stepped around her, the bat now in both hands. He was about to swing for the bleachers—that would be me. He was ready to do business, but so was I. With a much-practiced sweep of my right hand, I pulled my gun and aimed it at his chest. He was maybe eight feet from me and as big as the proverbial barn door. I couldn't have missed if I'd wanted to. He stopped dead and lowered the bat.

"Good thinking, Bat Man," I said, smiling. "Now drop it and step back."

He dropped it, then stepped back. He looked like a frickin' gorilla.

"Jacque," I said loudly. "Call Kate and tell her I need backup."

She didn't answer. She couldn't. I'd turned the volume down. I could only hope she'd heard me.

The ex-wife smiled and said, "I'm leaving."

"I don't think so," I said, wagging the gun back and forth between them. "Why don't you just sit down and we'll talk?"

"Screw you," she said and turned to the door.

I have to admit that at that point I was a little lost as to what to do next. I couldn't shoot either one of them; my life wasn't in danger, so I did the next best thing. I stepped forward and smacked Mullet upside the head, hard. He went down howling like a wolf.

"Your turn next, lady," I said. "Now do as I say and sit the hell down or I'll give you some of the same."

"You wouldn't dare," she said.

"Try me," I said, taking a step toward her.

She sat down.

I turned to Ruthman and said, "Now, Danny, you want to tell me what the hell's been going on?"

And he did.

It turned out that Mullet, aka Rufus, was the ex-wife's boyfriend and that Ruthman was one weak son of a bitch. At first she'd threatened to withhold visitation with his kids if he didn't pay her, a lot. When that didn't work, she'd turned Mullet loose on him. One visit from him and his baseball bat and Danny was putty in her fat little fingers, to the tune of almost a half-million dollars, and counting.

I picked up my phone and said, "Jacque? You get all that?"

She had, and she'd recorded the entire conversation from the time the two of them had stepped into the office.

I could hear sirens in the distance. Mrs. R and Mullet looked decidedly uncomfortable, but they stayed put. Kate and a fleet of cruisers arrived a couple of minutes later.

Captain Kate Gazzara stepped into the office followed by two uniforms, their weapons drawn.

"What's going on, Harry?" Kate asked as I slid my own gun back into its holster.

It was at that point I realized my hands were shaking... *What the hell?*

I ignored it, for the moment, and tried to hide it as I explained everything to Kate, then told her I'd have Jacque turn over the recording and the case files to her. Ruthman and the two extortionists sat sullenly by until Kate read them their rights and then had them cuffed and taken away.

And that was the end of it. The case was done, solved.

So, you say. *If that's all there is to it, why are you telling me? What does it have to do with anything?*

Well, let's see.

Me? I went back to my car and sat there for... I dunno. Ten minutes? Fifteen? More? Thinking.

The Ruthman case had worked out well, without too much confrontation. But I couldn't help but remember the thoughts I'd had while I was sitting out there in front of the site, about Amanda and Jade and the promises I'd made that I knew I couldn't keep.

I looked down at my hands. They were still shaking and, I have to admit it, not for the first time. It had been happening on odd occasions ever since we'd unloaded that nuclear weapon into the lake. Jacque had noticed it several times. Amanda? I don't know. She'd never mentioned it, but I'd seen her staring hard at me a couple of times over the last two months or so.

And on top of that... there was that moment when I'd thought Mullet was Duvon James. What was that about?

What the hell is happening to me? Am I going crazy?

No, I wasn't, but it was a pivotal moment for me and has a direct bearing on the story I'm about to tell you.

Chapter Two

It was late when I left the construction site that evening. The Ruthman case was, as far as I was concerned, nicely wrapped up. The bad guys were on their way to the lockup and I was driving home. I was on East Broad when I decided to call Jacque.

Even though she, Jacque, was now a part-owner of Harry Starke Investigations and my office manager, I still considered her my right-hand man, so to speak. I knew that as long as I was working, she'd still be at the office. The woman's a machine. I called her to make sure the Ruthman case had been properly handled. Of course, it had.

But then she asked me the question she'd asked so many times over the past several weeks.

"Harry, are you okay? How're you feeling?"

Okay, so it was two questions, but you get the idea, right?

I heaved a heavy sigh, shook my head and said, "I'm fine, Jacque. What the hell is it with you and these questions about my health?" And I could have bitten my tongue off.

"I'm sorry," I said quickly before she could answer. "It's been a long day. I'm tired and irritable. Forgive me?"

"There's nothin' to forgive. You t'ink I don't know what's goin' on?"

Jacque's Jamaican by birth, but she lost her accent a long time ago... except when she's pissed, which she was, and then it comes back with a vengeance. She doesn't mince words either.

"What d'you mean, you know what's going on?"

"I seen your hands shakin', and I know what you been thinkin' these last few months since the bomb. You got PTSD, is what you got."

I was stunned. I hadn't thought of that.

"We been steppin' around you like we was walkin' on eggs. You've been a bear, Harry Starke. We're all just worried about you, you know?"

I didn't know what to say. On thinking about it, though, which I hadn't—well, not much—I knew she was right.

"There's no need to worry, Jacque. I'm okay. I just have a lot on my mind, is all." *Boy, is that ever an understatement?* "I'm sorry. I'll try to do better."

"I hope so. What time will you be in tomorrow?"

The Jamaican accent was gone. I was back in her good graces. At least for now.

"The usual time. Eight-thirty... ish."

"Get some rest, Harry. You need it. Bye." And then she hung up.

As I turned off Highway 41 onto Scenic Highway and began the long haul up Lookout Mountain, I couldn't help but think about what she'd said. Was I really suffering from PTSD? I didn't think so, but what did I know? *Maybe I should get myself checked out... Nah, I'm just overworked, is all. I need a vacation... Maybe more than just a vacation.*

It was true the past few months had been traumatic, and I had to admit that I hadn't felt myself since the nuclear explosion and Amanda's near death... And then there was the aftermath of all that, the mess I'd found myself and my team in when I had to deal with Uncle

Joe's kidnapping and Nick Christmas. *Geez, that man was something else.*

And, finally, I'd lost my partner and best friend, Bob, to the CIA. *Yeah, I've been through a lot—we all have—but PTSD? I don't think so... Hah, maybe I'm losing my edge. I need to talk to Amanda.*

I found Amanda on a chaise lounge on the patio. She was in her pajamas. I thought for a minute that she was asleep, but she wasn't. She opened her eyes, raised herself up onto her elbows and looked up at me, smiling.

"You're late," she said. "I was just about to go to bed. How did it go tonight?"

I shrugged and said, "Fine. Ruthman and his wife and her boyfriend are on their way to the slammer. All's well that ends well, as they say."

I leaned in close and kissed her gently on the lips. She wrapped her arms around my neck and turned the kiss into an unmistakable declaration of her love for me.

"Wow," I said when she released me. "What was that all about?"

She shrugged, smiled shyly, but said nothing.

"I see," I said. "I need a drink. How about you? How's Jade?"

"I'll pass on the drink, but you have one. Jade's as adorable as ever. I put her to bed at six o'clock... It's late, Harry. I really need to go to bed, and so do you."

"No, please. Don't do that. Not yet. I need to talk to you."

She frowned, then said, "Is something wrong? Are you all right?"

There it was again, that question.

"Yes, I am, but that's what I want to talk to you about. Give me a minute. I'll be right back."

She looked up at me, frowning, but said nothing.

I returned a couple of minutes later with a glass containing three fingers of Laphroaig and a single ice cube, then sat down beside her, ignoring the look of disapproval.

"So tell me," she said. "What happened tonight? You look worn out."

So I told her, everything, including my conversation with Jacque and... my Duvon James moment. She listened intently; didn't say a word until I'd finished.

"Jacque's right," she said, swinging her legs off the chaise and sitting so she was facing me, her forearms on her knees, her hands clasped together. "I'm surprised, after all you've been through, that you're not a quivering wreck, locked up in a psychiatric ward. I asked you not to take chances anymore and what d'you do? You take on the Hulk and a baseball bat... What am I going to do with you, Harry?"

"Another kiss?" I asked, smiling hopefully. It didn't work.

All it took was "the look" for me to get back to being serious.

"Okay, I get it," I said, pulling a wry face. "Look, it wasn't as bad as it sounds. A gentle smack on his ear with the barrel of my gun was all it took to persuade him to drop the bat. After that... well, he was just a big old pussy cat."

"There you go again," she said. "More violence. Harry, you can't go on like this. You keep getting away with these violent confrontations. One of these days... One of these days you're going to meet your match and then... I can't lose you, Harry."

She leaned forward, took both my hands in hers and said, "We've had this conversation so many times since... well, you know. You're going to have to slow down, learn how to relax. You really are." She paused, stared into my eyes, then said, "Oh, what the hell. Come on. Let's go to bed. I know how to help you relax. We can talk about this PTSD thing in the morning."

And we did, and she did, relax me.

While Amanda did her best to put me at ease that night, sleep didn't come easy. It must have been sometime around two o'clock when I finally drifted off, only to awake from a nightmare some four hours later at six o'clock, sweating, shaking.

A nightmare? I don't usually remember my dreams, but that one... I did.

I'm in a huge, dark room; a basement, or maybe a warehouse. There's a woman strapped to a chair. Her back is to me. I can't see her face, but I know instinctively that it's Amanda. There's a man, a tall shadowy figure standing next to her. He has a gun to her head. I can't see his face either, but I can tell he's smiling at me and I... I think I know who he is, but I can't put a name to him. I know Amanda must be terrified, but I don't dare make a move to help her.

"How does it feel, Harry?" The voice echoes around the empty room.

I try to speak. I can't. I see his finger tighten on the trigger.

"Nooooo!"

The gun fires, and I wake up in a cold sweat.

I was lying on my back. Amanda was to my left, lying on her left side, her back to me. I reached out and put my hand on her waist. She stirred in her sleep. *Thank God. She's alive.*

I lay there for a few minutes staring up into the dark reaches of the ceiling, waiting for the monster that lives there to come. He's... It's an ethereal thing, bodiless, an oozing mass of sticky blackness without form. He didn't come, but I knew he was there somewhere, lurking, waiting.

The dream? Was it just that, a nightmare? Or was it something else, a portent of things to come?

All my life I've been blessed—maybe I should say cursed—with what I like to call heightened intuition. My team calls it second sight. I call it gut feelings. Call it what you will, it's real enough, and that morning I couldn't help but wonder if I'd just received some kind of warning.

I shook off the feeling of impending doom and got out of bed, trying my best not to wake Amanda. She stirred again, rolled over onto her back and took a deep breath, but didn't open her eyes.

As I looked down on her, sleeping peacefully as she was, I knew I had to do better. I had to do more to protect her and Jade from... I had no idea what.

Chapter Three

I wandered out onto the patio and went to the wall that separated it from the two acres of mountainside garden, and I looked down at the awakening city below. It never ceased to amaze me how beautiful it was. The sky was lightening, but most of the lights were still on, and the Tennessee River snaked around the city, dark and foreboding, toward the distant lights of the Sequoyah Nuclear Plant on the horizon.

I must have stood there for ten minutes or more, thinking about my dream, before I managed to shake off my fugue. Finally, though, I returned to the house, dressed in shorts, a T-shirt and sneakers, made coffee, took two minutes to drink a scalding cup, then went out for a quick sprint along East Brow and back again via North Hermitage Avenue, about three and a half miles.

Thirty minutes later I was back at my front gate, breathing hard but feeling a whole lot better. I looked in on Jade who was still sleeping, took Amanda a cup of coffee and one for myself, sat down on the bed beside her and kissed her awake.

"Ugh. You're all sweaty. Go shower, please, then come back to bed."

It was an offer I couldn't refuse, and for once I did as I was told. It was almost seven-thirty when we finally got to drink our coffee. By then it was stone cold.

"You feeling any better?" she asked, looking at me over the rim of her cup.

I looked thoughtfully at her, wondering if I should tell her about my dream. I decided not to.

"Yes," I said. "I am. I ran the loop in just over twenty-five minutes, and then... you. What's not to feel good about? How about you? Did you sleep well?"

"Like a dog," she replied.

"So we know how I feel," I said. "How about you?"

"Me?" She shrugged. "Better, I think... I need to get off the pills. Other than that, I have my moments, as you know."

I nodded. I did know. She was still recovering from a devastating accident... No, it wasn't an accident. Duvon James had tried to kill her. He ran her off the road on Lookout Mountain. She suffered three broken ribs, a broken left arm and a fractured skull, the result of which was an induced coma during which they had to take the baby... Jade. That was just over a year ago and she was still suffering from the aftereffects of the head injury. Jade, the second love of my life, had her first birthday just last week.

"Have you talked to Dr. Cartwright?" I asked.

"Every time I see him," she replied.

"And?"

"He said I could stop taking the pain pill—I'd already stopped taking them more than six months ago—but the others he wants me to continue with, for now anyway. Harry, they make me feel... awful."

I sighed, took the cup from her, set it down on the nightstand, leaned in close and kissed her gently on the lips, trying to ignore the angry red scar that started just above her right ear and continued diagonally up across her forehead, narrowly missing her right eye, to disappear into her hairline.

I sat upright again, turned to look at her, thinking how much she'd been through and how much I loved her.

"What?" she said, smiling.

I shrugged, then said, "I was just thinking how much I love you."

"I know you do, and I love you too. Now you need to get moving. You'll be late for work."

"So what? I need to eat something. You want a bagel?"

"That would be nice. Can I have butter and marmalade instead of cream cheese?"

"You can have anything you want, my love."

"I already have everything I want." She gave a happy chuckle. "But I do need to get moving. Rose will be here soon, and I need to get Jade up and fed."

Rose is, and I say this with tongue in cheek, my stepmother, because she's only two years older than me... but that's another story. Be that as it may, she's been helping Amanda with the baby and around the house.

"Fine, I'll go toast the bagels and make more coffee."

"Oh, by the way," she said. "I have a gift for you. Remind me to give it to you before you leave."

It was just after eight that morning when Rose arrived, and we all sat down together for breakfast, including Jade in her high chair.

I called Jacque and told her I was going to be late and, in return, received a caustic, "So what else is new?"

I had to smile. *That girl's come a long way since I hired her back in 2008,* I thought. *Almost eleven years ago. Wow, where's the time gone?*

"That girl's going to fire you one of these days, Harry," Rose said, picking up her mug of coffee.

Rose is my father's second wife. She's a stunningly beautiful woman and twenty years his junior. Her beauty, however, belies her character. While I couldn't think of her as my mother, Amanda considered her both a grandmother to Jade and her own best friend.

She's loving, kind, considerate and no more a trophy wife than I am, and I know my father, August, loves her dearly, as do I.

I smiled at her, shook my head and said, "You could be right. She's been on my case lately. She thinks I have PTSD, you know. Can you believe that?"

"I can," Rose said. "Your father said the same thing only yesterday. You need to see a doctor before you come apart at the seams, Harry."

"Oh, come on, Rose. I'm just tired, is all, and I have a lot on my—"

"Gaaah!" Jade said and threw a well-chewed hunk of bagel onto the table. *Geez, even she's giving it to me now.*

"That wasn't very ladylike, munchkin," I said. "Hmm, maybe it's time I taught you how to shoot. Joking, joking," I continued quickly when I saw the look on Rose's face. "Next year, perhaps, right, pickle?"

Then I saw the look on Amanda's face, shook my head and shut my mouth. There was no point in arguing with them. I gave up.

Jade looked at me as if I'd stolen her teddy bear, her mouth turned down and a deep frown on her brow.

"Okay, okay," I said. "Just gimme a kiss then. It's time I left for work."

"Here," Amanda said, as she tossed an envelope across the table to me.

"What is it?" I asked.

"I told you I had a gift for you. It will help you relax... Well, maybe it will. Knowing you, however—"

"All right, all right," I said, opening the envelope. "Enough's enough, okay?"

"Three massages?" I asked, not understanding. "It's a gift certificate. When did you go out and get this? You can forget it. I'm not—"

"Oh yes, you are," they both said in unison.

I looked first at Rose, then at Amanda. Both faces were set. Both brooked no argument. I looked at Jade, hoping for a little support.

There was none. She just grinned at me. Her mouth ringed with cream cheese.

I looked at the certificate. "Sheila Pervis? I've never heard of her. She any good?"

"I don't know," Amanda replied. "It came in the mail yesterday. It's a new business, I think. Can't hurt. It's free. If you don't like her, no loss, right? I made an appointment for you at noon today and for tomorrow and Thursday. Don't be late."

"Awww, hell. Okay, I'll give it a shot. Jacque won't like—"

"Jacque already knows," Amanda said, interrupting me, "and she agrees, absolutely. She's cleared your schedule. So don't think for one minute you can use her to get out of it."

I sighed, nodded, took a last sip of coffee, got up from the table, kissed Rose on the cheek, Amanda on the lips, Jade on top of the head and was rewarded by a slap on the forehead from a sticky hand.

The funny thing was, I was arguing with them more out of habit than to get out of the massage. Truth be told, I liked the idea and was... yes, I was looking forward to it.

I told them goodbye and turned to leave, but then I had a thought.

"Okay," I said. "How about this? I'll agree to the massages, but I'd like to hire a nanny for Jade. Rose, you've been a great help, but you have a life of your own. We've imposed on you long enough. How about it, Amanda?"

They looked at each other, then they both looked at Jade who was nodding enthusiastically and grinning while smashing cream cheese on the tray of her high chair.

"I'll think about it," Amanda said. "We can discuss it this evening."

"Fine," I said. "I'll call you later. You three have fun today, okay?"

And with that, I walked out to my car, smiling to myself and thinking, *Now all I need to do is find the right woman.*

Chapter Four

As I drove down the mountain on my way to work that morning, I passed, as I always did, the spot where Duvon James had run Amanda off the road. It was a constant and grim reminder of that awful day.

It wasn't something I like to dwell on. That day, however, the weather was particularly nice and I was in a happier mood, but I still had the dream and Duvon on my mind, so I pulled over into Cravens Terrace and parked.

I sat for a moment, wondering if I was doing the right thing, decided I was, and I got out of the car and walked the hundred or so yards to the spot where Duvon had rammed her car and sent her over the cliff.

I hadn't seen it—I hadn't stopped there—in almost a year and was surprised to see that it looked much the same as it did back then: the back yard of the house, some thirty feet below, still showed some of the damage done when Amanda's Jaguar had toppled over the edge, broken trees and branches and whatnot.

There'd been a witness, a woman driving down the mountain

some fifty yards behind Amanda. She'd seen a black SUV drive out of Cravens Terrace—where I was now parked—at high speed as Amanda passed. The big vehicle had slammed into Amanda's Jaguar, then it hit her a second time, forcing her off the road. The Jaguar smashed through the end of a roadside wooden fence, through the pull-off, over the edge and down the cliff, hit a tree, rolled, and landed on a fallen tree. A broken tree limb smashed through the windshield... That's what caused the worst of her injuries. The thick branch smashed through the airbag and hit her on the right side of the head. The first responders had to cut her out of the vehicle... Amanda was lucky to survive.

As I stood there on the roadside staring down into the trees, I had a clear vision of it, like a movie, in slow motion, it played before my eyes. My mouth was dry. I licked my lips. It didn't help. I looked at my hands. They were shaking. I went back to my car, slid in behind the wheel and sat there, waiting for the shakes to abate.

I closed my eyes, put my head against the headrest, and the nightmare from last night returned. It was even more vivid, more real than before. I snapped open my eyes. I shook my head. I put both hands on the wheel and gripped it, hard. My knuckles turned white... and then... nothing.

I rolled down the window and breathed deeply. The air was cool, crisp and invigorating.

I must have been sitting there for ten minutes, or more, when my phone rang. I tapped the Bluetooth button on the steering wheel.

"Starke," I said, my voice trembling. I hoped the caller didn't notice.

"Harry, where are you?" Jacque asked. "It's after nine. I thought you'd be here by now. Are you—"

"Don't say it, Jacque. I'm fine. I just stopped for a minute. I'll be there in ten, fifteen minutes." And I tapped the button and cut her off before she could say another word. *Hopefully, she got the message.*

I started the engine, pulled out onto the highway, drove to the

office and parked in my private, secure lot, then walked into my
offices through the side entrance. Jacque was at her desk, as was her
assistant, Lucy.

Jacque looked up at me, smiled, but said nothing. I felt bad. I was
turning into a hornet, and I knew it.

"Give me a minute to get some coffee and then join me in my
office," I told her as I walked to the breakroom.

I made myself a large mug of dark Italian roast and went to my
home away from home, my private office. It was actually more than
that. It was my sanctum. A place where I was comfortable, able to
think. Sure, it was luxurious, even a little over the top, but... well, I'm
sure you get the idea.

I went behind my desk, sat down, leaned back in my chair and
put my feet up on the desktop.

There was a knock on the door and Jacque stepped inside.

"Hey, you," I said. "Go get some coffee and we'll talk."

"I don't need coffee. I've had three already. Any more and I'll be
wound tighter than a spring. What's on your mind, boss?"

"Don't call me that. You know I hate it."

She looked sideways at me and shook her head—she looked exasperated—then said, "Do I need to take notes?"

"No. I just thought we'd chat for a bit, if you have the time."

She lowered her chin to her chest and stared at me through her
eyelashes, something she'd learned from watching Amanda.

I grinned at her. "This massage thing—"

"You're going. I promised Amanda."

"Yeah, yeah, I know. I wasn't about to argue. I was going to say...
Look, Jacque, I've been thinking about what you said last night, about
this PTSD thing. D'you really think that's what's wrong with me?"

"I don't know, Harry. I'm not a doctor, but you're certainly not
yourself. Maybe you're just stressed out, more than usual. It is, after
all, the anniversary of Amanda's accident."

"It was no accident, and you know it. Duvon James ran her off
the road, on Shady's orders. That son of a bitch almost had her killed,

and he's still out there, somewhere, lurking like a damn spider. He made me a promise that day they hauled his ass away, and I've not forgotten it. As long as he's still alive, Amanda's still in danger; we all are."

"Does Amanda know about Shady's promise?"

"No! Hell no, and she doesn't need to."

Jacque nodded and said, "Of course not but..."

"But what?"

"If you really think he meant it, you can't let her go running around all over the place without—"

"Protection," I finished for her. "That's what I want to talk to you about. I told Amanda this morning that Jade needs a nanny—"

"A nanny?" she said and snorted. "I was thinking she needs a bodyguard."

"Yes, that," I said. "But that would give the game away. She'd know something's up. She'd dig it out of me; I can't lie to her. What I need is a nanny with, shall we say, special talents? I'm thinking of someone like... like... What the hell was her name? Casey Wu. That was it. You don't think—"

"No, I don't," she interrupted me. "That woman is a psycho-pathic criminal. Besides, that was a long time ago and she's probably dead by now."

"Not her. I'd bet on it. Okay, so no Casey. How about... Okay, look. I'll leave it to you. You find someone, but remember, she has to pass the Amanda test. And she has to be great with kids. But most of all, she has to be able to protect her and Jade, and that means we're probably looking for an ex-cop or someone with military or government experience. I trust you to figure it out, and quickly. What's on my schedule today, apart from that damn massage?"

She looked at her watch, then at me and said, "You have an appointment in twenty minutes with a Ms. Jay Coin. She's the owner of a local modeling agency. Someone's stealing from her company, and she wants to know who."

"Oh geez. Can't someone else do it? How about T.J.? What's his schedule like?"

"She asked for you, Harry. She was quite specific."

I made a boss-like face and slowly shook my head, trying to stare her down. No dice.

"O-kay then," I said resignedly. "If that's the way it has to be."

Chapter Five

Jay Coin was an attractive woman in her late thirties. She was tall, about five-ten, slim with long blond hair, blue eyes and flawless skin. I couldn't make up my mind if her hair color was natural or not. If it wasn't, it must have cost her a bundle. The navy business suit was expensive: a blazer-style jacket over nothing but her skin and the skirt cut two inches above the knee. As I said, she was attractive, but she had a hard look about her. At first glance, I figured she was a tough bird and had probably come up the hard way. It wasn't until she spoke, however, that I realized I was wrong, that she was actually transgender.

Jacque showed her into my office and introduced her. She offered me her hand, palm down, as if she expected me to kiss it. I didn't. Instead, I took her hand and shook it. Her grip was firm but gentle.

"Please, Ms. Coin," I said, smiling at her, "sit down. Can I get you anything, coffee, tea, a glass of water?"

"No, thank you, and please call me Jay," she said as she sat down in one of the two guest chairs in front of my desk. She crossed her legs at the knee in one smooth, well-practiced movement and used both hands to smooth her skirt over her thigh.

"Thank you, Jacque," I said. "Please stay and take notes."

It wasn't that I needed her to do that, but I'd learned a long time ago that, in these present times, you never interview a female client without a witness present.

"So," I said, as Jacque took the seat next to her and opened her yellow pad. "What can I do for you, Ms. Coin?"

"I asked you to call me Jay," she said, a tiny smile on her lips.

"When I know you a little better, perhaps. What can I do for you?"

"As you wish..." she replied, as she placed her hands together on her thigh, one on top of the other. "I suppose I should tell you a little about my business first. I run a small but quite successful modeling agency here in Chattanooga. As of today, I have twenty-nine girls under contract, and I do business here, in Atlanta and in Nashville."

She paused, looked down at her hands, obviously thinking carefully about what she was going to say next. I decided to give her a prod.

"How did you find me, Ms. Coin? Did someone recommend me or... what?"

"You come highly recommended, Mr. Starke," she said, smiling.

"Anyone I know?" I was curious.

She just smiled and said, "Don't sell yourself short, Mr. Starke. You're quite famous, you know."

Hmm, she dodged the question, twice. I wonder why?

I leaned back in my chair and said, "Why are you here?"

"It's quite simple. I want to know who is stealing from me."

"Please, tell me about it," I said, leaning forward. Now she had my interest.

I looked at Jacque. I could see she wasn't impressed.

"Hmm," she said, tilting her head to one side. "Someone's taking money from my safe. Not a lot. Just small amounts. Never more than five hundred dollars. I don't miss the money, but it's annoying, an invasion of privacy more than anything."

"I understand," I said. "You say they're taking it from your safe. I need to know more. When and how?"

"At night. But never the same night. Several times a month."

"Okay, that's the when. Now tell me how."

"But that's the point. I don't know how."

I nodded, then said, "I'm sorry. I was being ambiguous. You said they were taking it from your safe. Tell me about the safe. Who knows the combination, other than you?"

"It doesn't have a combination. It's an antique. It has a key. I can show you a photo, if you like."

I liked, and she did. She took out her phone, flipped through several screens, found what she was looking for, then handed the phone to me, making sure she touched my hand as she did so. It was a practiced movement, one I was sure she used regularly.

The safe was a Burnaham 8000 built in Massachusetts in the late 1800s. It stood waist high and probably weighed better than eight hundred pounds. It had been beautifully restored: painted dark green and black. It wouldn't have been difficult to break into, not for an expert. *But why would an expert fool with such small amounts of cash?* I wondered. *And keep coming back for more.* The answer was, of course, he wouldn't. *So what the hell's going on?*

"How much money do you usually keep in the safe, Ms. Coin?"

"Several thou... I really don't see how that's relevant, Mr. Starke."

She was right. I wasn't, but her reluctance to tell me made me wonder why not.

I handed the phone back to her and said, "You say you have the only key. Where d'you keep it?"

"Well, it's big, you see, and heavy. It was designed to have been worn on a chain, like a watch. It's far too heavy to carry, so... Well, here, look at it." Again, she flipped through the screens and then handed the phone back to me.

She was right. It was big, and it looked heavy.

She looked embarrassed.

"And?" I prodded her.

She tsked, then said, "I keep it in my desk drawer. But no one can get it. I keep the drawer locked at all times and, besides, no one knows I keep it there."

Geez, how naive can you be?

"How many keys are there to your desk drawer, Ms. Coin?"

She pursed her lips, narrowed her eyes and frowned. "Two."

"And?"

"Two. That's it."

I sighed and said, "What I'm trying to get at, Ms. Coin, is... Could someone have gotten hold of one of the keys and had it copied, especially the key to the safe?"

"I don't see how." She pouted, obviously uncomfortable at the line of questioning. "Look," she continued impatiently. "Someone is entering my offices, at night, and they are taking money from my safe. That's unacceptable, Mr. Starke. Now, can you help me or not?"

Oh, I could help her all right. That wasn't my problem. My problem was there was something about the woman that didn't feel right. I couldn't put my finger on it, but there was something. I looked at Jacque. She shrugged. *Damn. Thanks for your help. A nod or a shake of your head would have done.*

"Have you reported it to the police?" I asked.

"Yes, of course I have, but they're no help. They came by, trampled dirt into my carpet, took a quick look at the safe and office exterior doors, and that was about it. They did say they'd keep an eye on the place... And they did for a couple of weeks, during which time the thievery stopped. When they quit watching, it started back up again. Mr. Starke. I'm convinced it's one of my employees. What you would call an inside job. Will you help me, please? I can afford to pay you whatever you ask."

Now that, too, sounded a little strange. She was losing... what? A couple of grand a month? And she was willing to pay me "whatever you ask." It made no sense.

I wanted to ask her the pertinent question, but I didn't want to piss her off: *Why don't you put your money in the bank like normal people do?*

I leaned back in my chair and stared at her. She didn't flinch. I looked at Jacque. She shrugged.

"I tell you what I'll do," I said, then paused for a minute longer to think, then continued, "I'll take your case. It shouldn't be too difficult to catch whoever's robbing you. How about I drop by your office this afternoon and take a look around? I'd like to do that before I decide on what course of action I need to take."

"Yes, yes, of course. That would be wonderful. What time should I expect you?"

"Let's say two o'clock. Now, if you'd go with Jacque, she'll do the paperwork and take a retainer."

"Thank you so much, Mr. Starke. You've no idea how much better that makes me feel."

They both stood, and Jacque took Jay Coin out to her desk. I sat and waited for Jacque to return, which she did about ten minutes later.

"Well?" I said.

"Well what?"

"Oh come on, Jacque. What did you think of her?"

"She seemed nice enough, I suppose. A bit flakey, if you ask me. That thing about the keys... Why on earth wouldn't she keep her money in the bank? To put it bluntly, who's really that stupid? Other than that, she's okay. But you don't think so, do you?"

I frowned, slowly shook my head and said, "Well, we don't know how much money she keeps in the safe, and who keeps large amounts of cash... anyway? Unless..." I left that thread unfinished, then said, "There's something off about her and I don't know what it is. But it's bugging the hell out of me, I know that, and it's not that she's trans, either."

She looked at her watch. "Harry, it's almost eleven thirty. You should go."

"Go? Go where?"

"For your massage, dummy."

"Oh yes, that."

Chapter Six

And go I did, but not before I went to see Tim.

"Hey, little buddy. Have you got a minute?"

Tim is not little, but he is my buddy. He's almost six feet tall, thin as a rail, wears horn-rimmed glasses and... he's a geek, and proud of it. He was just seventeen when I hired him back in 2008. I found him in an internet café in North Chattanooga hacking into the IRS database. I like to think I saved his ass from a life of crime. He is, without a doubt, my busiest and most valuable asset.

I entered the darkened room where he spends life, like an owl in the night, in front of the six huge flat-screen monitors—two over two over two—that are the focus of his world. A world that, to date, has set me back more than a hundred grand: four Dell 7910 towers, a Dell MX840c server, and a whole bunch of extras I didn't—and didn't want to—understand. And, of course, an assortment of laptops and tablets.

Tim handles my IT, which includes operating and maintaining the company website, handling background checks and skip searches, and a whole lot of stuff that often isn't quite... let's say, kosher.

He rolled his seat away from his desk... but I couldn't even call it his desk anymore. It looked like something from the Starship Enterprise.

He looked up at me, his eyes magnified by his glasses, and said, "What can I do for you, boss?"

"Don't call me that. I need you to run a full background check on this lady: rap sheet—if she has one—financials—hers and her company's—and, most importantly, where she keeps her money, the works. When you're done, run it by T.J. I'd like his opinion."

He took the Jay Coin file from me, opened it, glanced at the title sheet, turned on his wheels and dropped it on his desk, then turned back to me and said, "No problemo, chief."

"Don't call me that either. When?"

"Four, four-thirty."

"One-thirty. No later."

"Aw, man," I heard him wail as I left him there in the dark and headed out to my car.

***

The Tranquility Salon and Day Spa was across the river in North Chattanooga, about a fifteen-minute drive from my office. My appointment was at noon, so I started out a few minutes early, just in case I got caught in the lunchtime traffic. I wasn't a mile out from my office when I noticed a white Ford Escape two cars back and I was sure it was following me.

I made a couple of quick turns, just to make sure I wasn't imagining it. I wasn't. The Escape followed me. I slowed. The Escape slowed too. I slowed to a stop and parked curbside. The Escape accelerated and drove on past. I tried to see the driver. I couldn't. The windows were heavily tinted.

I waited for several minutes, but the Escape didn't return. I pulled away from the curb and drove on to my appointment. I kept watching through my rearview mirror, but there was no sign of a tail and I arrived at the spa five minutes late wondering if I'd been imagining things. I was pretty sure I wasn't, but...

The Tranquility Salon and Day Spa was a nice-looking place... Upscale, classy, expensive... exclusive. I stepped inside and was immediately surrounded by... well, it was quiet. So quiet it was almost palpable.

Sheila Pervis was waiting for me at the reception desk when I arrived, and when I tell you she was a big girl, she was a *big* girl. She was black, tall, muscular and dressed in a short white toga. It looked like something a Greek goddess might wear. She reminded me of Serena Williams, and I have to tell you, I was more than a little intimidated.

She welcomed me, introduced herself, asked me the usual questions: had I ever had a massage before? I had. Did I have any medical issues she should know about? I didn't. And so on, and then escorted me to a small room with a massage table therein and spa music playing the sounds of nature. Relaxing? If you like that kind of stuff. I don't. I find it annoying, but what the hell. I could stand it for thirty minutes.

"As it's your first time here, Mr. Starke," she said, "and you say you've had a massage before, would you like to tell me about your experience?"

"There's not much to tell," I replied. "I've stayed at several golf resorts in the past. Most of them had spas and a visit was part of the package... It's been a while though."

She nodded. "Nice. Did you enjoy them?"

"I did."

"Good. So, you know the routine. I'll leave you to get undressed. You can leave your underwear on, if you like, or not." She smiled at me and continued, "And then get on the table under the sheet and lie face down. I'll be back when you're ready."

She was right. I did know the routine and, just as I had in the past, I had to ask myself how the hell she would know when I was ready. Anyway, I did as I was told, sans my underwear, and lay down to wait. It couldn't have been thirty seconds later when she returned.

"So," she said, pulling the sheet down to my waist. "How would you like it? Light, deep or sports?"

Now, I'd had a sports massage at the Sawgrass Golf Resort in Florida and it hurt like hell, but it did me a lot of good.

I had my head on the table with my nose and mouth through the hole so I couldn't see her, but I did remember the impression she made on me when I first saw her in the reception area. This woman could hurt you. But, rather than have her think I was a wimp, I opted for the sports massage, and I was right.

She oiled her hands and began at my neck.

"Oh dear," she said. "You really are tight, aren't you?"

She dug her fingers into my trapezius muscles and I almost came off the table. I felt as if I'd been stabbed on both sides of my neck at the same time.

She didn't talk much. She asked me how it was feeling a couple of times and that was about it. I tried to make small talk, asking about her business and such, but her answers were less than encouraging. So, in the end I gave up, closed my eyes and let her get on with it.

Thirty minutes later, she turned me loose and suggested I take a hot shower. I felt like I'd been beaten all over with a baseball bat. Strangely, though, I actually felt better than I had in years, so I gratefully accepted the offer and took a long hot shower.

I walked out of the spa at a few minutes after one o'clock in the afternoon, looking forward to repeating the experience the following day.

I'd parked out front and as I walked to my car I looked around for the white Escape. It was nowhere to be seen. *Maybe I am paranoid.*

Chapter Seven

It was a little after one-fifteen when I walked into my office that afternoon and was immediately greeted by a barrage of questions about my experience at the spa, most of which I ignored, saying only that I enjoyed it and felt wonderful; this to Jacque's delight.

I asked her to grab Tim and T.J. and meet me in the conference room.

All three of them arrived together. T.J. with a yellow pad. Jacque also with a yellow pad. And Tim, well Tim being Tim, he came loaded down with a laptop, iPad and two phones. *Why the hell does he need two?*

"Okay, people," I said after they'd all settled down. "I have to be at the Coin Talent Agency at two, so we don't have much time. Tim, what d'you have for me?"

"Umm, yes, well, let me see," he said, pushing his glasses further up the bridge of his nose with the forefinger of one hand while opening his laptop with the other.

I drummed gently on the tabletop with my fingers.

"Jaylin Coin is thirty-seven years old. She was born in

Alpharetta, Georgia, where she graduated high school in 2000. She didn't go to college, but she did go to modeling school in Atlanta where she had a short career as a runway model. She moved to Chattanooga in 2015 and opened the Coin Talent Agency early in 2016. Back in 2009—and this is the good bit, Harry. While she was still in Atlanta, she was arrested for prostitution. The charges were, however, dropped. No reason was given. Since then, she has a clean record. Her agency has a good reputation. Revenue in 2018 topped seven-point-two million dollars. She pays her taxes, has no debt, and the property on McCallie is paid for. She's debt-free. And that's all I have. If I had more time—"

"That's okay, but I need to know where she banks, if she banks."

"First American on Broad Street."

"And it's all good and aboveboard?"

He nodded, did the thing with his glasses and said, "As far as I can tell without digging deeper."

I looked at T.J. and said, "She keeps a lot of money in a safe in her office. Why would she do that?"

"Any number of reasons, but none of them good that I can think of. How much?"

"She wouldn't tell me." I frowned and bit my lower lip. "And that's a red flag all by itself. Could it be drug money, d'you think?"

"It could," T.J. replied. "But, if it's just a couple of thousand, it's more likely she's doing jobs for cash and not declaring it. If it's more than that, I'd step very carefully, Harry. I'd say, judging from what Tim's just told us, that at some time in the distant past she was probably a high-class hooker, escort. And she might still be. If so, she will have some dubious connections, so watch what you're doing. You want me to come with you?"

"I was planning on it," I replied. "Escort? T.J., she's transgender."

"So?"

"So, okay... I guess."

I looked at my watch. It was almost one-forty-five.

"We have fifteen minutes. You ready to go?"

"I can be. Give me a couple of minutes, okay?"

T.J. Bron is... somewhat unusual. Just over a year ago, when he first came to me, he was a man on the streets, homeless, and ready to cash in his chips. That is until he discovered the body of a young woman in a back alley.

Kate Gazzara was the investigating officer, and when she interviewed him, she saw something in him that nobody else did. She also knew that my financial officer, Ronnie Hall, had just quit and headed for greener pastures—he turned pro poker player and went to Vegas to join the Tour.

Anyway, Kate brought T.J. to me. It turned out he's a highly decorated Vietnam vet—two tours, the first beginning in 1968 and then again in 1972. He's a United States Marine—there's no such thing as an ex-Marine—down on his luck... Actually, luck had nothing to do with it. T.J. was falsely accused of stealing from the bank where he worked. He did some time, and it ruined him. He lost everything: wife, kids, home, everything.

He has a degree in accounting, and at the time, I happened to be looking for a financial investigator, a replacement for Ronnie. And so, bearing in mind the man's military record, his Silver Star and two Purple Hearts, I figured I'd take a chance and hire him. Jacque found a place for him to live and here we are. At sixty-nine, he's... not a young man; he's the oldest member of my team. He's also in better shape than all of them, even me. This because of a rigorous workout regimen he started the day Jacque took him in hand and still continues to this day.

He's six feet tall, weighs one-ninety, with white hair and a heavily lined, deeply tanned face. He's also... crazy. Yes, that's what I said. He's nuts, and he's fiercely protective of me and the rest of my team. He's an expert with a knife, handgun, rifle and martial arts, and he will kill at the drop of a hat and not think a thing about it. Two tours in Vietnam will do that to a man. I haven't regretted hiring him, not for a single second, especially now that Bob Ryan has gone back to the CIA.

Anyway, he joined me in the outer office wearing a windbreaker to hide the Vietnam-era Colt .45 1911 model he wore in a shoulder holster. One similar to mine, only I carried a Heckler & Koch VP9.

"You ready?" I asked.

He nodded. "Let's do it!"

Chapter Eight

The Coin Talent Agency was located in a two-story building on McCallie just a block south of the strip mall from which, back in 2015, Lester "Shady" Tree had run his illegal enterprises. I was instrumental in bringing him down-along with Congressman Gordon "Little Billy" Harper, who died in prison a couple of years or so ago-but not before he caused me a whole lot of aggravation. As did Harper, right up until he checked out. That, as they say, is a whole nother story, but I thought it was worth mentioning anyway.

I parked out front, and T.J. and I entered what can only be described as unadulterated luxury. The décor in the foyer alone would have been the envy of any lawyer I knew, including my father. But instead of the dark paneling and leather furniture, all was white and bright, even the leather furniture which included two vast white couches and four armchairs.

On the walls, in a single neat row that started in one corner of the foyer and circled the room ending in the other corner, were some fifty large portraits, in identical white frames, of some of the most beautiful women I'd ever set eyes on. All past or present Coin Talent Agency models, I assumed.

The young lady at the ornate white table—no reception desk here—was, herself, a beauty with alabaster cheeks and straight, bleached white hair that hung to the tips of her breasts.

"Good afternoon, gentlemen," she said brightly as she stood and walked across the room to meet us. And when I say walked, I used the word advisedly because I don't know how to describe it... maybe undulated would be a better word. The kid could have been on a runway.

"How can I help you?" she asked.

"I'm Harry Starke. I have an appointment with Ms. Coin."

"Oh yes. She's expecting you. If you'll follow me, please."

And then she turned and did it again. Only this time the view was... spectacular. It was like... like a... It was like watching one of those giant American flags waving gently in the breeze.

Ms. Coin's office was a smaller version of her foyer: an ornate white desk with two matching, white straight-backed chairs in front of it, white carpet, and a small white coffee table flanked by two white leather love seats. The wall-to-wall, floor-to-ceiling window was flanked on either side by white fluted columns. On the wall behind her desk were three framed photos of herself in her younger days when she was a model. She had been lovely. Not quite so today, but still attractive, sophisticated and... even a little haughty. Also behind the desk was the green and black safe I'd seen in the photograph. It was a beauty, but it was out of place amid the all-white décor.

"Good afternoon, Mr. Starke," she said, rising from behind her desk upon which was nothing but a small, navy-blue clutch and a single piece of paper.

She stepped out from behind it and offered me her hand, again palm down. I shook it and introduced T.J. She shook his hand and gave him a funny look. I had to smile. I knew exactly what she was thinking: *Who the hell is this old man and what's he doing here?*

"T.J. is my financial investigator, among other things," I said by way of explanation. "Which is why I brought him along."

She was dressed to kill. The tailored, moss-green business suit and the matching handmade shoes must have set her back a tidy sum. And she was tall, taller than I remembered. The four-inch heels she was wearing might have had something to do with that.

As I looked at her, though, I once again had the feeling that something wasn't quite right. I couldn't figure out what it was that was bothering me, but something was. It could have been her demeanor or just the way she looked at me, and I can assure you it wasn't that she was flirting with me. She wasn't. I began to wonder if I was going nuts. Inwardly, I shook off the feeling and focused on what I was there for.

"So," I continued. "If you don't mind, I, that is we, have some questions for you, but first we'd like to take a look at that safe." I nodded in its direction.

"Of course," she said, taking a step sideways. "Be my guest."

T.J. and I stepped forward. We both crouched down and looked at the lock. T.J. grabbed the handle and tried to turn it. It didn't move.

"Would you mind opening it, please?" T.J. asked.

"Of course," she replied and went to her desk drawer. As she brushed past me, I caught a whiff of her perfume. It was heady.

"Here you go," she said, handing me the key.

I took it from her. She was right. It was huge and heavy, made of steel and it weighed a ton; it was not something to carry around.

I inserted the key in the lock. It turned easily. Whoever had restored the safe had done a great job. I nodded to T.J. He again grasped the handle and turned it. There was a satisfying clunk as the tumblers fell into place. He pulled on the handle and the heavy door swung silently open on well-oiled hinges.

We both peered inside. There were two shelves and two small drawers. We didn't touch anything. I didn't want her to get the idea we were investigating her, so we just looked.

On one of the shelves were four stacks of six, banded one-hundred-dollar bills: twenty-four thousand dollars. There was little else inside except for a file box and a Smith & Wesson Shield, semi-automatic 9mm handgun.

"You keep a lot of cash in here, Ms. Coin," T.J. said, "considering you're being systematically robbed. It seems to me you're offering the thief an open invitation to return to the candy store whenever he likes."

"And you have no security cameras," I added. "At least none that I've seen. I would have thought that would have been the first thing you would have done. Have you considered having a system installed?"

"This is a modeling agency, Mr. Starke. Not a bank."

"I understand that, but as Mr. Bron has pointed out, that's an awful lot of cash. Why d'you need to keep so much on hand? Don't you and your people believe in credit cards, or banks?"

"Not that it's any business of yours how much cash I keep on hand, but I'll tell you anyway. I use a lot of freelance photographers and makeup artists. Most of them like to be paid in cash. Yes, of course we use credit cards, and I bank at First American on Broad Street... as I'm sure you already know. But I can't see what any of that has to do with catching my thief."

She was all business now, and there was a hard edge to her voice that hadn't been there before.

I closed the safe door, locked it, removed the key and stood up. So did T.J., and we both turned to face her. I laid the big key down on the desk and opened my mouth to ask her a question, but I changed my mind and said, "Before we talk about your problem and how to fix it, I'd like to see the rest of the building, please."

"Of course," she said.

She went to her desk, picked up the key to the safe, put it in her desk drawer, locked it, put her keys in her clutch and fastened it.

"Please follow me," she said.

"The back entrance first, if you don't mind," I said.

She nodded and escorted us along a narrow corridor to the back door. The door was made of steel and featured the obligatory panic bar, but there was no security. Not even a bolt. Just a Yale lock and a keyed dead bolt.

I unlocked the door, pushed it open, and stepped out into a small courtyard surrounded by a six-foot-high brick wall with a gate on the north side. I walked to the gate, pulled the bolt, opened it and stepped out into an alleyway just wide enough for a single car or... a pickup. I stepped back inside, closed the gate, slid the bolt back into place, then looked around the courtyard. It was clear, except for two garbage cans. There was a single light fixed to the wall above the door. *How convenient for the thief, for you to enable him to see what the hell he's doing,* I thought, wryly.

We stepped back inside the building and Coin showed us the rest of the facility, which consisted mainly of a huge, open-plan photographic studio and three dressing rooms. Strangely, there were no models present, much to mine and T.J.'s disappointment.

Finally, we returned to her office and we all sat down: Coin behind her desk and T.J. and I on the two straight-backed chairs. They were not comfortable. And she knew it.

"It's all about posture, Mr. Starke," she explained. "I can't have my girls slouching when they sit, hence the uncomfortable chairs. Would you like to go to the love seats? You can sit by me. I'm sure you'll be more... comfortable." And hell if she didn't wink at me.

"We're fine where we are, thank you. So, if you wouldn't mind, we'll talk this thing through?"

"Fire away. I can't wait to hear your conclusions and, hopefully, a solution."

"First, let's talk about the safe," T.J. said. "It's beautiful, but it's not a safe. It's a tin box, albeit a damned heavy one. The key, in and of itself, is unique, but it could have been copied."

She opened her mouth to speak, but T.J. held up his hand to stop her and said, "If you'll allow me to finish, please, ma'am. As I said, the key could have been copied. That would be the easiest solution for your thief. If not, then he, or she, must have gotten hold of your desk drawer keys and had them copied.

"That's not possible," she said. "I have the only key to my desk. I keep it with me at all times. Here, in my clutch."

"If you'll excuse me for just a second," T.J. said, rising to his feet and walking around the desk to the drawer beside her.

He took a small pouch from the inside pocket of his windbreaker, revealing the grip of his Colt as he did so. She stared up at him. Her eyes wide. He grinned down at her, crouched, and proceeded to go about picking the desk drawer lock. No more than ten seconds later, he had it open. Coin looked at him in disbelief as he walked back to his chair.

"How about the back door?" T.J. asked. "Who has keys?"

"Just me, my secretary, Elana, and Louanne. You met her when you came in."

"At some point, Ms. Coin," T.J. said, "someone must have gained access to one of the keys. What about Elana and Louanne? Can you trust them?"

"Y-es... Yes, of course."

"You don't seem too sure," T.J. said.

"That's because I'd never thought about it before, but yes. I trust them both, implicitly."

T.J. looked at me and nodded.

"Let's talk about the alleyway out back," I said. "I assume you keep the gate locked at night, but anyone with a pickup truck could hop in the bed and then over the wall. It would take no more than a couple of seconds."

I paused, waiting for her to say something. She didn't. She just looked back at me, somewhat defiantly, I thought.

"Do you have any idea who the thief might be?" I asked.

"No, none. I've thought about it, of course. But I can't think of anyone."

"How about your—you called them girls? Could one of them have gotten hold of your keys?"

"I don't see how."

"How about your clutch?" I asked, looking at it on the desktop.

"What about it?"

"Do you always keep your keys in it?"

"Yes, of course," she said. "Well, in whatever one I happen to be carrying on any given day."

"And do you carry your clutch with you always?" I asked. "You pick it up every time you leave the room, even when you go to the restroom?"

"Well no, but—"

"No, you don't," I said. "You left it there on the desk when you showed us around. We were gone for just over ten minutes. Plenty of time for someone to enter your office and make an impression of the keys... including the key to the safe."

She stared at me, her top lip over the bottom one. I could see she didn't like what she was hearing.

"Look, Ms. Coin," I said quietly. "There's a simple solution to your problem. It's called security. Have someone install cameras, alarms and security lights in the courtyard out back. And have all the locks changed. That will cost you far less than I will have to charge you. I'll have Jacque return your retainer. It's been nice to meet you, Ms. Coin."

I was about to rise from my seat, but she beat me to it. She stood up, quickly, and said sharply, "No! That's not what I want, Mr. Starke. I want you to catch the thief. I will not be able to rest easy until I know who it is."

I shook my head in resignation and said, "If that's what you want."

"It is. I paid you and I expect you to do your job. When will you start work?"

"I'll have someone here tonight."

"Someone? I was expecting you to handle it yourself."

"I'm afraid I don't do that, Ms. Coin. My time is much too valuable. One of my investigators, Heather Stillwell, will be here before you close."

She didn't look happy about it, but she nodded, pushed a button under her desk and said, "Very well. Louanne will show you out."

Louanne appeared as if by magic and escorted us to the foyer, and once again, I came away with the same, nagging gut feeling something wasn't quite right about Ms. Jaylin Coin.

We sat together in the car for a moment, and I asked T.J. what he thought about Coin and the whole setup.

"I don't like it," he said. "I think she's full of it. Is she really being robbed or is it just a ploy to get you into the building, alone?"

"If it is, it didn't work, did it? She did have a logical reason for keeping that much money on hand, though."

"So what's the plan?" he asked. "Are you really going to have Heather babysit the place?"

"Yes. I want to see if we can find out what's really going on there. If we can catch her thief—if there really is one—so much the better. See to it, will you, T.J.?"

A movement outside across the street caught my eye. "Who the hell is that?"

"Who? Where?" T.J. asked.

"Over there. There's a guy in that doorway, and he has a camera."

Chapter Nine

I opened the car door, and as I did so the guy turned and ran.

I jumped out of the car and gave chase. It was no contest. The guy was hampered by a camera in one hand and a camera bag on his shoulder. I quickly caught up with him.

"Hold on, buddy," I said as I grabbed his arm.

I skidded to a stop and spun him around. He was young, maybe twenty-four, with long brown hair tied back in a short ponytail, glasses and a thin face with high cheekbones. He was wearing jeans, white sneakers and a black Lookouts windbreaker.

"What the hell d'you think you were doing?" I asked angrily.

"Nothing. Just taking a couple of photos, is all."

"You've been following me. Why?"

"I told you. I need some photos."

"Let me handle this, Harry," T.J. said as he joined me. He pulled the Colt from beneath his jacket and jammed the muzzle under the kid's chin, forcing his head back.

"Who are you and who sent you? Talk, you son of a bitch," he snarled, "or I'll plaster the street with your brains."

"O-kay. O-kay," he gasped, his eyes wide.

T.J. slackened the pressure, but not by much.

"My name's Roland Patrelli," he gasped. "I'm a freelance photojournalist. Nobody sent me. I'm doing an article on Mr. Starke, the hero of Chattanooga."

Shit! I put my hand on T.J.'s arm and told him to put the piece away. He nodded, took two steps back and holstered the weapon.

The kid also took several steps backward, staring wide-eyed, first at me then at T.J.

"Geez," he said, hitching his bag up onto his shoulder. It had fallen to the crook of his elbow when I grabbed his arm. "You guys are touchy. I just needed a couple of decent photos. Those they have at the stock agencies are—"

"Yeah, I know," I said. "They're crap, but they're going to have to do. Let me give you a piece of advice, kid. Pick up the phone and ask next time. Don't follow people around. You're likely to get your tail shot off. Now get the hell out of here and tell your buddies to quit following me, too."

"Buddies? I don't have any buddies. I'm freelance. I work alone."

"Do you drive a white Ford Escape?" I asked.

"No. I have a red Mustang, 2005 model. Over there, see?"

He pointed to the car parked a block away on the same side of the road as my BMW.

I stared at him for a long moment, then nodded and said, "Go, and don't let me catch you following me again."

He turned and ran down the street to his car. T.J. and I walked back to my car, watching as he drove away, almost as fast as the Mustang could carry him.

"What was that about a white Escape?" T.J. asked as he slammed his door shut and reached for his seatbelt.

"Nothing. I must have imagined it."

"You don't imagine things, Harry. What the hell happened, and when?"

So I sighed and told him what had happened on the way to the spa that morning.

"As I said, I must have overreacted, or maybe I'm going crazy... Did Jacque tell you she thinks I have PTSD as a result of what happened last year?"

"No, she didn't," he replied. "That's bullshit, Harry. She doesn't know what PTSD is, and neither do you for that matter. *I* know what PTSD is, and you haven't got it."

"I get the shakes, T.J., and I've started imagining things. I thought it was my gut kicking in, but now I'm not so sure. I almost hurt that kid. All he was doing was his job. Damn it. You were a little hard on him, too." I thumbed the starter and flipped the gas pedal a couple of times, then eased out onto the street.

"Maybe he was doing his job. Maybe he wasn't. You think I was hard on him? I wasn't, but you were too easy. We should have looked in that bag of his. It was big enough to hold a Mac10."

"Now whose imagination's running wild?" I said, grinning sideways at him.

Chapter Ten

I dropped T.J. off at the office and drove to Carter's Shooting Supply on Highway 58. I'd been carrying an H&K VP9 for several years, and I felt like a change. I had it in mind to try out one of the Czech-made CZ 75s. I also needed to practice, something I'd neglected of late.

I told the guy behind the counter what I was looking for. He nodded, opened the glass-fronted cabinet and put several different models on the counter in front of me. A full size, a compact, a CZ75b and a TSO.

I hefted each one in turn and I liked the feel and the balance of all of them, but not enough to switch.

I sighed and said, "They're nice, but I think I'll stick with my VP9, for now, anyway."

He nodded, cocked his head to one side, looked at me and said, "You're that Harry Starke, aren't you?"

I looked at him. He was smiling. I nodded. "*That* Harry Starke? That's a first."

"I thought I recognized you. Hell, I should, shouldn't I? You were all over the news last year, and even before that. Wow, you're a celebrity. We don't get any of those in here. What are you looking for, Mr. Starke?"

"Not really anything. To be honest, I was on my way home and thought I'd stop by and take a look at the CZ, and maybe put a few down range. I'm getting a little rusty."

"It's a nice weapon," he said, nodding enthusiastically.

"It is, but so's my VP9."

"I agree, but... Can you wait just a minute? I have something I'd like to show you."

I nodded, and he went to a safe at the far end of the shop and returned a moment later with a small black gun case. He placed it on the counter in front of me, opened it, and reverently removed the weapon and handed it to me.

"What d'you think of that?" he asked.

I was holding a 9mm CZ Shadow 2 with blue grips. I'd heard of the weapon, but I'd never handled one.

I hefted it. Held it by the grip. It was heavier than the VP9. Quite a bit heavier in fact, but it felt good. I looked at him, my eyebrows raised in question.

"Seventeen in the mag plus one in the chamber. It's a competition pistol. A frickin' nail driver. Two-and-a-quarter-pound trigger; works like butter. The thing's a work of art, man."

"How much?"

He pulled one of those widemouthed toothy faces and didn't answer.

"That much, huh? C'mon, spill it."

"Thirteen fifty-nine." Again, he made with the face.

"Can I try it?"

He shook his head. "Sorry, Mr. Starke. You shoot it, you buy it."

I looked down at it. It really did look good, but more important it felt even better. "It's a competition pistol, you said?"

"Yup. Best there is... in my opinion."

I thought for a minute, looked up at him, tilted my head to one side and said, "Throw in a box of ammo and you have a deal."

"You got it, Mr. Starke."

I reached for my wallet and handed him my American Express card, my carry permit, and my PI license.

"I'm going to go shoot this thing while you do the paperwork, okay?"

"Yes, sir," he said, handing me a box of 9mm, one hundred and fifteen grain cartridges. "The range is that way. End of the store and turn left through the door. You can't miss it."

He was right. The gun was a dream. Hell, I'd never fired it before and I was able to put a full mag, seventeen rounds, into a three-inch circle at thirty feet. I fired two more full mags, and by the time I was done, I'd reduced the circle to two and a half inches and I was grinning like a fool. I was sold. Hell, like it or not, I was sold anyway the minute I pulled the trigger for the first time.

I put the weapon back in its box, went back into the store.

"So," the clerk said. "What d'you think of it. Sweet, huh?"

"Sweet indeed," I replied. "Are we all done?"

"Sure are. I just need you to sign here, here, and here and you're good to go. Do you need ammo? How about that fiber optic front sight? Ain't that something?"

The guy was almost as excited about the weapon as I was. I smiled at him, shook my head and signed the paperwork, retrieved my Am-Ex card, told the guy thank you and headed home.

***

It was almost seven-thirty when I arrived home that evening. Amanda was putting Jade to bed, so I was able to kiss my sweet little baby goodnight. Something that didn't happen very often, but I was determined to change that, somehow, sooner or later.

We tucked her in and I followed Amanda to the kitchen, where I sat down at the table while she made me a ham and cheese sandwich. She also made me a drink and poured herself a glass of white wine.

Then she, too, sat down at the table and... a look of expectation on her beautiful face.

"This is delicious," I said through a mouthful of sandwich, thinking she wanted me to comment on her culinary skills. "Hits the spot."

"Well?" she replied, still smiling.

"Well what?"

"Are you going to tell me about your massage or not?"

"Oh... that." I took another bite of my sandwich. She watched as I chewed.

"It was... interesting," I said finally. "Sheila is... also interesting. I can still feel where she dug her fingers into my neck and shoulders. I do feel better for it, though... Well, I did. It's kind of worn off now."

"But you did enjoy it?"

"Yes, of course. It wasn't the first massage I've ever had, you know."

"What was the spa like?"

"Nice, high-end. Expensive. Yeah... It was nice."

"That's good, because I was worried. I didn't know what I was sending you to. The gift card came in the mail. There was no return address on the envelope and just a hand-written note that said, 'Enjoy.' No signature. And it was addressed to both of us. I would have gone myself, but I'm still having physical therapy and I didn't think the two would mix."

I frowned. The hair on the back of my neck was beginning to tickle.

"D'you still have it? The envelope and the note?"

She nodded. "They are in your office. I put them on your desk. Do you want me to go get them for you? Is something wrong?"

I had a feeling something *was* indeed wrong, but I wasn't going to tell her that. Nor was I going to tell her I thought I was being followed, either by Patrelli or the Ford Escape.

"No," I said. "I was just curious, is all. I'll look at them later."

Look at them later, hell! I'm going to run them by Kate and ask her to have them dusted for prints. I want to know who the hell sent it.

"I'm sure it's okay," I lied. I hated lying to her, even when it was in her best interest. "It's a brand-new place, and the gift card is probably a promotion sent by her ad agency to bring in new customers."

"So you'll keep your appointment tomorrow?"

"Of course. Why wouldn't I?"

Why wouldn't I indeed.

Chapter Eleven

Irose early again the next morning, as stiff as a board. The result of the extreme massage, I assumed. I went for my usual six-mile run, and by the time I returned at around six o'clock, I was as loose as a goose and feeling better than I had in many a long month. And I was looking forward to my next massage... for more reasons than just one.

Amanda was already up and about when I returned and was about to cook breakfast. I asked her to give me a few minutes to shower and dress, and then I'd join her. Which I did.

Fifteen minutes later, dressed in jeans and a black polo shirt, I sat down with her to scrambled eggs, sausage, fried tomatoes and mushrooms.

"You look perky this morning," she said, taking a sip of her coffee.

I nodded. "I feel pretty good, actually. I enjoyed my run. It got rid of the cobwebs, and the stiffness from the massage yesterday. How about you?"

"I'm fine. I just need to get out of the house. I think maybe I'll take Jade to see your father and Rose."

"Good luck with that," I said. "Rose, yes, but August. He'll be in his office by eight. You never know though."

And we made more such small talk for the next fifteen minutes or so until finally I rose, kissed her on top of her head and made ready to leave.

When I did, Amanda, carrying a still sleepy Jade, walked me out into the garage to my car.

"Have a good day, Harry," she said as I opened the car door. "And enjoy your massage."

I tilted my head, looked at her, kissed her on the lips, kissed Jade on her cheek, and then said, wryly, "Yeah, that! You have a good day too." And with that, I climbed in behind the wheel and rolled out onto West Brow and headed for Scenic Highway and my office, keeping a lookout for the white Ford Escape. There was no sign of it, or of a tail of any sort. *Yeah, so maybe I was overreacting yesterday.*

It was exactly seven-thirty when I arrived at my office, an hour earlier than usual. I was hoping to have the place to myself so that I could do some thinking. But, as always, Jacque beat me to it and so, believe it or not, did Tim.

I told Jacque that I didn't want to be disturbed, not before nine, anyway, and made myself coffee. Then I went to my office and closed the door.

I do my best thinking in my office and I wanted to try to make sense of the Coin situation. Not only did I feel uncomfortable about the entire situation—and no, it had nothing to do with her being transgender—nothing about the case made any sense.

I took a yellow legal pad from my desk drawer and began to write.

Why does she want me to handle the case personally?

If she's been robbed, why hasn't she had a security system installed?

If she's being robbed on a regular basis, why would she continue to keep a large amount of money in the safe?

The answer, Harry, I told myself, *is that she's not being robbed, at all.*

If that's the case, what's her game? What's her motive?
If that's the case, who put her up to it? Who's behind it?
What about the Ford Escape? Is it connected to the Coin case?
If not, who's behind that?
Who sent that damn gift card?
Something's going on! What?

I sat there for a moment, looking at what I'd written and twiddling my thumbs. *Too many questions. No answers!*

I looked at my watch. It was just after nine. I picked up the phone, buzzed Jacque, and asked her to grab Heather and join me.

Heather Stillwell has worked for me for more than eight years. She spent the first two years of her law enforcement career as a street cop in Atlanta, until the GBI —the Georgia Bureau of Investigation— recruited her. How that happened, I have no idea. She never would tell me. Maybe she knew someone. Hell, maybe it was because she's a good detective.

I'd met her on several occasions during the course of one investigation or another, and we'd gotten along. Then, one day, she called me wanting to know if I had any openings. It just so happened I did. Things were beginning to move for my company, and Bob Ryan and I were so busy we hadn't had a day off in months, so I hired her. It worked out well, even though she's kind of reclusive... you know, quiet. I still don't know why she left the GBI, but I'm glad she did.

"Hey, Heather," I said when she and Jacque joined me. "Take a seat and tell me about last night."

"There's really not much to tell," she said, taking out her notebook and flipping through the pages.

"I arrived at the client's location on McCallie at seven, as arranged, and entered the premises. There were several... There was a lot of people there, working." She flipped through a couple more pages and continued, "These included Coin, her receptionist, Louanne, her secretary, Alana, two photographers—a Michael Hollins and Rudy Shea, a female—and nine models, all skimpily dressed. I have their names if you want them."

"You can give them to Jacque. Please continue, Heather."

"The two photographers worked until nine-forty-five when they left. During the time from seven when I arrived until Coin left for the evening, she received five calls on her cell phone. She left the room each time to take the calls. I didn't hear anything. After each of four of the calls, though, she returned to the studio—where I was observing the photographers—and called a model by name—I made note of their names—and they, Coin and the model, left the room together. Coin returned a few minutes later; the model did not."

She looked up from her notes and stared at me. She obviously was trying to make a point.

"That it?" I asked.

"Pretty much. I stayed the night on the premises. I slept on one of those big couches in the lobby." She smiled at me. "Oh, don't worry. I'm a light sleeper. I would have heard if anything had happened. Anyway, I had Coin check her safe before she left for the night and as soon as she came in this morning... at eight, more for my benefit than hers. I don't trust that woman. Anyway, that's it; nothing else to report. You want me to try again tonight?"

"Yes, but I think it's a waste of time... About the four girls, the ones that left after the phone calls. What was your impression of them?"

She looked at me and frowned. "Lovely, all of them. Sophisticat-ed..." She paused, hesitated.

"And?" I said.

"I think they were high-class escorts."

Now why doesn't that surprise me?

"I have no reason to say that," she continued. "It's just my impression."

I looked at my own notes and added, *Escort service?*

"Well," I said. "T.J. thinks so, too. I really don't care if that's what she's doing. What I do care is, what the hell is she up to?"

Thank God I was smart enough not to go in there alone.

"Okay, ladies," I said. "That'll do it for now, and thanks, Heather.

Yes, give it another try tonight. I'm pretty sure we're wasting our time, but you never know."

They left my office together. Me? I looked back through my notes, at those first three questions I'd asked myself.

Why does she want me to handle the case personally?

If she's been robbed, why hasn't she had a security system installed?

If she's being robbed on a regular basis, why would she continue to keep a large amount of money in the safe?

I stared at them, and the more I thought about it, the more convinced I became that it had to be some kind of a hoax. Or worse, a trap of some kind. But why? What could she possibly hope to gain? Maybe T.J. was right. Maybe she wanted to get her hooks into me for some reason. Why she would want to, I had no idea.

What the hell is her game?

I didn't know and I couldn't figure it out, so I called her.

"The Coin Agency. How may I direct your call?"

"This is Harry Starke. I'd like to speak to Ms. Coin, please."

"Hello, Mr. Starke. This is Louanne. I'm afraid Ms. Coin is out of the office. She should be back later. Is there anything I can help you with?"

"If you wouldn't mind, please tell her I'll drop by later."

"I'll do that. Do you have any idea what time?"

"Let's say five o'clock... ish."

"I'll tell her. If it's not convenient, I'll call and let you know."

I thanked her and hung up.

I piddled around the office for the next hour and a half, making a nuisance of myself to one and all, especially Jacque who finally told me to get the hell out of there and go for my massage, which I did.

I drove to the spa in North Chattanooga without incident—no white Escape, no tail.

During the massage I casually asked Sheila about the gift card and how come I'd received it. She didn't seem disconcerted by the question, which I thought she might have been if something untoward was going on.

She said she'd bought a mailing list of the most influential families in Hamilton County and had mailed a gift card to everyone on the list in the hopes it would bring in new business and, she was happy to say, it did. It was a good answer, and I saw no reason to disbelieve her, so I thanked her and settled down and enjoyed my treatment.

I left Sheila around twelve-forty-five after a rigorous massage and a scalding shower, feeling like I'd just gone three rounds with Mike Tyson, and I was happy to see that my hands were no longer shaking and, I felt surprisingly calm. I'd also made up my mind that I liked her, Sheila. She was funny and jolly, and she had this... this way of putting me at ease.

Amanda's right. I have been on edge lately... Holy shit! What the hell?

I'd stepped out of the front entrance onto the street to find that all four of my tires had been slashed.

Chapter Twelve

I was pissed... No, I was frickin' mad as hell. I stood beside my year-old Beamer and my blood boiled. Something bad was happening to me and I didn't know what it was. I felt damn helpless.

I called the dealership and asked them to fetch the car. Next, I photographed both sides of the vehicle with my phone and called my insurance company. Finally, I called Kate Gazzara, told her what had happened and asked her to come pick me up; as a reward, I'd buy her lunch. She told me she was just finishing up at a crime scene on Jersey Pike and could be with me in thirty minutes, which was okay because the wrecker was supposed to arrive at the same time. So I slid in behind the wheel and settled down to wait.

It was about five minutes later when I saw a white Ford Escape cruise slowly by coming from the opposite direction. I could see through the windshield there were at least two males in the small SUV. Unfortunately, they had both their sun visors down so I could see only the bottom half of their faces, and they were smiling, both of them. And my gut was telling me it was the same car that had followed me the day before, but because of the four slashed tires, there was nothing I could do about it.

I didn't get the license plate number then, and I couldn't get it now—we don't have front license plates in Tennessee. I tried to turn in my seat, but the damn car accelerated and sped away as it went past. All I could do was just sit there, gripping the wheel and gnashing my teeth. Somehow, though, I also knew that sooner or later... they'd pay dearly for those tires.

Kate arrived just a couple of minutes before the wrecker.

"It looks to me like you've pissed somebody off, big time," she said as she walked around my car. "You do seem to make a habit of doing that, don't you, Harry?"

"Ain't that the truth?" I replied.

I took what I needed from the car, told the driver to have them install four new tires and that I'd be at the dealership to pick it up in an hour.

That, I thought, was asking a bit much, but I tipped the driver a twenty and asked him to tell the guy in the tire shop there'd be one for him too if he had the car ready for me by two-thirty.

"What the hell was that all about, Harry?" Kate asked as I slid into the passenger seat of her unmarked Interceptor.

"The tires? I have no idea... Well, I might, but it's a long story. Where would you like to go for lunch?"

"I fancy some manicotti," she replied. "How about Provino's?"

"Sounds good to me."

I've known Kate for more than eighteen years, since she was a rookie cop. She's a classic beauty, almost six feet tall, slender, huge hazel eyes and long tawny hair she usually keeps tied back in a pony-tail. Back in the day, when I was still a cop, she and I were partners and... yes, lovers, too, until I managed to screw it up. But that was a long time ago. Now we're just good friends and sometimes even partners in crime... fighting, that is. I have a great team, but there are some things they just can't do, even Tim. Fingerprint analysis is one, ballistics is another. Kate is my go-to for that kind of help, and for backup, when I need it, which isn't often.

"So," she said as we sat down to eat, "are you going to tell me or not? Who slashed your tires?"

"What d'you know about a Jay, or should I say Jaylin, Coin?" I said, ignoring her question. "She runs a modeling agency on McCallie."

She wrinkled her nose, then said, "I know the name. Why? Does she have something to do with your tires?"

"No... at least I don't think so. The truth is, I don't know. She came into my office yesterday morning with a cock and bull story that she was being systematically robbed. I had a gut feeling there's something off about it. So T.J. and I went for a look-see yesterday afternoon, and I think she's full of it."

I looked up at our server and asked her to give us another minute then continued.

"She has twenty-four grand in hundred-dollar bills stashed in an old safe that was made before the turn of the last century and claims someone is stealing it. Just small amounts. Five hundred or less, and regularly. She has no security and, as far as I could ascertain, no intention of putting any in. It's frickin' weird, Kate. T.J. thinks it's me she's after. But why would she? I don't know her. I'd never even met her before she walked into my office yesterday."

Kate just sat there and stared at me, chewing slowly. Then she put down her fork and said, "I'd say someone's pulling her strings. What you've just told me... That and the tires... I told you. You've pissed somebody off, Harry. You'd better watch your back."

She picked up her fork again.

"I take it you've had Tim put her through the wringer, right?" she asked. "What did he come up with?"

"Not a whole lot... Well, nothing. The woman's clean, except for an arrest in Atlanta for prostitution way back when. No charges were filed."

"She's a hooker, then?"

"I'd hardly call her that," I replied. "She's one classy, sophisticated woman. Her agency paid taxes on more than seven mill last year. But here's the thing, Heather spent last night there. She thinks Coin could be a madam and that the agency is a high-end escort agency. But that's not all."

And then I told her about the gift card and that I thought I was being followed.

I handed her the envelope and note, encapsulated in a plastic baggie.

She took it, looked at it, turned it over and said, "No return address, no signature... weird. And it's addressed to both you and Amanda, also weird. Amanda? Yes. You? I don't think so. You want me to have it run for prints?"

"If you wouldn't mind, please... Look, you know me. I have this gut feeling that there's something off about the Coin woman and I can't figure it out. My gut is never—"

"Your gut is never wrong," she finished for me. "I know that, so what would you like me to do?"

"I was thinking, maybe you could run her name by Vice and see if they know anything."

She nodded, then said, "You're at it again, Harry. If you don't feel good about her, drop it. If she has anything to do with your tires... All I'm saying is, if they'll slash your tires, they probably wouldn't think twice about slashing your throat."

She had a point.

We ate for a while in silence. Me? My mind was elsewhere. One, I didn't think Coin and the slashers were connected. Two, I had a sinking feeling that something from my past was coming back to haunt me, though I had no idea what it could be, and that's what bothered me most.

"Why is your hand shaking, Harry?" Kate asked, interrupting my thoughts.

I looked at the fork in my right hand. It was trembling slightly.

"It's not," I lied. "It's just the way my forearm is resting on the table." I put the fork down and held out my hand. "See? Steady as a rock."

It was at that point my phone rang. I looked at the screen. I didn't recognize the number so I declined it. Two minutes later, it rang again, same number.

I sighed and looked at Kate. She nodded, and I answered it.

"Harry Starke."

"Hi, Mr. Starke, it's me, Roland Patrelli. I was wondering if maybe—"

"Are you serious?" I asked, interrupting him. "I thought I told you to stay out of my way."

"You did, and I'm sorry, sir, but I'm going to write my story whether or not you cooperate. It would be best though if I could interview you, get your input. Could you spare me say, thirty minutes?"

"Look, son," I said. "I'm not even sure how much longer I'm going to be in this business." I saw Kate raise her eyebrows. "And I don't do interviews, ever. Ask my wife. She'll tell you... No, don't ask her. And that thing about me not knowing how long; it's off the record. Don't you dare print it. I'll sue your ass if you do... What exactly is it you want from me, Roland?"

"Just some personal stuff. A quote or two... Okay, what I'd really like is an exclusive story about how you handled the terrorist attack and the bomb."

"Tell you what, Roland. You stay out of my way for the next couple of weeks and we'll talk about it."

"Oh wow, that's great, Mr. Starke—"

"No promises, Roland," I said, interrupting him again. "Just talk."

"Thanks—" but by then I'd hung up.

"Sorry about that, Kate. Some damn kid journalist wanting an exclusive. Now where were we?"

"Your hand was shaking."

"No, it... Oh hell." And I told her about the PTSD thing. I also told her that T.J. had pooh-poohed the idea and that I didn't believe it either.

Kate, however, thought differently and said I should "see someone."

"Yeah, right," I said. "I need to see the son of a bitch who slashed my tires. How about giving me a ride to the dealership?"

And she did.

Chapter Thirteen

Kate dropped me off at the dealership just as they rolled my Beamer out of the tire shop. I handed the guy the twenty, as promised, paid the bill and drove to my office. It was two-fifty when I walked into the outer office to see Jacque talking to a woman I'd never seen before.

I nodded to the woman but didn't take much notice of her.

I went to Tim's office, had a quick word with him, then went to my own office to close out some paperwork and to think before keeping my appointment with the inimitable Ms. Jay Coin. Barely had I closed the door when Jacque knocked and walked right on in.

"Did you see her?" she asked.

"Who? The woman you were talking to? Yes, I saw her. What about her?"

"She's here to apply for your nanny job."

"Really? Where did you find her?"

"Well, that's... Actually, I didn't find her. Wendy did."

Wendy Tanner was, and still is, Jacque's life partner. She was once a... No, she had been... No, I'm not going to say it. She's a lovely lady, and she loves Jacque dearly. They met several days after Police Chief Johnston's daughter, Emily, went missing. He asked me to find her, Emily. We did. Unfortunately, we were too late. She was dead, murdered. Wendy was the key to our solving the case. But all of that is another story.

"Wendy found her? Where? How?"

"Wendy knows people. I asked her to ask around, and she did. I think you'll like her. Her name's Maria Boylan and—"

"Hold on a minute, Jacque," I said and picked up the phone and buzzed Tim.

"Yeah, boss?"

"Tim, I need you to run a quick background for me. The name's Maria Boylan."

"I already did that for Jacque. Didn't she give it to you?"

I looked up at Jacque. She had her lips pursed, her arms folded across her chest, and she was slowly shaking her head.

"Thanks, Tim. I got it." I hung up and grinned at her.

"You didn't give me time to tell you," she said, the Jamaican accent thick on her tongue. "You always in a hurry, Harry Starke. No wonder you shakin' like you are, you know. Now, you gonna let me tell you, or what?"

"Sit down, Jacque," I said dryly, "and lose the accent."

Hell, what was I thinking? The woman's been working for me for eleven years. Of course she ran the woman's background.

"I'm sorry," I said. "Please continue."

"I've been talking to her. I think she's perfect. She's a former agent—Alcohol, Tobacco, and Firearms—but she was dismissed when... Oh, don't look at me like that. Just talk to her, okay? You'll see."

I shook my head, lowered my chin to my chest, stared at my shaking hands. *God knows I need someone, and quickly, but a disgraced ATF agent? I don't know. Shit, if someone's after me, and they are, maybe...* I took a deep breath as I thought of Amanda and Jade up there all alone.

I shook my head, looked at Jacque and said, "Okay. I'll talk to her. Bring her in."

A minute later, Jacque escorted the woman into my office. "Good afternoon, Ms. Boylan," I said, offering her my hand. Her grip was firm, almost manly.

She was of average height, perhaps a little overweight, but not noticeably so. I had her figured to be about thirty-five with dark, shoulder-length red hair—not her natural color—tied back in a pony-tail, blue eyes and full lips. *Botox?* I wondered. Her oval face was not unattractive, but there was a hardness about it that gave away her background. Even if I hadn't known, I would have pegged her as a cop.

"Mr. Starke," she said.

"Please, sit down, Ms. Boylan."

She sat on one of the two guest chairs in front of my desk.

"Jacque, I'd like you to stay, too," I said, looking at her.

Jacque handed me the background report, stepped away, and perched on the edge of one of the two couches.

"I understand you're looking for a bodyguard for your wife and a nanny for your child," Maria said, without preamble. "I can start tomorrow."

"Wow," I said, looking past her at Jacque, who was smiling. "You don't beat around the bush, do you?"

"There's no point in wasting your time and mine. I assume you know all about me. You wouldn't be much of a detective if you didn't."

I burst out laughing. T.J. could learn a thing or two from this woman. "It doesn't work like that, Ms. Boylan. I need to know about you, not from this." I picked up the paperwork and dropped it again. "Besides, I haven't had time to read it yet. Give me a moment, please."

I flipped through the three pages, glancing at the information as I did so. She was, according to the report, thirty-nine years old. Her credit score was 773, excellent, as were her references from the two security companies she'd worked for since leaving the ATF, under a cloud, and that was the one fly in the ointment, as they say.

I pushed the papers away, leaned back in my chair and stared at her. I could tell she knew exactly what I was thinking, and she didn't flinch or look away.

"I didn't do it," she said defiantly.

"Do what?" I asked.

"You know, what I was accused of. I didn't do it. I was set up."

"You want to tell me about it?"

"There's not much to tell. I was accused of assaulting a suspect and he had the marks on his face to prove it. I wasn't even there, but I didn't have an alibi. He had a witness, so I was charged. The charges were eventually dropped for lack of evidence and the witness's lack of credibility. I, however, was let go. I could have appealed the dismissal, but I was pissed off, so I walked. That's about it." She shrugged and shook her head.

"So," she said. "That it? You want me to leave now?"

"Not yet," I replied. The truth was I liked her. I liked her forthrightness, and my gut was saying she was telling the truth.

"Tell me about yourself, Maria. Is it all right if I call you by your first name?"

She nodded, then said, "I graduated UA in 2003 with a degree in political science and applied to the ATF. The process took thirteen months and I was inducted in 2004. I left in 2015 with the rank of G9 after eleven years on the job." She sounded bitter.

"Since then I've worked for two security companies specializing in personal protection." She sighed and shook her head. "In other words," she continued, "I was a bodyguard. I have a license to carry and I'm an expert shot. I know what you need, Mr. Starke, and I can do it. And I love kids, so how about it?"

I cocked my head, looked at her, took out my wallet and handed her a photo of my wife and Jade.

She took it from me, and I watched her reaction. Her face softened and she smiled.

"You have a lovely family, Mr. Starke. I'd be honored to look after them. I'm good with kids. I can't have any of my own, but I have a sister here in Chattanooga. She has three girls aged three to nine. I spend a lot of time with them. They love their Aunt Maria. You can call my sister if you want to. She'll be glad to talk to you."

She took out her wallet and showed me a photo of her with three nice-looking kids. I was sold, but she still had to pass the Amanda test.

"How about this?" I said, handing back her wallet. "Come to dinner at my home tonight and meet them both and let's see how it goes."

"Hmm, that's a first," she said thoughtfully. "Very well. I can do that."

I gave her the address and my phone number and asked her to be there at seven-thirty. That worked for her, so I stood, thanked her for her time, and Jacque showed her out.

I called Amanda and told her what I'd done, and that Maria would be our guest for dinner... If I told you she was underwhelmed, I would be exaggerating. But she agreed, much to my relief. Then, thinking it wouldn't be a bad idea to get a couple more opinions, I asked her to invite August and Rose.

I didn't tell her that Maria would have a dual function as a nanny and bodyguard, for two reasons: One, I didn't want to frighten her and two, I wasn't sure how she'd react to having a hard-nosed, former ATF agent as Jade's nanny. I figured I was going to have a tough enough fight on my hands without having to climb that wall.

In the meantime, I had an appointment to keep.

Chapter Fourteen

I t was right at five o'clock that afternoon when I arrived on Jay Coin's doorstep, figuratively speaking, of course.

Louanne greeted me enthusiastically and escorted me through to Coin's office where she was seated behind her desk. She reminded me somehow of a predatory spider. Don't ask. I don't know why. It was just an impression I had.

"Mr. Starke," she said, rising from her seat. "How nice to see you again."

Louanne left, closing the door behind her.

Coin was wearing a white business suit over a white blouse. She was also wearing white pumps. If I told you it was almost difficult to see her amid all the white in the room, you'd have an idea of just how over the top it all was.

Her voice was... oily, and I knew right away that she wasn't pleased to see me at all.

"Please, won't you sit down? To what do I owe this visit? Have you found out who my thief is?"

"You know, Jay," I said and paused for just a second, "you really are something."

"How so? Is that a compliment or...?"

"It's or," I replied. "Do you really think I believed all your BS? I didn't. You're not being systematically robbed. In fact, I'd be willing to bet you're not out one single penny. What I think you are, what your agency is, is a front for a high-end escort service. And that's okay. It's none of my business. It's illegal, but you do provide a service. What I don't get is why you had to get me involved. Did you think you could hook me up with one of your models and blackmail me? Or is someone paying you to set me up?"

All the time I was speaking, I was watching her. The color drained from her face, but she said nothing until I'd finished.

When I did, she simply shook her head and said, "Wow."

"Is that it?" I asked. "Is that all you have to say?"

"Oh, I could say plenty, but you seem to have made up your mind."

She rose to her feet, stepped around her desk, went to the door, opened it and said, "I think we're done, Mr. Starke. It's been... interesting, to say the least. Please send your invoice and I'll see that you're paid for your... efforts."

I stood and joined her at the door, put out my hand and pushed it closed.

"Come on, Jay," I said. "Talk to me. What the hell were you trying to do?"

"As I told you, Harry. I hired you to catch a thief. It seems I made a mistake. You're obviously not all you're cracked up to be. Now, I insist that you leave, and don't come back... Oh, and I don't have to tell you to drop your investigation, do I?"

I smiled at her, opened the door and stepped out into the corridor, but then I had a thought. I turned, offered her my card and said, "If you change your mind and would like to talk, that has my private cell number. Or, should you ever need help... well, call me."

She took the card from me and tore it in half, then she looked me in the eye and said, "I don't need your help, Harry, now or ever. Now, if you don't mind, I have work to do." And she closed the door.

I smiled down at my feet, then turned and walked quickly to the foyer, said goodbye to Louanne and went to my car.

I slipped in behind the wheel, tapped the Bluetooth, called Heather and told her what had happened and that she was no longer needed at the Coin Agency.

Her reply? "Why am I not surprised?" She's a woman of few words, is our Heather.

Next, I called T.J. and brought him up to speed. I also told him I wanted him and Tim to keep on digging into the Coin Agency. I might have been fired, but I wasn't about to quit. Someone had me in their sights and I didn't know if Coin was involved or not, but I wasn't about to turn my back on the idea that she might be. If she was, I wanted to know who she was working for.

I told T.J. that we'd all get together the following morning, then I hung up, looked again at the Coin Agency front entrance and shook my head. *What the hell is it about that woman that's bugging me?*

Chapter Fifteen

Dinner that evening was... interesting.

I arrived home at a little after seven. August and Rose were already there. Rose had Jade on her lap and was playing peekaboo with her. Jade was squealing with delight.

Amanda? She was in the kitchen putting the final touches to the dinner, and I could see that she wasn't too happy. After all, I dropped it on her without any warning.

"Who, exactly, is this woman, Harry?" she asked as she stirred the gravy. "What do you know about her?"

Now that last one was a question I really didn't want to answer, so I dodged it.

"You'll love her," I said. "We can talk about it later," I added, stepping up behind her and kissing her neck, "after she's gone. Right now, I need a shower."

She opened her mouth to speak, but before she could I kissed her on her open lips and all but ran from the kitchen.

I showered, dressed in comfortable clothes and then looked at the clock. It was already seven-thirty-five. *Damn it!*

I hurried from the bedroom to the kitchen to find it empty, but I could hear laughing coming from the living room.

Maria had arrived and was standing in the middle of the room holding a giggling Jade in her arms.

She looked different. Instead of the ponytail, her shoulder-length hair was clipped back to show her ears and a pair of diamond studs that looked to be a couple of carats each. She was wearing the quintessential little black dress under a white cardigan, and three-inch heels. A black, oversize clutch lay on the coffee table, and I could tell by the bulge that the lady was packing.

"Sorry I'm late to the party," I said. "I see you've met everyone. Can I get you a drink, Maria?"

"Just some Perrier water, if you have it, please." And she handed Jade back to Rose.

I poured myself a small measure of Laphroaig and a large one for my father. Amanda declined, saying she'd have wine with dinner. I looked at Rose. She shook her head.

"Please sit down, Maria," I said, handing her a glass of Perrier water on ice.

She sat on the couch next to Rose and the baby. I sat on the loveseat next to Amanda.

"Dad, Rose," I said. "I know you've already met this lovely lady but let me tell you why we're all here. Her name is Maria Boylan... Okay, I need to start over."

I took a sip of my drink before continuing. This needed to be worded correctly or I'd be sleeping on the couch.

"Amanda and I have decided we need a nanny for Jade. Jacque and I interviewed Maria earlier today and... well, while I haven't made a decision yet, I thought it might be a good idea if she met the family."

"*You* decided Jade needs a nanny," Amanda said. "I'm not so sure."

August turned in his chair to look at her. I could almost hear the wheels grinding away inside his head.

Rose, who was sitting next to Maria, turned her head to look at her, smiled and winked. *Well, at least Rose likes her,* I thought.

"Why don't you tell us a little about yourself, Maria," August said, frowning.

Typical, I thought. *Always the skeptical lawyer.*

"Why don't we have dinner first," Amanda said, rising to her feet. "We can talk about it after."

Amanda had prepared roast pork loin, saturated in herbs and garlic, with roasted potatoes, brussels sprouts, and mashed sweet potatoes with coconut cream pie to follow. I opened a couple of bottles of Pinot Grigio.

Dinner was a bit of a strain. I kept trying to make small talk while August kept trying to grill the woman about where she came from, her education, her experience as a nanny, her interests and, of course, her job history. And the reaction to her answer to that... well, you can imagine.

"I have three nieces whom I adore, and I served eleven years in the ATF and four in private security."

The room went quiet. Everyone stopped chewing, even me.

"Well," Amanda said, finally, "that's interesting. Why on earth do you want to be a nanny?"

Maria looked at me. She was practically screaming for help. I smiled at her and nodded.

She smiled back, shrugged and said, "I was wanting to make a change. I know Wendy Tanner quite well, and when she told me the famous Harry Starke was looking for a nanny, I was intrigued. I researched you, Harry. I liked what I found and called Jacque. I thought it was a good idea at the time. Now, I'm not so sure. You guys are way above my pay grade. So," she said and started to rise to her feet, "I'll leave you to enjoy—"

"Sit down, please, Maria," August said. "Harry, Amanda, can I talk to you both, in private, please?"

I nodded and we went to the kitchen.

"Sit down, please," August said. We did, and he continued. "Talk to me, Harry. Who the hell is this woman and what are you playing at?"

"You heard what she said. Amanda's still not well and needs help with the baby. Jacque and I interviewed her, and we were both impressed. I would have hired her then, but I thought it best that Amanda met her first. You, Dad, were an afterthought."

"What do you know about her?" he asked.

"I know she was fired from the ATF for something she didn't do. I had Tim run her background. Other than her getting fired, she has a clean record, good credit and great references. And, damn it, I like her... Look, I can't be with Amanda and the baby all day, every day. I worry about them when I'm not around. You know my lifestyle and I don't want... Oh hell, let's say it like it is. I want them protected from... anything. I think Maria has what it takes to do that."

"So," Amanda said, "What you're really saying is that you want to hire a bodyguard to protect me. I—"

"Yes, but," I said, interrupting her. "But Jade also needs a nanny and Maria loves kids. You should have seen the look on her face when I showed her your photograph. She's... She's perfect. I don't think I could find anybody more suited to what we need."

"What you need," Amanda said, her arms folded across her chest. "I'm not so sure."

"I'd like to know a little more about her," August said.

And so the conversation went on, and on, for more than fifteen minutes until finally I'd had enough and suggested we rejoin the others, which we did.

They'd left the dining room and were in the living room. Jade was asleep in Maria's arms.

That was good enough for me. I turned, looked triumphantly at Amanda and August, then turned to Maria and said, "If you still want the job, Maria, it's yours. You told me earlier that you could start tomorrow. Right?"

"Yes, I can start tomorrow."

"Good. Jacque will be in the office at eight. She'll get you up and running. I'll be there at eight-thirty. I'd like you here at the house by nine. Now," I said and looked around the room. "That's done, so let's relax, have a drink and see if we can get to know each other."

I looked at Amanda. She was smiling. *Whew! Thank the Lord.*

Chapter Sixteen

Maria left a little before ten o'clock that evening. August and Rose followed a few minutes later.

I was a little apprehensive to see them go. I had no idea what Amanda would say when we were finally alone. She said nothing, and I took her silence to mean she was angry, so I decided to find out. My old granny once told me never go to bed angry. I always remembered that.

"You're quiet," I said as we lay down in bed together. "What's on your mind?"

"I like her," she said.

"O-kay," I said. "And?"

"And that's it."

"But—"

"Don't push it, Harry. Now, make love to me like you mean it, for a change." And she climbed on top of me.

"But, what if—"

"No buts. I'm okay. You can't hurt me."

"Well, if you insist."

She did.

* * *

I was early into the office the following morning. I wanted to have a quick chat with Maria before she headed up the mountain.

I found her in the outer office sitting to one side of Jacque's desk. They were just finishing up the paperwork.

"*Good* morning," I said brightly. "You made it I see. Welcome aboard, Maria."

"Thank you, sir."

"Whoa," I said. "We don't do that here. My name's Harry, not boss," I looked at Jacque. She smiled innocently up at me. "Or chief, just Harry."

"Very well, sir, I mean Harry, and thank you. I won't let you down."

"I'm sure you won't," I said.

"Jacque, when you get done here, I'd like to see you both in my office."

"Five minutes, boss."

"Don't... What did I just...? Oh, hell, never mind."

I left them to it and went to get myself some coffee.

"All square and shipshape?" I asked when they sat down together in front of my desk.

"Yes, of course," Jacque replied.

"I just wanted to make sure you're happy," I said to Maria. "Do you have any questions about your duties?"

"I do," she replied. "I want to clarify that you hired me to be a nanny for Jade, as well as a bodyguard for both Amanda and Jade. Last night, I got the impression that Amanda wasn't aware of the bodyguard aspect of my job."

I nodded and said, "She is aware now, and I didn't have to tell her. She's... quite astute, is Amanda." I paused for a moment, thinking about what I wanted to say next, then continued, "I've made a lot of enemies over the past twenty years, especially since I put Billy Harper away. You do know what happened to Amanda last year?"

"Yes, Jacque told me. I'm so sorry that happened to her."

"Yes, well. I can't let it happen again, so yes, your duties are to help her with the baby, but your first priority is their safety, to protect them."

"I think I'm going to like this job. Is Amanda happy about it?"

"She told me she likes you, so that's a good beginning. Something to build on, right?"

She nodded.

"Okay, now for the bad news," I said. "I hate to throw you in at the deep end, but someone's been following me and whoever it was also slashed my tires. That could mean that someone has me in their sights. So you'll need to keep your wits about you. Amanda will fill you in on the security system at the house and... do you have a laptop?"

"Yes, an old one."

"Jacque, have Tim fix her up with a MacBook, an iPad and a dedicated phone. I'll need the number, so will you... All right," I said when I saw the look on her face. "I was just saying."

Jacque nodded and wrote in her notebook.

"What are you carrying, Maria?"

She opened her clutch, took out a Glock 17, dropped the magazine, cleared the chamber and handed it across the desk to me. I quickly stripped it and inspected it. It was clean and oiled.

"Can I see the mag, please?"

She handed it to me. I looked at the rounds. They were Liberty Civil Defense hollow points, fifty grain, two thousand feet per second. I was impressed.

"You don't mess around, do you?" I said as I reassembled the weapon.

She smiled. "I can't afford to."

I nodded, handed the weapon and magazine back to her, and looked at my watch. It was eight-forty-five.

"Jacque, give Amanda a call and tell her Maria will be a few minutes late."

Jacque nodded, raised her eyebrows, and wrote in her notebook again.

"What are you driving, Maria?"

"A 2017 Nissan Maxima."

"No way," I said. "You're kidding, right? I drove one of those for years. Loved it."

"Me too. It's reliable and fast, when I need it to be."

"That it is, that it is."

I looked at Jacque; she was smiling.

"Okay, I think that's it... unless you have any more questions."

"None that I can think of right now."

They rose from their seats together.

I nodded. "Okay then. Jacque, take her back and introduce her to the others, be sure Tim orders what she needs. Don't take too long. She needs to join Amanda ASAP."

"Thank you for the opportunity, sir," Maria said. "I'm very grateful and, as I said, I won't let you down."

"I know you won't, and remember... don't call me sir, or boss," I said, glaring at Jacque who smiled sweetly back at me.

"Don't take any notice of him. He thinks he runs this..." I heard Jacque say as she closed the door behind them.

I would have liked to hear the rest, but I knew she was joking and had meant for me to hear that one-liner.

I settled back in my chair, linked my hands behind my neck and closed my eyes. I was feeling really good about Maria, and that Amanda was willing to give her a chance was icing on the cake.

Five minutes later I rallied myself and went to get more coffee. Jacque was seeing Maria out of the door, so I waited, then asked her to give me ten minutes and then ask Tim and T.J. to join her in my office. And then I called Kate.

Chapter Seventeen

"Hey, you," I said when Kate answered my call. "Any word on that envelope?"

"Harry, I was just going to call you. Mike's people found one set of prints. They belong to Sheila Pervis."

"How do you know? Does she have a record?"

"No, but she does have a concealed carry license, so her prints are on record."

"So the invitation was legit, then?"

"I'd say so."

"Hmm. Okay, how about Jay Coin and her modeling agency? Did you run it by Vice?"

"I did. I talked to Dick Tracy. You remember him, right? He was my first partner after you left the force. He was a... Never mind. He said they checked her out several months ago and gave her a pass. They still have their suspicions, but other than that... nothing."

"Yes, I remember Tracy. How is he?"

"Hah, still a flirtatious pig. He'll never change... He did say one thing of interest, though. He said they think she has a partner."

"No kiddin'? Did you get a name?"

"Nope. He didn't have one."

"Okay. Well, thanks, Kate. Look, I'm sorry, but I have to go. I have a meeting. Can we talk later?"

"Sure. You know where I'll be." And she hung up.

Me? I sat at my desk, thinking, *So, the gift card's legit. Whew, that's a relief. I'm enjoying those massages.*

There was a knock on the door. It opened, and Jacque stuck her head inside and asked if I was ready for them. I was, and I told her I'd join them in the conference room.

She nodded, backed out and left the door open. I buzzed Heather and asked her to join us, too.

T.J., Tim, and Heather sat at the table with their backs to the door. Jacque and I sat together on the opposite side of the table.

"So," I said. "Talk to me about Jaylin Coin and her business. You first, Tim."

He nodded, opened a file box and took out a stack of 8x10 photographs.

"These are surveillance photos Heather shot last night," he said as he handed them to me. "They are the best of more than fifty. Most of the others are almost identical to these, you know, images taken from in her car, in bursts of three, or more..." He'd noticed the look I was giving him, did the thing with his glasses and leaned back in his chair.

There were twelve images, including a headshot of Coin herself.

"Nice shot, Heather."

"Thanks. She was leaving the premises. I didn't know if you had a good one of her or not."

"I do now."

I flipped through the rest of the images. The photos were time and date stamped, and of different girls leaving the agency property. All of them were lovely, all were young, and all were scantily dressed. They looked like models, but what did I know?

"What do you think, Heather?" I asked. "Is Coin legit?"

"From what I saw going on in the studio on Tuesday, I think she could be—"

"She is," Tim said, interrupting her. "Here's a list of her clients. You'll recognize a number of names—most of them local ad agencies —and they most definitely are legit." He handed a sheet of paper to me across the table.

"As I was saying," Heather said, with an edge to her voice as she glared at Tim.

Tim grinned back at her. I smiled.

"I think she could be 'legit.'" She made finger quotes. "But I also observed the way she acted when she received those calls. And then there are those." She pointed at the images on the table in front of me.

"As I said yesterday," she continued, "I think she's running two businesses: the legitimate modeling agency as a cover for an escort service."

"I agree," T.J. said. "That would account for the large amount of cash in the safe. What I don't get is why she would want to involve us."

"Me neither," I said. "Tim?"

"I can't find anything, other than the arrest. She's clean, Harry. So's the business. No red flags."

"Kate says Vice thinks she has a partner," I said. "Any sign of one?"

"If she does," Tim said, "I haven't found him, or her. I'll keep digging though."

"T.J.?" I asked.

"As far as her finances go, she's meticulous. She pays her taxes. She draws cash from the bank every week, in varying amounts anywhere from fifteen hundred to a high of eleven grand—that would be the float in the safe—and she declares it as miscellaneous expenses, whatever that means. If she's taking in large amounts from the escort service, she's hiding it well."

"What about credit card receipts? Johns use them all the time."

"That's true," T.J. said. "If it is an escort service, she's running it separately. In which case, credit card receipts would be untraceable and are probably going into an off-shore account."

I thought for a minute, then shook my head and said, "I get the feeling we're wasting our time. Whatever it is she's doing... It may be illegal, but I don't think it concerns us."

It was at that point I noticed something I hadn't seen before.

What the hell?

I picked up one of the images. It was a headshot of Coin, one taken some years ago. I stared at it. *No, it can't be,* I thought, my brain in turmoil.

I picked up the one Heather had taken the night before. There it was again. I shook my head in disbelief.

"Tim, do you have these on your laptop?" I asked.

He nodded. "Yes, of course."

"Pull them up for me, please."

He did, then turned the machine around so that I could see the screen. I reached across the table and grabbed it, set it down in front of me, flipped through the images until I found the headshot. I stared at it for a moment, slowly shaking my head. I tapped the keys and zoomed in closer.

"Holy shit," I whispered.

Chapter Eighteen

"What?" Tim said. "What is it? Is something wrong?"

"Yes, something's wrong," I replied, "but it's no fault of yours. It's what's been bugging me ever since I first met the woman. How the hell didn't I spot it sooner?"

It was a rhetorical question and I didn't expect an answer.

I leaned back in my chair, linked my fingers together at the back of my neck and stared at the enlarged image—wondering what the hell—as my head filled with images from the past.

"Jacque?" I turned the computer slightly so she could see it.

"Oh, dear Lord," she said. "It can't be. Can it?"

I nodded. "I think it is."

"Well," T.J. said. "Are you going to share it with us or not?"

"You won't remember this, T.J., but Tim and Heather will."

I turned the laptop around to face them.

For a moment no one said a word. They just stared at the screen, then Tim whispered, "Frickin' hell," and looked across the table at me, his face pale. Tim never swears. It was a first.

"Oh my, really?" was all Heather said.

"What?" T.J. said. "All I can see is a necklace."

"Yeah, it's that all right," Tim said.

Around Jay Coin's neck was a thin gold chain from which hung a tiny gold circlet—two snakes entwined eating each other's tail—and oh how it brought back memories.

"Yes," I said, "it's a necklace, a very special necklace. The circlet is an Ouroboros or, in this case, its Hindu symbolism, kundalini. The two snakes represent eternity, but this necklace represents something else entirely."

I paused for a moment, thinking, remembering. "It was before your time, T.J., a case we handled back in early 2015. It concerned a young woman, Tabitha Willard. She had one just like it. I'd never met the girl, well, I did, in a way, in Doc Sheddon's lab. I was also there when she committed suicide... threw herself off the Walnut Street bridge. I tried to stop her, but..." I paused again as my heart seemed to well up in my throat as I remembered that awful night in December 2014.

"But that's a long and complicated story," I continued. "She was wearing one of those when she jumped." I nodded at the laptop. "It was the key to solving the case. I put away Congressman Harper and two members of his staff. Harper died in prison a couple of years later, but not before hiring a hitman—a woman, actually—to kill Amanda and me. The assassin almost got me and would have but for you and Amanda." I looked at Tim when I said that.

He simply grinned, put his forefinger to the bridge of his glasses and shoved them further up the bridge of his nose, looking embarrassed.

"Anyway," I continued, "as I said, that necklace was key to solving the case, but it was also the key to something else. Billy Harper was blackmailing high-ranking members of congress and the senate. To be able to do that he photographed and videotaped them in compromising situations. Through his influence, they were introduced to Mystica, a sort of sex club... It was actually more complicated than that, but that will cover it for now. If you want the details, T.J., you can get them from Tim some other time. Anyway, Mystica was located in a strip mall just a block from the Coin Agency off McCallie."

T.J. nodded, then said, "If you solved the case, how does it affect us today?"

"That, my friend, is the crux of the matter."

I turned to Jacque and said, "Do me a favor, Jacque, and call Sheila Pervis. Tell her I'm not going to be able to make my appointment this morning and ask her if she can reschedule me for later this afternoon."

She nodded, got up and left the room.

"To answer your question, T.J., I think the necklace answers a couple of questions. One, it tells me who her partner is and two, it tells me who's been following me and who slashed my damn tires."

I looked at Tim. His eyes were wide. He obviously knew what was coming next.

"Mystica, as I said, was the brainchild of Congressman Gordon 'Little Billy' Harper, but he didn't run it. He was too high profile to get personally involved in something like that. He employed a rascal by the name of Lester Tree, aka Shady Tree, to run it for him. I first met Shady back when I was a cop. In fact, I put a bullet through his arm and put him away for five years, something he never forgave me for. We've been running into each other ever since. He was responsible for the death of my brother Henry. The last time I saw him was last year, after I... after Duvon James disappeared," I said, catching myself. *No wonder I've been seeing his damn ghost.* "Shady had cut himself some sort of deal with the Feds and was entering the witness protection program."

I paused as I remembered his final words to me.

And remember how I told ya I wasn't finished with ya? Well, I ain't. One of these days, Starke, when you ain't expectin' it, I'll be there, in the dark, waitin'... Hahahahaha!

"He promised to return one day and get his revenge," I continued. "I have a feeling this is the day."

"So, what are we going to do about it?" T.J. asked.

It was then that Jacque returned.

"Sheila can't do it this afternoon," she said as she returned to her seat next to me, "but she penciled you in for two-thirty tomorrow afternoon. Is that okay?"

I nodded, then continued, "That necklace is identical to the one that Tabitha Willard wore and... that several other members of Mystica wore. It was like a membership card, and used as an invitation to other members... That tells me that Jay Coin knows Shady; she may even have been a member of Mystica. It also means that he may be her mysterious partner. There's only one way to find out, and that's to talk to her, like now."

I stood up and started pacing. "T.J., I want you to come with me. Tim, see what you can find about Shady. I want to know where he is. If you have to hack into the WITSEC system to find out, do it, but for God's sake, don't get caught. All right, people. Let's get to it. T.J., I have a couple of quick calls to make first."

The first call I made was to Maria to put her on high alert. If Tree was behind Coin's interest in me, Amanda and Jade could be in deadly danger.

The second call was to Jay Coin.

"Jay," I said. "It's Harry Starke. I need to talk to you, urgently. Can you meet me somewhere?"

"I told you I wanted nothing more to do with you and that you were to stop your investigation. I suggest you go straight to h—"

"Don't hang up, Jay," I interrupted her. "This isn't about the investigation. It's about you. It's about that necklace you're wearing. I think you're in a world of trouble and don't even know it. Look, I can help you, but we have to talk, *please*."

We argued back and forth until, finally, she agreed to meet me at a Starbucks on Hamilton Place Boulevard.

Chapter Nineteen

There are several routes from my offices on Georgia Avenue to Hamilton Place. The shortest is via Bailey Avenue. The quickest—about fifteen minutes—is via I-24. For some reason, I decided on Bailey. I think it was a psychological thing, to take the shortest route, even if it takes longer.

Anyway, that's what I did. T.J. was in a talkative mood and as I turned left onto ML King, he began by asking me if I really thought Shady could be involved somehow. He knew who Shady was through past dealings we'd had with him since he, T.J., had come on board; namely when we were dealing with the terrorists whose plan it was to lay waste to the city and the Nicholas Christmas affair.

Any other time I would have answered him, but not that time. You see, when you're driving in downtown Chattanooga you have to keep your wits about you. Me? As I turned left onto ML King, I checked each rearview mirror in turn. And, as I checked the one above the dash, I noticed a white Ford Escape with two people up front some three cars back. They made the turn after me. *This time, you son of a bitch, I gotcha.*

I knew if I stopped, they'd just speed up and drive on past, so I hit the gas, made a left on Houston, another left on Flynn, another left on Lindsey, and finally left again back onto ML King behind the Escape. My plan was to force them to stop and then confront them. Only it didn't work out like that. I got caught two cars back from the red light at the corner of Lindsey and ML King. When I finally was able to make the turn, I hit the gas and tried to catch them, but they'd disappeared. They must have realized what I was doing and bailed. *Damn it all to hell!*

I slowed down to the speed limit and T.J. and I chatted all the way to Hamilton Place about the possibilities of ever finding them or Shady Tree. He was, as usual, skeptical. His argument being that if Shady had entered the WITSEC program, the Feds would be keeping a close watch on him.

"You don't know Shady," I muttered.

We arrived at Starbucks no more than a couple of minutes late. I parked across from the entrance and we went inside and looked around. The place wasn't busy, so it was easy to see that Coin hadn't arrived yet. We ordered coffee and sat down to wait... and wait...

I'd arranged to meet her at two o'clock. By the time two-thirty rolled around I was beginning to get worried, so I called her. My call went straight to voice mail.

I looked at T.J. and said, "Either she's changed her mind, or something's wrong. I'm thinking the latter. Drink up and let's go."

We arrived at the Coin Agency back on McCallie some twenty minutes later at five minutes to three. The place was empty, except for two dead bodies. Louanne was on the floor behind her table with two bullets in her head, one in the ear and one in the forehead. Jay Coin was in her office, still seated at her desk, her hands dangling at her sides, her head thrown all the way back. She also had a bullet in her head and another in her chest.

Frickin' hell. This just turned into a shitstorm.

"Go back to the car, T.J., and wait for me."

He nodded and backed carefully out of the foyer.

I took out my phone, looked at it, debating whether or not to make the call. Decided not, put the phone back in my pocket and took a few minutes to look around. First, I checked the two bodies again. The wounds appeared to have been made by a small caliber weapon, probably a suppressed .22. There were no shell casings, so either the killer picked them up or he used a revolver. I figured it was the former. A revolver is not usually the weapon of choice for a professional killer.

Someone wanted the lady silenced, I thought as I toured the building, being careful not to touch anything. I found nothing. Other than the two bodies, the place was deserted. I took one last quick look around Jay Coin's office. I have to admit, I felt kind of sorry for the woman.

I stepped outside and called 911 and then Kate.

Chapter Twenty

"Wow, you really do have the touch of death, don't you, Harry?" Kate said as she stepped out of her unmarked cruiser and joined me at the curbside. "How long have you known the woman? Two days, three? You're frickin' dangerous just to know, my friend." She shook her head.

"Kate," I said. "This is Shady's work. I'm certain of it."

"Oh come on, Harry. Tree is in the WITSEC program. You know that."

"You think? Well, I'll know for sure soon enough, I hope. If it's not him, it's one hell of a coincidence. Here, take a look at this."

I handed her Jay Coin's headshot and waited for her reaction.

She glanced at it, turned it over, looked at the back, then said. "It's the Coin woman. So what?"

"Geez, Kate. Look at the necklace."

She looked again. Looked at me, then again at the photograph, cocked her head to one side and said, "Oh... my God. I don't believe it, Harry. It's a coincidence. She could have gotten that thing on eBay."

"She could have, but I'm willing to bet she didn't. She was

involved somehow with Shady. I think he's her mystery business partner. It had to have been that son of a bitch that slashed my tires. He's like a damn dog with a bone. He never gives up. He promised me he'd be back. You know that. And he is."

She sighed, handed me the photograph, and said, "Talk to me, Harry. I have two dead bodies in there. One of them was your client. What the hell happened here?"

"She wasn't my client. She fired me, yesterday."

"Geez, that had to have been the shortest contract you ever made. Why'd she fire you?"

"Because I told her she was full of shit, and that she was little more than a high-class madam. She didn't take it too well. Look, I arranged to meet her at Starbucks at Hamilton Place, her choice of venue. I was on my way to meet her and had just turned off Georgia when I spotted that damn Ford Escape following me again. I tried to grab 'em, but that damn red light at Lindsey and ML King put a stop to that. We need to find it, and them. I'd bet my entire 401k that Shady was in that car."

"You don't have a 401k," she said, smiling snidely at me.

"I did," I said. "I rolled it over. Hell, Kate. Stop kidding around, will you? I'm being serious here."

"Okay, but I'm not buying Shady. I'll have someone take your statement and then get you out of here. What's your next step?"

Now that question floored me, because I had no earthly idea what my next step was going to be. With Coin gone, I had no leads. All I could do was wait for Shady to make his next move.

And he did, or so I thought. Two minutes later, while I was in the middle of making my statement, my phone rang. I looked at the screen. It was Amanda.

I took the call and said, "Hi, sweetie. To what do I—"

"Harry," she said, interrupting me. "There's someone here, watching the house, taking photographs. I'm scared. What should I do?"

"Don't worry. Put Maria on."

"How d'you want me to handle it, Harry?" Maria asked when she came on. "You want me to go out there and grab the son of a bitch, I will."

"No, don't do that. Take Amanda and Jade to the basement. There's a panic room down there. Then go back upstairs, stay by the security monitors and keep an eye on him. Keep that Glock handy. Make sure the security system is on and the cameras are recording. If anyone enters, shoot to kill. If it's who I think it is, you'll get only one chance. I'll be there as soon as I can."

It took almost twenty minutes for me to get from McCallie to my house, and I burned rubber all the way. I was less than a block away when I spotted the familiar red Mustang.

That little prick. When I get my hands around his throat, I'll throttle him to death.

Chapter Twenty-One

Kate arrived at my house five minutes after I did. By then, however, I had Roland Patrelli by the collar and it was all I could do to stop myself from doing him serious injury.

"D'you have any frickin' idea of what you've done, what trouble you've caused?" I snarled as I swung him around and shoved him onto his ass on the grass verge. Oh yes, I was boiling.

"You've upset my wife and she called me away from a frickin' crime scene. I oughta bust your a—"

"Take it easy, Harry," Kate said, then looked down at Roland. "Who are you and what were you doing?"

"I'm a journalist," he said, looking up at her. "Mr. Starke said I could have an exclusive interview. I was just getting some background material, some nice photos of his house and such. I meant no harm. I'm sorry if I caused any trouble."

I looked down at him. He looked like a wounded puppy. *Oh geez,* I thought as my anger subsided.

"I didn't say I'd give you an exclusive." I leaned toward him. "I said we'd talk about it. I ought to smack you silly."

"I think you'd better leave, before he does just that," Kate said to Roland.

I gave him a look that said he'd better get out of my sight. "Yeah, I think so too, and stay the hell away from me. D'you understand?"

He nodded and looked at me wide-eyed. I knew what he was thinking.

"Go on, get out of here," I said. "Call me in a couple of weeks... and don't pull this kind of shit again."

He struggled to his feet, grabbed his camera and bag, and said, "Thank you, sir." Then he almost ran to his car, threw his gear onto the back seat, jumped inside and drove away.

"Bit hard on him, weren't you?" Kate asked, smiling as we walked to the house.

"Maybe. You want some coffee? You can say hello to Jade."

They were all waiting for me. Amanda holding Jade in her arms. Maria sitting at the kitchen table, her Glock on the tabletop. Not good. I could tell by the look on Amanda's face, and Kate's.

"Everything all right?" I asked as I walked into the kitchen.

"Are you serious?" Amanda replied. "What the hell is that all about?" She nodded at Maria's Glock.

"Yes, I'd like to know that, too," Kate said.

"You didn't tell me she had a weapon," Amanda continued before I could answer. "And I don't like it. Having you walking around with one is bad enough, but now this. I won't have it."

"Calm down, honey," I said. "It's not what you think..." And that was the wrong thing to say, because it was exactly what Amanda was thinking, and she knew it.

"Okay, okay," I said. "I understand how you feel about guns, but I can assure you Maria is better qualified to handle one than I am." I didn't know if she was or not, but it seemed like the right thing to say.

"I worry about you both when I'm not here," I continued.

She looked at Maria, then at me. Then she sat down at the table. Jade stuck her fist in her mouth and gurgled.

"Look, sweetheart. You didn't hesitate to use a gun when you thought Calaway Jones was about to kill me."

"That was different."

"How was it different?" I asked. "Do you think I wouldn't do the same if the roles were reversed, if you and Jade were in danger? Come on. You know I would, but if I'm not here... Maria will keep you both safe."

She looked at Maria. Amanda's face softened and she said, "I'm sorry, Maria. Thank you. And I do feel better knowing you're here."

Whew. That was a tough one.

She turned to look at Kate, who was still standing just inside the door, and said, "Hi, Kate. Come on in and sit down. I'll make coffee."

"I can make it for you, if you like," Maria said, standing up.

"No, I'll do it. I know where everything is. Just taking Jade for me would be a big help." And she did.

Amanda looked at Kate and said, "You haven't met Maria, have you? Harry hired her. She's Jade's *nanny*." She emphasized the word and glared at me.

"Harry," Kate said. "If you'd give me a moment, I'd like a few words with your *nanny*."

Oh shit. Now I have you to contend with, too? It ain't like I don't already have enough to worry about.

"Sure," I said and left them to it and joined Amanda in the kitchen.

I put my arm around her shoulder and nibbled her ear.

"Quit it. Don't think you can get around me like that. It won't work. What were you thinking, Harry?"

"I was thinking how much I love you and how I need to protect you both. Now come on, admit it. You felt safer with Maria here, now didn't you?"

She turned around, threw her arms around my neck and squeezed. "Oh, Harry," she whispered. "I was so scared. Maria was an angel, except for the gun. You know how I hate them."

"Yes, I know, sweetheart, and I'm sorry."

It was a nice moment, but soon over. I didn't mention it to Amanda, but I still had Shady Tree front and center in my mind.

Even so, just to be sure, I called Tim and had him run a background check on one Roland Patrelli.

"I want to know everything there is to know," I told him. "If he has a record, who his friends are, who he works for, everything. And I want it first thing tomorrow morning. And I want to know where Shady is."

I ended the call, went back into the living room and put my cell phone down on the table. It was then that I noticed my hand was shaking like a leaf in the wind. I was pretty sure everyone else noticed it, too, but no one said a word.

Chapter Twenty-Two

hen I arrived at my office the following morning, Kate
was already there waiting for me.

"You want coffee?" I asked.

"Sure."

"Well," I said, as we sat down together in my office. "Spill it. Why
are you here?"

"I didn't tell you this last night because I didn't know if you'd told
Amanda or not," she said, "but after I dropped you off at the dealership on Wednesday, I put out a BOLO for your white Ford Escape."

"I didn't tell her," I said. "I didn't want to frighten her."

"That's what I thought. Anyway, throughout the day yesterday
Traffic pulled over several dozen such vehicles. Only one fit the
description: late model with two toughs up front."

"You got him then?" I asked, holding my breath. "You got
Shady?"

"No. Not quite." She paused and took a sip of her coffee.

"Not quite? What the hell is that supposed to mean?"

"Shady was not one of the two gentlemen in the Escape, though

461

one of them is a one-time 'associate' of his." She emphasized the word with air quotes.

"Then who the hell are they and what d'you mean, 'one-time'?"

"A patrol officer pulled them over on Hixson Pike. He ran the driver's license and insurance and the passenger's ID. The driver was a DeAnté King. The passenger was Hector Santos."

"DeAnté King?" I asked. "I've heard that name... somewhere."

"I'm sure you have," she said. "He used to work for Shady when he hung out on Bailey."

"See, I told you."

She shook her head and said, "I don't think so, Harry. I said he *used* to work for him, but not since Shady left for WITSEC pastures unknown."

She took a sip of her coffee and looked at me with a curious expression. I wasn't sure what to make of it.

"As you know," she continued, "Shady was into just about every shady—no pun intended—deal in town, including prostitution, drugs and extortion. When Shady disappeared, DeAnté took up some of the slack. He took over the protection part of Shady's empire and has been putting the squeeze on his, Shady's, customers ever since."

"But can you tie him to Shady now?" I asked.

Again, she shook her head. "No. As far as we know, he's had no contact with Shady in almost a year. There's no evidence to suggest he's still working for him, though it wouldn't surprise me if he was."

"You think?" I asked. "Do you think for one minute that Shady would give it all up and just fade away? He wouldn't, and you know it. Somehow, he's still running King, and others. I just know he is."

"Well, whatever. Traffic had to let them go. The two were clean, no warrants, not even a ticket. They refused the officer's request to search the car, which they had every right to do. The officer didn't have probable cause."

"He could have hauled them in for questioning," I said.

"Even you know better than that, Harry."

"Did you get an address?"

She nodded. "The Cascade Long-stay Suites on Rossville Boulevard."

"That's it then. Let's go talk to them," I said, standing up.

"Sit down, Harry," she said. She sounded tired. "You might be able to, but I can't harass them. Not anymore, not these days, not without probable cause, and we don't have any... Harry, I'm sorry, but there's zero evidence that Shady is involved in any of this."

"Then why are they following me? Why did they slash my tires?"

"We don't know that they are or even that they did. There are a lot of white Ford Escapes out there. These two operators... It could be, and probably is, just a coincidence. You've upset a lot of people over the years, Harry. You may be The Hero of Chattanooga, but you sure as hell aren't popular. Look, if it is these two clowns, now that we're onto them, they'll probably lie low for a while. If not, they're going to get caught, sooner or later."

"Yeah, well. I need sooner. I'm going to talk to them. You can come, or not. Please yourself."

"I don't think so, Harry. You want to protect your family. I'm telling you to stay away from those two creeps. All you'll do is get yourself into trouble, maybe even killed. Let me take care of it. I'll put a tail on them, and I'll tell you immediately if we find anything."

I stared at her. Deep down I knew she was right. Not only that, but she had the manpower. I didn't. So, reluctantly, I nodded and sat back down.

"And there's one more thing I want to talk to you about."

"Oh yes, and what might that be?" I asked cautiously.

"How long have you and I been friends, Harry?"

She knew the answer to that better than I did, but I played along. "Fifteen, sixteen years?"

"Try eighteen. Harry, I'm worried about you. You have a problem. You're almost... I've never seen you like this before. Not even when Duvon killed your brother. You're on edge all the time, you fly off the handle, you've become paranoid, and you're obsessed with

Lester Tree. I saw your hands shaking last night, and I know Amanda did. Look at them; they're shaking now."

I looked at them. They were trembling slightly.

I took a deep breath and clenched my fists. Much as I hated to admit it, when I thought about it, I knew Kate was right.

I nodded. "Okay, you win. You handle King and Santos, but if..."

She cocked her head and widened her eyes.

"I have a massage this afternoon," I said, trying to change the subject.

She just shook her head, stood up and said, "I gotta go, Harry. Enjoy your massage, but take it easy. You hear?"

"Yeah, yeah," I said as she closed the door behind her.

Chapter Twenty-Three

After Kate left I sat there at my desk, thinking about Shady, DeAnté King and Jay Coin. I knew there had to be an answer, a connection there somewhere, but I just couldn't put my finger on it.

Kate had said that King's presence was probably just a coincidence, but I don't believe in coincidences, especially where Shady Tree is concerned. Besides, my gut was telling me different. What were the chances of King, one of Shady's lieutenants, being in the same place as me, not once, but three times? It didn't compute. I buzzed Tim.

"Hey," I said when he picked up. "I need you to run a couple of backgrounds for me. How long will it take?"

"It depends who they are... but, say ten, fifteen minutes."

"Good. Their names are DeAnté King and Hector Santos. I need them ASAP, and then I need you in my office."

"You got it, b... Harry."

I looked at my hands. They were still trembling slightly. *Damn it,* I thought as I balled them into fists and stood up.

For five minutes I stood there, behind my desk, doing deep

breathing exercises. Finally, I sat down again and looked at my hands and convinced myself the trembling had stopped.

There was a knock on my door.

"Come in," I shouted.

Tim entered, loaded up as usual, and sat down in front of my desk, dumped his gear on the desktop, then leaned back in his chair and looked at me, smiling.

I stared back at him, thinking to myself, *What a breath of fresh air he always is.* It was then I noticed something about him that I should have noticed before.

"Tim," I said. "Have you been working out?"

He was wearing jeans and a fitted, short-sleeve golf shirt. The fabric was stretched tight around his biceps.

He looked embarrassed, poked his glasses with his forefinger and said, "Well, I err... Yes... some. I've been taking Krav Maga ever since we had to deal with Nick Christmas." His eyes narrowed for a second before continuing, "I go three times a week. I'm at level two. I have an orange belt. I thought that maybe it was a good idea to be able to defend myself."

I couldn't help it. I wanted to laugh, but I didn't. Instead, I smiled at him and said, "Wow. That's amazing, but Krav is as much offensive as it is defensive. It's an aggressive art, developed by the Israelis. Why did you pick that one?"

"I remembered what you told me about Calaway Jones, and I knew first-hand how good she was, so..."

I just looked at him and shook my head, smiling. Somehow, I just couldn't see our Tim as aggressive in any situation. *But the kid's earned an orange belt. That's something special. It means he's worked hard and stuck with it. No wonder he's building muscle.*

"Well, okay then," I said, getting back to work. "Nicely done, young Jedi." When he heard that, he really colored up.

"So," I said, "what about King and Santos?"

"They both have extensive rap sheets. King has multiple arrests for acts of violence here in Chattanooga. Santos has been in trouble in Laredo, Texas, ever since he was sixteen. But as far as I can tell, they've stayed clean for the last couple of years." He paused for a minute, then continued, "Harry, you also asked me to check on Lester Tree. You're not going to like what I found. He never made it into the witness protection program."

I frickin' knew it!

"Go on, Tim."

"I talked to an FBI friend of mine. He didn't know much, but he did know that Mr. Tree had spent nearly six weeks in custody... 'spilling his guts' was how my contact put it. Then he was finally being transported to... well, my contact didn't know exactly, but somewhere along the way Mr. Tree had to go to the bathroom. That's when he disappeared, and there's been no sign of him since. They think he must have made it out of the country."

I leaned back in my chair, sucked in my top lip and then blew out a deep breath.

"So," I said. "That was what, nine, ten months ago?"

Tim nodded.

"And you haven't been able to trace any of his movements?"

"Not a one."

"So he could be here, then, in Chattanooga?"

"He could be anywhere."

"This is not good," I muttered, more to myself than to Tim.

Tim said nothing.

"What about the journalist, Roland Patrelli?" I asked after a long pause.

"He is what he says he is, a freelance journalist. He graduated Northwestern in 2015. Then he worked for a small daily in Charlotte before stepping out on his own a year ago. I found nothing suspicious, except that he's broke with a credit score of 623. No criminal record. He's clean."

I nodded. "I figured he was," I said, deep in thought.

I looked at my watch. It was almost eleven, and I'd arranged to meet Amanda for lunch at the Red Lobster at eleven-thirty.

"Okay, Tim," I said finally after another long pause. "That should do it for now, I think. We'll talk again later."

He nodded, stood, gathered up his gear and left.

I tried to shake off the deep feeling I had of impending doom. I couldn't. I left the office feeling like shit and drove to Hamilton Place, looking over my shoulder every yard of the way, but I saw nothing. Did that make me feel any better? Hell no.

* * *

Lunch with Amanda and Jade that morning was kind of strange, mostly because Maria sat by herself two tables away. She said it was to give us some space, a little privacy, but I knew different. She was keeping a lookout in case of trouble.

We chose the Red Lobster because it's kid-friendly and because I like their cheesy biscuits.

Amanda looked beautiful with her shiny blond hair and pink cheeks. Jade looked adorable with her crazy hair and messy face. I loved the normalcy of enjoying lunch with my wife and daughter, and I loved them. Being a husband and father was... something I never thought I'd experience. I would do just about anything to keep them safe.

We were just about finished eating and I'd ordered coffee when Amanda asked me what was wrong.

"Wrong?" I asked. "Nothing. Why d'you ask?"

"Yes, there is. I know you too well, Harry. What is it?"

You think for one minute I was going to tell her about Shady Tree? Hell no. So, instead, I said, "Nothing, really. I just have a lot on my mind, is all... And... Oh hell, Amanda, sometimes these last few days I feel like I'm coming apart at the seams."

Involuntarily, I looked down at my hands. They were steady as a rock. That alone cheered me up, but sitting there, in the dark reaches of my mind, was Shady Tree, and he was smiling.

"You're not still thinking of quitting, are you?" she asked.

I shrugged. "No, not really."

"What kind of answer is that?" she asked.

"The only one I have."

"I think you need a vacation, Harry. We all do. How about it? Let's go somewhere nice. Calypso Key? I love that island."

"I'll... think about it."

She looked at her watch, then said, "I have some shopping to do. Don't forget your massage. It's at two-thirty."

"Oh hell," I said. "I'd forgotten all about that."

Chapter Twenty-Four

A manda, Jade and Maria left for shops unknown a few minutes later, but not before I managed to sidetrack Maria and tell her to stay sharp, that there might be trouble in the offing, but I didn't mention Shady.

Me? I had some thinking to do. I had a couple of hours before my massage, so I decided to visit a dear old friend—and when I say friend, I'm being facetious—and maybe learn something.

The Sorbonne doesn't open until four in the afternoon, so I parked outside the rear entrance and rang the bell, and then I rang it again. I had to ring it three times before I heard a voice on the other side of the steel door shouting, "All right, all right. I'm coming, damn it."

A lock clicked, then another, and then I heard a bolt being drawn. The door opened a crack and a frowsy pair of eyes peered out at me.

"Oh hell, it's you," Benny Hinkle said as he opened the door wide to let me in.

Benny is a weird little man, a creature of the night, a member of the walking dead. No, he's not a vampire... at least I don't think he is. He's a fat, greasy unshaven slob that creeps out of his lair—his office—

after dark to short his customers with watered liquor and deafen them with the brain-numbing rap music that the younger generation seem happy to call music. No, he's not a vampire, but he very well could be.

"Geez, Harry. Couldn't you wait until I opened? I need my sleep, you know?"

"You don't sleep, Benny," I replied. "You're like a frickin' raccoon, a nasty little nocturnal predator. Can we go to the bar? I need a drink, and not that crap you serve to the tourists. Besides, I don't think I could handle more than ten minutes in that rat trap you call your office."

"Geez, Harry. Who kicked your dog? Okay, but it had better not take all afternoon."

He closed the steel door and locked it, and I followed the fat little man as he waddled along the dark corridor, past his "office," and into the bar where a single light was burning over the cash register. It was like walking into Azkaban. Only the Dementors were missing, and I say that advisedly because I had an idea that Benny might himself be one. He did manage to find some decent scotch, though, and on the house, too. That was a first.

"So what is it you want, Harry? Spit it out. I ain't got all day."

"What do you know about Shady Tree?"

He pulled his chin back into his neck. It almost disappeared. He looked at me, his eyes narrowed, and said, warily, "Nothing. I ain't heard nothing about him in more'n a year. Last I heard, he was in the witness protection program. Why?"

"I dunno," I replied. "But I have a nasty feeling I'm about to find out... How about DeAnté King and Hector Santos?"

"Yeah, I see them now and again; not often. I heard DeAnté took over Shady's protection racket, but they don't bother me none. I already got protection." He grinned at me.

"Oh yeah, and who provides that?"

"You do, Harry. You do. All I have to do is mention your name and any would-be gangbangers back right off. DeAnté tried it more'n six months ago. I told him to get the hell out or I'd turn you loose on him. I didn't think he'd be impressed, but he backed right off. He's never mentioned it since, so thanks, Harry. You want another?"

His grin widened until he looked like that damn fat Cheshire cat in *Alice's Adventures in Wonderland*.

"Yeah, a small one, and you're welcome."

Unfortunately, there was not much more he could tell me. I hung around for a little while longer chatting about old times, and then I headed out to my massage, feeling a little better. I put that down to the two measures of scotch, and not to Benny's scintillating conversation... or company.

Chapter Twenty-Five

I t was just after two when I left the Sorbonne and headed across the river to the Tranquility Salon and Day Spa. Again, I watched for the white Ford Escape, but there was no sign of it.

Just to be safe, though, and to protect my new tires, I parked around the back of the building and entered through the rear door.

Sheila was a little quieter than usual when she greeted me, but I thought nothing of it. I undressed as usual and slid under the sheet and waited, listening to the music.

"Good afternoon, Mr. Starke," she said. "And how are we feeling today?"

"Better than I deserve," I said, parroting that financial guy on the radio. "How about you?"

"Me? I'm fine, just a little frazzled, is all."

"Staying busy, huh?" I asked, wishing she'd shut up and get on with it.

"Yes, that."

She seemed bright and cheery enough, but the longer I lay there with her fingers kneading my shoulders, the stronger the feeling became that something was wrong.

And then she stopped, stepped away for a second, and then stepped back again.

I thought she'd put more oil on her hands and waited for her to begin again, but she didn't. Instead, she began to sob. I sat up, gathered the sheet around me and looked at her.

"What's the matt—" And then I saw the syringe in her hand.

I jumped up off the table, the sheet falling away. I grabbed her wrist with one hand and carefully removed the syringe from her hand with the other.

"What the hell is this, Sheila?" I asked.

By then she was crying freely.

"They're going to kill my daughter. I'm sorry," she said while sobbing. "I just couldn't do it. Now they'll kill my little girl."

I stood there, naked, staring at her, the syringe in my hand.

"What's in this?" I asked. I said it quietly, but inside I was seething with mixed emotions: anger for what had happened and a deep feeling of relief at my narrow escape. *Holy... Oh my God. If it had been anyone else...*

"It's... a... tranquilizer... I... think," she said between sobs.

I grabbed the sheet and wrapped it around me. Not because I was shy, but because I felt vulnerable.

"You're going to have to talk to me, Sheila. If you don't, I'm going to have to call the police. What the hell were you thinking? What's going on? For God's sake talk to me."

She couldn't talk. She was crying too hard. It must have taken me five minutes to get her to calm down enough so that she *could* talk, and when she did... *Frickin' hell!*

"After you left the other day, you hadn't been gone long when two men came in. They asked if you were coming back again. I told them you were, and then they threatened me. They showed me a picture they'd taken of Sheree. She's my daughter. They said they knew where to find her and that if I didn't do as they said, they'd kill her. I had no choice, Harry. I had to do it, but... I couldn't." And she started to cry again.

"Now they'll do it." She sobbed. "They'll kill her. What am I going to do?"

"Calm down, Sheila. They don't know you couldn't go through with it, and they won't. Not until... Who were they? Do you know?"

"No."

"Can you describe them?" I didn't need her to do that. I already had a good idea who they were. And I was right. She described DeAnté King and Hector Santos.

"Turn your back while I get dressed, Sheila."

She did, and while I dressed I tried to think. I couldn't let anything happen to the kid. She was my first priority. So now I had to catch these two before they found out I wasn't incapacitated, or worse... and then I had another thought.

"All right, Sheila. You can turn around now. You said you thought the syringe contained tranquilizer. What made you think that?" I asked as I slipped on my shoes.

"They told me. I said I wouldn't kill you. They said that's not what they wanted. All they wanted was to knock you out, so I agreed. Now they'll kill my little girl."

"No, they won't. I won't let them... But did they say why? What was supposed to happen after you administered the drug?"

"I'm supposed to call them. They said they'd come and get you and take you somewhere safe. They said they just wanted to talk to you."

I looked at my watch. It was almost three o'clock. I didn't have much time, if any. I thought quickly and then made a decision.

"Okay, give me fifteen minutes, then make the call."

"But what if—"

"There's nothing for you to worry about. I'm not going to let anything happen to you or Sheree, okay? So just sit tight and give me time to get organized, *please*."

She nodded, tears still rolling down her cheeks. I called T.J., gave him the address of the spa, and told him to get there ASAP and park out of sight at the back of the building. Then I went to my car and retrieved my new weapon, the CZ Shadow, checked the load, made sure there was one in the chamber, thumbed the hammer back, put the safety on, then slipped it into its holster and returned to the massage room where Sheila was still sitting, sniveling quietly.

The fifteen minutes clicked slowly by until, finally, I nodded and Sheila made the call.

I heard someone on the other end say, "Yeah?"

"It's done," Sheila said, and then she listened, said "Okay," and then hung up.

"And?" I asked.

"They'll be here in twenty minutes."

That's cutting it a bit close, I thought. *I hope to hell T.J. doesn't get stuck in traffic.*

He didn't. He arrived just five minutes before they did.

Sheila showed them into the massage room, where I was laid out covered by the sheet all the way up to my neck. Then I heard her walking quickly away.

"Hello, boys," T.J. said, emerging from behind the door, his vintage .45 in his hand. "Please don't do anything stupid. Just take out your weapons—slowly, two fingers only—and drop them on the floor, then put your hands on the back of your necks. If you even think about doing anything else, I'll drop you both where you stand."

Neither one said a word. They did as they were told, and I sat up and swung my legs off the table.

"Now your phones," I said. "Put them on the table."

Again, they did as they were told.

"DeAnté and Hector, I presume," I said, smiling at them both. "You two owe me nine hundred dollars for a new set of tires."

They didn't answer. Why was I not surprised?

"Who hired you, DeAnté?" I asked. "Who sent you after me?"

Again, there was no answer from either one of them.

"T.J.," I said, taking my CZ from its holster.

He nodded, put his weapon away, stepped up behind them and

then secured each of them in turn with zip ties, their hands behind their backs, and then he patted them down.

"They're clean," he said, having lifted a small revolver from DeAnté's ankle holster.

"So," I said pleasantly as I sat on the side of the table, the CZ dangling from my finger by the trigger guard. "What's the plan? Now you've got me, what are you going to do with me?"

"Go to hell, Starke."

"Oh, now that wasn't nice, DeAnté, and me being so affable and all. What d'you think, T.J.?"

"Not nice at all, Harry. You want me to clip his ear?"

"No, I don't think that will be necessary... not yet, anyway. I'll ask you again, DeAnté. Who hired you and what's the plan?"

He didn't answer. He just stood there, staring at me, defiantly.

I almost hated to do it, but I nodded to T.J. anyway.

He stepped forward and around them to stand in front of DeAnté.

"Last chance, dumb ass," he snarled.

DeAnté stiffened but said nothing.

T.J. grinned, then slowly undid DeAnté's belt and unzipped his pants.

DeAnté stiffened even further and closed his eyes. He seemed to grow at least two inches taller.

T.J. pushed his pants and his underwear down to his ankles, then stepped back and said, admiringly, "My, you *were* a big boy," he said, emphasizing the word "were." Then he took a pocket knife from his pocket and flipped it open with a loud click.

At that, DeAnté's eyes snapped open and he yelped, "Okay, okay. I'll tell yuh. It wuz Shady Tree. We's supposed to take yuh to a house on Dodson Avenue an' hand you over. That's it. That's all I know."

"Hah! You ain't so tough as you think you are," T.J. said as he closed the knife and put it away.

"Screw you, pimp," DeAnté muttered.

"Excuse me?" T.J. said and grabbed the man's naked package in his huge right hand and squeezed it. "What did you say?"

The man howled.

"Okay, T.J., that's enough," I said, smiling. "I need him in one piece."

T.J. released DeAnté's family jewels and stepped away.

"Now, DeAnté," I said, "here's how we're going to play this. And you're going to cooperate, both of you." I looked at Santos. He blinked rapidly but said nothing. "If you don't," I continued, "I'll turn T.J. loose again and I can assure you, you don't want me to do that. He learned things in Vietnam you wouldn't believe. Now, what's it to be?"

DeAnté looked at Hector. They both nodded.

"Hell," DeAnté said. "I don't owe that man nothin'. What's yo' wanna do?"

"First, you're going to tell me how this was supposed to go down."

"The bitch was supposed to put you out, then we wuz supposed to come git you and take you to Shady, is all, but first I wuz supposed to call him and tell him we wuz on the way."

I nodded. "That sounds reasonable. Which one is yours?" I asked, looking at the two phones on the table.

"The one with the gold case."

I picked it up, looked at it, set it down again, then said to T.J., "Keep an eye on them. I'll be right back."

Chapter Twenty-Six

I left Shady's two soldiers in T.J.'s loving care for a few minutes, then went to the foyer and thanked Sheila and told her not to worry, that I was going to end it, now, today. Then I went out to my car, opened the trunk, took out my Kevlar vest and put it on. That done, I called Kate.

"Hey," I said when she picked up. "I'm at the spa and have DeAnté and Hector—"

"You what? What the hell, Harry?"

"Calm down, Kate. Everything's going to work out fine. They're working for Shady. Didn't I tell you? But you wouldn't believe me. Now..."

And then I spent the next couple of minutes explaining what had happened, then I asked her to send protection for Sheila's daughter and, finally, I told her what I was about to do. Kate, ever the cop, didn't like it; not one bit, but after arguing the potential consequences, she finally gave in and agreed to join us at the house on Dodson Avenue.

I went back inside to find T.J. still sitting on the massage table and Hector and DeAnté still standing there; DeAnté with his pants still around his ankles.

I clipped the zip tie with my pocketknife to release his hands and told him to get dressed, then I had T.J. secure his hands again.

I returned to the table, picked up DeAnté's phone and tapped the button. *Damn. It needs a thumbprint.*

I went to DeAnté, stepped around behind him, grabbed his thumb, twisted it and pressed the ball against the screen. He howled like a stuck pig, whatever that sounds like. Then I flipped to his contact list and found one labeled Shady.

"Here we go," I said, showing it to him. "Now, listen to me and listen very carefully. You screw this up and I'll have T.J. turn your balls into mincemeat."

I explained what I needed, then dialed the number and held the phone up to his ear.

"We got 'im," DeAnté said. "Yeah... Yeah, no, they was no problem... Fifteen, twenty minutes. No more'n that... Yeah. Okay."

I heard a click as Shady hung up.

I closed out the phone and slipped it into my pants pocket. Then I called Kate.

"We're on. Twenty minutes." I hung up without waiting for an answer. I was in a hurry and didn't have time to talk.

T.J. stuffed his hands into DeAnté's pants pocket, found his keys, went out front and drove the Escape round back. Then we hauled our two heroes out and sat them in the front seats, DeAnté behind the wheel.

That done, I told T.J. to suit up—put on his vest—and then I climbed into the driver's-side rear seat, took the CZ from its holster, cut DeAnté's hands loose, then stuck the gun in his ear and told him to drive.

Five minutes later we were headed across the river on Veteran's Bridge to Riverside Drive, and from there to Wilcox Boulevard and the house on Dodson Avenue, with T.J. following about a half a block behind.

DeAnté parked the white Escape in front of the house.

What would happen next was crucial to my plan. I was sure that there would be a lookout in the front window, so the next couple of minutes had to be choreographed to perfection.

I was supposed to be drugged, right? So, I leaned forward and freed Hector's hands, then I told him to get out and come around and open my door while I kept the CZ to DeAnté's ear.

"Do it!" DeAnté said to Hector. And he did.

My side of the car was the side furthest from the front of the house, so what happened next was shielded by the SUV.

I ducked down and out, stayed low, and told DeAnté to exit the car and step back to join Hector. Now this was the weak point in my plan. If DeAnté decided to make a run for it, or if Hector decided to make a move, I was screwed.

I saw DeAnté hesitate.

"Don't even think about it, DeAnté. You'll never make it."

He didn't try. Instead, he came around and between them. They took my arms and made a great show of dragging my drugged body to the front steps, my CZ jammed hard into the soft tissue of DeAnté's right side.

When we reached the steps, I regained my feet and pushed DeAnté and Hector up the steps in front of me.

DeAnté knocked on the door and yelled, "Hey, it's me. We're here. Open up."

No answer.

DeAnté knocked again. Same result.

"Try the door," I said.

He did. It opened and we stepped inside.

Chapter Twenty-Seven

The house was... strangely silent. I didn't like it.

"Stand still, boys," I said. "Don't make a move."

I stood still, listening.

"What's happening?" T.J. said as he stepped through the open front door and found us all standing there like three frickin' fence posts.

"I don't know," I replied. "I don't think there's anyone here."

I paused, listened for a moment, then said, "What the hell is this, DeAnté? You wouldn't be screwing with us, now would you?"

"Uh-uh. No, sir. He wuz here when we left to come git you. I swear he wuz."

I nodded. "Keep an eye on them, T.J., while I take a look around. Sounds like Kate's here." I could hear sirens in the distance, but I went to look around anyway.

I made it no further than the next room, the living room. There was no one in there. The room was bare except for a table and a chair... and a laptop computer on the table facing me. The chair, which had its back to me, was facing the screen. There was a roll of duct tape and some rope on the table next to the computer, and some tools. Pliers. A hammer. A car battery and jumper cables. Knives. *Someone was planning a party, and I think I was to be the guest of honor.*

The laptop was on, its screen bright and suddenly... there he was.

"Hiya, Harry. Long time no see. Have you missed me?"

"Well, well," I said. "Now why am I not surprised that you didn't have the balls to meet me face to face?"

"Oh, but I do," he said. "I fully intended to. I was all prepared for you. Welcome to the wonders of Zoom, by the way. You want to know why I'm not there, Harry? I'll tell you why, you dumb son of a bitch. DeAnté didn't give me the safe word when he called, and I knew you had him. I wasn't surprised though. You always were tenacious, and DeAnté? Well, let's just say he's one French fry short of being a happy meal, and Hector's no better." He sighed, then said, "It's so difficult to get good help these days, don't you think, Harry?"

Shady had changed a lot over the years. Gone was the street jock with the do-rag, the Ebonics, the street slang. The accent was almost refined, but not quite.

"I intended to take you apart piece by piece all by myself," he continued. "Well, with a little help from my friends, of course. Where are they, by the way?"

"I have them nicely tucked away," Kate said from behind me.

"Ah, there she is. The lovely Kate Gazzara. Now why didn't I think of inviting you to my party as well as John Wick here? That would have been kinda fun, don't you think? I always did have a thing for you, Kate."

"Cut the crap, Shady," I said. "It's over. What is it you want?"

"Want? What do I want? I'll tell you what I want, you self-centered, smug son of a bitch. I want you dead, but first I want you to suffer, like you made me suffer all these years. I've hated you from the moment you put a bullet through my arm back in oh-seven, and then last year when you took my frickin' finger, I hated you even more and I swore I'd make you pay for it. What kinda man are you, Harry, to treat another human being like that? I was going to take all of your fingers, but now it looks like I'll have to wait a little longer."

There was something about the tone of his voice. He should have been totally pissed off, but he wasn't. He was gloating.

"You managed to screw up everything I've ever done," he continued, "and now you've won again." And at that he grinned like a happy kid. "But have you, Harry? Remember what I told you last time we met?"

"Yes, I remember, Shady. You were going to get me and make me pay. Same old Shady, all mouth and no balls. You're here in the city somewhere, my friend, and we'll get you... I'll get you. And when I do, you'll wish you'd gone into that witness protection program, because this time I'm going to put you into a box."

"Whoo, listen to you. You do realize I'm recording this, and what is it you guys always say? Oh yes, I know, 'it can be used in a court of law.' But I don't think it will get that far. You think you won, Harry? You didn't. The game's not over yet, not even close. I think we're done here. Goodbye, Kate, until the next time. Take care, Harry. The game, as they say, is afoot. Hmm. Who did say that? Sherlock Holmes, I think. Oh, and say hello to Jacque for me, will you?"

The screen went black. He was gone. I stared at the blank screen. I stuffed the CZ back in its holster and stuffed my shaking hands deep into my pockets so no one could see them.

The son of a bitch has done it again. He's always one step ahead. What the hell did he mean by that? The game's afoot.

I felt a hand on my shoulder. It was Kate.

"I'm sorry, Harry," she said. "I'll have forensics go through the place, but I doubt we'll find anything. He's smart. He's playing mind games with you and he's winning. Don't let him win, Harry."

"I'm taking the computer, Kate," I said and stepped over to the table.

"You can't, Harry. It's evidence."

"Evidence of what? Nothing. This isn't a crime scene. The only crime committed here was one of stupidity, my stupidity. I'm taking the computer. Live with it."

"Nope, not going to do it. I'll have you arrested if you try to remove it. If you want to have Tim come here and check it out, fine. I can live with that, but it stays here with me."

"Fine. I'll do that then."

And I did.

Chapter Twenty-Eight

I called Tim and told him what I wanted.

"The only thing I care about finding on it," I told him, "is what Shady's up to. What I need to know is where he is, and I need to find him, like now!"

That done, I called Amanda to make sure everything there was okay. I also talked to Maria and told her to be on high alert, but not to tell my wife.

The game's afoot! What frickin' game?

I had no clue.

I had T.J. take me back to the spa to get my car, then I returned to the house on Dodson Avenue. I wasn't about to leave until Tim had hacked what I needed, or not. I found him sitting at the computer, surrounded by forensic techs processing the house.

The hours passed slowly as I watched Tim work his way through the computer. Forensics continued to pick the place clean, looking for fingerprints and fibers, but they found little to even place Shady in the house. He'd obviously chosen it for one purpose and one purpose only, to take me apart. I looked at the tools on the table and shuddered at the thought of what might have happened to me if Sheila

Pervis had done as she was told. *Shit! I'd probably be dead by now, or worse.*

It was a little after ten o'clock that evening when I decided to call it a night. Yes, Shady *had* learned a lot over the years since I'd first met him. He'd deleted almost all his files before he installed Zoom on the computer. To anyone else but Tim, it would have taken days to recover them. He, Tim, however, had written some proprietary software to do the job. Even so, it took him several hours to track it all down and then, nothing, other than several dozen porn sites and hundreds of emails that didn't even belong to Shady. Tim was of the opinion that Shady had bought a used machine, wiped it and then used it for nothing other than his conversation with me. Wiping it was just a ploy to waste our time, a diversion. And that's exactly what it turned out to be: a diversion.

As to the forensics, there was nothing there either. There were piles of old clothes in the bedrooms. Dirty plates in the kitchen. The garbage cans were all full. Mike Willis, the forensics supervisor, figured the place was actually a squat for the homeless of our fair city, and that it would take weeks to process it all.

Me? I was tired, disappointed and... yes, I was pissed off. So, I took out my phone to call Amanda to let her know I was on my way home, but then I noticed there was a text message from Jacque timed at six-forty-eight that evening. How I'd missed it, I didn't know. Actually, I did. I'd been consumed with trying to find Shady when the message came in.

Anyway, she'd messaged me to tell me that a large box had just been delivered and that she was about to leave and go home.

A large box? I didn't order anything...

It was at that very moment when I recalled the smile on Shady's face. *The game's afoot... Oh, no. Oh hell no!*

I ran out of the front door, jumped into my car and drove like a maniac back to my office. I turned off East 4th onto Georgia and was literally blocks away when I saw the lights of the fire trucks and police cruisers.

Blair Howard

I slammed on the brakes, jumped out of the car and ran the three blocks to what once had been my offices. The building was in ruins. It had totally collapsed. All that was left was a pile of flaming bricks and ruins. There was debris all over the street: huge chunks of masonry, glass. Most of the windows in the buildings opposite had been blown out. The electricity was out: the streetlights were dark, so were the stoplights. The flashing red and blue lights from almost two dozen emergency vehicles had turned the street into a kaleidoscopic nightmare.

I stood there for a moment, my mind in turmoil. I couldn't think straight. Hell, I couldn't think at all. I leaned forward, put my hands on my knees, breathing hard, and I stared at the ruins, and then... *Oh my God. Jacque!*

I called her. It went to voice mail.

I shoved the phone back in my pocket, ran to the fire captain, identified myself and asked him if anyone had been in the building. The answer was, of course, he didn't know.

Horrified, I called Wendy.

She'd seen the early reports on the news channels, and she hadn't heard from Jacque. Wendy had called and called, but her calls all went to voice mail. She was beside herself with worry.

There was nothing I could say to her, so I told her I'd call her as soon as I knew something, anything, and I hung up.

Chapter Twenty-Nine

I didn't sleep that night. Nobody did. T.J., Tim, Kate, Heather, the rest of my small staff, and Wendy... all joined me at the scene and we stayed there through the night. Only Jacque was missing.

It wasn't that we had any intentions of trying to salvage anything from the ruins. There was nothing left to salvage. They just wanted to be there, for me, yes, but mostly for Jacque.

By dawn the following morning, Saturday, in the cold light of day, the devastation became a sharp reality. The building was gone, and so was half of the one next to it.

The press were already calling it an act of domestic terrorism, and they were right, of course. Only this time, what they didn't know, was that it wasn't directed at the government. It was directed at one person... me!

I'd stayed in contact with Amanda throughout the night, and as it grew lighter, I decided to send T.J. to my home to augment my security there.

It was at around five-thirty that morning when I received a tap on the shoulder.

"Harry?"

I turned around. It was Roland Patrelli. I looked at him and shook my head.

He nodded respectfully and backed away.

"Some other time, Roland," I said as I turned back to the devastation. "I promise."

By seven o'clock that morning, the last flames had been extinguished and only a vast pile of smoking embers remained of what once had been the pride of my professional life, my suite of offices.

Jacque, I was sure, was under there somewhere. It was now a matter of recovering her body. The first responders had most of the street taped off and had already started searching the debris. The fire captain told me it might be days before they recovered her.

Wendy? Wendy was unhinged, crying uncontrollably. I put my arm around her and squeezed her to me. I was in no better condition myself. Wendy had lost her soul mate and I'd lost my right arm.

Finally, realizing there was nothing to be done, I gathered my people together and told them to go to my home on the mountain. Then I put my arm around Wendy's waist and steered her gently to my car. And then I followed them up the mountain.

It was Saturday and Kate was supposed to have the weekend off. Given the circumstances, however, she'd been called in just after six that morning. She told me she'd catch up with me as soon as she could.

Fortunately, as I learned later, there had been no one in any of the adjoining buildings, or those across the street, so the only casualty of the blast was Jacque.

Wendy and I rode up the mountain in silence, except for her sobbing. There was nothing I could say to comfort her, so I didn't try. I did tell her, though, that she could stay with us until... for as long as she liked.

It was just after eight when we arrived at my home on East Brow Road that morning to find the street lined with cars. All nine members of my staff were there, as well as a half dozen media vehicles of one sort or another.

I weaved my way through the melee, hit the button to open my electronic gate, drove inside and closed it again.

I took Wendy inside and... If I said I handed her off to Amanda, that would be wrong. Amanda took her from me, sat her down, gave her a large mug of coffee laced with brandy, then sat down beside her, took her hand and did what she could to comfort her.

Me? I gathered my staff, including Maria, together in the living room. We had no offices, no equipment and, worst of all, no tech, except for Tim's MacBook and iPad, that is. He never goes anywhere without them.

The mood in my living room that morning was somber. Jacque was on everyone's mind, and would be until...

"I know how we're all feeling," I said to the group, who were scattered around the room, most of them drinking coffee. "But we have to move forward, and we have to find... whoever did this. We have no offices so, as inconvenient for y'all as it is, we'll have to work from here. We have a large basement. We can turn that into a temporary office. T.J., you can organize that when we're done here. Tim..." I noticed he was seated at the coffee table, his laptop open, and he was tapping away like a fiend.

"Tim," I said. "I need you to pay attention for a minute."

"No, you don't," he said, without looking up from the screen.

"*What?*" I was stunned. It was so unlike him.

"Just give me a minute, will you, Harry? This is important."

I stared at him. So did everyone else.

He continued to tap the keys and then suddenly he looked up, jumped to his feet, did a fist pump and yelled at the top of his voice, "*YES! She's okay.* Well, I don't know if she's okay, but she's alive. *Jacque is alive.*"

"What did you say?" I couldn't believe it. The rest of the group was silent. Most of them had their mouths open.

"I said, she's alive." And he did a little jig, waving his arms in the air.

And then everybody began talking at once, some of them even cheering.

I quieted everyone down, then told him to explain.

"Well, as you know, we lost all of my equipment," he began, "including all of the security cameras inside the building and out, but..." He paused for effect, smiling. "We didn't lose the data, not any of it. You see, I back everything up to the Cloud... well I don't. It's automatic, every fifteen minutes. The security system backs itself up the same way. I have the security footage, here." He looked down at the laptop. "Jacque was kidnapped a few minutes before seven o'clock: two hours before the explosion."

I can't tell you how I felt. Mixed emotions don't get it. I was relieved, elated, angry and stunned, all at the same time.

"You want to see?" he asked, grinning like a fool.

"Hell, yes, I want to see it." And I went and sat down beside him on the couch. T.J. did the same. The rest of the group gathered around behind us.

"So," Tim said, as he tapped once, and the image began to play. "This is at six-thirty. Watch."

The screen showed the interior of the outer office. Jacque was at her desk doing... whatever it was. I watched the time stamp at the bottom of the screen.

At six-thirty-five she looked up. There was no audio, so I had to assume someone had knocked at the front door.

She rose from her desk, went to the door and looked out through the glass pane, then she opened it. She said something, nodded, then stepped aside and a man wearing a blue uniform pushed a two-wheeler inside with a large wooden crate on it.

Jacque had the guy wheel the crate through to... either the break room or my office. That much we couldn't see. When they returned to the outer office, she signed the guy's clipboard, went to her desk, took out two five-dollar bills from a drawer, and handed them to the

Backlash

man, who nodded, smiled at her and left. Then she went back to her desk again and picked up her cell phone and... the time stamp at the bottom of the screen read six-forty-four.

"There," I said. "She's texting me."

Tim nodded and said, "Now wait." And he fast-forwarded to six-fifty-five.

Jacques was back at her desk. She looked up again, rose to her feet, walked to the door and opened it. *Bad move, Jacque,* I thought.

No sooner had she unlocked the door and begun to open it than the door was flung inward, knocking her off her feet, and the delivery guy, along with another thug, burst in and grabbed her. Delivery guy stuck a needle in her neck and she went limp almost immediately. I couldn't help but wonder if it was the same stuff they'd meant for me. I continued to watch as they carried her out the door.

"Okay," Tim said. "Now watch this."

He tapped another button and the view changed to one of the outside cameras. A dark blue van pulled up outside the front door. The two thugs carried Jacque out. The side door opened. They threw her inside. One of the two thugs jumped in after her. The other ran back, closed the office door, then jumped into the van through the front passenger side door, and the van drove away going north toward either Veteran's Bridge or Riverside Drive.

I sat back on the couch and stared at the screen. Tim was right, Jacque was alive, *but for how long,* I wondered.

"That's going to depend on you, Harry!" I swear to God, I heard Shady say those words somewhere in the back of my mind.

Tim tapped again. The screen showed the interior of my now empty outer office. He fast-forwarded until the time stamp showed eight-fifty-eight. At eight-fifty-nine, the screen went dark.

"That's when the bomb exploded," Tim said, stating the obvious.

"I'd say that the box must have been loaded with some high-yield explosive," Tim added.

T.J. nodded and said, "Semtex, most likely. They must have put

493

Blair Howard

the crate in the break room. It's small and would have concentrated the blast, which is why it demolished the entire building."

I nodded. I was too angry to speak. I went to the bar and poured myself a large measure of brandy. Yes, I know. It wasn't even ten o'clock in the morning yet, but I needed something to steady my nerves... and my shaking hands.

I stood for a moment looking out the window, seeing nothing but the needle going into Jacque's neck, and I was super pissed, scared for Jacque, and feeling guilty, all at the same time.

"I'll be back in a minute," I said and went to the kitchen.

"Wendy," I said. "She's alive. I don't know where she is, but she's alive, and I'll get her back for you, I promise."

Wendy burst into tears. I couldn't stand it. I left her to Amanda and went back into the living room.

"If I'd only seen the message sooner—" I muttered more to myself than to the others.

"You would have been too late no matter what, Harry," T.J. said, interrupting me. "This isn't on you. It's on Shady. Focus on that."

"That's exactly what I plan to do."

Chapter Thirty

I gave instructions to my staff to begin converting the basement of my house into a temporary office. I already knew that replacing everything that had been lost was going to cost a fortune, but I didn't care; I could afford it and, besides, I was insured.

I instructed Tim to make a list of everything he needed and get it ordered and have it FedExed to the house or, even better, go fetch it.

Then I went back to the kitchen, sat down at the table opposite Wendy and Amanda, put my elbows on the table and my head in my hands and thought... about nothing. Then I sat upright again. I looked at Wendy. Her face was streaked with tears. Amanda looked at me, her eyes pleading. I didn't know what to say. I was hurting for both of them, Wendy and Jacque.

"I'm sorry, Wendy. I don't know anything except that I do know she's alive and that I'm going to get her back for you."

She nodded. I rose to my feet.

"I'll be in my office, if you need me," I said to Amanda. "Where's Jade, by the way?"

"Rose has her. I called her right after you called me, and she came and got her. She's fine."

I nodded, left the room, and went to my office, a small room at the far end of the house with two views: Chattanooga and the river on the one side and East Brow Road looking north on the other.

The road was packed solid with media vans, cars and trucks. There must have been a dozen of them and at least double that reporters and cameramen.

I sat down at my small desk to think. That was one of the hardest things I'd ever done. My brain was mush and my frickin' hands were trembling again.

Tough as it was, the more I thought about it, the more I realized there was only one thing I could do. So I upped and walked outside, out through the front door, and out through the gate into the melee and was immediately surrounded by the yammering press.

I raised my arms over my head and called for silence. Then I looked around the mob until I spotted... you've got it, Roland Patrelli.

I pushed my way through the crowd, grabbed him by the arm, and hauled him in through the gate into the front yard, then closed the gate shutting the rest of the mob out.

"You want an exclusive?" I said to him. "You've got it, but first I need a favor."

"Whatever I can do, Mr. Starke."

"What d'you know about social media? Twitter in particular."

Tim had mentioned when he talked about Patrelli's background that he, Patrelli, had a large following.

"I know my way around," Patrelli replied guardedly. "What do you—"

"I need you to tweet something for me, then ask your following to retweet it and keep on retweeting it. Can you do that?"

He could, so I told him what I wanted and then I let him take a couple of photographs of me.

That done, we both went outside the gate again and he disappeared into the crowd as the mob closed in around me.

Again, I raised both hands above my head and called for silence. The mob quieted down.

"I'd like to make a statement," I said. "A very short statement."

Every camera lens was directed at me. Every microphone was pushed toward my face.

I looked directly into the camera in front of me and said, "You win, Shady. Let her go. Let her go and you can have me."

And with that, I turned and went back into the house.

I don't know if it was Patrelli's tweet that did it, or the one-liner I gave the media, but it couldn't have been more than five minutes later when my phone rang.

I didn't recognize the number, but I knew who it was.

I smiled, shook my head in disbelief, and took the call.

"I'm touched, Harry. I really am. Let's make a trade."

Chapter Thirty-One

"Where is she, Shady?" I asked. My phone was on speaker with Tim and T.J. listening.

"Patience, Harry. Patience. Let me tell you how it's going to go down. You're going to do exactly as I tell you. If you don't, I'm going to blow this pretty little girl's head right off her shoulders."

"You touch—"

"One hair of her head?" he finished for me. It wasn't exactly what I was going to say, but whatever. "Oh dear, Harry," he continued. "That's so cliché. Now listen to me. I have myself a nice little place just off Hickory Valley Road. I'm going to give you directions and you're going to come to me, and you're going to come alone and unarmed. D'you understand?"

"And you said I was cliché... Yes, I understand."

"Good, because if you decide to screw with me, it's goodbye pretty face... On the other hand, though, it really doesn't matter, does it? I win either way. You do as I say, and I get my revenge. You don't, and I still get my revenge and you have to live with what happens to your girlfriend. That's kinda cool, don't you think?"

Girlfriend? "I get it. Now tell me."

And he told me. He gave me the GPS coordinates, and as he did so, Tim brought the location up on his laptop. It turned out to be a small complex of four buildings on a section of the old Volunteer Ammunition Plant, and that was something I was very familiar with.

The Volunteer Army Munitions Plant was and still is—though there's not much of it left to see these days—located on the north side of the city. Most of what's left is ringed by Hickory Valley Road and South Hickory Valley Road. For years it manufactured munitions for the WWII war effort.

The complex closed for good a very long time ago and fell into disrepair—a word that doesn't adequately describe the overgrown wilderness it's become today, a wilderness that covers more than six thousand acres; a dozen square miles.

Volkswagen has since built a plant on the east side of what once was a vast industrial complex, and so has Amazon and several other large companies, but what remains is... a veritable jungle dotted with ruined structures: old warehouses, workshops, garages and large and small structures that long ago housed... God only knows what; all of them now in ruins.

"Five o'clock this afternoon, Harry. Not a moment later, not a moment sooner. I'll be waiting." And he hung up.

I sat back in my chair and looked at Tim's laptop screen. I looked at my watch. It was a little after twelve noon.

"We have five hours," I said to T.J., "and we don't have any weapons other than those we have on us, and an AR I have here at the house."

"I take it you're not going to do as he says," T.J. said.

"Yes, I am. If I don't, he'll kill Jacque. I have to go in there alone and unarmed."

"So what's the plan, then?" Tim asked.

"Well look at the place," I said, pointing at the screen. "Not the best choice he could have made, wouldn't you say? The place is approachable from here, here, here and here."

"He's smarter than that, Harry," T.J. said. "He'll have people watching those entry points."

"He will..." I paused and thought for a minute, then said, "T.J., that friend of yours, the sniper. The old guy we took to Georgia when we took down Nick Christmas. Is he still around?"

"Old guy? Seriously? I wouldn't let him hear you say that, but yes. They both are."

"Can you get ahold of them and ask them to join us? I'll pay them well."

"Just give me a minute while I make the call. I'll be right back."

"Tell them to bring weapons."

He nodded and left the room, to return a few minutes later.

"They're on the way. They'll be here by three."

I sucked in my breath and said, "That gives us just two hours. It's going to be cutting it a bit close, but we don't have a choice. We'll just have to make it work. Let's get to it."

Chapter Thirty-Two

Monty and Chuck arrived early in a beat-up old Ford F-150 pickup truck at a little after two-forty-five.

Now you have to meet these two to believe what I'm about to tell you.

They are both Vietnam vets and close friends of T.J.'s.

It had been more than a year since I'd last seen them, and neither of them had changed a bit. They were still, in my opinion, grizzly old men who should have stayed home, rocking on the front porch whittling sticks and drinking shine.

I'd first met them when the thing with Nick Christmas had gotten way out of hand. We were up in the mountains of Northwest Georgia, outnumbered and outgunned, and we needed help in the worst way. These two were what T.J. came up with. They were old friends of his, living in a homeless shelter—which is a sad reflection on how we treat our veteran heroes—but they turned up and... I don't think I'm exaggerating when I tell you they saved the day. With T.J. they make an extraordinary trio.

"Hi, fellas," I said as they climbed out of the truck and T.J. closed the gate behind them.

"Harry, m'boy," Chuck growled as he wrapped his arms around me in a bear hug. "How you bin, fella? It's good to see you, man. Where's that good-lookin' cop? Katie, her name was. She around?"

I could barely breathe, but I managed to gasp, "It's good to see you too, Chuck. No, she's not here... Not yet anyway." I somehow managed to release myself from his gorilla-like grasp and turned to his friend.

"Monty. It's good to see you too," I said, grasping his hand and pulling him to me to hug him, too.

"Hey, Harry," he said. "T.J. told us what happened. I was sorry to hear it, man."

I nodded and said, "How have you both been keeping? Come on inside. We need to talk."

Gunnery Sergeant Montgomery "Monty" Fowler was seventy-two at the time. He'd completed three tours in Vietnam; won a Silver Star, a Bronze Star, and two Purple Hearts. The man was a true American hero, as was his buddy, Staff Sergeant Charles Wilson Massey - Chuck to his friends - of which I was proud to count myself one.

Chuck, the hugger, was a huge black man and one of the most likable guys I've ever met. He was seventy-one back then, and he too had completed three tours. He was a sniper credited with sixty-two kills, confirmed, but T.J. will tell you it was more like ninety. Chuck had taken a round to the shin and thus has a prosthetic leg. He also has a Bronze Star and two Purple Hearts.

Without them, the outcome of that mess in north Georgia would certainly have been different. I doubt any of us would have lived through it.

We spent a few moments greeting one another and chatting about old times. Amanda made carafe after carafe of coffee and a mound of ham and cheese sandwiches. Then I gathered my troops together.

"We don't have a lot of time," I said, "so let's get down to business. T.J., Monty, Chuck, gather round."

By then, my living room was getting crowded, and Tim's laptop was less than adequate for the job he was asking it to do. The tech was fine, but memory was limited, and the screen was too small for all of us to see at once, so I asked Heather to take the non-essentials—actually, the non-combatants—to the basement and supervise its conversion to an office. I was about to lose my gym, and a whole lot more, but there were no other alternatives. I had to keep my people at work.

Unfortunately, Tim couldn't access the satellites either, so we had to settle for Google Earth. It showed the terrain, the roads—what was left of them—and the buildings, but not in real time, so there was no way we could determine Shady's numbers.

"This is Shady's lair," Tim said, zooming in on a small complex of four derelict buildings. "As you can see, it's surrounded by... trees, a jungle. Visibility from the ground is restricted, almost nonexistent from... I dunno, twenty, twenty-five yards out, and Shady's smart so he'll be expecting the unexpected, right?"

He looked up at me. I nodded but didn't take my eyes off the screen. Tim was right. The terrain around the complex was tight. The complex itself consisted of one large, two-story rectangular building with an exterior iron staircase—fire escapes—at each end and, from what we could see, at least five exterior doors. The other three buildings were smaller and in various stages of disrepair.

"The main access is here, on Hickory Valley Road," Tim continued, pointing to the 3D image, "but there are three more potential access roads, also on Hickory Valley Road, here, here and here. There's also a fourth access road to the east, here. That road can be accessed by at least a dozen separate routes from South Hickory Valley Road. As T.J. said, all of these access points will certainly be watched. There is, however, a fifth way to access Shady's complex that he may or may not be aware of, here."

He zoomed in slightly, enlarged the image, and pointed to what appeared to be an overgrown, tree-lined hiking trail. I knew that it wasn't. The entire area was off-limits to the general public. But that didn't stop the kids and homeless from trespassing whenever they felt like it. No, what we were looking at had once been a paved road, but the years had not been kind to it. In places, it looked almost impassable.

"As you can see," Tim continued, "it's not paved—it was once, but that was a long time ago. You can still see bits of paving if you look closely. Time and tide... Oh. Sorry. So, my suggestion is, we use this fifth option as our point of access. Harry, I assume you'll go in from Hickory Valley Road as instructed. I'll take T.J., Monty, and Chuck and we'll make access off of South Hickory Road here." He zoomed out slightly. "I'll drop Chuck first at the base of this water tower— more about that in a minute—and then drop you guys here. You won't have too far to walk," he said, grinning up at the two vets.

"You cheeky young monkey," Chuck growled. "I've a good mind to whack you upside the head."

"Yeah, right!" Tim replied. "You'd have to catch me first. So, as I said, I'll drop you guys off, then park somewhere in this area here and keep an eye on things, and listen in, too."

"Wait a minute," I said. "What d'you mean, keep an eye on things? I thought you'd lost everything in the explosion."

"I did," he replied. "But I still have a few... small things in my car." He grinned sideways at me.

His car was a pristine, wood-paneled 1990 Jeep Wagoneer. I stared at him and shook my head. *The boy never ceases to amaze me.*

"So what's your plan then, Tim?" I asked. "I go in alone, distract him, and then the three musketeers come charging in guns blazing?"

"Well, something like that, but—"

"Yeah, gotcha," I said.

"You could let me finish, Harry." The boy looked at me like a wounded puppy.

"Well, I can't think of anything better," I said, "so go ahead."

"As I said," Tim continued. "We four will go in my vehicle and I'll drop you guys off." He turned to look at Chuck. "I estimate this old water tower to be about a hundred and fifty yards from Shady's hidey-hole, which I assume will be the large building. The others don't look habitable to me. Anyway," he said and paused, did the thing with his glasses, and then continued, "from there it's a direct line of sight. See?"

He enlarged the image.

"So, Chuck, you'll be on the water tower. There are windows all along the north side of the large building, here, as you can see. The other side... I can't see it so don't know. Anyway, you'll be able to cover the windows, the roof and stairs at the east end of the buildings. With a bit of luck, you should be able to see inside through your scope... You did bring your rifle with you, right?"

"Are you kidding me?" Chuck replied. "Of course I did... I like it, Harry. One hundred fifty yards? Hell, I can reach out and spit at 'em at that range."

"Right," Tim said.

I grinned. I knew Tim too well. The boy was concentrating on his plan, so he hadn't heard a word Chuck said.

"So, you two," Tim looked at T.J. and Monty. "You disembark here and take the trail to this point here, then you wait for my signal, as do you, Chuck."

"Wait. What?" I said. "What signal?"

"I have comms in the car." Again he made with the grin.

"Geez," T.J. said. "Are you serious?"

"I am. C'mon, let's go get my stuff."

"Wait," T.J. said. "How about I hide in the trunk of Harry's car?"

I shook my head and said, "Too risky. If they decide to search the car, we'd be done. You're dead, and so am I and Jacque. No, I have to go in alone. We stick to Tim's plan. Now, let's go get that gear."

We followed him out to his car—it was more of a land yacht than a car—and he opened the rear hatch, rummaged around inside a big blue plastic storage bin and retrieved six small boxes, each about the size of a fifty-count cigar box.

"One each for the five of us," he said, handing them out, "and the comms center for me. I'll explain how they work in a minute."

"Come on, Tim," I said. "We don't have much time."

"Okay, but I have one more thing, Harry. I bought this for myself, with my own money."

"Wow, that's a first," I said.

He turned his head and grinned at me, then reached further into the vehicle and retrieved a much larger box.

"Say hello to my leetle friend," he said triumphantly. "This is a drone. Not an ordinary drone. It features something called active tracking. I can have it read your body shape, Harry, and it will find you and keep you in sight. With the new battery I've installed, I have about thirty-five minutes of flight time, which should be plenty. I can fly it right outside Shady's windows, and it will transmit 4K images to me and to Chuck's phone. I need a little time to set it all up, say forty-five minutes, but it will work."

"You have thirty," I said. "Let's do it, guys. C'mon, Tim, move it, move it."

"I need to fit you up with the comms first," he said.

"Geez," I said, looking at my watch. "How long?"

"Just a couple of minutes, okay?"

I nodded.

The comms device was also something I'd not seen before. It was small, so small Tim could insert it right inside my right ear, completely out of sight. The microphone was almost as small as the earpiece, and he installed that inside the lining of the front of my ball cap. I could now hear him, and he could hear me and anyone else close enough to me.

"What's the range of these things, Tim?" I asked.

"Not far. About a half-mile, which is why I chose the spot I did for me. It's less than four hundred yards from Shady's hideout. It's a little more than that from the water tower, but it should work fine."

Shady had said for me to come unarmed, so we had to assume he'd have me patted down. I would be without a weapon, but I wouldn't be out of communication, and that made me feel a whole lot better about what I was about to do; put myself, and Jacque, at Shady's mercy.

"Okay," Tim said. "A quick test and you're done."

The test was nothing more than a couple of words each way. I could hear him perfectly and he could hear me, so he began to fit the others.

It was right about then that Kate arrived and, of course, she wanted to take over, but that was out of the question. She wanted to send in the cavalry right away, rescue Jacque and take down Shady. I couldn't risk it. At the first sign of trouble, Shady wouldn't hesitate to kill Jacque. No, I had to go in alone and put my trust in Tim and T.J.'s has-beens. On thinking about it, though, I couldn't have been in better hands.

"Harry," she said finally. "You know I can't condone what you're planning to do, right?"

"You can't stop me either, Kate. I'm going to do what has to be done to protect Jacque. No argument."

She took a deep breath, shook her head and said, "It's on your head, Harry. You do this and it goes sideways... If Jacque dies, I won't be able to protect you from the consequences."

"I know, but if Jacque dies, so will I, and I don't intend for that to happen. I have a wife and child to think of, remember?"

She nodded. Her face was pale, and I could see she was deeply troubled.

"How about you stand by and wait for Tim to call and *then* bring in the cavalry?" I asked.

"I don't know, Harry. I just don't know."

"That's the best I can do, Kate. If I don't turn up as instructed, she's dead. This way, at least we have a chance."

She nodded. There was no point in talking about it further, so I turned to Tim and said, "How about you? You ready?"

"There's one last thing I need to do before we go, Harry. I need to get you entered into the drone's system. It'll take but a minute."

"How are you going to do that?" I asked.

"I'm not. She is."

"She? Who's she?"

"The drone of course."

"Well be quick about it. We need to get out of here."

"Let's go out onto the patio," Tim said.

Two minutes later I was standing still, my arms at my sides with the little red drone hovering six feet away from me at eye level. It seemed to stare right into my eyes—well, that's what I felt it was like —then it slowly circled me once and then landed on one of the patio tables.

Tim scooped it up and said, "Got it. I'm ready. Let's go."

I turned to Chuck—they'd all turned out to watch the drone performance—and said, "Chuck, what goodies have you guys brought for us?"

"Not too much, I'm afraid," Monty replied. "Let's go out to the truck."

Not too much turned out to be four fully automatic M4 carbines, two thousand rounds of 5.56 ammo for the M4s, and a Savage semi-auto sniper rifle chambered for 6.5 Creedmore.

"That it?" I asked.

"Hell, Harry," Chuck replied. "There are only three of us, right? We have three spare thirty-round mags for each of the M4s—that's a hundred and twenty rounds per weapon. Enough to take on the damn Taliban—and I have what I need for the Savage. We're loaded, man."

It made sense, so I nodded and told them to get ready to leave, then I turned to Kate.

"Kate, I need your help."

She glared at me and cocked her head to the right.

"I knew that was coming," she said. "What d'you need?"

"The road out there is packed with media. The minute we exit the gate they'll be on us. They'll follow us."

She nodded and said, "I'll do what I can. Let me know when you're ready to leave."

I looked at my watch. It was just after four.

"How about now?" I said. "You can start moving them out. Back them away to the north. We'll go south, down the mountain."

I turned to Tim who was packing his gear into his Wagoneer.

"How much longer, Tim?"

"I'm done," he said, closing the hatch.

"Okay, guys," I said, turning to face them. "Suit up and load up into Tim's truck, and let's get the hell out of here." By suit up, I meant for them to don their tactical gear. Me? I was unarmed. My only protection was a lightweight Kevlar vest under my shirt and Tim's comms unit in my ear and in my ball cap. Without the CZ, I felt naked.

I turned again to Tim, grabbed him, hugged him and whispered in his ear. "Take care, young Jedi."

Chapter Thirty-Three

W hen I finally exited my front yard onto East Brow Road —Tim first with me bringing up the rear—I could see that Kate had her unmarked cruiser parked catty-corner across the road with her blue lights flashing and that she was out of the car holding back the frenzied reporters.

Smart, I thought.

But not smart enough, because as I turned onto Scenic Highway, I noticed two vehicles—one with the familiar red and yellow cladding of Channel 7 TV—come streaking out of North Hermitage and glue themselves to my rear bumper.

I smiled to myself and slowed down. I knew that Tim would have noticed it too. I also knew which way he was going to go to get to South Hickory Valley Road, so I drove sedately down the mountain, keeping the media behind me.

By the time I reached the bottom of the mountain, Tim had disappeared. Me, I had a wagon train trailing along behind me. I stayed on Lee Highway, still trailing the media, then took a left onto St. Elmo Avenue and hit the gas. At West 40th I made a hard right, then a hard left onto Alton Park Boulevard to Market Street, then took the ramp up onto I-24. By then I'd lost them and was less than twenty minutes from my destination. I was going to make it with a few minutes to spare.

I didn't learn until I finally pulled over a couple of hundred yards short of my destination for one last comms check, that Tim had completed his journey without incident and he and his team— his team? Sounds good, doesn't it?—had properly deployed. Tim was already parked and out of his vehicle and at the rear gate. Chuck was climbing the water tower, and T.J. and Monty were already en route toward Shady's compound—if you could call it that.

Having ascertained that the comms was working properly, I drove slowly to the driveway, turned in, and drove even more slowly to the large, though essentially derelict, two-story building wherein I assumed Shady was holding Jacque.

At first glance, the place appeared to be deserted. Then I noticed a red Dodge Charger, a black Chevy Suburban and a dark blue van parked among the trees, so I figured I must be at the right place. Then, when I spotted two men with automatic weapons on the roof watching me, I knew for certain I was. On closer inspection, I spotted two more near the vehicles and then two more walked out from behind the building as I drove by. *Damn! That's six so far and I'm not inside the damn building yet.*

I parked in front of the main entrance—at least I assumed that's what it was—and sat there for a moment, thinking and watching the circling vultures. And, even though I knew I wasn't, feeling utterly alone. Finally, I took a deep breath and, just as two more thugs stepped out of the door, I exited the car. One took me by the arm while the other, sure enough, popped the trunk. Had we gone with T.J.'s idea, he could have died right there and then.

As it was, I was escorted into the building where one of them patted me down, took my ball cap off my head, looked inside it, found nothing and handed it back to me. They found nothing on me but my iPhone, which thug number one dropped on the floor and ground under his heel. *You'll pay for that, you son of a bitch,* I thought, the anger rising like bile in my craw.

I took several deep breaths and, as they escorted me further into the wreckage of the one-time warehouse, I counted slowly to ten to calm myself. This wasn't the time to let my nerves get the best of me. And, as we walked, I was counting bad guys silently to myself: *two men on the roof, two in the trees, two outside, two at the front door who'd patted me down and were now escorting me inside*—we came to a large open area—*and two, no, three more here. That makes eleven so far. How many more are there?* I wondered.

I can probably take these *two clowns,* I thought, *but three more, and Shady? I don't think so.* And I had a sinking feeling that Kate may well have been right, and that I should have let her handle it. But there was no going back. I had to try.

The three of us stepped into the open area and my heart rose into my mouth.

It was full daylight, but the windows were, for the most part, dirty. Some, though, had recently been washed, though not very well. They were still dirty, and streaked, but at least you could see through them and they did let some light in. Somewhere, I could hear a generator running. It was the generator, no doubt, that was powering the string of ten or more LED bulbs.

But it was none of that that had caused my heart to leap. It was the chair in the middle of the open space, its back to me, and seated on it with her arms taped to the chair, was... Jacque.

It was my dream incarnate. No, it wasn't Amanda I had thought was in that chair. It was Jacque, and beside her, with a gun to her head, stood Lester Shady Tree, an evil smile on his lips. And I could feel my hands shaking.

Chapter Thirty-Four

"So, you made it then?" Shady said conversationally, the weapon steady in his hand.

"Yes, Shady. I'm here. Now turn her loose and let her go."

"Umm, umm, umm." Jacque struggled against her bonds when she heard my voice and tried to turn her head. I could see then that her mouth was taped.

"Oh come on, Harry," Shady said. "That's no fun. Besides, I'm in a good mood and of a mind to talk a little. You want to talk a little, Harry?"

"No. I want you to keep your word and let her go."

Shady sighed, shook his head and tapped the muzzle of the gun on the backrest of Jacque's chair, making her jump.

I took a step forward but was immediately restrained by my two escorts.

"Take it easy, Harry," Shady said. "I'm not going to hurt her... yet."

He grinned, and I couldn't help but notice how white his teeth were. I didn't answer.

"You know, Harry, we've known each other for a long time, you and me. How long has it been?" He stared up at the ceiling, the muzzle of the gun tapping gently, rhythmically, on the back of Jacque's chair. "Twelve, thirteen years?"

Again, I didn't answer.

"And I've hated you from day one, ever since you put that bullet through my arm. And then, you sorry son of a bitch, you took my pinky finger." He held his hand up, fingers spread, as if to prove what I'd done.

"I would have taken a lot more than that if you hadn't spilled your guts, crying like a baby," I said, cutting him off.

"Well said, Harry, my friend. And talking of crying, how about that brother of yours? Henry, I think, was his name. He cried too. He begged. He was not half the man you are, Harry, but you know what? You're going to cry too before I'm done with you."

He paused for a moment, then he screamed at the top of his voice, "I hate you, Harry Starke."

Jacque jumped so hard she almost tipped her chair over.

Then he sucked in a huge gulp of air, shuddered, coughed violently, breathed deeply two or three times and seemed to calm down.

"And I'm going to make you pay for everything you've ever done to me."

"Hold on, Harry," I heard Tim whisper in my ear. "I'm getting it all. Chuck is in position. I'll give you the word when the time's right. Over and out, for now."

For now? I thought. *Holy crap, how long's it going to take before the time's right?*

"I won, Harry," Shady said, his voice gentle now. "I won, but you know what? I never thought I'd live to see this day, but here we are."

The man was obviously full of rage, but somehow he'd managed to get a grip on himself and calm down.

"You're all wind and piss, Shady," I said. "And you're a liar. I did what you asked. Now let her go."

"Am I now? Well, we'll see. I'm not going to kill you, Harry. No, I'm not going to do that. I'm not going to let you off that easy. Billy Harper—remember him, Harry? I'm sure you do. He taught me that. 'Make him suffer,' he told me when he had me hire that Jones woman to kill you. She almost pulled it off, too. Me? I gotcha, Harry, and I've made special arrangements for you. I'll be long gone by the time you realize what I've done. And you, my friend, will be ruined, ruined forever. For now, though, you'll stay here and watch your friend die."

"You said you'd let her go."

"I lied, but here's the thing..."

But by then I wasn't hearing him as he droned on, so full of himself and the fact that he had me at his mercy. I was deep in thought. My mind was a kaleidoscope of scenarios and wild thoughts and what-ifs.

What if I somehow get the upper hand tonight? Even if Shady ends up dead, has he really won? He said he's made sure that, after he's gone, I'll be ruined. How? How could he do that? What the hell is he talking about?

All the time I was thinking, I was breathing deeply, trying to stay calm and assess the situation. In the meantime, two more thugs had entered the room at the far end. I figured I could probably take my two, but that would leave five more, plus those outside, plus Shady, and I knew he wouldn't hesitate to shoot Jacque in the head the moment I made my move.

Where the hell is T.J.... and Monty? What the hell's Tim doing? And then my mind made a sideways track. It's strange how the mind works in times of stress.

I remembered when I first met Tim, a young kid caught up in hacking. A young kid headed for disaster and a life of crime. But now? Now, Tim is working for the good guys. *He's turned into a responsible, helpful young man. And what about T.J.? T.J. has a dark side, a savage streak. But he also has a good heart and is a valued member of my team. And, surprisingly, his best talents aren't behind the butt of a gun but in his forensic accounting abilities.*

And what about Jacque? She doesn't deserve this. What would I do without her? Where would I be without her? A young woman with spunk who runs my office like the captain of a submarine. I'd be dead even now but for her. And what about Kate? Amanda? Even August? Haven't they all saved my damn skin—or soul—over the years?

Deep inside, I was slowly working myself up into a terrible, burning rage. But I knew I couldn't let him get to me. My primary goal was to save Jacque, and at that precise moment, I couldn't see it happening.

And then I returned to the moment. My hand had stopped shaking. I was calm.

"Are you even listening to me, Starke?" Shady yelled, his voice echoing around the vast, empty room.

And then I noticed that, in his confusion, or whatever his state of mind was, he'd lowered his weapon slightly. It was no longer pointing at Jacque's head.

C'mon, Tim. The time is right, now!

And then, out of the corner of my eye, I spotted it. The little red drone was at the window peering inside. As if on cue, there was a dull thud outside one of the broken windows as a man fell from the roof and his already-dead body hit the floor.

"Harry, move! Now!" Tim's voice yelled in my ear with an urgency I'd never heard from him before.

And I did.

Chapter Thirty-Five

I snapped into action. I took the thug to my left, who was staring at the window, completely by surprise with a straight-finger punch to the throat. He dropped his weapon, grasped his throat with both hands, and went down gagging. A solid kick to the side of the knee and the guy to my right went down screaming in pain, and suddenly I was standing there alone, concentrating on Shady.

Sniper shots fired in through the windows were, to me, little more than a distraction, though each in turn found their mark, taking out two more of Shady's thugs.

Shady was in a state of stunned confusion. He looked first one way and then the other, the gun in his hand whipping back and forth, sweeping the room. Jacque, it seemed, was forgotten.

Instinctively, I reached under my jacket for my weapon and then realized I didn't have one. I had no choice. If I didn't do something, and fast, Jacque was a gone goose. I was more than twenty yards from him, and I didn't like my odds.

I dodged two steps sideways and then charged towards him. He raised the gun and fired at me twice, three times. I ducked and weaved. In his panic, fortunately for me, he'd forgotten the basic rules and was shooting at me one-handed. He missed with all three shots.

He realized his mistake, grabbed the weapon with two hands, tried to lock onto me, and fired three times so fast it sounded like one. But I was moving fast, and the range was down to maybe thirty feet, and a moving target is hard to hit with a handgun at any range.

It was at that moment that T.J. came crashing in through one of the windows, followed by the little red drone that, like a lost puppy, immediately rushed to my side and stuck there, like glue, hovering five feet away from me, mimicking every move I made.

How did T.J. do that? He's almost seventy years old. I couldn't help but wonder as I dodged the drone. Try as I might, I couldn't lose the annoying little bugger that stuck to me like glue.

Shady spun around at the sound of smashing glass, brought his weapon to bear on T.J., and snapped off two shots—both of them missed—as I came under automatic fire from one of the two thugs that had entered the building at the far end. He was covering his buddy and Shady while I was making like a ball, rolling across the floor, trying to draw his fire away from Jacque.

T.J. rolled and came up on his feet spraying automatic fire at the two thugs, taking both of them down. Shady snapped off two more shots, then turned and ran towards an open door to my right. By then, of the original three, Chuck had taken down two and the other had disappeared. Where to I had no idea. Shady, too, was gone, out through the open door into some kind of corridor.

Damn it, he's escaped... or has he? I thought when I heard the crack of Chuck's rifle in the distance.

"T.J.," I shouted as I ran to Jacque, the little red drone at my side. "I think one went that way." I pointed at the door through which I'd entered. "And take care of those two." I pointed at my would-be escorts. "I think the one on the right is dead." That was the one I'd straight-fingered, and I was right, he was. I heard a short burst of automatic fire behind me, and I didn't have to turn around to know that T.J. had "taken care" of the other.

"Tim," I yelled as I bent down beside Jacque. "Get this damn thing out of my hair."

"I can't, Harry. She's locked onto you. Besides, through her I can see what's happening. I can see Jacque. Is she okay?"

"I don't know, yet."

"You're right," T.J. said as he joined me at Jacque's side. He was breathing hard. "They're dead," he said as he tossed two handguns he'd taken from the dead thugs onto the floor beside me. "The other guy? I dunno, but Monty's still outside. He'll get him. He and Chuck are keeping 'em penned in. They ain't gonna get away this time, Harry." He looked at Jacque as I gently removed the tape from her mouth. "How is she?" he asked.

"Damn it, T.J.," I replied. "There was no need to kill that guy."

"I'm fine, damn it," Jacque responded with spirit as the tape came away.

A sharp burst of automatic fire sounded outside, beyond the end of the building, followed by several more bursts, and then all went quiet.

"Don't you bother about me, Harry," Jacque shouted, her Jamaican accent stronger than I'd ever heard it. "You go get 'im. You go get dat Shady, you hear? Let me be. Go, go. Go!"

"Look after her, T.J.," I said and took a step back. Then I picked up one of the handguns from the floor—a Glock 17. I dropped the mag and checked the load. It was full. I reinserted it, chambered a round, then nodded at T.J. and ran to the open door through which Shady had disappeared, the drone close by my right side.

The corridor ran the full length of the building. There were no doors, just windows and a flight of stone stairs at each end. I couldn't remember which way Shady had gone, but something at the back of my brain told me to go left, and I did. I ran like a cat being chased by a mockingbird—the damn drone—along the corridor, up the stairs and charged through an open door into a vast room that mirrored the one below, the one I'd just left.

Big mistake. Shady was waiting for me behind the door.

He jumped out at me, swinging a length of two-by-four at my head, and he would have made it too, had it not been for him being distracted by the drone. As it was, he managed to smash the plank down on my left hand as I raised my arm to protect myself. It hurt like hell and I was sure he'd broken something. Instead of taking advantage though, and pressing his attack, he threw the piece of wood down, pulled his gun from his pants pocket, leveled it at me and then backed away into the middle of the room, coughing.

I leveled my Glock at him, pain shooting through my hand and up my left arm, and said, "You're done, Shady. There's no way out of here. I have a man outside, another downstairs, and a sniper on the water tower and, by now, the cops are already on their way."

"That they are," Tim said in my ear. The drone hovered at my side, five feet off the ground.

"Tim," I said. "You have to do something about your girl here. She keeps distracting me."

Obediently, the little red machine sank slowly to the floor and its turbines slowed and stopped turning.

"Thank you," I said.

"You're welcome."

"So, Shady," I said. "It looks like we have a Mexican standoff. You shoot me, and you still lose. You have nowhere to go. I shoot you... you're dead. Not much of an alternative, is it? So why don't you just give yourself up and let's get the hell out of here?"

"You're wrong, Harry. You already lost, even before you got here, even before I blew up your offices—yeah that was me—and before I took your girl. I wasn't really going to hurt her, by the way. I did all that just to get your attention, and I did, didn't I? You've lost, Harry. You just don't know it yet. Even after I'm gone. I'm the Pacman, remember? I always get my man. We still have to play the end game. Goodbye, Harry."

He smiled at me, put the barrel of the gun into his mouth and pulled the trigger. The back of his head exploded in a mist of blood and bone and he fell over backwards, the gun falling from his lifeless fingers.

I was stunned. I stood there for a moment staring at his body, realizing at last that it was truly over. Shady Tree was dead.

I heard something behind me. I spun around as T.J. walked in through the open door.

He took one look at what was left of Shady, stepped over to him and put two bullets into the man's already very-dead body. Then he turned, looked at me, smiled and said, "I thought he was reaching for his gun."

Chapter Thirty-Six

Jacque and I were sitting together on the steps outside the entrance to the warehouse and T.J. was pacing back and forth a few yards away when Tim arrived, followed a couple of minutes later by Kate, three cruisers and two EMT vehicles. By then, there was no sign of Chuck and Monty. They had disappeared. Officially, they were never there.

Tim scooped up the red drone—yes, I'd brought her downstairs—like it was a naughty puppy. Grinning happily, he gently returned it to its box in the back of his Wagoneer.

When Kate appeared, she didn't look happy. No, she was extremely angry.

"I'm glad to see you're safe, Jacque," she said. "Are you hurt?"

"No," Jacque replied, "just stiff from sitting for almost twenty-four hours, and I'm hungry and thirsty. That SOB didn't give me anything to eat. Nothin'."

Kate nodded and then signaled to the EMTs, two of which came and helped Jacque up and walked her slowly to one of the ambulances. I remained seated.

"How many, Harry?" Kate asked when we were alone. She was

standing with her hands on her hips and I knew exactly what was going through her head: How the hell am I supposed to explain all this?

I shrugged, looked up at her and said, "How many what?"

"Don't play games with me, Harry. I'm not in the mood. How many dead?"

"All of them, I think. Except for one that might have gotten away." *I somehow doubt that though,* I thought, looking at the body lying in the dirt a few yards away from where I was sitting, thinking that Chuck up there on the tower must have taken him down.

"Shady's dead, too," I continued. "He shot himself. You'll find his body on the upper floor."

"So where is everybody?" she asked. "I see Tim and T.J. over there. Where are Chuck and Monty?"

"Who?" I asked.

"I see," she replied. "So that's how you want to play it?"

Again, I shrugged. I stood, brushed myself off, then offered her my hands for the cuffs.

"That's a nasty bruise you've got there," she said, looking at my hand.

"Courtesy of Shady," I said.

"Put 'em down, Harry, and stop playing the fool. It doesn't become you."

Just then we were joined by a uniformed sergeant.

"Captain? You got a minute?"

She turned. "What is it, Riley?"

"Whew." He shook his head. "We've got a total of thirteen dead, including the guy that shot himself."

"Did you get the one on the roof?" I asked. He hadn't, and I was wrong, turns out there were two up there, but they didn't find that out until five or ten minutes later.

"Go take a look," she said to Riley, who turned and ran toward the end of the building.

"Geez, Harry," she said. "You're a fricking wrecking machine. How the hell am I supposed to explain all... this?"

"Rival drug gangs battling it out over territory?" I asked brightly.

"You really are something else," she said. "How the hell Amanda puts up with you, I don't know. How many have you killed? T.J. I can understand, but you... Don't you have any feelings about that?"

I shrugged and said, "I'm not a sociopath, but no, not really. It was kill or be killed. All I was concerned with was Jacque... and finally putting an end to this thing between me and Shady. In the end, though, I didn't have to. He did that himself."

"Where are they?" she asked again. "I need to talk to them, both of them. We have at least thirteen dead, for God's sake. I can't brush that under the rug."

"I'm telling you, Kate. I don't know. I arrived here at a couple of minutes to five. I never saw either of them. That's the truth." And it was.

"Screw you, Harry," she said, then turned and walked over to where Tim was sitting in his Wagoneer with the door open.

She talked to him for several minutes. I could see enough to tell she was becoming angrier by the moment, and that Tim's answers to her questions were short and restricted mostly to nods or shakes of the head. In the end she took a step back and pointed angrily at the way out. Tim? He closed his door, started the motor and drove out of the complex without a backward look, at her or me.

Shit! That's not good.

She stood with her hands on her hips and watched him go. I heard a phone ring. It was hers. She answered it, walked slowly around in circles, her head down as she listened and talked. Every now and then she'd glance over at me. Then she nodded, said something, closed out the call and walked back to me.

"Let's go, Harry," she said, a hard edge to her voice. "The Chief wants to talk to you."

Oh shit! Again, not good.

"Geez... Okay, but can I use your phone first to call Amanda and let her know that everything's okay? One of Shady's thugs smashed mine."

"Everything is not okay, but yes. Go ahead."

* * *

I'm not going to go into all of the details of what became a very confrontational meeting between me and Chief Wesley Johnston. Let's just say we didn't like each other and had never gotten along.

The crux of the conversation was that he wanted to know exactly what had happened and, in particular, who the sniper was. And that was something I wasn't about to give him. I did my best to keep Kate out of it, too, not entirely successfully.

"Harry," he said finally. "We have a problem. We have fourteen dead, including Lester Tree. And we have Jaylin Coin, also dead. I don't think for one minute that you had anything to do with that—that's down to Tree, if we can ever prove it. But what I do know is that you and your crew are responsible for what happened out on Hickory Valley Road. We've managed to identify most of the dead. They are all bad guys, the worst. But that's no excuse for wholesale slaughter. Harry, I have no alternative but to hand the whole thing over to the district attorney."

"You're right, Chief. It doesn't. But I acted in self-defense. I went into that building alone and unarmed to try to talk Shady into letting Jacque Hale go—he was also responsible for the bombing of my offices on Georgia, by the way—but he wasn't having any of it. He threatened me, and he threatened to kill Jacque. I was in fear for my life and for Jacque's. I felt I had no alternative but to incapacitate my captors and take one of their weapons. T.J. did not enter the building until after Shady and his people opened fire... on me. Yes, I took T.J. with me. And yes, he was armed. I'd have been damn stupid if I didn't. But, as I said, he didn't enter the building until I was already under fire, and I have the recordings, *and video*, to prove it." *Thank God for my little red friend.*

"Video? How can you possibly have video of what went down *inside* that building?"

I explained about my personal drone, and as soon as I did, I knew I'd made a mistake.

"Oh yes?" he said, his eyes narrowed and he smirked. "And who was operating the drone?"

"It was locked onto me," I said, trying not to lie to him.

Fortunately, he didn't push it. He looked skeptically at me, but he let it go. I couldn't help but wonder why.

"What about the guys on the roof?" he asked.

Now there he had me. I had no answer to that so, like Brer Rabbit, I said nothing. If you say nothing, you can't incriminate yourself... Well, that's my theory.

"You think I don't know you had a sniper?" he snarled. "That's not self-defense. I don't know of a single handgun that shoots 6.5 Creedmore."

Yes, I thought. *That was a mistake.*

Again, I laid low and said nothing.

He looked at Kate.

I heard her take a deep breath, but she too said nothing.

"Damn it, Harry. If the press gets hold of this—"

"It was a gang war," I finished for him.

"You're asking me to lie for you?" he asked. He was incredulous.

I said nothing. You could have cut the silence with a knife.

"I'll do it," Kate said. "If you arrest him, you'll have the mayor and every mover and shaker, not to mention the general public, down on your head like... Let's put it this way; that bomb he saved the city from would be nothing by comparison. Chief, you wouldn't even be sitting there now, but for Harry. I'll handle it."

He stared at her, stunned.

"Get the hell out of here. Both of you."

And we did.

Chapter Thirty-Seven

The truth was, that for all his bullshit and bluster, neither the Chief nor anyone else wanted to look too deeply into the incident at Hickory Valley Road. The bad guys had lost, and that alone was good enough for most people.

And so, after several very uncomfortable hours, T.J. and I were released. Kate, during that conversation with Tim at Hickory Valley Road, had already sent him home with strict instructions to keep his mouth shut, so he was never involved... officially. Nor were Chuck and Monty. They'd disappeared as soon as they heard the sirens.

I finally arrived home that night at a little after midnight. Kate had had an officer drive my car to the police department, so I dropped T.J. off at his apartment on the way.

I arrived home tired, drained and totally wiped out. The funny thing was though, that ever since that moment when I confronted Shady in the warehouse, not once had I had the shakes, and I still haven't. Whether or not it was the fact that it was all over, I can't say, but they were gone, hopefully for good. *PTSD? Hah. Not hardly.*

I had a tearful moment with Amanda. She knew that Shady was gone—I'd told her when I called her just before I went with Kate to the police department. She hugged me tightly, the tears running down her cheeks. Me? I felt like... Hell, I don't know what I felt like.

I rose early that following morning and went for my usual run. My intention was to take the rest of the day off and spend it quietly with Amanda and Jade. But, having cleared my head during my fast clip along East Brow Road, I realized it wasn't to be. That I had things I needed to do.

Thanks to Shady, my professional life was in ruins, literally, so I had some decisions to make.

I ate breakfast with my two girls, then I made some calls, quite a few calls actually, and asked everyone to join us at the house for brunch.

The last call I made was to Jacque. She was at home, having been released from the hospital late the previous evening. Miraculously, Shady hadn't laid a hand on her—maybe he really didn't intend to hurt her—aside from taping her up and not feeding her, that is. So, when I called her, she sounded chipper enough, so I asked her to join us and bring Wendy, and she agreed.

It was a nice day, so Amanda insisted we all meet outside on the patio. Rose and August came by, ostensibly to help Amanda make lunch, but I felt that what I had to say affected them so I asked them to join us, too.

"You're probably wondering what this is all about," I said, after we'd eaten and when I had them all gathered together with drinks in their hands. "Well, I'll tell you. I've come to a decision that will affect all of you."

I paused and looked around the gathering.

"I have decided that... I'm going to continue as CEO of Harry Starke Investigations."

They all began to clap, but I held up my hand and said, "Whoa. Don't get carried away. There's more to it than that. Let me finish, please."

My audience went quiet.

"As you all know, the last ten years... The first ten years of Harry

Starke Investigations have not been easy. Yes, we've had some good times and we've solved a lot of cases... a *lot* of cases. But there have been some bad times too, not financially. I mean dangerous, and that bothers me, *a lot*, and it should bother you, too."

Again, I glanced around the group. All were quiet, watching me. So I continued.

"In the early days, when I just had myself to worry about, that was bad enough. But I've been thinking about the danger I put y'all in, more times than I care to remember. Now, though..." I looked at Amanda, who was holding Jade, and I smiled. "I have a family of my own to think about, but I have so much more to protect. I have to protect each one of you." I pointed to each of them in turn.

"So, here's the thing. I've already talked it through with Amanda and my father and Rose, and they are on board and will support me whatever happens here this afternoon.

"The world is full of bad people, people like Shady Tree and many others we've been instrumental in putting away over the years. I've made a lot of enemies. That's true whether Harry Starke Investigations continues or not... I can't promise that there's not another Shady out there, because I know there is, and that means danger for you all. And that really bothers me, but I can't run away from it. The best I can hope to do is to try to make the world a little safer for us all, for you, my family and for Jade."

I had to be careful how I phrased what was to come next.

"But I can't ask that of you. You, too, have families to consider. So, it's your decision to make; will you join me or not? If not, I won't blame you, not one bit. If you're with me, please raise your hand. If you need time to think about it, that's okay, too. Take all the time you need. Thank you."

I sat down. All was quiet.

Tim was the first to raise his hand, followed almost immediately by T.J., then Jacque raised hers. I looked at Wendy. She smiled and raised her hand, too. I was touched. One by one, they all agreed to stay. Me? I was overwhelmed, and I know I teared up.

"Wow," I said. "Thank you, that's a rare compliment indeed. I'll try to make sure you won't regret it."

I stood up again, raised my almost empty glass and said, "Let's drink to the new Harry Starke Investigations." And they did. My company had just taken a new lease on life, and I was proud of them.

Later that afternoon, just as they were leaving, Jacque took me to one side and asked me why I'd changed my mind about quitting.

The truth was, I really didn't know. The only thing I could think of was the thought process I went through in the warehouse when she was taped to the chair and I was filled with fear about what Shady might be about to do, especially to her.

"I suddenly realized," I said to her, "that all these years I've been thinking and operating as if I was all alone. But then I realized that I wasn't alone at all, that I had you, and the rest of my team, and that I couldn't do what I do without you, all of you. You guys are my family just as much as Amanda, Jade, Rose and my father, and we have something special together, all of us."

I looked down at her. Her eyes were watering.

"Now look who's tearing up," I said, using my finger to wipe the tears away as they rolled down her cheeks.

"Stop it, you silly old bugger," she muttered, sniffing and reaching into her purse for a tissue.

She wiped away the tears, then flung her arms around my neck and whispered in my ear, "I love you, Harry Starke."

"I know you do," I said. "And I love you, too. Look, why don't you take a few days off, rest a little—"

"What you t'ink?" she said, interrupting me. "Dat I can't handle a little danger? I'll be at work bright and early tomorrow mornin', you know, and you better be, too. Besides, I have to find us some new offices."

I laughed, assured her I would be and sent her and Wendy on their way.

It took more than thirty minutes for the rest of them to leave.

Everyone, so it seemed, had something encouraging to say to me. And then, only Tim was left.

"Thanks for all you do for me... us, Tim," I said, taking his hand in both of mine.

He colored up, nodded, and I turned him loose, but he just stood there, and I could tell he wanted to say something.

"What is it, Tim?"

"I heard what Shady said, Harry. I was the only one that did. You haven't mentioned it. What did he mean? What does he have planned? What's the end game?"

I stood there for a moment, looking at him, wondering what to say. The truth was, I didn't know.

"It was just BS, Tim. You know how Shady was, all talk. He's dead. It's over. There's nothing he can do." *I just hope you're right, Harry,* I thought.

"Go home, Tim. I'll see you bright and early in the morning."

And he did. And I watched him go, wondering if I was right... or if I'd just lied to him.

Chapter Thirty-Eight

Two days later, while I was having lunch at the Boathouse on Riverside Drive with Amanda, Jade and Maria—those three really seemed to be getting along, much to my relief—I received a call from Kate. She was with Doc Sheddon for Shady's autopsy. They were just about to wrap things up and she was wondering if I'd like to join them.

My first inclination was to say no. I'd had a lifetime of Lester Tree and enough was enough, but I hadn't seen or heard from Kate since our interview with Chief Johnston so, against my better judgment, I agreed to meet her there at the Forensic Center. I was only a couple of miles away, but I still had to finish lunch, so I told her I'd be there in thirty minutes.

I took my leave of the girls some twenty minutes later and drove on over and parked out front.

Kate was waiting for me in the lobby, and I could tell she had something on her mind.

She gave me a quick hug, then stepped away and said, "Before we go in, Harry, I should tell you that the Chief has insisted that... I'm not sure exactly what he was getting at, but it boiled down to this. Our relationship... It has to stop, professionally, anyway. I can't help you anymore. He's not stupid. He knows I had a hand in what happened on Saturday... Well, whatever." She sighed, then continued.

"So, you were never here, okay? If he finds out, I'll lose my job."

I can't say I was surprised, but hearing it... well, I suddenly had a hollow feeling in the pit of my stomach. My relationship with Kate, though often rocky, stretched back more than eighteen years, and now it was over? That was a hard pill to swallow.

"I'm sorry, Kate. Give him time. Maybe he'll come around," was all I could say. What else was there?

She nodded, then said, "Come on. Doc has something interesting to share, and so have I, for the last time, I think."

I shook my head and followed her through to Doc Sheddon's office.

Hamilton County's Chief Medical Examiner was seated behind his desk, but he rose quickly to his feet and came to greet me, his hand extended.

"Harry, m'boy," he said as I shook his hand. "These are sad times, sad times indeed. Kate told me about her run-in with the Chief. Give it time. He'll get over it. But how about you? How are you, Harry? That's what's important. Take a seat, take a seat."

Doc and I go back a long way, even further than my relationship with Kate. He's a strange little man, but I'd always been proud to call him my friend, and I still do today.

"I'm fine, Doc. The more so now that this thing with Shady is finally at an end."

"Yes, yes, there is that," he said, returning to his desk.

"About that," he continued, sorting through the untidy heap of papers on his desk. "He was terminal, you know. Pancreatic cancer."

"Get out of here..." Now that, I wasn't expecting. "How long d'you think he had left, Doc?"

He shrugged. "Less than three months, I'd say. He probably found out about it a few months ago."

"So that was it," I said. "Typical Shady. He took the easy way out, just like always."

We sat together in silence for a moment, not out of respect or even sympathy for Shady, but just to contemplate the moment.

"I told you I had something to share with you, too," Kate said suddenly.

I nodded absently. I was still thinking about Shady and our long and turbulent history.

"You did," I said.

"We charged DeAnté King with the murder of Jaylin Coin."

"No surprise there," I said.

"We also charged Hector Santos."

"And?"

She sighed and said, "Unlike DeAnté, Santos has no prior connections to Shady, at least none that we could find, and that puzzled me, so I kept digging. It turns out that he was running drugs in San Antonio, Texas. In fact, he's wanted by the FBI, DEA and Border Patrol for running drugs, immigrants, and human trafficking from Laredo to San Antonio."

"I think I get the connection," I said. "We know that Shady spent time in Nuevo Laredo with the cartels. That was how he met those Iranian terrorists. He must have recruited Santos while he was there and..."

And suddenly, some of what Shady had said back there in the warehouse began to make sense: "I'm not going to kill you, Harry. Make you suffer. After I'm gone. Ruined, ruined forever... End game." He knew he was dying and... Yes, it began to make sense, only it didn't.

I spent a few more minutes talking to Doc and Kate, then I told them goodbye and went to my car and called Amanda. She and Jade, and Maria of course, were on their way to the Aquarium to see the sharks. Me? I had already come to the realization that I needed to make Amanda and Jade a priority in my life, so I decided to join them.

As I pulled out onto Amnicola Highway going south toward the city center, a thought popped into my head.

What the hell did he mean, end game?

The End

One more thing

So what about Shady's promise? Will there be an End Game for Harry Starke? Yes, of course. Harry Starke, Book 16, END GAME is available NOW at a discounted rate. CLICK HERE.

Made in the USA
Middletown, DE
10 October 2023

40531305R00300